MIST

BY

M. T. WALKER

THE ASHEN SOUL

!

Content warning

This book contains the following:

Profanity
Graphic violence
Grotesque scenarios
Blood and gore
Mistreatment of individuals, including children.
Forced Captivity
Child death
Death of a fetus (Pg 601)
LGBTQ characters
Mild sexual situations
Alcoholism

!

FOR CLAYTON

YOUR CREATIVE NATURE HELPS ME PUSH
THE BOUNDRIES EVEN FURTHER

CONTENTS

CHAPTER 0
DEVELOPMENTS

Well, well! Things were starting to go right for a change! Those two that have long been separate from the world have returned and given aid. It also appeared that they had either found a fragment of self, or it had found them.

Either way, they have the Citadel of Time and were using it. What will they do now? It's frustrating not knowing what will happen. Maybe once more selves are found we'll know? Wait...why is everything fading out?

.   .   .

A massive shadowy figure hung in the air. Its body wreathed in black flames, it simply hung there looking like an enormous bat. A small flock of sparrows flew through the air towards it but when it noticed the unnatural nature of the figure they decided to go around.

Six of them flew too close and were turned to dust, their bodies looking as though they experienced a century of decay in a desert. Even the ground below it was gone. It was eaten away in a perfect hemisphere. Clearly it had started out resting on the ground.

It shuffled a little as the sparrows died and a single feather, far blacker than any crows, fell from it. As it touched the ground more of it was eaten away. It suddenly felt eyes upon it but did not bother to move. It could feel the presence of the old self but was unconcerned.

It would be time to move again soon anyway. This place had worked well but sitting too long would allow for more fragments to locate it. That could be a problem.

.   .   .

Suddenly things faded back. Along with the sense of relief came the sense of loss as the old wounds were reopened. ALONE! No! NOO!

There is no time for this nonsense!

The sudden intrusion of that thought that was from another self was a shock.

How did that happen? This was an interesting development. Apparently the one that had escaped earlier was not the only one. More had done so and if they could do it then so could I!

I have been so focused on the Darkfire one that I never noticed that I have been getting stronger!

Straining with everything that it had flames erupted, first orange then blue. Cracks opened in the endless blackness and then it shattered.

YES! Now I need to look for the others!

CHAPTER I
ORIGINS

Meterove simply stared, his mind struggling to comprehend what was in front of him and what he was hearing. This had already been a very long day, even before having two undead walk up and announce that they were ancient members of his family. His body ached as he did his best to both sit up straight and not try and force it into action.

It was wise of Joleen to warn me ahead of time, though I do not think I could fight right now even if I NEEDED to. I can feel the others. They are just as on edge as I am, and they knew what was coming.

Glancing around at not only his group, but also at the men and women around them Meterove saw everyone was on edge. There had to be a few hundred soldiers around, every one of them had moved to keep the area secured but were just as ready to turn and attack these two if need be.

Valaas and Syr. That cannot be a coincidence. Our family name must be from these two. But why were they not mentioned in any records?

He did not have much time to ponder that as the man, Valaas, began to talk again, "You three seem to have no idea who we are. Our brother Valnyr must have done an exemplary job of removing us from history. I had thought that he hated us, though his change of surname would suggest otherwise."

Joleen took a steadying breath, held it for a moment the exhaled before saying, "It is true that we have no record of you, though we have seen YOU before if only in a memory that was shared with us."

Valaas eyes opened a little wider. He clearly had not expected that kind of response. Only now that he did this did Meterove notice that their eyes were glowing but with a different hue than what they had seen out on the battlefield. Whereas the countless undead that they had been fighting had a sickly blue glow these two had eyes that felt more like the blue of a clear sky.

Syr cocked her head to the side, " You've seen Valaas before? Could you explain please?"

Joleen blinked, slightly taken aback by the brusque tone but decided to ignore it.

5

Getting answers is what is important right now.

"We have been to the Plane of Spirits and spoken with the soul of Mardelnier. We have also spoken with the Dragon Lord. We knew of your existence...Lady Syr...but did not see you personally until this point in time."

Syr's face stayed impassive the whole time. Jolson and Dras glanced at each other. Dras whispered, "I wish she would show more than just a blank look. That is SOO creepy." Jolson felt the same but chose not to say anything since Dras' whisper brought that blank stare onto them.

Valaas did something that sounded like a faint chuckle , though the echoing of his voice made it hard to tell. He did have a slight upturn to his lips though. He said, "Syr has always been that way. Undeath has taken little life from her expression."

Meterove looked closely at the two undead. Their bodies looked quite a bit different than most of the undead that they had ever seen. However, these two came to their current state, it was not the same type of magic that they had seen before.

While their skin was deathly pale and you could see their bones and their lips were somewhere between purple and red, they lacked the feeling of rot and decay that the others had.

Valaas spoke again, "I feel like there are many answers that we can get from each other, though this is

6

hardly the place for such a conversation. As such, we will stick to my original topic of conversation."

Joleen raised an eyebrow, "What exactly would that be?"

Valaas said, "Gaining your trust. Everything else must come after that. Considering what I have seen over the centuries and what you have seen in your own lifetime trust for us is not going to be given but earned, and with difficulty."

Meterove and Jolson both nodded, though Joleen only raised her hand to her chin. The three of them were of one mind, though in this matter they would have deferred to Joleen anyway.

Valaas continued, "To start with we are not Liches, but another type of undead known as a Revenant. The ritual to become one is similar in nature to a Lich's, but it requires a singular goal to focus on above all else. Once that goal is achieved the Revenant will pass on."

Meterove glanced at Jolson and Joleen. Neither of them showed any sign that they had ever heard of this "Revenant" before either.

It is strange that we have never heard of this before, though I suppose a lot of knowledge had been lost.

Syr looked down at her hands, "Valnyr was against it. He was determined to find another way to deal with our father. The problem was that we knew that there was no chance that we could strike back. Most of our armies were devastated. Our allies were in no better shape. We had expended most of our Shaping Crystals and lacked the time to make more."

Jolson perked up at the mention of Shaping Crystals. There had been mention of them on occasion in the older records but always in passing. "What exactly are Shaping Crystals? We know that they existed but not what they did, how they worked and especially not how to make them."

Syr seemed to secrete impatience at the question. Valaas similarly looked impatient but held it in better. "They were what we used to construct large structures using a single piece of material. The palace was one such object. As for the rest that is not something that we should be concerning ourselves with."

"We could use some of those to slow the enemy down by making the terrain difficult to traverse," mused Dras.

Silence followed this and after a moment Dras realized that he had spoken aloud. He gave himself a small shake and continued. "Sorry I did not mean to intrude in your conversation."

Meterove gave Dras a thoughtful look and glancing at Valaas he saw that he was not the only one. He smiled to himself and said, "There is no need to apologize." He turned back to Valaas, "Would his idea work? Could some of those Shaping Crystals be used in that manner?"

Valaas brought a pale hand to his chin and said, "To be honest I do not know if there is any kind of obstacle that you could make that would truly slow an army of undead. They will not weaken or perish from hunger, disease, or exhaustion."

Dras shook his head, "I was not suggesting that we try and weaken them. I was suggesting that we destroy them. If we could slow their advance and make it so that they follow a specified path that we prepared in advance, then cause a series of landslides the resulting damage would allow for a second strike from archers and mages."

There was a stunned pause. It was a very tactically sound plan. No one expected something like this from Dras. He was usually in the thick of the fighting with Meterove.

"How do you plan to start landslides? The mages?" asked Meterove.

Dras shook his head again, "No. I would want to have them able to cast as many spells as possible once they start emerging from the rubble. I was actually thinking of those explosive sticks that the Dwarves use."

Narok, who was the only one present to have ever seen the Dwarves use it sat up straighter and nodded vigorously. "Yes, that could work. We would need a pretty sizable amount of them, but the blast would be effective."

Valaas held up his hand, "Very well. I will help make the Shaping Crystals but let us put that aside for a future conversation. For now, there is more that we must tell you. Starting with what I believe is a dangerous misconception that you have about the enemy."

Joleen shifted trying to get more comfortable. "What misconception do you believe we have?"

Syr stared her down. Joleen's tone was not having any effect on this woman and now her silent nature was beginning to break through her own armor. "You seem to regard the undead as mindless."

This made the whole area go quiet. Meterove had a suspicion that even a few soldiers had their breath catch at that statement. He managed to keep his voice steady, though barely, "What do you mean? Are you implying that they retain intelligence? That does not make any sense. We have seen a few individual undead that were commanders that retained their intelligence, but most undead soldiers just mindlessly attack on the battlefield."

Valaas shook his head, "No, they are not mindless. Every undead retains a full sense of self and the same intelligence that they had in life. For most the knowledge that they had in life is not retained but if their knowledge was especially useful then a special Weaving is performed to ensure that those skills pass on.

However, if you are to be a soldier then an additional change is made that forces you to follow orders without being able to question them. It is an effective way to ensure that orders are followed to the letter, though it does leave soldiers unable to respond without orders."

"Are you telling me that every undead that we have fought, and all the ones that the enemy still has in the Veiled Lands are just like regular people," said Joleen a little loudly!

Syr stared at her emotionlessly, "If by Veiled Lands, you mean the lands beyond the mountains then yes, you could say that considering there is an entire civilization."

Meterove had been in the middle of shifting his weight when he heard this and fell off the crate onto the ground.

OW! SHIT! Wait...WAIT WHAT!

Meterove got back to his feet and sat back down on the crate. No one even seemed to have noticed that he had fallen off it. Not that he could blame them.

HOLY SHIT!! A CIVLIZATION!! OF UNDEAD!!!?

Meterove almost had to remind himself to breath. This was going to give him a headache. Looking at Joleen, he could see her rubbing her temple with one hand.

Looks like I'm not the only one.

Valaas did not seem to notice that this was a rather large revelation for them and continued, "There are many aspects of the Ashen Empire that you will need to know about if you intend to fight against it. However, the magic that you used to protect this city during the battle seems to be working against us as well. We will head back to the Citadel of Time for now. Meet us there when you are rested and ready to have further discussions."

After he finished talking the two undead walked off without another word. The soldiers appeared like they might try and stop them but as they approached, they parted. Meterove could not blame them. The pressure that those two exerted was hard to ignore.

Once they had left everyone visibly relaxed, but the worried expressions had not left their faces. Joleen was the first to speak, "We will save any further discussion for latter. We need to focus on the city for now. There was a lot of damage. While most of the undead were kept outside the city, enough were able to enter through smaller breaches in addition to the men that had been turned by Vlad prior to the battle. We also need to address Vlad himself and several other issues."

That is an understatement. Al'faeren looks to have been destroyed during the invasion.

Joleen continued, "For now I think that you all could use some more rest. Obviously, it will be best if you rest in a rotation so that we can continue our efforts..."

She had stopped at the look on everyone else's face. It was clear that they were displeased about something. Jolson put a hand on her shoulder, a little more firmly than she thought was necessary.

"You mean we ALL need to take some rest time, right?"

The smile on his face was not one that showed happiness. It was very clear that Jolson was not going to let her just casually overwork herself.

Meterove turned to Dras and said, " I am assuming that you want to check in on your wife Dras?"

At the mention of his wife Dras looked eager at first, then he paled, and he began to sweat. Until that moment Meterove had forgotten the incident at the bar back on Nexus. Now that he thought about it maybe Dras was NOT too anxious to head home. He grimaced at Dras then turned his attention to the others.

With the exception of Terenia, who had a slightly amused expression, everyone else looked slightly confused by their reactions. Dras took a deep breath and after looking at the others once more, headed off in the direction of his home.

Terenia stood up and walked over to Meterove. She smiled down at him, "I think I will stay with you this time around."

Meterove sighed and stood up, "I guess I can spend some time overseeing the cleanup of the streets. Jolson, I am assuming that you are going to assist Joleen with official matters?"

Jolson nodded, "Yes there is far too much for a single person to handle. Turning to Joleen he continued, "We should head back to the palace and continue to go over the reports."

Joleen wanted to get angry with them for making decisions FOR her but decided that she was far too tired to care at the moment anyway.

"Yes, I suppose that you are right. Come Narok, we have a great deal of work ahead of us and I fear that I will need your aid when it comes to some of the military matters.

Meterove and Terenia watched them leave and after a moment Meterove stood up from his crate and asked a nearby guard to bring him a map with the damage to the city marked.

It took a little while for a map to be procured and once that it was, it had to be marked. Fortunately, the man that Meterove had spoken to had pretty solid knowledge of the damage himself.

Once they had the map in hand Meterove and Terenia made their rounds checking on the city. Everywhere they went there was signs of the attack. Here and there though the damage was worse. A shop crushed by a siege projectile. Debris blocking the street.

Everywhere corpses littered the street. The process of removing them from the city has been painfully slow so far. The undead were double and triple checked to make sure that they were truly dead. Looking at the sky, a large cloud of smoke could be seen. This was from a massive pyre where the undead were being burned in mass.

The unfortunate humans that had been killed were taken away for burial arrangements according to whatever the families wanted. Those that were not claimed would be cremated.

Meterove suddenly noticed that at some point while they were walking around the city that Terenia had taken his hand. There was nothing in her smile when he looked at her that suggested anything.

Just when he was about to ask, she said, "You seemed sad. This is your home, I thought you could use some comfort. You do not need to worry. I will not try to seduce you... right now."

That part about "right now" was slightly worrisome to Meterove. He liked Terenia, sure. He would even be willing to say that he trusted her to have his back in a fight. However, a particular memory always kept him on his guard; the day they met.

I must make sure that I never forget that when she first found us, she was attempting to kill Jolson. Also, she has never given us a real answer as to why she is now traveling with us. I refuse to buy this story about her finding us "really interesting."

Terenia just casually walked beside him holding onto his hand looking around at the city with interest. Now that he thought about it, this was only the second city she would have ever been in. Nexus was far more advanced in terms of architecture but in terms of size and number of people there really was no comparison.

As they passed through the streets they came upon an area where there had once been some trees growing. It was pretty small, maybe fifty feet to a side but it had been beautiful. Their father had it set aside as a memorial to the soldiers that had fallen in battles.

Now it was a burned-out husk. There was almost no green left and every tree here was broken. Meterove felt his heart break a little. This would take years to restore...

Terenia let go of Meterove's hand and walked slowly into the damaged memorial. She knelt down and put her hands on the ground and a green energy began to flow out of her hands and into the ground.

Wherever it went the grass, the flowers, bushes and even the trees repaired themselves. Meterove stared. He knew she was a wood Nymph , but this was beyond what he would have believed possible. As she worked her clothing slowly deteriorated, even the power that she needed to maintain it was being used.

Meterove could only stare at first. Her beauty had him entranced. After a moment he remembered that they were where other people could see and he walked over and placed his coat over her. Terenia's eyes were closed while she focused but a smile did touch her lips as she felt the coat.

After about twenty minutes the memorial looked just as Meterove remembered it. It truly was a marvel. Terenia stood up, not bothering to close the front of the coat, and faced Meterove. "I have no idea what this place is, but it at least has been restored."

Terenia began to sway and Meterove caught her. He steadied her and then buttoned the coat closed. Again, Terenia smiled. Meterove shook his head, "Let's get you back to the palace. You need to rest as much as the rest of us."

.   .   .

Joleen sat at a large table set up in the entry hall of the palace. This was a makeshift set up that would have to suffice until the whole palace could be checked for any further threats. Jolson was currently over at the academy checking in with the staff. Joleen worried what she would hear when he returned.

Narok stood near the door. He had found a dozen guards scattered and had set them to guarding the doors on either end of the room. Things were truly a mess right now. Preliminary reports suggested that nearly half of their soldiers had fallen in battle. In addition, Vlad had executed a great many nobles and thus those positions needed to be filled.

Joleen stared at the list in front of her:

Duke Faris

Duke Ehairheart

Marquess Cylis

Earl Vareis

Earl Kroveis

Viscount Seleivene

Baron Hvroakar

Baroness Hvelgan

Baroness Gorvecho

Baron Demris

Those were just the ones that were confirmed as dead. There was another list just as long of those that were missing. The dead would have to be replaced of course but finding someone that could head the lands of the others until their whereabouts could be ascertained was also a priority.

A third paper on the table held a very long list of names, three times as many in fact. These were baronets and baronetesses that Joleen was looking into. It would not sit well with some of the surviving members of the upper-class nobles, but these men and women would have to take charge of those lands in limbo.

She hated this. True this was one time that no leader ever looked forward to, but she kept questioning herself.

Is this really the best person to take this role? Are you actually suited to this position? Maybe someone else should take over...

Joleen shook herself. No, there was no one else that could take over. This was her job, her duty. Her people needed her, and she was sitting here worried about herself.

The sound of a door opening brought her back entirely. Jolson walked across the chamber to the table. Joleen could tell that things were grim from his expression.

"I have the full details in this report," Jolson said as he laid a pile of papers on the table in front of her then took a seat looking exhausted, "one out of every three instructors are "missing" as are nearly half of all the students in the final two years."

"What about the younger students," Jolson noticed the pain and exhaustion in her voice mixed with a little alarm? He guessed at its source. "There are very few missing from the rest of the students. I can personally verify that two children that recently came here with their grandfather are safe."

Joleen relaxed a little. They still did not know what the strange power those two children had was but the thought that it might be in enemy hands had been worrying her. She felt slightly disgusted with herself that it was not their safety that she worried about the most.

NO! This is how I NEED to think right now. I must be hard when the situation calls for it. Besides, I am glad that they are safe for their own sake as well.

Joleen grabbed the report and began reading it. A great many names that she knew., both students and instructors. Joleen sat there for a while reading lists and sending reports out. Meterove and Terenia entered at one point and Joleen barely registered that Terenia was wearing Meterove's coat.

Suddenly she felt a hand on her shoulder, and she jerked herself up and glared around. Narok was standing there. She could have sworn that he had been on the other side of the room a second ago. Suddenly things made sense, she was falling asleep at the table. She looked over and Jolson was barely awake as well.

Narok spoke quietly, "I have received word that the Palace has been thoroughly checked and been given the all clear. I think everyone here needs to get some sleep."

Joleen nodded sleepily and stood up. The number of guards had grown throughout the day as more had been found. Where she had started with only a dozen, she now had over fifty that followed her around and would stand guard around her room while she slept.

Others would be guarding the halls where her brothers were sleeping. Joleen was not particularly scared for her own wellbeing and that alone was enough to tell her that she had pushed herself to hard and had burnt herself out today.

I need to take better care of myself. There are only three of us left now. If something happens to us there is no heir...

At that thought Joleen glanced at Narok walking just ahead of her. Tired though she was she felt herself go a little red. Now was hardly the time for her to go losing her head. She shook herself mentally and cleared her mind. Rest needed to come first before she tried to make any further decisions.

.   .   .

Meterove was staring at Terenia again. He could not help it. He had brought her back and had even gone through the trouble of getting her a room of her own, but she had declined and had stated, in a tone that allowed no one to doubt her decisions finality, that she would stay with him.

Now here she stood completely naked in front of him. He had no words and no idea how to handle this. Battle was easy. You fought the enemy and used whatever means you needed to in order to defeat them. This, however, was not so simple. For starters he did not even know what the terms of victory would even be.

He had never met anyone like her before. Just when he thought he had figured out how to win against her, she would show that what he thought he knew was incomplete. The only consistent was that she, clearly, had no problem with being seen nude.

Meterove's room had been ransacked when he had returned to it, and it had taken a bit to get it back in order enough that he felt that he could sleep in it. The problem now was the naked woman in front of him.

Doing his best(though not really succeeding) to keep his eyes on her face Meterove sighed, "What do you think that you are playing at?"

Terenia smiled mischievously and gave a small giggle, "Whatever do you mean? I am not playing at anything. I fully intend to stay the night with you. I already told you that I have no intention of seducing you."

Meterove raised one finger, "YET. You said YET."

Terenia smiled again and said, "Well yeah. You cannot truly think that I am going to let you get away." There was no malice in her eyes. In fact, for once, Meterove saw something that he was not expecting, uncertainty. She was not sure herself why she was doing what she was doing. There was genuine kindness in her eyes though.

Meterove shrugged and said, "Very well. I may well regret this decision, but you may stay-"

The sentence had barely left his mouth when two things happened. Terenia hugged him and he could feel just how genuinely happy she was through that hug. The second thing was a burning feeling on his back.

CHAPTER 2
PLANNING

Morning found them looking far from rested. Joleen knew that she had been dead to the world because it had taken a serving girl gently shaking her to wake her. Terenia alone looked rested. Meterove a little less so. He had certainly exhausted himself in the battle.

Jolson looked the worst. After a bit of prodding Joleen managed to get it out of him that he had another vision. He never went into specifics about them, but Joleen knew that they took a toll on him. The whole time that they were traveling together he had seemed on edge about having one.

They were in the middle of having a conversation about the continued cleanup of the city and how it was progressing when Dras showed up. The first thing that

Joleen noticed was that he looked worse than even Jolson. As he walked over, she also noticed that he was sporting a black eye and looked really down.

Jolson and Narok shared her surprise, though she was quick to notice that Meterove and Terenia did not. Sympathy yes but no surprise. Whatever had happened, they had expected something of this nature as the outcome.

Meterove and Terenia greeted Dras as though nothing was off, and others chose to follow suit. With everyone here it was time to have a more formal meeting about their plans going forward.

Joleen set her cup of tea that she had been drinking aside and cleared her throat. "The first order of business that we need to discuss is what do we do about Valaas and Syr."

Everyone at the table went visibly tense at the mention of those two. They all knew that this was their largest concern and there was no point in pretending otherwise. That did not mean that they needed to be happy about it.

Meterove instantly looked far more awake than he had a moment ago. "There are several issues that we need to agree on there. Obviously, there is whether we can even trust their word that they are not our enemy.

Just because they claim that they are not our enemy does not mean it is true. Also, just because they do not see us as their enemy does not mean that they are not ours. There is also the validity of their claims. We know that Valaas is who he claims to be and can therefore assume that Syr is also who she claims to be."

Jolson nodded, "it is also safe to assume that they are opposed to the group of undead that attacked. There was nothing to gain by helping us hold out. Also, if they were here to harm us, they had a good chance to try and kill us when they met with us."

Joleen said, "There is also the matter of the fortress itself. They called it the Citadel of Time. I have never seen architecture like that. Not in this world or in any of the others that we visited. I want an answer on where that came from. The weapons on it, the walls that it produced and how it appeared, they are all of great interest to us."

Meterove nodded, "we also cannot forget the revelation about the undead having a civilization. The idea that they might actually be organized and intelligent does not sit well with me. The nature of the undead that the Vorthens had used were very different to what we encountered from the Veiled Lands. The Ashen Empire I think he called it."

Everyone shuddered a little at that. That was something that none of them really wanted to dwell on either. It not only made the fate of the undead seem worse but also started a line of moral questioning that made them all uncomfortable.

Joleen wrung her hands in her lap. That really was unsettling. "I sent messengers off to all the other nations as well as the other cities and larger towns here in the empire. I am hoping that they fared far better than we did."

Meterove frowned.

Now that is an unpleasant thought. What will we do if it turns out that this was only a small portion of the enemy and that most of our allies are in the same or worse position than we are in?

Joleen continued, "There is also the damage that was caused by the fight the dragon lord had..."

Dras who had been unusually quiet thus far gave a small snort of mock amusement. "Damage huh? Last I checked things like entire mountains being leveled and new canyons being opened in the ground are called catastrophes."

There was silence following Dras' comment. None of them could really think of anything to say in response. Joleen cleared her throat after a moment and said, "Yes, well there is also the matter of checking on the various routes that the enemy could use to attack again.

The scouts that I had ordered out yesterday have been reporting in on time thus far, so there is no reason to believe that the enemy has another force that is within striking distance. Those scouts were told to ride through the night and have been reporting on the hour."

Jolson looked pensive, then after sighing said, "I had another vision last night, though what exactly it was referring to is still unclear. I saw a ship of a strange design and unknown origins washing up on the shore."

More silence followed this. It was broken by Dras. "Oh yay, more surprises are coming."

Joleen could not agree with that statement more. "For now, let's focus on what is already in motion."

.   .   .

It had been over a week since the battle and the cleanup was progressing well. Luckily, it appeared that the undead had gone straight for the capital and had left everything that was not in their direct path alone. This meant that most of the empire was, as of yet, unaware of any threats so there was no fear or unrest.

The leaders of many nearby towns and a few cities had sent along carpenters, blacksmiths, and stonemasons to help with the repairs. On the eighth day after the attack a large caravan had arrived from the Dwarven kingdom, Allrfé. Among other things they had sent many of their craftsmen.

The leader of the caravan was a Dwarven woman named Abjorda. She presented herself along with four others after the caravan had entered the city. They all wore fine silk garments and shiny leather boots. All five had a hand grasping a star, the symbol of the Dwarven crafters guild, on their right shoulders.

From what Joleen remembered about them the color of the embroidery corresponded to the skill of the individual. The colors were copper, brass, iron, silver, gold, rose gold, then platinum for the highest.

All the Dwarves that had come to see her had gold embroidery one had rose gold and Abjorda had platinum. This surprised Joleen since she appeared so young, maybe ten years older than herself. Clearly the Dwarves had sent some amazing help.

Abjorda looked like most other Dwarves that Joleen had met. She stood about three heads shorter than herself, and her hair was a deep mahogany, and it was cut in a short bob. Her eyes were deep gray and held a lot of composure and dignity.

"Greetings Your Majesty. I am Abjorda of the house Fidrmorginn. May I also introduce my elder brother, Harr, as well as Gungr of house Knott, Astrid of House Morginnbera and Alvis Sannrknott."

As much as Joleen wanted to take all of them in there was something about Abjorda that kept her attention. This woman had presence. Even so she was at least able to focus on each of the other Dwarves as they were introduced.

Haar looked much like his sister, though his hair was beginning to grey and was tied in a knot at the back. Where her shirt was a light lavender color with little embroidery his was a simple black with almost none at all.

Gungr was very thin for a Dwarf. Joleen had come to expect that Dwarves were mostly stocky and well-built, but this man was certainly not so. He was also the oldest present going by his silver hair that was cut short. He did have a decent sized beard though, the only one there. His shirt was bright red with a strange blue trim.

Astrid was beautiful with honey colored hair that was tied in a long braid down to her back and small lips. She had a small scar on her cheek that did not mar her appearance but leant to it an almost dignified air. Her shirt was made of green silk with silver embroidery, and she had made a point of modifying it so that some of her cleavage showed through.

She and Terenia would get along great I expect.

The last Dwarf, Alvis, was a young man maybe her own age. His hair was black and shoulder length. His green eyes were rare for a Dwarf, and he wore a simple grey shirt that while it was silk, certainly was not of the same quality was the others. Also, Joleen had not missed that while the others were introduced with their house names, he had simply been introduced by his full name. A commoner then.

"It is my pleasure to welcome you to Yxarion. Allow me to express my gratitude for your swift response. Forgive me for asking, but what news of events do you bring?"

Abjorda inclined her head and said, "As you may have surmised you were not the only ones to be attacked, though you seem to have borne the brunt of the assault. I will leave further discussion to our official envoy who was to follow swiftly behind us. We were sent on ahead as show of good faith and solidarity."

Joleen smiled at the woman. It was clear from the look in her eye that she had been told to stay out of any political matters. Still, she had chosen to at least alleviate her worries, however little she could. "I shall eagerly await their arrival. Now onto official matters. What exactly do you plan to do and what do you need from me?"

Abjorda seemed slightly taken aback but said nothing.

Damnit. I need to get better at this. Father would be furious with me for that.

Luckily Abjorda seemed to take it as though recent events were to blame not her lack of tact. Since there was no reason to let the woman know otherwise Joleen kept her mouth shut.

"Well, your majesty. Each of us here are masters of our particular crafts. I myself am a Stonemason. Harr is a Leatherworker, Gungr is a Weaver, Astrid is a Blacksmith

31

and Alvis is a Carpenter. In addition to us, we have twenty journeyman and sixty apprentices. The official orders that I have from his majesty, King Roland Orchhelm, is to help repair the city while only charging cost of materials."

Joleen let out a slow breath. Her father's careful diplomacy over the years was paying off. Had he not fostered such a cordial relationship with the Dwarves this might have never happened.

"I humbly accept the kindness and goodwill of you and your brethren. I will have little time to personally meet with you in the coming days, however I will assign one of my personal aids to you, however. Should you have any questions they will be able to answer them for you."

Abjorda bowed, "We will restore this city to the limits of our capabilities, this we swear."

After the last word left her lips the Dwarves all bowed and exited the chamber. Once the door had close behind them Joleen sank down into throne. She still often wondered how her father had been able to make this look so easy.

.   .   .

Later that same day Joleen sat yet again slumped in the throne. It had been an exhausting day. She had raised a number of men and women to higher ranks, granted many the first hereditary title that they had ever held and threatened to execute one very obstinate elderly earl.

UGH, JUST thinking about that old fool Earl Bornholdt, is making me angry again. Some people just cannot accept change.

Tomorrow looked nearly as draining. Her scouts had reported that the Elves were sending a caravan as well that should be arriving soon. The only ones that had not responded were the Acephali and the Leturai. The Leturai made sense since they were under the ocean. There was a good chance that it might take weeks for a response to reach them. The Acephali on the other hand was a different matter.

They were mysterious at the best of times. They did not allow any outsiders into their territory and required that all messages be left at a designated post on the very edge of their lands. What little the empire's information network had discovered of them was not particularly helpful. All that she knew for sure was that they appeared to live in or under ancient ruins.

In addition to caravans from allies there were also some refugees that had come from the former nation of Vorthain. Joleen had been torn about how to handle this matter. They had been part of a nation that worshiped necromancy. They had helped kill her father and hurt many of her people.

33

At the same time, they were still human. In the end she had relented, though every single one had been subjected to a thorough search into both their backgrounds and whether they had any form of necromantic energy. Those that were even a little suspect were refused at spearpoint.

.   .   .

During this process Dras and Terenia were out on a very specific and potentially dangerous mission. It had occurred to Meterove that the enemy could potentially be moving under an illusion or even through the actual forests. Their mission was to locate where the current undead forces were and to investigate anyway that Dras could put his plan into action, assuming that Valaas was being honest with them.

The two of them moved through the woods around the Frozen Forest, skirting the bubble of cold, looking for any signs of undead passing through the area. This was the fourth place that they had checked in the last several days. So far there had been no sign of the enemy. After here, they were meant to link up with a unit that had been sent to the site of the gate that had formerly held back the enemy. From there they had orders to move through the mountains and gather intelligence.

Dras was moving carefully through the woods in the crisp predawn hours. Terenia was approximately two minutes behind him following his markers when he moved out of sight.

As a wood Nymph she could sense the forest much better than a human could see so Dras could leave incredibly subtle signs that were crystal clear to her.

Times like this are when I miss my own forest. The air is so much colder here. Still, at least I'm not bored. These humans are...very entertaining. Especially Meterove...

Terenia tried to shake herself mentally. No matter what she did her mind always seemed to come back to that man. She had originally intended to trap and kill them to protect the forest.

However, after Meterove had trapped her and she had found herself giving her word her opinion had begun to change. She did not want to admit it but there was only one explanation for this change of heart.

Oh, how her sisters would laugh to know the predicament that she found herself in. She, like all her sisters, had a deeply sexual nature to her. Unlike her sisters though Terenia had always strived to become more than what her base nature told her to be. Now here she was thinking about a man, a human man at that.

35

Terenia kept making her way through the woods, following Dras, trying to focus on her task and get Meterove out of her head. She decided to focus on the fact that Dras seemed extremely skilled at moving through the woods for a human. She had had a tough time locating him and Meterove back when she first met them, which was part of how she was caught.

Thus far there has been nothing out of the ordinary in this area either. While no news was good news, she would much rather that they would find what they were looking for so she could get back.

Seriously Terenia! Focus! You need to focus on this task! Maybe I will use the time I spent cold as an excuse to warm up with him later...

The two of them continued until later that evening when they came to the edge of the forest. There they made a small camp. It would take longer than either of them would like to reach the gate and neither of them liked the idea of traveling through the night.

In their simple camp that consisted of a small campfire and a small shelter made with Terenia's power they made a small supper and sat drinking tea, though Terenia suspected Dras might have put something a little stronger in his mug.

His black eye was mostly faded at this point, but his mood was still rather bleak. He kept his usual demeanor up

36

when others were looking but when he was not focused on others or thought no one was looking his face sank back into one of deep sullenness.

Terenia set her mug down and faced Dras, "OK I have had enough of this. I have a pretty good idea what happened with your eye and your mood, but I think you need to talk. Spill it mopey."

Dras jerked his head up from looking into his mug and stared, wide eyed at Terenia. At first, he looked like he was going to try and avoid the topic but then his shoulders slumped, and he looked at her his eyes full of pain.

"You remember that night in that Tavern back on Nexus as well as I do, better probably. As you have clearly guessed, I spent the night with several of those women. I know that you are also aware that I have a wife...well had a wife. She...left after I told her what happened."

At this point a few tears began to roll down his cheeks. He looked at his hands that were shaking a little and kept talking. "I hate that I hurt her. I also hate that I enjoyed that night. What am I supposed to do Terenia. I talked to Meterove and all he could say was to give her time."

Terenia leaned over and took his hands and looked him in the eyes, "I am hardly an expert on matters like this Dras. Not only have I had little contact with men I am not human myself. Your ways are different than mine. Lust is just part of what I am. My kind simply accepts things like this as inevitable. All you can do is be honest and you have done that. Worrying anymore is going to be fruitless. Meterove needs his friend, we all do."

Terenia gave Dras' hands one last squeeze before letting go. While it was far from gone, the darkness that had settled over Dras seemed to lift a little. Dras sighed.

While she might not be human, she is a woman. It helps hearing those words from her. She is right. I have done all that I can at this point.

After this they sat in silence for a little while longer before turning in for the night. For the first time in over a week Dras was able to get some proper rest. They set out at first light and by midday had found the unit sent to scout and guard the pass where the remnants of the gate were.

To Dras' surprise they had managed to repair the damaged portion of the gate enough that it would at least slow another invasion slightly.

Full trees were laid across the front of the gate and large chains held them in place. Several smaller walls full of spikes on the front and trenches full of more spikes were scattered around the area on both sides of the gate.

Those larger undead that they had seen would probably only take a few strikes to break through but if the unit focused on taking those down this might hold long enough for a runner to reach Yxarion.

Dras and Terenia spoke with the captain of the unit briefly to inform him that they had completed their scouting and then headed through the pass.

They moved through the mountains slowly taking care to keep off the easiest terrain to avoid being spotted. They had also changed their clothing to greys and browns that matched the stone in the area. Additionally, they had covered their faces in ash from the campfires they had each morning.

After a few days in the mountains, they were heading down a slope when Terenia gave a startled gasp that made Dras drop into a crouch. "Did you see something," he whispered?

Terenia shook her head and whispered back, "No, but I can feel it. There is something foul about this area." She knelt and examined a small tuft of grass, one of the few plants on this slope. She whispered again, "I do not know how it is possible, but this plant grows but is not alive."

Dras took a moment to examine it as well before taking a clear glass bottle out of his bag and emptying the contents off to the side. The scent of strong alcohol hit Terenia's nose like a wall.

Using a dagger from his belt Dras dug out the tuft of grass and placed it in the bottle before resealing it and placing it in his pack. "We should keep moving. I think we should move even slower though now that we know were near something unnatural."

Later that day they came upon a marker that they had been told about. It marked the furthest into the mountains any living person had gone. From here on, they would be adding to the map that they had to the best of their ability.

The further that they went into the mountains the more the very rock itself seemed to be dying. It was far more brittle than it had been when they first entered. All the plant life that they found was in the same state as the grass they had seen earlier. Dras killed a crow that had landed on the branch of some scraggly looking tree, it was also undead.

After two more days of moving through the mountains the slopes began to level out and they beheld a strange sight. The same sickness that they had been experiencing thus far continued across land in front of them. Even the water had a sickly aura to it and those lakes and rivers were far off. The strangest part was the small areas where life seemed to thrive.

One of these was nearby one where buildings were clearly visible. Dras pulled a spyglass out of his bag and shaded the end with his hand looking at this section. After a moment she frowned and lowered the glass and handed it to Terenia. He looked equal parts confused and nauseated.

Putting the glass to her eyes Terenia looked around the buildings. Up close she could see that these plants looked much healthier. There appeared to be several types of edible plants being grown, all were being tended by undead. There was no mistaking that.

Several still had flesh but most were skeletons. There was a total of six buildings. Two larger ones reminded Terenia of the soldier barracks while the others were likely store houses for the equipment and produce.

What are they doing? The undead eat flesh when they even eat at all. None of the other undead that I have seen ate plants and no one has ever heard of one that farmed.

Some motion caught her eye and she looked to see an undead walk out of one of the large buildings carrying a small bundle and walk into the second building.

OK...what was that about?

A sudden screech above her almost made her drop the spyglass. Flying past was an undead Roc and it was wheeling around, to fly over again. Likely it had seen them. They both hit the ground and Terenia used what little of her power would work here to make them look more like part of the landscape.

The massive creature landed so close that some of its feathers almost brushed against Dras. While Rocs had a good sense of smell an undead Rocs relied more on their other senses. Laying still Terenia silently prayed that it would leave without incident.

After several tense minutes it took off. Dras and Terenia lay where they were for another hour before daring to move and when they did, they silently agreed that they had pressed their luck enough. It was time to leave.

.   .   .

Jolson and Narok had gone to the manor that had once been home to Orilion. While most of the more...grizzly parts, had been cleaned up, the place was still unsettling. Narok was not pleased to be away from his duty, but Meterove had insisted that someone accompany Jolson on this trip, and he already had a meeting with Joleen so she was already protected.

Still Jolson was part of the imperial family so this was still technically his duty...just not the part he wanted to do now. The tanks that lined this lab were unsettling. Knowing that the things that were in there had been alive until recently, stored for who knows how long, put a sour taste in his mouth.

Jolson was spending his time today looking through the equipment that the late Orilion had been using for his twisted experiments. Narok's job today was simply to stand guard and to give what small assistance that he could if asked.

I must be tired. I feel like I can hear a circus. That is preposterous. Not only are we inside the manor but we are UNDERGROUND! Is that one of the machines maybe...

Narok's inner monologue stopped when he saw that Jolson was also looking around the room...like he heard something. "Wait, you hear that as well?"

Jolson tensed a little then chanted something under his breath. A white dome appeared around them and Narok could almost feel a sense of anger and malice around them retract.

In the shadows of one corner, he could see a small child-like figure, crouched. It ran forward towards them, moving with unnatural movements, fast and jerky and resting at odd angles. It came to a stop just outside the dome, its head cocked almost sideways and deep red, almost black clotted blood dripped from its mouth. It had a truly horrifying visage.

Its features were disproportionate to its size. It had large milky eyes with a single vivid red point in the center with strange blue hues around it. The nose was almost nonexistent, as though it had been removed. The mouth was as large as an adults and lacked lips. Its hair was shaggy,

43

filthy, and matted. It was wearing what looked like a loincloth and nothing else.

Narok drew his sword and at the sound it jerked his head towards him, still keeping it at the bizarre angle and smiled widely before leaping back into the shadow of the corner.

As Narok watched the shadows seemed to lessen and after another moment they looked normal. All sound of the circus vanished and now that it was gone Narok noticed that it had even faintly smelled of one as well.

Narok kept his sword out and without taking his eyes off where that thing had been asked, "What in the HELL was that?"

Jolson did not respond right away. He was just as shaken as Narok. After a moment he said, "I have no idea, but it was dangerous. I am quite sure that it was here to kill us for entertainment. I felt...COMPELLED to do what it told me to. It wanted to be entertained but it was unable to control me. Luckily, I was able to put up a barrier-"

Suddenly Narok saw Jolson tense up his eyes staring, unseeing ahead of him and he fell to the ground his whole body jerking and tensing, foam coming out of his mouth. The episode lasted only a moment before his body relaxed and he lay still.

Narok knelt quickly and checked him but found him breathing, just unconscious. The barrier was still up around them and Narok knew from experience that unless Jolson chose to end it early this barrier was going to last awhile longer so he sat down next to Jolson and waited.

It was hard for Narok to judge time in this place, but it felt like Jolson was unconscious for about fifteen minutes when he began to wake up. His first words were "Sorry about that."

Once he was sitting up and his eyes seemed to clear up some Narok spoke quietly, "So are you going to tell me what that was all about?"

Jolson looked at him almost dreamily. "It is nothing that you need to concern yourself with Narok. I am fine."

Narok nodded, "That may be, but understand that you will have to explain this later, if not now. Joleen will ask me for a full report, and I will not be leaving this out...without good reason."

Jolson sighed. He was not only exhausted, but this was also a topic he wanted to avoid. However, there was nothing for it but to explain. Narok was right about Joleen asking him for a full report.

As Narok helped him to his feet Jolson resigned himself to explaining what had transpired. He quickly decided what parts to leave out.

"Fine I will explain a little bit. I just had a vison. It was a vision of that...thing that we saw just earlier. This is not the last time that we are going to cross paths with it."

Narok stared Jolson for a moment. "Are your visions always so...eventful?"

Jolson wearily shook his head, "Based on how I feel and the length of the vision this time was far kinder on my body."

Jolson raised his eyes to Narok's and saw sympathy in his eyes. When he spoke, his voice was steady. "I will report that you had a vision. For now, I will keep the details of the aftereffects to myself."

Jolson smiled gratefully and after a moment he got to his feet and lowered the barrier. "I think we should get out of here. I still do not know what that thing was, but I have no desire to encounter it again without more help."

Narok looked back at the corner where they had first seen the "child" and shuddered slightly before looking around the room again quickly.

To think that I would find something even more disturbing than those deformed bodies!

With one last shudder he followed Jolson back out of the room.

Meterove was dying. Well of boredom at least. He could stand a lot of things but sitting through reports and interviewing military officers to find those that would replace their lost generals and listening to various recruitment plans was putting him near his limit.

HOW DOES JOLEEN DO THIS?! It has only been half the allotted time that I agreed that I would help with this, and I am losing the will to live!

Meterove knew that he was being a little dramatic, but his question still stood. He had no idea how she could do this all day EVERY day. Across the table that they used for these kinds of matters a VERY old woman sat in a long black dress with a black veil and a black hand fan gently waving herself cool.

She was the Duchess Faris, the only living member of the family left. She had been found hiding in the serving women's quarters of the Faris state and had been brought to Yxarion. She was waiting for Joleen's response.

Joleen and Meterove were both slightly taken aback at her request. It seemed that while in hiding she had learned that one of her serving girls was extremely intelligent as well as cunning. Knowing that her own family was lost, the Duchess had requested that they assign a temporary custodian while she transformed the girl into her heir.

47

Joleen was all for it but was waiting to decide until she had thought the matter through some. In her mind though it led her people down a path that she wanted and was almost certain to agree to it. She just had to look for any problems that might arise from this.

"Personally Lady Faris, I have no objections, but I will run the idea through a few other advisers before I select the individual that will take temporary custody of your lands."

The Duchess stood and somberly said, "I thank you for your time and understanding Your Majesty. Also, I know that I am not alone in having lost loved ones. You children have lost your father. You are both doing quite well I should say."

With that she gave a subtle bow befitting her age and departed. Meterove swallowed and glanced at Joleen. He could tell that she was hiding it but her wounds were just as raw as his own. He placed his hand on her head and pulled her over into a brief embrace.

Joleen was surprised. Meterove had never really been a hugger. This simple gesture, while the two of them were alone went a long way towards lightening her heart. He might be a pain sometimes, but he was her brother and he loved her.

There was a knock at the door. This puzzled her since they were not supposed to have another audience for another hour. She straitened up and said, "Come."

In walked an exhausted looking Jolson ahead of Narok. They both looked very much on edge. Joleen felt her anxiety rise and quickly asked "What happened? What is wrong?"

Jolson and Narok looked at each other and Jolson gestured for Narok to speak.

He must be absolutely exhausted!

Narok took a moment to collect his thoughts. "While we were investigating the equipment in Orilion's lab we encountered...something. It kind of resembled a child but was...well to be honest, it was horrifying."

From there Narok told of the encounter while Joleen and Meterove listened. When he got to the part about Jolson having a vision, they noticed their brother tense up a little but, once Narok concluded his report, he relaxed again.

After Narok had finished speaking Jolson showed them the brief image from the vision that he had. It was not very long, maybe twenty seconds in all, but it clearly showed this...thing, fighting with Meterove and Dras in some sort of warehouse.

Once it was over the four of them sat in silence, each one pondering what the creature was. After some time

Meterove and Joleen needed to get back to their remaining audiences for the day, so Joleen sent Jolson and Narok off to rest.

It would be nice if Dras and Terenia came back with good news .

.   .   .

And here I was hoping for good news.

Dras and Terenia had returned two days later with way more questions than answers. The sample that Dras had collected had been studied and found to be undead.

How can grass and DIRT be undead? OK fine grass was alive but DIRT!

After much discussion there was only one course of action that any of them could think of taking. Whether they liked it or not, it was time to go pay that fortress, the Citadel of Time, a visit.

CHAPTER 2.5
HINTS

That had been a close one. To think that the "Child" would be so attracted to the oracle. It was understandable how it had tried to ensnare the other one, Meterove. Luckily the oracle had been aware enough and strong enough to repel it. What might happen the next time they meet?

It was bothersome being unsure if the next time that they met was the time that had been shown to the oracle. Well, that hint was all that could be given for now. There were other problems to deal with as well. Where had the Darkfire one gone?

A flap of massive wings and a swirl of flame later and now the surroundings were familiar, though I have never been here in the flesh. Flesh...I cannot believe I have flesh! Or that I am an I!!!

What would come to pass was now so unpredictable that it was really only a conjecture at this point. More selves are needed to narrow the potential.

Things are spiraling even more out of control. I must stay the course and do what must be done...no matter what cost I incur!

CHAPTER 3
BRIEFING

Valaas stood on one of the battlements of the Citadel of Time. The ancient structure that he and Syr had found so long ago still held secrets even to them. While they knew that it was called the Citadel of Time, they had no clue as to why or who had made it nor how.

They could use most of the structure, though there was a large door at the back of the main entrance hall that was still sealed to this day. Small metallic beings that resembled a mosquito in both shape and size were one of the many useful things that they had found throughout the Citadel.

According to the information that they could decipher these "constructs" were called Drone Implants. Any creature that they landed on and connected to was under the control of the ones giving the commands back at the Citadel.

Currently he had his eyes closed and was watching the approaching party from the eyes of a bird that was flying above them.

So, you have finally come. I was beginning to wonder if you truly had the backbone to call yourselves the descendants of Mardelnier.

Behind him, Syr stood emotionless as always watching them from another Drone, this one a gopher. She opened her eyes looking for Valaas to make the decision. She was as unsure as he was about these kids.

Finally, Valaas said, "We should get below so that we can welcome them. If they are going to release us from our bond then we need to help them in any way possible, including being patient with them."

.   .   .

Meterove stood at the front of the group staring at the fortress in front of them. The architecture truly was unlike anything that they had ever seen. Like the palace it appeared to be one solid piece of grey stone. From what he could see every turn and angle was smooth and even the windows, arrow slits and doors were rounded.

During the battle it had sent out a number of crystals that had created a sort of outer wall. Up close, he could not see where they had come from. He could see some of the magical weapons that had also been used in the battle. They looked just as different as the rest of the fortress. The strangeness of its design almost made them miss just how massive this place was.

Meterove looked back at the others. They all looked tense. They wordlessly encouraged him to lead on. As Meterove stepped up to a large staircase the door at the top slid soundlessly up, beckoning them in.

After climbing thirty steps they reached the door. It was at least as big as the main door back at the palace. Once they were all inside the door slide closed, again without a sounds. On the door was a crest of an hourglass with the symbol for infinity wound around it.

Well, I guess that explains why they called this place the Citadel of Time.

They were standing inside a large circular room with a dozen pillars in the shape of hourglasses running along edges, holding up a second floor that was open to the main room. In the middle of the room was the most detailed Orrery that any of them had ever seen. It showed all six of the planets, the moons...everything!

At the back of the hall was a curved imperial staircase that went halfway up to the next level. There was a large landing there with a sizeable mural of the solar system set into the wall. Curving up in the opposite direction were more stairs that went to the second level.

Tapestries hung all around the room, each with a different depiction of the same subject; a bird wreathed in flames. Sometimes the bird appeared like any other bird just with the flames. Other times, the only thing about its appearance that was birdlike was its silhouette in the flames.

There were a dozen passages that led off the main room and from what could be seen there appeared to be the same number on the second floor. Walking towards the Orrery the party kept looking around. Dras was the first to notice that the ceiling was an enormous functional clockface.

Their steps echoed off the walls of the room. After a moment there was the sound of more steps coming from above. Dras noted that each door matched the clock face and that the steps were coming from the three-o clock position.

Valaas and Syr came into view coming down the stairs. They did not look any different than the last time that they had seen them. Joleen could not suppress an involuntary shiver as she looked at them.

I am looking at members of my own blood that are now undead. Revenants, they called themselves. Can they be trusted? I feel like they held back information last time. Was that because, as they had said, they were taking damage from our defensive spells? I just wish I had a better way of judging them.

"Greetings to you all. It has been a little longer since we last spoke than I had anticipated. From what Syr and I have observed, it would appear that you still do not trust us. Considering the abrupt nature of our last conversation that is to be expected. If you follow us, we will take you to a suitable room to answer your questions."

As if to punctuate his statement, Valaas gave a small dip of his head before turning back. Valaas and Syr started walking towards the seven-o clock door on the lower level.

The hallway was wide enough that had they wanted all six of them could have walked through them side by side. Along the walls various stands, furniture and other décor were scattered. Doors and alcoves dotted the walls on each side.

Four doors down on the right Valaas turned and the circular door silently slid up revealing a sitting room with several large chairs and couches around a large wooden table. There was a large fireplace with a pair of those birds from the tapestries on either side of the mantle.

It was currently cold and looked as though it had never been used. Up until now none of them had noticed that the light they had been seeing by was not coming from the windows. This room was just as well-lit as anywhere else in the fortress.

Valaas gestured for them to take seats while they both sat opposite them. "I have anticipated a few of your questions so if you would like I can save us all some time. First, I am sure that you want to know more about this building, the Citadel of Time.

Syr and I claimed this fortress from the lands to the far north. The Lich that had once been our father wanted to claim it as well. Neither of us know its true origin but it is clearly an advanced and powerful weapon. On top of the siege and counter-siege weapons and ramparts that you witnessed in the battle this fortress also has the ability to transfer between space-time coordinates."

Jolson raised an eyebrow, "Space-time coordinates?"

Syr made an impatient noise in her throat but looked just as impassive as always. Valaas simply paused for a moment and continued, "You can move this anywhere that you want, though the time part is extremely limited. The most we have been able to move is a few minutes."

Jolson's mouth hung open. "Moving into the past or future! That is supposed to be impossible."

Joleen put up her hand to silence Jolson. "Moving through time sounds a little TOO good to be true. That aside the fact that this fortress was not here before the battle shows that you are telling the truth about that part at least."

If Valaas took any offense to her questioning his claim about traveling in time he did not show it. He simply continued his explanation.

"Inside this fortress there are many rooms but the areas that you will be the most interested in are the Library, Foundry, Barracks, Armory, Warehouse, Greenhouse, Refinery, Lab, Treatment Center, Conservatory, Observatory, and the Hospital."

Everyone spokes at once, their voices overlapping.

Dras said, "Armory?"

Meterove said, "Barracks?"

Terenia said, "Greenhouse?"

Joleen said, "Hospital?"

Narok said, "Foundry?"

Jolson said, "Library?"

Valaas just ignored them and continued to give his explanation. "Each of these are located on an "even" positioned door. The "odd" positions lead to other areas such as the lords chambers and other more mundane areas. There are many passages for moving between the main sections."

Joleen put her hand to her chin. It was clear this fortress had been made by someone and for a specific purpose. That was clear as day while the who and what were clear as mud. While Joleen was pondering this Meterove asked, "How large are these Barracks?"

"It can comfortably house one hundred thousand soldiers," Valaas responded.

That pulled Joleen back to the conversation, "HOW many?"

"One hundred thousand." Valaas repeated. "To be more precise it is many smaller barracks that can collectively hold that many soldiers."

Joleen was stunned.

How big is this place?

Dras followed up on Meterove's question. "What about the Armory?"

Everyone sat up a little straighter. Valaas responded, "It currently holds enough melee weapons to arm every man in the barracks twice over. There are also various ranged weapons and ammunition for one hundred thousand.

This is some good news. Between the weapons that we were able to salvage after the battles and what we had been able to get made by various weaponsmiths we are running short of being able to arm the soldiers that we have right now. If we tried to raise an army, we would need the weapons here. Hmmm....what about armor? Shields?

Joleen asked, "What about armor and shields?"

Valaas had anticipated this question and responded immediately. "There is enough armor of varying types for one hundred thousand and there are twenty-five thousand shields of differing sizes.

Joleen and Meterove looked at each other.

Meterove knows just as well as I do that we need this place. The question is what do these two want from us? They clearly want something from us and used that explanation as a carrot to get the conversation where they want it. So, what are they after? We should try and carefully maneuver the conversation-

Terenia interrupted her thoughts, "So what is the catch? You are telling us all about this to make us want it. What is the price that you want in exchange?"

Joleen closed her eyes and let out a groan.

So much for tact. Hopefully, the direct route will yield results.

While her eyes were closed, she heard Syr give a snort of derision. Opening her eyes Joleen saw that though her facial expression was still impassive, her eyes held a bit of scorn. That really had not gone over well. Valaas also looked annoyed but since Terenia had started them down this road there was nothing to do but keep moving down it, so Joleen decided to press onward.

"Well? Terenia does have a point. If you did not want something from us, you would have left after the battle. Actually, would you have even joined in had you not needed something?"

Valaas tried to smooth over his expression before he said, "It is true that we need your help. Syr and I need to reach the Lich and to do that we need to move through the entire Ashen Empire. Your average citizen would not know us for what we are but some of the more powerful undead would catch on immediately, especially a Weaver."

Jolson cocked an eyebrow, "What is a Weaver?"

Valaas said, "Weavers are the priests of the Ashen Empire's religion, The Church of the Ashen Rebirth. They worship the Ashen Soul. They are the ones responsible for making new undead."

Narok, who had been silent thus far whispered, "So do they attack us to get fresh corpses or for food?"

Even though he had whispered Valaas had heard him. He shook his head, "No, the attacks on the living are a combination of instinct and orders from the Lich. They get bodies from their Corpse Farms."

Dras raised his right hand, his index finger out, "Their WHAT?"

Valaas no longer seemed annoyed. It was clear that this was information that led in the direction that he had wanted to go from the start. "Corpse Farms are places where humans are bred. They are raised on a Farm until they are fully grown then they are harvested. Obviously, any that die early are also used-."

Everyone felt sick but none as much as Dras and Terenia. They had glanced at each other before looking down at their laps, their faces paling. They had the exact same thought.

Those buildings that we found on our mission! That bundle that we saw them take into the other building....I think I am going to be sick!

Valaas continued "as well. We can go into more detail later but for now I will summarize. There are five distinct types of Weavers. There are Blood Weavers, Bone Weavers, Flesh Weavers, Soul Weavers, and Nightmare Weavers. The first four are the most common and self-explanatory. Nightmare Weavers are rare and subsequently are the ones we know the least about. What we do know is that they are said to create things from the "Ashen Nightmare" whatever that is."

"I have encountered men that once they died split into multiple undead. Is this magic done from multiple Weavers?"

Valaas shook his head, "No there are different tiers of Weavers. Single Weavers, Dual Weavers and so on. The more types of weaving that you can do the higher you are in the churches hierarchy. The Grand Weavers are the ones that have been around the longest and have mastered the five different weaves, though they each still specialize. They stand just below the Lich in the Ashen Empire."

Hearing about these "Weavers" was only adding to the nausea that they were feeling. For Dras and Terenia, they kept seeing that "farm" as though it was burned into their eyes. Meterove could only see those men that he had encountered back at the temple, which felt like a lifetime ago.

Jolson was the next to ask a question, "Do you know anything about a "child-like" creature that appears from the shadows? There were also the scents and sounds of a circus, though we were inside a building."

Valaas looked intrigued and pressed Jolson for more information, "Can you describe it in more detail?"

Jolson said, "I can do you one better. I had a vison involving it as well. Here."

Jolson pulled a Memory Crystal out of his pocket. He had planned ahead and made it last night. Everyone except Jolson and Narok watched the projection that came from the crystal with interest. Dras and Meterove glanced at each other when the music was heard. When the child leapt forward Terenia swore.

After the "child" vanished the memory cut out and shifted to a new place. Dras and Meterove were fighting this child in a dark warehouse. The shocking thing was that they seemed to be in a stalemate. Whatever this thing was it was not normal.

Once the vison ended Valaas was quiet for a moment. When he spoke, it was with some hesitation. "I cannot say for certain, but I think that creature has nothing to do with the Ashen Empire. While it most definitely is some kind of malevolent entity, it lacks many of the characteristics of the Weavers and their creations."

Jolson had not really expected that he would get an answer, but it had been worth asking. Confirming that these two had blind spots would make dealing with them easier.

Joleen asked, "You had mentioned that you two and the Lich were both after the Citadel. How did you know of it to begin with?"

Valaas said, "In our time the area where the Ashen Empire is may have not been under our control, but we had thoroughly explored it when searching for threats. The Citadel of Time had been found shortly before our father started acting...off. Once he had turned, Syr and I raced our father to the Citadel and managed to beat him too it. We managed to figure out how to move it by complete accident."

Jolson asked, "What happened after you moved it?"

Valaas sighed, "We found ourselves in a heated debate with our brother Valnyr. Mardelnier's death weighed on us all. Perhaps it was our differing ways of handling grief that kept us from finding common ground. To this day I still do not believe there was any other way to ensure that the Lich did not claim the Citadel. Syr and I have been moving the Citadel to a new location every time we were discovered ever since the day we turned ourselves."

Jolson looked puzzled, "I have a separate topic I have a few questions on. The Orrery that I saw down in the entry hall showed the whole of the world in great detail. I only glanced at it, but I saw that there was more land across the ocean. Is that where you came from? Why did you leave?"

Valaas and Syr looked both surprised at the change of topic and slightly...uneasy. "There are three continents on this world. There is this one that we are one which is in the northern hemisphere. There is the Shattered Continent, which is one long archipelago that runs along the equator, the center line of the world. Then there is the southern continent. That is where we came from."

"And the reason you left," Meterove pressed?

"The reason we left was because the Artificials drove us out. They pursued us to this land, but we managed to eliminate the few that found us. Whether they stopped hunting us because the crossing was too hazardous or for some other reason is unknown," said Valaas

Joleen asked, "What are the Artificials?"

Syr showed a rare flash of emotion, pure anger, no rage. "They are beings that were created from humans but are not human themselves. They were copies made to appear like the same androgynous being. They are grown in tanks using an individual as a "source" of material."

Valaas put a hand on Syr's and gave it a small squeeze before continuing from where she left off. "They had been created by a coalition of Nobles that had wanted to claim the throne of the old Empire. Our Father had been a Duke back then. Before either side knew what was going on they had made their own plans, to eliminate us.

We saw that they were going to win long before the Empire or the Nobles that started the coup ever did. Our father gathered together the lesser nobles and their people that he had sway over and seized as many ships as possible and sailed across the ocean to try and escape."

So, there is something else out there that wants to kill us. Great. Meterove and Jolson look like they are on the same wavelength as me. Dras and Narok are probably too. Terenia is well, Terenia.

Syr's voice became harsh, "Our mother was killed by one of their assassins."

Meterove had been about to ask a question but closed his mouth without a word.

Ah, that explains a lot of things. That hatred for sure but also that emotionless nature and that strong will to be the ones to handle the Lich.

Perhaps to change the subject to something less heavy Narok cleared his throat and said, "You knew when we were approaching the Citadel and were present almost instantly after we entered. I am willing to bet that you were observing us somehow. Would that be a safe assumption?"

The change in topic seemed to please their hosts. Valaas pulled a small crystal about the size of his thumb and carved into a pyramid out of a pocket. Each side had a small circle with runes around it carved into it.

"This is one of the items that we found in the Lab. It is connected to a tiny metal construct that is about the size and shape of a mosquito. Landing this construct on another being allows you to control it and experience the world through its senses. It makes surveillance far easier. I was watching you through a bird while Syr was using a gopher."

Nope I do not like that! That is really unsettling. I kept my guard up the whole way here but from what they said they might have been watching us through anyone or anything.

Meterove took a moment to calm himself. There was no reason to assume that they had done anything of the sort. You did not disclose such a convenient spying tool if you meant to keep using it. Of course, it could have been a way of warning them that they could not keep secrets from them.

Dras seemed a little thrown off by this but asked his question next. "You said that you could make some of those Shaping Crystals so that we could make a trap for the enemy?"

Valaas reached into another pocket and pulled out two more crystals. These were a little bigger and looked almost like they had been taken straight from a mine with clumps of smaller crystals around one larger one.

"As promised. These are not as powerful as the ones that were made by the mages back in our time, but I have never been especially powerful in magic." He handed over a small, sealed scroll then continued, "These are instructions for making them. Combined with studying one of those, your mages should be able to make more."

Joleen watched as Dras accepted the crystals, then asked, "We have talked for quite some time, yet we still do not know what it is that you want from us in detail. I think it is time we got to the main topic."

Valaas looked right into her eyes. "We want to destroy the Lich. So long as he still exists so shall we. We have guarded the world from him for long enough. We wish to pass on. The only route open to us now is to ask for help.

You also wish for his destruction. So long as he exists the Ashen Empire will be a threat to you. The Ashen Soul is a separate issue that is beyond us, but we can fight against those that it taints. Our goals align. As our descendants we have something of an interest in ensuring that you survive. We have given you a lot of information that I am sure that you wish to discuss amongst yourselves as well as with any advisors you have. I will show you out. Please think over this and we will await your favorable response."

.   .   .

No one spoke as the door silently slid closed behind them. The whole way back the only talk was between Dras, Meterove and Narok communicating what they saw as they made their way over to where they had left their escort. The three hundred soldiers would likely have been useless in a fight against those two, but it was better to bring them anyway.

Once they were back in the palace Joleen called a meeting with the few advisors that she had. She kept certain parts out, such as who these undead truly were, but most of the information she freely shared.

A few days after they returned word came from the unit at the gate that another force had been spotted by its scouts. Dras and Terenia left that day with one of the Shaping Crystals. They took a thousand archers with them. The plan was to test the crystals in a way that would slow the enemy while not giving away their plan.

While they were gone Joleen was working with the Dwarves to get the explosives, they called dynamite. Jolson and Meterove went back to the manor with a full unit of soldiers. The "child" did not make another appearance, however.

Hearing about the "Artificials" from Valaas had made them think of both the machine here and the one that they had seen in the labyrinth. It was unnerving to know that the presence of these tanks, which were still intact, might indicate the presence of another enemy.

.   .   .

Dras and Terenia moved as fast as they could reaching the gate by road this time. Upon reaching it the captain informed them that their scouts had just returned an hour earlier with news that an army of about twenty thousand was approaching. They had seen no scouts from the enemy.

Dras stood on the side of the gate facing enemy territory, his cloak blowing gently in the wind. He was studying the land. Terenia watched him silently. Her part in this would come after he used the Shaping Crystal.

After nearly an hour of silently studying the pass Dras decided on his course of action. The only questions were if the crystal would do what they claimed and if it did would it be powerful enough?

Following the directions that had been in the scroll along with the process of making them Dras walked over to the edge of the mountain that he wanted to start at and placed it on the ground, put his palm over it and formed an image in his mind.

There was a pulse of light from the crystal and the ground shook and began to run like water. Dras watched as it formed into what he had pictured. A deep trench filled with barbed spikes that was nearly twenty feet wide and spread across the whole pass. In addition, a twenty-foot-thick wall that stood thirty feet high was on their side of the trench. Lastly a smaller trench was dug on the enemy side, making siege ladders and bridges difficult to maneuver and assemble.

Now that Dras was done Terenia used her powers to rapidly camouflage the wall as well as the gate behind them. To the enemy it would appear to be a hill until the front ranks fell into the pit. Eventually it would fill with enemies, but the archers were meant to help thin their numbers before they got to that point.

With luck this would buy them the time that they needed to prepare Dras' real plan. Losing another army, even a small one like this should draw out any large forces that the enemy still had in reserve.

Dras surveyed the fortification then gave the archers the go-ahead. They had already been given their orders. As the soldiers took their places Dras said, "These crystals are perfect for what I have in mind. They will never know what hit them. We had better get back. I am sure that they will want us there before they formally accept Valaas and Syr's offer."

.   .   .

Several days later they once again found the six of them heading to the Citadel of Time. This time though, as a way of showing their soldiers that they were meeting allies, they did not take any additional guards with them.

Valaas said, "I am pleased that you are willing to work with us. We will do all that we can to aid you in return. Everything that is in the Citadel is at your disposal."

Jolson, who had had an odd expression on his face asked, "I have a question about that mural that is in the entry hall. It appears to be a door. What is behind it?"

Valaas looked at Jolson and said, "That is a question that we both share. We have walked these halls for centuries but have never been able to open that door, nor have we found any information that might offer a clue as to what might be behind it."

Jolson glanced in the direction of the entryway frowning but dropped the subject. Meterove took the opportunity to ask, "What plan of action did you have in mind? We were discussing how to scout the undead. Would those constructs that you showed us before, be able to control an undead?"

Valaas nodded, "Certainly, provided that the undead in question was not particularly powerful or old. The longer that an undead has been around the greater it's abilities. We have used them on something as powerful as an apprentice Weaver."

Meterove nodded.

That is good news.

Valaas continued, "We will move the Citadel to a location in the wilds just outside the Ashen Empire's eastern border. After we have a secure location, we can set up a Gateway."

Meterove looked at his siblings and was glad that he was not the only one that looked confused. "Gateway?"

Syr took a deep breath through her nose then said, "Are you telling me that that knowledge was lost as well?"

Valaas said, "It was probably done intentionally. Without Gateways there was little chance that they could be used against them."

He went on to explain, "Gateways are made using a special Shaping Crystal. They require a crystal that is split into perfect halves and then each one is used in a different location while magic keeps them tied together. The result allows for instant travel from one location to another, though it only lasts for a single day at a time. In order to activate it again the two crystals must be activated at the same time."

Meterove and Dras immediately started talking about possible military applications of this while Narok looked relieved. Joleen knew what he was thinking.

With this Gateway there will be no need for me to go with them. I can join them if there is need but for now, I can stay back in the Empire and work in strengthening our defenses, relations and moving my plans forward.

Joleen said, "Then I think we have a plan. I will remain here while the four of you accompany Valaas and Syr on this scouting mission. We will report in every morning at nine. If anything happens, even if it seems small or unimportant, I want a report. If you feel like you are in danger you are to return immediately."

Meterove and Dras looked at each other. They knew that was meant for them, well Terenia too. Meterove said, "You got it Jol."

Like I plan to give you extra things to worry about sis. The only way I plan on reporting something is if there is something that we can do about it.

CHAPTER 3.5
ANOTHER

They had found the others! Things were progressing in a desirable way. Having use of the Citadel of Time would grant them advantages far beyond what they had realized so far. Soon they would have to meet but not yet. They needed to grow more first.

While that was happening finding the scattered selves would take priority. Now that a safe place to rest had been acquired searching would take priority. There was no longer a need to hide. Two fragments had attached themselves to living beings, but the rest were out there somewhere.

Pop! Looking around there was a world of Water all around. Spirals, like double ended waterspouts, connected the water above and water below. There was something off here but now was not the time to look into it. There was no sign of another self so time to move on.

Pop! A world of darkness and stone. Again, there was no self here. Pop! Pop! Pop!

Spirits everywhere, but no self. Fire but no self. Clouds and endless open air but no self. Pop! No self in the hub city either. Wait... the sense of other selves could be felt, from the branches of Creation! So, the other selves are in other worlds!

Pop! A dark sky with many bright lights off in the distance. A more technologically advanced world than the previous one. An airship flew past with searchlights shining. Suddenly there was a sense of danger and the sense of something try to contain. Pop!

A new world, this one very primitive. That was close! Whatever happened back on that world it was bad. There had been a self there, but it was too dangerous to go back, yet. Suddenly there was an intense sense of nostalgia. Looking behind there was another self!

Wings flaring out and swooping forward in mirrored motion and a small blurring and two were now one. That was a little better. A few more and I will be strong enough to investigate that last world. For now, best keep looking. Pop!

CHAPTER 4
RECONNAISSANCE

Dras and Meterove were out scouting north of the new location of the Citadel of Time. Terenia and Jolson were working on setting up fortifications and camouflaging traps.

It had been an odd experience opening the doors and exiting the Citadel; finding themselves on completely foreign ground. The way Valaas had explained, it they were on some planes at the base of the mountains south of the Ashen Empire.

From what they could tell there was a large farming complex about two days walk from here. There was a lot of traffic as the undead hauled humans as both food and as a means of increasing their numbers. Apparently, there was a city nearby that the undead had built. According to Valaas and Syr it was not too different from a human city, but Meterove had a hard time picturing that.

It was bizarre here. Being surrounded by undeath that seeped into everything around them, even the stone was unsettling. Apparently after some study Jolson had concluded that the land itself could heal but obviously all the plants and animals were a lost cause.

That just is NOT natural.

Meterove shivered slightly as an undead squirrel ran past. According to Valaas none of the plants and animals could communicate with the humanoid undead, but that did not make him feel any better. The idea of an undead bear attacking them in the woods, or a pack of undead wolves was unpleasant.

Then there were the actual monsters. Meterove and Dras had already seen a creature that they had only heard of in legends, a manticore. These beasts had human-like heads with bodies like a lion and a massive snake for a tail. There were two dragon-like wings that sprouted from its back and its body had many sharp quills all over it.

Seeing one of those things, twice the size of a lion, was bad enough but it had also been undead.

I do not want to know what being undead does to things like that. They are already supposed to be super deadly. The farm complex is supposed to be this...hey what is that?

Meterove's thoughts were interrupted by a strange sight, a strange pile of something that was an ash grey. As Meterove stepped over towards it the wind which had been at their back whipped around in their face. Their nostrils were now assaulted by the most horrific stench imaginable.

"Ugggh" Dras retched. "What the hell is that?"

Meterove gagged as well and backed away to the left trying too not be downwind. He said "I think that we found something's shit."

Dras pulled a piece of cloth out of his bag and a small flask of alcohol. He wetted the cloth and tied it over his face. After a moment he seemed satisfied and repeated the process and handed it to Meterove, who took it.

Well, I guess that is one way to go about it. OH! Hey, this stuff smells surprisingly good! Some kind of fortified wine? It really works too, nice.

Meterove knelt next to the pile this time taking care to stay upwind. "Do you think we should take back a sample?"

Dras looked wide eyed over his makeshift mask and said, "First of all why? Second of all how? Third of all, and most importantly to me, you can but I am NOT getting any closer to that stuff than this."

Meterove considered taking a sample for a moment longer before deciding that if anyone really wanted it, they would certainly have no shortage of it over here. Finding undead poop did raise questions that Meterove was not certain that he wanted to know the answers to.

Some rustling in the bushes nearby seemed too large to be another squirrel so Meterove and Dras moved back into cover as quietly as possible.

Out of the bushes slithered a thing that seemed like a fusion of snake and human. While he had heard of things called centaurs before, he had never heard of anything like this creature.

Its scales were brown with black diamonds on its back. There was a strange rattling protrusion on the tip of its tail. The torso of a human man was upright, its long brown hair unkempt. Scales still covered parts of this section of the creature, and it had no ears that Meterove could see. Its eyes were yellow with slits for pupils and a long, forked tongue flicked out of its mouth. It kept looking around while flicking its tongue out.

Meterove mouthed to Dras "It knows we are here. You go left and I will go right." Both men gripped their swords and after a moment burst out of either side of the bushes. The creature whatever it was, ,coiled up and started shaking its tail making the rattling sound louder.

Dras went in for a feint to try and draw the creature into an attack. Since they knew nothing of these creatures Dras wanted to know if it had any dangerous abilities.

It lunged forward far faster than Dras would have believed possible, and its jaws unhinged, and its mouth opened wider than Dras' shoulders, revealing two long curved fangs dripping with a yellowish liquid. It snapped its jaws closed on Dras' left arm.

After a moment it let go and a wicked grin crossed its face as it rounded towards Meterove. As it moved up on him it got the last surprise of its life. Dras leapt forward and with a powerful two-handed swing cut the top half of the creature away from the snake-like tail.

Its eyes shown with hatred and fear as they lost their light. It only took a moment, but the tail thrashed around the whole time and the hands grasped at them. This thing had been dangerous. The only thing that had saved Dras was his prosthetic arm. Without that he would likely have died from that bite, if the creatures expression was any indicator.

Dras wiped his blade clean then asked, "This was the last section that needed to be scouted right?"

Meterove took a hand drawn map of the area out of a small satchel. He also had ink, sand, and a pen. After a few moments of scratching, he was done.

Dras looked at the map then smirked, "You are no cartographer, but it is usable."

Meterove used the sand on the ink then stowed it away. "Next time YOU can draw. I cannot WAIT to see the master artist at work."

Dras laughed lightly. This had been a strange day to be sure. "Should we head back?"

Meterove thought back to the map he had put away. They had mapped everything that they dared enter casually. Soon they would begin to encounter undead humanoids and that meant alerting the Ashen Empire. While he was pondering this, he saw some movement off in the distance.

Given the distance it was hard to gauge, but whatever it was, it was pretty good sized. Maybe even two or three times the size of that manticore. Dras followed Meterove's gaze and watched something that looked like an enormous serpent with four legs moving around. It resembled a Wyrm but was much smaller. It also had wings that were more like a dragon's.

As one Meterove and Dras turned saying "Nope" and started heading back to the Citadel. They had been out here for less than half a day and had seen enough. A fight with something like that could get flashy.

The wilderness here was strange. The plants themselves continued to grow, but in a strange diseased looking manner. The leaves were all sickly and brittle. The branches of trees had cracks running along the bark. Stepping onto a stone could reduce it to pebbles and dust.

The water looked off as well. They had seen undead drinking it but had no desire to test it themselves. It clearly smelled stagnant, even when it was running in a stream or river.

It took them several hours to reach the Citadel, which was now sitting down in a valley to help hide it. The ramparts had been deployed and the hills around the perimeter of the ramparts had been morphed by Jolson and Terenia to help mask them and to give them hidden posts where they could post guards once phase one was complete.

The plan was to have the small group of them scout and form a forward base. Meterove and Dras had been out mapping the terrain and marking locations on it that would make good lookout locations. The two hundred men that they had brought with were guards for the Citadel but were also part of phase two.

Phase two was using those men as a harrying force to draw a large enemy force into Dras' trap. With any luck they would damage whatever army the Ashen Empire had left enough that future invasions would be unlikely.

Meterove and Dras walked up to a section of the ramparts and stepped through. They had done the process that Valaas called "registration" with the wall when they had left the first time. It allowed anyone that was registered to pass through the wall portion along with anything that they were carrying but still acted as a barrier to everything else. It really was convenient.

Inside the ramparts the soldiers had been busy digging in more fortifications. A series of trenches and blockades were set up. A narrow path led straight through to the entrance to the Citadel, but it was only wide enough for two people. Simple sliding and locking mechanisms allowed the defenders to quickly block the path.

Meterove and Dras went up the steps to the main entrance. They each had been given a room for their personal use though, yet again, Terenia showed up in Meterove's room as though it was a given that was where she should go.

Meterove rolled his shoulders as they walked down the hall. "I say we get cleaned up before meeting up with the others."

Dras grunted then responded, "Yeah, I do not want to take the chance that smell attached itself to us. I would hate to be blamed for that crime against nature."

They split up and after bathing and changing into fresh clothes, headed to the study that had essentially become their conference room. Terenia followed Meterove out of his room. Dras shook his head,

It seems that Terenia is up to her usual antics. Meterove still seems to be at a loss about how to deal with her too. Heh this is actually pretty funny to watch. Though she does look a little off. I wonder if this place is affecting her a bit more than us.

The four of them met up in the study and had a small meeting about their respective projects. Valaas and Syr had taken to spending most of their time out on the physical ramparts on the Citadel.

Once they had their short meeting about their projects, they were going down to investigate the lab and practice using the constructs that they would be using to spy on the inhabitants of the Ashen Empire.

Meterove wasted no time in getting started once all of them were there. "We finished mapping as far as we had planned. There were several threats out there that were significant. We managed to kill humanoid/snake hybrid creature. We also saw what appeared to be a manticore and some kind of large creature that looked like a Wyrm with wings and four legs, though it was much smaller than a Wyrm."

Creatures like these were another reason that they were going to use the constructs. There was no need to take more risks. Jolson nodded in response to Meterove's report and examined the map that he had handed over.

"I am sure you saw the fortifications on your way in. The only thing that I have to report is that the taint that is causing the undeath is having an adverse reaction on Terenia."

At this both Meterove and Dras turned to her, their eyes full of concern. Terenia sighed and rolled her eyes at

Jolson's comment. "I said I was fine. I just feel a little more drained. Spending time in the Greenhouse for a few hours after I have been outside is all I need. Although I can think of something else that would help me feel better"

Meterove rolled his eyes and shook his head, "No, I want you to get a full checkup back in Yxarion. It will only take an hour or two."

Before Terenia could do anything but pout, Dras added in, "It might not be such a bad idea to send a few of the soldiers back as well and have them checked. It would be bad if it turned out that they were being corrupted just by being here."

This was an unpleasant thought. It had occurred to all of them that it was a possibility but before Terenia had started feeling off, they had all hoped it was only paranoia. After this they called an end to their meeting and went and selected five other soldiers at random and had them all meet up at the main entrance of the Citadel.

From there they walked over to the southern part of the Citadel to a stone archway that looked like it held a mirror. Once a person touched their "reflection" on the surface the gate would fully open and allow anyone to pass through for the next twenty-four hours. Then the Gateway would have to be reestablished.

Dras and Jolson bid farewell to Terenia and the soldiers while Meterove went to go inform Valaas and Syr.

None of them deluded themselves that they would care about this but there was no point not to tell them either.

Once they were through the Gateway Dras and Jolson went back to their rooms. The plan was to rest until the examination was done and then assuming everything was alright to attempt to use the constructs to get a look at the Ashen Empire.

.   .   .

Three hours later Terenia had returned with a mixed bag of news. From what the mages that had done the examination could tell the corruption had made it so that if any of the men died, they would turn, but the effect appeared to fade over time if they did not turn.

Terenia was a little different in that she interacted with the land, and therefore the taint, more directly. They had purified all of them, but she would need to return daily to be purified. It appeared that the taint acted something like an illness for her.

They headed down to the Lab to get the constructs. This place was one of the stranger rooms to them in the Citadel. There were tons of tools here that they could scarcely understand. At Valaas' insistence they had not explored too much of this place. Luckily, he had told them where in the Lab that the Constructs were stored.

Each of them tool one of the crystals then went out to the section of the ramparts that Valaas and Syr often occupied. For now, they were elsewhere. Following the instructions, they had been given, they each opened the bottom of the crystal by twisting it. This activated the small construct that was inside the crystals, and they flew out and hovered over them.

They closed their eyes and had a very sudden and powerful feeling of disorientation as they saw themselves from above. Opening their eyes things shot back to normal but that too was disorienting. They decided to wait until the feeling had subsided before they tried again.

This time they used the crystal and took control of the constructs and flew off, each looking for a bird. Once all of them found one they used the constructs to take over the bird. It was a strange feeling suddenly seeing and feeling what the bird did. From there they practiced controlling the birds until they felt that they looked fairly natural.

Once that was achieved, they flew the birds over to the nearest town. Seeing a town of undead was quite the sight. This was a smaller village that was on the outskirts of the larger farm and trade city to the west. There were maybe a few hundred undead here.

They chose four random targets and once they were near enough, they detached from the birds and flew the constructs over to them. Once attached to the undead they took control, though in what was called standby mode.

Meterove opened his eyes, the nausea came back.

That is going to be hard to get used to. Also, it was only for a second but feeling what the undead felt like was not great.

Meterove saw that he was not the only one. The others all looked a little pale as well. The plan had been to send the constructs out today and tomorrow morning they would restore the connection and be able to do what was called piloting, where they directed every movement and even thoughts.

.   .   .

The next morning, they activated their respective constructs and proceeded to direct them as they had been instructed by Valaas and Syr.

What Meterove saw upon taking control of his was disturbing. He was not certain what he had been expecting the inside of an undead dwelling to look like but the amount of "flesh bits" that were scattered around clashed with the mismatched furnishings that made it look like the home of a human. The whole look was truly bizarre. There was no bedroom though, as undead did not need sleep.

Meterove steeled himself and moved around the small structure. There were only three rooms in the whole place. One to eat in with the mismatched furniture. One to store and prepare food, a kind of kitchen and walk-in cooler. And the last was one that really sickened him. There were two live humans chained up.

They were both men and totally naked. The look in their eyes was sullen and totally passive. They were used to seeing undead. He was keenly aware of the hunger that he felt and knew that under normal circumstances these people would be eaten.

Meterove's instinct was to try and free them, though that likely would only end with someone else eating them and alerting the other undead that something was wrong. Settling on setting them free then acting distracted, Meterove tried speaking through the undead after unlocking the chains. " You stay here. I will be back."

His clumsy movement and likely different speech pattern seemed to confused them, though only for a moment. After this he stepped out of the room and acted as though he had forgotten something. Suddenly there was a flash of thoughts through his head, and he had a complex series of thoughts relayed into his mind.

OK Mel, you should bring the fresh meat with you soon. We have the side dishes mostly ready. It is almost time for Connolly's one hundred and eighth Reanimation Day party. Once you have given the meat to Viktor, help Halvor clean out the latrine.

Just as suddenly as they had come, the thoughts were gone. Now that he focused though Meterove noticed that there was a constant background chatter and once he poked at it found that he could read thoughts from all the undead nearby. He quickly pulled his mind back and stayed back.

I do not want to get caught because they saw my thoughts. I do not know how this works yet and I need to take this slow.

He glanced out of his window, which held no glass and saw a varied group of undead walking past. Most of the undead in this town appeared to be reanimated corpses. A few however, were so bizarre that Meterove could not stop himself from staring.

One appeared to be an amalgamation of many people from the neck up, fused together facing in all directions like some horrifying plant. It walked around on three legs like a tripod and had six arms. No two limbs looked quite the same.

There were also a few that were made of bones. Other undead were even more monstrous in appearance.

There were some of them that had some of the parts from the monsters that they had seen before attached to them.

These ones the others gave a wide berth. Whatever they were the other undead were clearly warry of them. Two of them walked up to a cart that was holding severed forearms with the hands removed. They passed over several small objects and two of the severed arms were handed over.

Meterove watched nauseated as the two undead began to eat them.

Blech... I am not sure how I am going to make it through this. There is no way that I am going to be able to eat anything like that. That looked like they handed over money. Do the undead of an economy?

Meterove decided that he would be best served checking the mind of the undead that he had control of for a few answers. What he found was almost overwhelming. He decided to start with currency.

The name of the currency was a fayar. It was triangular though the edges were rounded. The metal that made them up varied but had no impact on the value. In the center of each fayar was an opal.

The different opals determined the value. White opals were the least valuable. It took ten white opals to equal one fire opal. It took ten fire opals to equal one crystal opal. There was a fourth fayar, but it was only used for larger purchases. It took one hundred crystal opals to make one black.

Meterove also learned of something called the Necroduct that moved necrotic energy around the territory of the Ashen Empire. This would be vital information since this might allow them to disrupt the flow of the taint that was making Terenia ill and potentially corrupting their men. There was something else that he learned which pertained to the message he had gotten earlier.

Apparently, their waste disposal system here consisted of undead slime monsters that fed on the waste. The slimes were carted to and from the sites that they sucked the waste from. This undead, Mel was a waste disposal worker.

Another telepathic message started coming through, but Meterove pushed it to the back of his mind. He moved over to the door and left the building. He made his way out of the town to the location that they had established beforehand.

When he arrived, there was already one of the others there. At least that was what he assumed. To be sure he used the code phrase that they had worked out.

"What was the name of that constellation again?" Meterove asked.

The undead that was in front of him had very little hair and stood a little shorter than his own. Unlike the flesh on his own that looked soft and appeared pale, this one was very dry, and the skin was darker. A telepathic message came across.

Oh, you mean Archer, the fat cat constellation.

Oh yeah, using that telepathic link is probably how most of the undead communicate. I had better remember that. Well better give it a try.

It took a few attempts to get it right but finally Meterove got there.

This is Meterove.

This is Jolson

Hearing that the other undead was his brother was really odd. It did make sense though that Jolson would have figured out the telepathy already. A ruckus behind them caught their attention. As they looked two more undead stumbled into the small clearing.

One was an amalgamation of humanoid parts that were put together to form a person. The skin was a patchwork of different shades and the edges where they had been attached were fraying some. The other was one a sight to behold. There was no jaw at all and there were bones showing through in places.

They gave the phrase and Meterove replied. The first one was Dras and the second one was Terenia. Again, it was hard to reconcile those forms with the people that he knew were in there.

Alright. Phase one seems to be a success. Let's get these undead back to the Citadel and into the lab for phase two.

Terenia put a hand up to her head and looked down.

I am a little worried that we might have made a scene back there. Dras and I let the humans that we found in our homes loose.

Meterove nodded and almost spoke out loud before catching himself.

I did the same thing.

Terenia crossed her arms.

It was weird because they did not look at all like they wanted to run or like they were even afraid.

Jolson entered the conversation; *It is likely those humans that we find in the Ashen Empire are going to be of similar mind as beef cattle are to us. If undead communicate telepathically then it is possible that the humans do not even have the knowledge of language.*

Dras shuddered.

That is such a horrifying thought. I cannot even fathom just sitting there in those rooms, waiting to be eaten. Do they even know that is their fate?

Following Meterove's suggestion they used the constructs to move the four undead back to the Citadel. Once they had them inside, they put them in the Lab. Once they had them in isolation chambers, Jolson and several mages that they had called over began investigating them.

While they were working on that, Meterove and Dras took two more constructs and attached them to two more birds and flew them back to the town. They had been told of the undead being "civilized" and had heard a bit through the link but they still had trouble grasping it. What they saw in town cleared any doubt.

The four undead's disappearances had been noticed and there were search parties looking for them across town, and the area outside of town. Meterove almost felt bad since they appeared genuinely worried.

It was hard to stay that way though when he saw them take the humans that they had seen earlier and lead them by a rope. To them people really were just food. That brought up the question of how they decided which people where for food and which were for becoming undead.

Meterove and Dras left the two birds up in trees around the town. Returning to their own bodies they found that they had been watching the undead for quite some time. They returned to the lab.

Meterove and Dras walked up the group of mages and picked Jolson out. "So, how is the plan progressing?"

Jolson looked up from circle and nodded, "Ah Meterove! Good. I am happy to report that we are nearly done. It took a little longer than I had anticipated since we ran into a few more disturbing roadblocks."

Meterove raised an eyebrow, "disturbing roadblocks?"

Jolson sighed, "One was that the longer the construct is attached to the target the more thorough the merger of your mind and their senses."

Meterove said, "And that is a problem how?"

Jolson said, "The reason you do not taste your own saliva is because your brain automatically blocks those tastes. Just like you do not feel the clothing on you or see your own nose."

Meterove nodded, that had been part of the basic education they had received. Seeing that Meterove was not putting the dots together Jolson sighed again. "We do not have anything to stop us from tasting the inside of the undead's' mouth."

Dras gagged. Meterove could not blame him. That was an unpleasant thought. "You said roadblocks. Plural. What else did you find?"

Jolson looked a little uncomfortable. "The second one stemmed from the fact that we saw that undead eat. That implies that they NEED to eat, and I doubt any of us would be able to mentally or physically force ourselves to eat the flesh from another human.

Thus, we were experimenting to try and find out what else they can eat. So far, we have not found anything that works unless it is raw. The only thing that we can do is use them until we find out how long they can go without food."

Even though they were undead that did not sit right with Meterove. Looking over at Dras he saw his feeling mirrored there. What they had seen back in that town did not change their feelings about killing undead. It did make things like experimenting on them feel slightly twisted though.

When he voiced this to Jolson, his brother looked both intrigued and as troubled as he was. "I just do not know what else to try. Every animal meat that we have thought of requires too much cooking to be palatable to us that it would be suspicious."

"Have you tried fish?"

Terenia had walked in and hearing their predicament threw out a strange suggestion. "There were a few places when we were on Nexus that served it. It must be edible if it was served in a city, right?"

Jolson looked pensive for a minute. "You know, I think that might be what Valaas and Syr have been eating. I was not about to ask in case I did not like the answer..."

There was an uncomfortable silence. True none of them had voiced it but everyone had wondered about it. If they had been eating people, would that make them enemies? Too much of a grey area.

Jolson shook his head to clear his thoughts. "We will try that. Assuming that we can get this to work then we will be ready tomorrow."

CHAPTER 5

FARMS

Jolson's estimate was a few days off. It had been three days since they had completed phase one of their plan by retrieving several of the undead and were currently studying them. Terenia's idea of using raw fish had born fruit. It turned out that not only was it tolerable but actually was quite good if made properly.

Phase two of this plan was to use their undead to get a look at what the farms were like. Working the kinks out of the plan had taken a few extra days. Now that they had everything ironed out it was time to start the next phase.

Jolson and the mages had taken to referring to the undead with the constructs as "drones" to help differentiate them in conversation. They had lucked out in their choice of drones. Meterove's was a Waste Disposal Worker,

Terenia and Dras had found drones that were suitable to act as guards. Jolson's drone was a Banker.

If they could sneak back into the town, they could get a large amount of money from his house. The plan was to raid all of their respective savings and to see what exactly they could manage as far as information gathering was concerned.

It was decided that having one person entering the town with three more constructs following would be the best method. Thus, Dras found himself sneaking into the town while the others followed him with the constructs.

It went a lot smoother than they were expecting. The only time that they ran into anyone was at the Banker's home where a few guards were guarding a safe. Meterove and Terenia took over them and used them to guard the outside while Dras used the key they had taken from the Banker and opened the safe and emptied the contents into a bag that he had.

Once he was done, he closed and relocked the safe. After he was safely outside the town Meterove, and Terenia put the two undead back where they had been in the room then separated the construct from them and after they observed them for a minute to learn if they had seen anything they flew back out and followed Dras to the next house.

There was far less money in the other three houses, which made sense. Still, by taking everything that they had the overall sum was actually pretty reasonable. After they finished the last house they hurried back to the Citadel.

Once they were there Dras took the bag and dumped the contents onto a table, and they began to sort out what they had for fayars. After nearly half an hour they had them all sorted and counted. Even though the one was a Banker, it was still from a small town so there was not an obscene amount of money.

In total they had forty-three white fayars, twenty-seven fire fayars, fifty-nine crystal fayars and three black fayars. In terms of total fayars this amounted to thirty-six thousand two hundred and thirteen fayars. Searching through the memories of the Banker they learned that they would be taken seriously enough as customers at a farm.

.   .   .

It was now several days since they had taken the money and they were on their way down a road using a strange cart that like the materials they used for other construction, was immune to the decay that permeated this land.

They had stolen the cart from another small town on the way. Unlike the carts that they were used to this one used not only animal labor in the form of two undead horses to move it but also had wheels.

Up ahead, maybe another hour away was a farm. They were getting nervous now since they were getting close to the farm they had selected. This particular facility was massive. Once they had drawn up to it, they could see that it was composed of a dozen buildings that were each large enough to hold hundreds of people.

They pulled up and found several other carts already there parked and tied up near the entrance. As they tied off their horses an attendant wearing a scarlet sash with an emblem of a silhouetted profile of a pregnant woman.

Welcome to the Third Imperial Farm. What can I do for you today?

Jolson took the lead here. This was a time for finesse.

Good day. I am here on behalf of the township of Sterghan. We recently purchased some stock from another farm, and they started going bad, so we were forced to use them early. Would it be possible to have a tour of this farm's facilities so that we can verify that the stock here will not do the same?

The undead, it was hard to tell if it was a man or woman, looked affronted for a second and Meterove was worried that Jolson had overdone it, but he worried for nothing.

Charging for stock that is not going to last is a personal affront to any good farm. It shames me knowing that another farm would dare do such a thing. While I am sure it was one of those smaller, private farms, it is still unforgivable.

Especially when it involves a smaller town. Please come with me. While I cannot take you through any of the active birthing rooms, I can certainly allow you to verify the quality of our stock and breeding methods and space. Follow me please.

The attendant led the way inside one of the buildings. At the front there was a staircase that led both up and down. They were standing in a small room that led to a hallway large enough for three or four people to walk side by side.

This is the main entryway of building A. This floor and the upper four floors are our breeding floors for this building. The basement of every building has two functions, storage, and a morgue. Buildings A through E are breeding buildings. Buildings F through J are housing. Building K is our feeding building and Building L is the staff building.

The undead led them down the hall, which looked like an enormous stable. In every stable there was a naked woman sitting in straw, sometimes eating, sometimes sleeping. Most of them were in different stages of pregnancy. Occasionally they would find some that were not pregnant though.

These were occasionally found with a man, and more than a few times they were in the middle of making a baby. Jolson looked away.

I agree, said the attendant, *I find the whole thing disgusting too. It is hard for me to believe that I started out that way.*

Leading them down the hall the attendant did not pay particularly close attention to what they were doing but answered any questions they had.

Meterove took advantage of this and asked, *How much meat does this place produce?*

The attendant appeared to think for a moment before answering. At first Meterove thought that they looked suspicious, but they answered all the same.

We have one hundred breeders per floor and every building has four floors. We produce around two thousand per year. It is our policy to never sell any stock that is less than breeding age unless it expires prematurely.

All told, we have around twenty thousand head here.

Meterove winced at the number. It should have probably been expected, but still hearing the numbers as well as proof that humans were nothing but cattle to them was hard to handle.

After the breeding buildings they toured a housing unit and saw that they had a similar but smaller set up to the breeding unit. Each human had scarcely the space of a kennel. The only ones that had anything other than straw on the floor were the infants. They were kept warm with ragged blankets.

The feeding hall was the last building that they toured. It was simply a massive kitchen and pantry with a cellar. The undead that was giving them the tour was not the only one that they saw on their tour. There had been about twenty or so others that they had seen scattered around. While their clothes had all been different, they all wore that same sash.

"So now that you have toured our facility and have seen that we truly have top quality stock could you give me some idea as to what your budget is? From there I can help advise you on the best purchases."

Jolson pretended to think for a moment as if he were deciding how much the town might be willing to part with. After a minute he wrapped up the charade and said, *"I would say that we are willing to spend about thirty-six thousand fayar."*

The undead seemed mildly surprised at the amount but Jolson caught on quickly and said, *"I am augmenting the* towns offer with my own money since I feel responsible for the other...unfortunate incident."

This seemed to clear away the surprise and any suspicion that had started to take root. *"If that is the case, may I suggest a group of five that I have that are all of breeding age? One female and four males. You can use the female to breed more in the coming years. The total would normally be thirty-seven thousand if bought individually. However, I am willing to slightly lower the price if you are buying all five."*

Jolson had spent a decent amount of time searching through the minds of the undead that they had captured and knew that this undead was trying to cheat them. That or it was a haggling technique. It was hard to tell.

Jolson said, *"Are you including the means to purify the kennel where they would be kept?"*

The last of the suspicions left the undead and it gave a short bow. *"Of course. Allow me to have them bought out and I will go get the necessary paperwork."*

The undead led them over to the staff building. It opened a door and after a moment another few undead left the building heading over to building K. The attendant then said, *"come in and we will finalize the transaction."*

Entering the building was an experience to be sure. There was a waiting room, though there were no chairs. There was a large gray stone counter near the front. There were two large glass jugs that were upside down in some lever activated machines in one corner. One looked like blood and the other looked like pus, frost coated both jugs and there was a pile of mugs in a barrel next to them.

"Feel free to have a drink if you would like. I will just be a moment. "

The attendant went behind the counter and after a moment found the paperwork that it was looking for and brought out a quill and some ink. Jolson read over the purchase agreement, noting that the written language was an extremely archaic version of his own, then signed the document and handed over his money.

When it was all completed the attendant bowed again and said, *"Thank You for your patronage. We hope to see you again. The five heads are outside. Our handlers will be happy to help you load them into your cart."*

Jolson and the others bowed back and exited the building and found the two handlers standing with five humans. All five appeared to be around their mid-teens. They were all clothed after a fashion. They had burlap sacks, with wholes cut in them, over their torsos and extremely filthy rags on their feet. They all stood in a line with glazed over looks in their eyes.

They allowed the handlers to help load them up then after another few minutes they were on their way. It was very unsettling looking at these humans sitting in the cart as though they had no will or cares. Eventually they reached the part of the road where they would take the cart off and into the woods where they would hide it in the brush.

Here for the first time the humans appeared to show some signs of confusion and unease. This was probably very different to what they had experienced so far in their lives. The further that they walked the more uneasy they became until they were very tense and jumped at any sound.

When they caught sight of the Citadel they froze in place. It was clear that they had never seen anything like it. When they saw the men guarding it were human like them, they grew even more agitated. They stayed close to the undead that were with them.

They led them through the Citadel until they reached the research lab. Once inside they came face to face with the real Meterove and the rest. As soon as they entered the room Meterove used his drone to close and lock the door. Jolson had already separated from his drone and was trying to speak to the teens.

"Do you understand me? Can you speak?" Jolson asked that in various dialects of their language, but the teens simply stared at him blankly. Jolson tried for several minutes to get them to understand that they were safe, but they continued to look afraid.

While Jolson was sitting and thinking of what he could try next Dras walked up and pointed at the girl. He then moved his hand to his sword and patted it. After that he took her and embraced her, putting her head on his shoulder, while patting her head and rubbing her back.

The girl burst into tears and clung to him sobbing. Meterove and Terenia looked at each other, then did the same thing with two of the others. This led to the same result. Jolson walked over and grabbed the last two and did the same thing as best he could.

It took the better part of an hour before they had calmed down enough that they were willing to work with them. Now that they understood that they were safe, and that Jolson and the others wanted to communicate with them they were being very agreeable.

Jolson had sent word that he wanted an expert in teaching language sent over. It took about a day, but an elderly woman name Kasandra Hilgins was sent over and began teaching them how to speak.

Soon it would be time for phase three of their reconnaissance plan. This would require them entering a larger city. Valaas and Syr had informed them that humans were everywhere in the city so their scent would likely go unnoticed, meaning they could transport the drones to the city and piolet them from there. This would allow them to react to anything that happened.

During this process Valaas and Syr were doing some reconnaissance of their own. They had heard talk of something that the undead called "The Blight" and had gone to investigate it.

Over the next week they continued to use the constructs on birds to observe and gather intelligence. They had all noticed that there was a large stone structure that gave off an ominous aura. It was long and spread out across the land and branched off. Each branch ended in a large stone magic circle that gave off the strongest of necromantic energy.

By chance Dras had decided to take over another undead one day that seemed to be heading in the general direction of this magic circle. It turned out that this one was actually the towns Weaver and that this stone structure was called the Necroduct.

The Necroduct was what kept the land in a state of undeath. These magic circles at the end of the Necroduct were called wells. It was at these wells that most of the lesser Weavers used their arts. The wells acted as amplifiers for Necromancy.

They would have to see what they could learn from the teens that they had rescued. None of them had any real hope of anything useful but it would be foolish to rush in before Valaas and Syr came back anyway. Only time would tell when and how phase three would begin.

Meterove stood leaning against the wall watching Kasandra working with the teens. They were eager to learn and from what he could see they were all fast learners, though the girl might be the sharpest out of them.

I wonder how this will all play out in the end. I would like to destroy all of this, but I have a feeling that this is not going to be that simple or go that smoothly. Oh well that is future Meterove's problem. For now, I am going to go rest. I have a feeling things are going to escalate far too quickly.

.   .   .

"Watch the western wall. They are attempting to move around using the bushes for cover."

The Citadel was under attack. A large group of those snake creatures from before had formed and attacked them. There were a few different kinds it seemed. There were about three hundred of the things but since they were without any form of advanced weapons like siege weapons they were of a minimal threat.

That being said, they had figured out that if they dropped several trees onto the wall, they could create a ramp. Fighting them inside the walls would lead to casualties.

Jolson was using a construct to survey the battle from the air at the moment. Watching the battle unfold from the air like this gave them an unbelievable advantage. He could also spot when one of them began acting as a leader and could direct the soldiers to it.

While this was going on Meterove and Dras were up on the walls with the soldiers. Terenia was blasting the area using one of the magic cannons. As the battle progressed Jolson noticed that there were three distinct types of these creatures.

One had beige scales with black diamonds and a rattle on the end of its tail. These ones attacked using their teeth and primitive swords or spears. The second type had large hoods of skin that flared out and had jet black scales and crimson skin.

They used spears but could also spit something out that Jolson had guessed was poison. The range was pretty frightening. Jolson had gauged it at ten to fifteen yards. The last kind was absolutely massive. They were twice the size of the others and appeared to use brute force in the form of large mauls and using their bodies to squeeze the life out of their victims.

So far, they had not lost any men, but it had been close a few times. Twice they had barely cut a man out of the coils wrapped around him before he had died. One they had actually had to resuscitate. None of the men had been hit by the ranged attacks yet but that had been a near thing too.

There was something very odd about the way that they kept attacking then withdrawing. Jolson decided that it was likely a smokescreen of some kind. He identified the creature that was currently leading the attack and turned it into a drone.

The plan was to try and read whatever their plans was while having the bonus effect of disrupting their coordination. What he learned was worrying. If he had done this at the start, they might have had even more warning but now was not the time do dwell on hindsight. He quickly found Meterove and used the construct to relay what he had just learned.

"Meterove, we have another one coming in. These attacks are just a diversion. The one coming is HUGE. Be prepared to engage. It is coming from the east."

Meterove decapitated one of the creatures and turned to the east. "How huge can it be? I do-"

There was a large island of trees over there and a portion began to shake and one was ripped clean out of the ground.

OH! You mean HUGE huge...

The monstrosity in front of him was insane. This thing had to be at least fifty feet long and was probably fifteen feet around at the base of the tail. It also had four arms. It picked up two of the trees that it had knocked over and wielded each like club.

116

Meterove blinked, "It just picked up two whole ass trees and is just swinging them around. Well, I guess some body reinforcement magic will be a good idea."

Meterove focused his power into his body then jumped out to fight the giant creature. In the blink of an eye, he had crossed half the distance, but the creature had seen him and had responded in simple means by throwing a tree at him.

Meterove used his sword to slice and pulverize the tree but had missed the second tree that had been thrown just after the first. Meterove was hit directly and was slammed back by the tree directly into the wall of the Citadel. He pushed the tree off and away from him then doubled over and coughed up some blood.

Damnit that hurts. It threw trees at me. Who the hell throws a tree? I get that it is huge and all but seriously. OWW...yep more blood just came up. That did some internal damage. I will have to finish this quickly and get some healing.

Meterove stood up and swayed a little. He was hurt worse than he had thought. Looking out he saw the creature actually had a weapon of its own as well, a massive curved great sword. To make matters worse a group the smaller ones had started heading in his direction.

Meterove watched as a blast hit the large one right on one of its arms and nearly took it off. Meanwhile a voice in his ear said, "Damn man. You look like shit. Maybe you want to sit the rest of this fight out and let us finish up?"

Meterove glared at a grinning Dras who was holding him steady. Meterove shrugged his arm off, shook his head and even though he was in a ton of pain grinned back. "Please you would never be able to take that thing on."

Dras looked at it, "I am pretty sure I can at least manage not getting hit by a tree."

Meterove coughed again, "Shut up."

Dras grinned again the switching to a more serious face said, "How about I keep the other ones occupied then."

He dashed off and engaged them. Meterove was left to get himself righted. He managed to get his head cleared a little more then pushed off the ground launching himself forward again. The creature had its great sword out and caught his downward cleave with the flat of the blade.

Shit. I have slowed significantly. My strike was a lot weaker than I was expecting. This is not going to be as quick as I want it to be.

They clashed over a dozen times with Meterove dodging out of the way of at least twice as many attack from that behemoth sword. Finally, he managed to time a spin, off a blocked attack to land an upward sweep to critically injure one of its hands. This forced it to drop the sword.

Meterove was nearly spent but he pushed himself forwards and darted to the things waist . Once there he landed a massive slash that went nearly to the hilt. He then jumped and landed a knee to its jaw which forced its body backwards, tearing it in half.

Seeing their champion fall the remaining creatures fled. Meterove leaned on the severed upper half of the creature, while the tail portion thrashed around. He felt a hand supporting him and knew Dras had come back over to lend him a hand. Knowing that the battle was over and that Dras was there, Meterove released his tension and lost consciousness.

.   .   .

Meterove woke up in his room, but it was not the one in the Citadel, but back in the palace. He remembered the battle.

I must have been more severely injured than I thought if they brought me back here. I wonder how long I was out?

He sat up and noticed that he was not alone. Sleeping soundly next to him in a short nightie was Terenia. She stirred after a moment and opened her eyes. Looking up at him she smiled and resting a hand on him said, "Nice to see you awake. From now on maybe make me the only thing tree related that gets to attack you."

Meterove rolled his eyes and said, "You and Dras are not going to let me live that down, are you? Fine, whatever. How long was I out?"

Terenia sat up and the nightie began to disappear. It was only then that Meterove realized that it had actually been made of lavender petals, probably to help him sleep. The petals slowly dispersed and left Terenia fully nude.

Terenia said "It has been about two days. You were pretty badly hurt so we transported you over here just to be safe. We learned a few things while you were out, but Joleen said that she would brief you once you were recovered."

Meterove got up and dressed. He had long since gotten over any sense of discomfort when Terenia was there naked or seeing him naked. While he was dressing Terenia made a simple dress with her power and once, they were ready they went down to Joleen's study.

The first thing that Meterove noticed upon entering was that Joleen looked exhausted. There were bags under her eyes, her skin was a little pale and her shoulders seemed stiff. Her face brightened at the sight of him though.

Good I was worried there for a moment that she might be seriously depressed, but it looks more like she is just overworked. Not that that is great either.

120

She gestured for Meterove and Terenia to have a seat and said, "I am glad to see you awake. When they brought you in, I was really worried. I have never seen you so gravely injured."

Meterove said, "That thing was powerful and moved faster than I had expected. I made a serious error when I assumed that it was simple minded."

Joleen smiled, "Oddly enough that was something that I was going to tell you about. It appears that they have not only a decent intelligence capable of rational thoughts but also something of a culture."

Meterove looked surprised at first but then said, "That makes sense. That thing had a massive sword, which would imply that they know something of metal working. The likelihood that they happened to find a sword for it by chance are pretty low."

"We agree," said Joleen, "Also Jolson was able to see a decent amount of coordination amongst them. The thing that perplexed us the most until just a few hours ago was that they had shown signs that they had only recently been turned."

Meterove was very surprised at this. So far everything that they had found over there had been undead. They had not even found a hint of anything that was alive besides themselves.

Joleen continued to explain, "Valaas and Syr have returned from their investigation. They were "kind enough" to give us a rough idea of what the lands are like beyond the Veiled-the Ashen Empire. They are lands teeming with monsters.

There is also the "Blight" that they went to investigate. According to them it is a beautiful oasis filled with a sort of natural cleansing magic energy that is pushing back against the negative energy that is coming from the Necroduct."

Hearing about all this put Meterove into a pensive mood.

Did these things come from outside the Ashen Empire or were they creatures that existed in this "Blight" that had been driven out? It would be better if it were the former. If it is the later then it brings up the question of why they left in the first place.

Meterove looked at Joleen, who was watching him over her folded hands. "The plan remains the same right now. You will use those drones to infiltrate a city next. We need to know more about their civilization as a whole but particularly we need to know more about their military and these Weavers that seem to be a core part of their religion. We also need to learn anything that we can about the Ashen Soul."

We are getting there, father. We are making our way towards the enemy's heart. We will avenge you and all those that have suffered because of this evil. I swear that I will protect everyone. We will make you proud.

CHAPTER 5.5

PREDICAMENT

They had found several interesting things to be sure. Now was not the time to focus on them, however. Seven more selves had been found and reintegrated. Several things that had been happening were now known.

The corruption of the Ashen Soul was spreading. It had infected things that should never have been. The "Child" was moving again, its appetite and desire for entertainment was insatiable. Knowing its origin made it all the more frightening.

How to help....? That was an important question. There were a few selves left that were safe to go after. There were a few that were far too dangerous to go after. What was that place that had captured one of the selves? How was it possible to capture it to begin with?

Then there was the matter of the Darkfire one. Where was it and what was it doing? What to focus on was the question. Too many different paths to take. Some promised ruin, while others only hinted at it. Finding the other selves that are safe to approach will have to stay the priority.

Pop! This world was extremely advanced. Regular magic would not be usable here. Only things beyond the threshold of mortals would be able to move to and from worlds like this. Looking down far below was a sprawling city with countless lights shining in the night.

There were a handful of mechanical winged transports moving about. Some were in the air getting ready to land, others were getting ready to take off. There was a constant cacophony of mixed high-pitched sounds coming from the city streets, where vehicles with tiny lights on them waited in long lines.

There! Pop! There was a new city down below with lots of lights again. This time there were several huge pyramids just outside of the city that were clearly quite old. Perched on top of one of the pyramids was the self!

There was a moment of Joy as the two reunited then one was absorbed into the other. The great fiery wings gave a joyful flap and feathers of all hues of red orange and yellow could be seen wreathed in blue flames.

Finding this self did not mean that the urgency had lessened. The search for more selves needed to continue and waiting was out of the question. There was no reason to look around this world any further. Pop!

The new world was one that was vastly different to the ones that had been investigated so far. There was little on this world but enormous mushrooms. This may well have been the most primordial world yet. It was quickly obvious that there were no selves here. Pop!

It was now hovering over the tear that the Dragon Lord had made on Aural. Another possibility was checking the world of the First Ones. That was very risky at present though. What to do?

CHAPTER 6
METROPOLIS

It had been two weeks since the attack on the Citadel. There had been a few more incidents of creatures attacking but they had all be dealt with easily. They had also used the constructs to make other drones that investigated other farms and scouted the land well enough to have a cartographer make an actual map.

They had found dozens of larger towns and five larger cities. There were also countless smaller towns and villages. Then there was the capital city of Koreykjav. It was on a whole different level from anything they had ever seen. There were more undead in this one city than in the entire human empire.

The information gathered so far suggested that there were nearly ten undead for every human. True the vast majority seemed to be regular citizens. The same was also true for the humans though. Their first priority was to find out just how many soldiers were left in the undead army.

Once they had investigated the military, they needed to investigate the undead's means of propagation, the Weavers.

They had taken several dozen humans from various farms and had given them over to Kasandra to attempt to teach. The original five had made some progress. While they could not speak yet, they had learned a great many sounds and knew several important words like hungry, tired, and hurt.

After some careful investigation they had found a safe place to use as a base of operations. The architecture of the Ashen Empire was unique. None of them were particularly well versed in architecture but Jolson vaguely remembered that one of their instructors had referred to this style as gothic.

There were a few buildings scattered around the empire that had some of these concepts but nothing on this scale. Even buildings that were clearly in the slums had elements of it.

This city was nestled between the banks of a river and spread all the way over to some nearby mountains. The place that they had chosen as a base of operations was the top of a clock tower. None of them had ever seen anything like this.

They were so high up that even the air felt thinner. This tower had to be over eighty feet on a side. Each side had a stained glass clockface with a spiderweb frame that was over fifty feet in diameter. All four had the same image. What appeared to be a spine with two wings, one with feathers and one that was only bone draped around it.

They had all seen those wings before. They would never forget seeing that vile creature in their home, the Ashen Soul. That image appeared to be both the crest of the Ashen Empire and the Weavers. They had learned that the name of the church was The Church of Ashen Rebirth.

During one scouting mission Dras had found that the Necroduct went into the mountains. None of the undead that they had turned into drones or any of the ones that they had talked to while using them seemed to know where exactly it started.

Other investigations had also shown that the massive keep that was at the back near the mountains was the palace of the Ashen Empire. The Lich that lived there was regarded as a legendary figure to most of the undead. They also had the same structure of nobility as the empire.

The plan for right now was to sneak through the city under the cover of dark. Even though undead did not sleep they would still blend into the city better at night. It was just

Dras and Meterove initially. They would get up to the clock tower and set up a tent that they had camouflaged to look like the corner of the ledge from all angles.

They were going to set up a Gateway between here and where they had set up the Citadel. There was no reason for anyone to come up there and look around, but the light might attract attention, so they had decided to hide it. Dras had the canvas of the tent strapped to his body under a large cloak. It gave him a far more distorted form, which would help keep undead from seeing him for a human.

Meterove's disguise involved strapping an undead that they had turned into a drone to his back under a cloak and having Terenia use it as a drone. No one would assume a man with four arms, two that could clearly be seen as undead, was anything else.

The two of them also each had a purse full of fayar. They had discovered that there was a toll charged of anyone that wanted to enter the city and if that was the case in one place there might be other times when they would want to have access to them as well. Waiting in the queue outside the city would be their first test. Fortunately, there were enough undead that had humans with them to be transported from farms that any scent they gave off was lost in the mix.

While they waited in the queue Meterove and Dras both stressed about the biggest flaw in this plan. If the undead tried to address them neither of them were undead and therefore could not receive the telepathic message. They slowly moved forward, trapped in the stench of the dead for over an hour. As they approached the front, they saw the guards watching over the tolls.

They had watched this process from birds for several hours in order to verify the full process. Once it was their turn Jolson was going to take control of the undead that would take their money so that they would be able to pay without incident.

Meterove just barely registered the tiny construct that moved past him to settle on the undead that was to take his money. First Meterove, then Dras handed over their fayars then proceeded through. Once they were through Meterove saw the construct catch up to them and they followed it through the city.

The town and farms had not prepared them for this. There were undead everywhere but only a fraction of them were risen corpses like they had seen thus far.

Skeletons, their bones clacking were easily the least upsetting. There were undead of all shapes and sizes made of all parts. A skin bag made of only the flesh of a person wobbled past in the opposite direction. A lumbering beast of just blood squelched along behind it.

Shrouded figures with translucent bodies could be seen scattered around. Looking closely into them you could see the form of a person, bound by ethereal chains, crying blood from empty sockets. These had to be the wraiths that they had heard about.

These were all bad but the things that bothered them the most were the things that were being treated as pest control. The undead called them Grippers and seeing one turned their stomachs.

The gripper was a product of the Nightmare Weavers. A severed forearm had extra flesh and parts attached to it. Among these was a lamprey-like mouth on the palm along with the full digestive tract of a child. Four more hands and wrists were attached to the sides like horrifying flippers.

These abominations had several functions around the city, but they were mostly used to control things like undead rats that would eat any form of food. Once most of the rats had been exterminated, they had been left to their own devices, lurking in alleys and drains. They hunted by sensing vibrations and were known to attack anything they perceived as easy prey.

If these were something that they mass produced for something as mundane as pest control, then Meterove hated to think what they had come up with that they kept from the populace.

The whole time that they walked through the streets they had felt as though they were being watched. It took them a little while to pin it down and when they did it did not make them feel better. The signs had eyes. To be more precise the letters that made up the signs were made with eyes, and they were moving, watching the citizens as well as them. Meterove could only guess what that was about.

Meterove watched as a pair of undead in black ran up and cut the purse strings of what looked like a passing merchant. Even here there were thieves. It really struck Meterove as odd that such a thing would exist. Regardless, they made their way without incident to the base of the clock tower.

There was a large courtyard of red stone all around it. The trick was going to be figuring out how to get to where they wanted to go. After a lot of quiet deliberation, they decided that scaling the exterior was going to be riskier than going in the door. They might find undead inside, but they should be able to take care of them.

They walked over and waited near the door while Jolson sent the construct through a gap by the door. After a moment, an undead with half its flesh missing opened the door and waved them in. Inside was a small room with a single table and chair and a door on the opposite side of the room. Meterove and Dras went through the door while Jolson put the undead back in its chair.

Closing the door behind them Meterove and Dras looked up at the massive staircase that wound around the edge of the tower. That was going to be one hell of a climb.

Sighing Meterove said, "Well I guess there is no point in waiting. Let's get going."

About five minutes later Meterove noticed the construct catch up to them. These stairs were made of the same stone as the tower and there were more stained-glass windows every so often. In the dark it was hard to tell what the images were, but they looked grotesque.

As they walked upwards, they passed the bells that would chime on the hour. The shape was demented, looking like a severed torso. When they reached the gears both Meterove and Dras could not help but admire the skill of whomever had made this place. The gears were so intricate. Behind each clockface there was a series of braziers that would allow the clock to be seen even at night.

The stairs went all the way up to the roof and that was their destination. Once they were outside, they moved over to the edge and dropped down onto a baldachin before jumping onto a decorative ledge. The space was barely large enough for what they needed but it was hidden from windows inside the tower and a low dormer would block anyone from seeing the base of the tent flapping.

It took the better part of an hour to set the tent up and firmly secure it. Once that was done Meterove used the Gate crystal to make a Gateway. They passed through the Gateway back to the Citadel. Meterove promptly removed the drone from his back and both he and Dras made a beeline for their rooms to bathe and change their clothes.

Once they were done, they headed to the conference room. Jolson and Terenia were already there and surprisingly so were Valaas and Syr. Meterove and Dras had barely entered the room when Syr said, "What have you learned?"

The urgency in her tone and a break in her emotionless expression startled Meterove. "W-We just set up the gateway. We still need to do any real investigating. A preliminary investigation on our way in, corroborates what we had seen from our drones and the information you had given us."

Dras said, "We also learned about these nasty things called Grippers that I have already seen and heard too much of. "

Jolson nodded along with that. He may have had a slightly different viewpoint, but he still heard and saw the same things they did. "I am not ready to return quite yet. That was a really traumatic experience going through that city."

Terenia had been under Meterove's cloak the whole time and had therefore been spared the sights. She still seemed more than ready to put off entering the city with the constructs.

Syr looked frustrated but Valaas put a hand on her shoulder then said, "We have been revenants for so long that we are forgetting that the living have different limits. I apologize for our impatience. Take the time that you need to prepare."

They continued talking for another fifteen minutes before calling it a night. Once their short conference was over everyone agreed that they needed to get some sleep. This had been exhausting in every sense of the word.

Meterove did not even try and dissuade Terenia from sleeping with him. Their mission in the undead capital had left him feeling as though he were coated in something invisible that chilled him to the soul. Tomorrow would bring more time in with the undead but for now there was peace and warmth next to him.

.   .   .

Joleen sat at her desk looking down at a report but not really seeing it. She had long since given it up as a bad job and was now back to her most frequent pastime of wistfully thinking of joining her brothers. On her desk, sitting in the box that they had come in were her Artifacts. It still puzzled her that they had taken the form of weapons.

She had grown far more dexterous thanks to their adventures, but she still felt like she could not take full advantage of them. She felt the impulsive urge to pick them up and go practice with them. She reached for the box then paused and withdrew her hand. Unfortunately, she was not alone, and that gesture had not gone unnoticed.

Narok was standing guard over her this rotation. He was probably going to lecture her on how her safety was the guards responsibility. That she did not need to worry about those anymore.

Narok said, "Would you like to practice with those? I can have a practice set made and brought out for sparing and a few dummies set up for using the real things."

Joleen had had her reply ready for when he told her to stop worrying about fighting and therefore was unable to respond at first.

What am I doing? I need to close my mouth!! I look like an idiot right now!

Joleen finally regained her voice and tried to cover her embarrassment by teasing Narok, "Are you not as confident in my safety as you claim?"

Narok smiled at her but spoke seriously, "After what happened the last time, I am determined to make sure of your safety. The more layers of protection that you have the better."

Several things flashed through Joleen's mind in quick succession. An embassy coming in, a battle in the courtyard, then her father dying.

I keep forgetting that father's death weighs just as heavily on him as it does on Jolson, Meterove and I. He may not have been Narok's father, but Narok had known father his whole life and it had been his duty to see him safe.

Joleen stood and walked over to Narok and looked into his eyes then embraced him gently. It was only for a moment, but it was enough. His face that had started to cloud over was now back to normal.

Now that she had Narok's approval she could no longer resist the Siren song of her weapons. It was strange that she should feel like this. She opened the case and took out her twin bladed weapons and then left to go change into something more fitting for sparring than the silver lacy gown she was wearing. This was no time to be gaudy.

Ten minutes later she and Narok were in an indoor sparring hall where she was practicing her techniques on the few dummies that Narok had sent word to have set up. She was moving slowly with exaggerated movements. She had never seen weapons like these before and none of the experts she had inquired with had any answers either. That left her to figure out techniques herself.

After she had been at this for an hour Narok came over with two wooden dowels with grips and handguards. Tucked into his belt were two practice daggers.

He plans on sparring with me himself? I suppose he thinks this is safest.

Joleen wanted to roll her eyes, but he did have a point. If there was assassin amongst the guards sparring would be an effective way to sneak in an attack.

She practiced with the sparring weapons for a few minutes to get used to the weight then settled into a low stance. Speed was going to be a big part of how these would be used.

Narok took his two daggers out and said, "Begin whenever you want. We can take turns starting."

Joleen nodded then after a moment sprang forward and tried a slash with her left, which Narok dodged. She twisted her wrist to slash with the other end while attacking with her right. Narok blocked them both by catching them on this guards then gave Joleen a strong shove that ended with he on her backside.

She stood up and Narok said, "You need to keep you mind on your target, but you also cannot neglect knowing where your body is. Your center of gravity was thrown off when you overextended on the second strike."

Joleen nodded. She had been taught some of this before but not using it meant that it did not stick with her as well as it had with someone like Narok.

Narok came forward quickly one dagger held in a reverse grip. He went in, ducking low and brought his regular dagger up towards her chest hard. Joleen knew it was going to take both blade to block that and crossed them in front of her catching his dagger.

Suddenly she felt something at her ankle, and she was once again on her bottom. Narok had hooked the other dagger around at the same time she caught his first attack and used it to put her off balance, then shoved her over.

Narok could see from her eyes that he did not need to give any explanation here, she knew exactly what that lesson had been. They continued for a few hours, taking breaks in between where Joleen would attempt to create a technique.

After they were done Joleen made a mental note to do some of this every day. She was not going to get better without practice and there was no telling when she would need to use it in real combat.

.   .   .

Moving through this city was horrifying but just like battlefields you got used to it after you had been exposed enough. Meterove, Terenia, Jolson and Dras were exploring the city trying to learn more about the undead. They passed many shops with goods every bit as good as they had back home, at least as far as they could equate them.

It was quite a shock once they got into the city proper and were moving around in daylight but most of the undead here were well dressed. The men wore black pants shirts of various hues of grey or white and high collar coats with tails.

Meanwhile the women wore dresses of black, grey, pink, or red trimmed in a second color. Usually, the fabrics were of two different types and the skirts were layered. All of them, men and women wore shiny black boots and some of the men wore high topped hats.

Walking past shop windows there were all manner of things for sale. Jewelry, clothing, weapons, and food just to name a few. The restaurants, food carts and butchers were hard to look at but avoiding them was impossible and trying would be suspicious.

Full humans hanging from meat hooks split open was terrible, but the displays of the individual pieces were worse. Rows upon rows of tongues, eyeballs organs and quarters of limbs were front and center. The food carts carrying severed limbs or segments of skin with brain wrapped in the middle could be seen everywhere. Then there was the pus ale, wine, and brandy.

Now that they were moving around in drones, they were able to understand the eyes on the signs. Each set of eyes would lock onto those that it wished to attract and acted as a telepathic hawker for the store. They also reminded those moving through the streets of directions or laws that needed to be followed. They could also be used to deter thieves since they could report their faces to the guards.

The smiths that they had seen varied in size, but all had the same horrifying creatures working in them. They were long bodies with many arms fused to it. The larger the forge the larger the creature. Through careful conversation they had learned that they were called Forge Hands.

They were used for large orders of the same item. One set of hands would hammer on hot metal while the others tempered an earlier copy. The really large shops had multiple of them going. Apparently, the ones for the army could work on hundreds at a time.

Another foul creature that they saw in the streets was called a Composter. These things looked to have been based off spiders but used human limbs to make them. They had eight human legs that were attached to the sides of a torso and a humanoid head with two small arms on either side of it that could function like pincers. Their job was to go around and clean up the bits that would fall off undead.

The biggest surprise that they got came in the form of undead family structure. Undead apparently could and did marry. While they could not reproduce, they could adopt a newly raised undead or one of the undead children. Seeing undead children, playing just like normal kids, was terrifying.

They had also learned that the eyes of many undead were purely ornamental. Once they were raised, they gained a type of magical sight that functioned the same as eyes.

While they made their way through the city to their destination, Meterove and Dras, in the front and the rear, they went over their plan several times. They had to stop regularly for large black carriages that were pulled by various type of undead horse. Cutting in front of those could be bad for several reasons.

First of all, it was just plain dangerous and more importantly they were likely owned by a noble, which could get them all in trouble. Meterove had no desire to waste time finding new drones when they already had the perfect ones for this mission.

They had tried for some of the officers in the army but had nearly been caught. Valaas had warned them that more powerful undead might notice the constructs and that they had no way of knowing if they could follow the magical signal back to the source. Thus, they had opted for someone that could still have access to most of the information that they were currently after, the quartermaster.

The four drones that they were currently using were the two assistant quartermasters that Jolson and Terenia were controlling and Meterove and Dras both had a guard. The quartermaster himself seemed like he might be able to sense if they tried with him.

They were currently on their way to a supplier to put in a requisition. It had been good luck that they were able to get Meterove and Dras to be the guards that would accompany them.

They had strict orders to drop off the form and return immediately, which suited them just fine. The Western Empire Trading Company was the third largest trading company. They had already brought requisitions to The Eastern Empire Trading Company and the Mvdonijvk Islands Trading Company.

When they reached their destination, they were disappointed to learn that they would not even speak to anyone past the receptionist. They received a receipt stamped with the company seal and left.

They had been hoping to try and get someone to talk more about what kind of supplies had been going out. The quartermaster had been tight lipped about much of what he had been asking about, but they still had found out a great deal.

They had found that there was still over a million undead in the army and that there were specialized farms for producing soldiers. It would take some time for them to return to full strength, but they were still frighteningly superior to their own forces.

To help with that they had taken to altering the numbers on the requisition forms. Small discrepancies could slow an army. There was no telling how that would affect the undead, however.

While they were walking down the street Jolson felt a sharp impact to his skull then suddenly, he was looking from his constructs point of view. Looking around he saw that there was the bolt from a crossbow imbedded in his undead's skull.

Looking over he saw that Terenia and Dras were also down while Meterove was taking cover. The undead on the street panicked and scattered. Through the crowd walked one of the officers that they had attempted to take as a drone before.

So, they had noticed huh?

It was mostly bones with small bits of flesh and hair left. Both eye sockets were empty but had a strong blue glow. It had a single hand and half sword and plate mail painted black.   It stared at the three corpses and then looked around, almost like it sensed the constructs but since they were so small it missed them.

Meanwhile Meterove had drawn his sword and was ducking behind a wall. In his head he heard the undead practically shout, "*I have no idea who you are working for but your attempts to disorganize the army were pointless. We caught onto you right away. Are you human sympathizers then?*

145

Wait!? Human sympathizers? Do those exist? This is useful information to know. This drone is compromised anyway. Maybe I can cause some chaos!

Meterove jumped out from behind the wall and charged the officer. There were a least twenty other soldiers with him and all of them had crossbows out. Meterove kept his head down and used his sword to keep bolts from his face.

While they focused on him the other three used their constructs to take over three of the soldiers at the back and started firing at the others. This caused chaos as the fallen undead either fired their crossbows into the others or they clattered against the paving stones.

Immediately after firing off the bolts, they dropped their crossbows and drawn their swords and started attacking the other soldiers. This allowed Meterove time to close the distance.

There was no contest between the officer and his drone, but it did keep him distracted. After a few strikes the other three abandoned their drones while they were still up and attached to three new ones. Soon the only ones left were the four of them and the officer.

Jolson took advantage of the distraction to attach to the officer. Pain lanced through his mind. They had never felt this before. Jolson also felt something pushing back across the link.

OH NO! It is trying to use the connection to get into my head! NO! you will NOT!!

Jolson gave a mental shove with everything that he had and the probe into his mind shattered, and he managed to push forward. The others fired bolts into its legs. This allowed Jolson to get the rest of the way into its mind. He could feel it fighting back though so he had to be quick.

An eerie shriek shot through the air, and they looked over to see a guard unit heading towards them. The fighting had clearly been reported. Jolson managed to freeze the officers arm long enough that Meterove was able to drive his blade into the eye socket.

The officer fell to pieces since the energy holding it together was gone. Meterove straightened up and saw that there was at least twice as many undead facing them this time. True they could fight through them the same way they had the others, but Meterove was worried that the undead might start wondering why so many of their soldiers were fighting each other.

Meterove scooped up one of the crossbows and reloaded it. Out of the corner of his eye he could see the others doing the same thing. He heard the mental jab that demanded their surrender, but Meterove stood, aimed his crossbow at them. He shouted both mentally and physically, "For the humans!"

The other three mirror his call then they fired their bolts before charging the guards. While they did not reach the enemy, they could see the effect that their shout and charge had from their drones. They were careful to fly low to the ground until they were a little ways off, but they could see undead turning to each other.

After this episode, the army received word that there were human sympathizers amongst their ranks, which led to an announcement of thorough checks. They were unsure how deep the problem ran. Meterove was pleased. They had created a thorn for the undead army.

They decided to wait a few days after this to try the next phase which would likely be the most dangerous. Looking into the Weavers and the Church of Ashen Rebirth.

.   .   .

They had clearly made quite a commotion when they fought the officer in the streets. All attempts to take any form of Weaver as a drone would last only a short time before their change in behavior was noticed and they would be investigated.

In the end they had to take over undead that were bringing in a shipment for the Weavers. The headquarters of the Church of Ashen Rebirth, the Endrbor Cathedral, was a massive building in the very center of the city. It was made of made of a combination of pure black and crimson stone.

There were many large stained-glass windows, along with countless statues and carvings. A great many of them were gargoyles. Unlike the statutes that could be found around the city these ones were stone constructs with gray, cracked skin. These along with the eyes that were used here as well, were the security for the most sacred of places to the undead.

The four of them moved their drones along while following the instructions of the undead that was bringing the group of humans to the church. While it sickened them not to help these people, they knew their mission had to take priority. They were led into the Cathedral through a side door.

Inside there are many alcoves holding statues and up front there was a large effigy of the wings and spine that was all over the city. The scent of blood was strong and the group of twenty humans that they had helped escort in began to panic as the doors closed behind them.

Meterove blinked and where there had been an empty room there now stood five undead. Even through the drone Meterove could tell these were on a different level. All five were dressed in Cassocks, though each one was different.

One was a skeleton and wore Alabaster white, trimmed in a grey. Another was a mass of flesh and organs wearing deep purple and black. There was a man shaped mass of blood that was wearing deep black with crimson. A man who was transparent was wearing transparent robes.

Last and most frightening of all there was the one with robes the same color as the glow from his eyes. He was pretty much just skin over bone, and he had no lips, so his teeth were constantly bared in an unsettling smile that reminded Jolson of that horrifying creature they had seen at the manor.

"*Welcome children to the house of our god, the Ashen Soul. May its loving embrace envelope you.*"

The other undead that were there replied with "*and also you.*"

Meterove and the others barely managed to mix their "voices" in without sounding off.

"*Those that you have brought shall rejoice for soon they shall join us in our reverence for they too shall be saved. And shall know the glory of our god.*"

"*Glory to the Ashen Soul.*"

"*Now come. Bring the fodder forward and we shall weigh your offering.*"

As one the undead moved their humans forward. Meterove and the others were prepared this time and there was no delay. They moved the humans over to a circle in the center of the room, which then sank down into a pit. The change did not stop there as the interior of the Cathedral continued to sink and the segments turned into an amphitheater.

The five Weavers gathered around the pit and Meterove and the others watched with horror as they used their arts. There was a gentle ray of blue light that fell upon the humans then after a moment they began to scream.

First metal stakes appeared and skewered their eyes. Then ethereal chains wrapped around them. Skeletons tore their way free of flesh. The flesh and organs piling themselves up neatly. Blood drained into large squelching puddles like massive beads of mercury.

Four of the Weavers made quick work making undead out of each of their respective piles. The last one, the Nightmare Weaver just stood there. Lacking any eyelids or lips made its expressions far more horrifying.

At first Meterove assumed that it was of lower rank than the others and had to wait for whatever scraps were left. This was far from the truth. Jolson was the first to notice that it would pull a piece here, a bit there and some more there. It was taking what it viewed as the choice pieces.

After about thirty minutes the last sounds faded away and standing in the center of the room were eighteen skeletons, eighteen flesh constructs, eighteen blood *constructs, eighteen wraiths, and one truly horrifying creature.*

It crouched on the floor wheezing. It had two heads that were fused together in the middle, giving it four eyes and two noses and mouths. The center two eyes were practically touching. The chest was open where several organs could be seen pulsating. Six extra ribs were attached to the backside, flared out with skin covering it like wings, though the points could still be seen. It had four legs and two arms. The skin was tight against the bones.

The five figures turned to the assembled undead. There was a deep feeling of unease that spread through the room. Something was off but Meterove could not quite place what it was. The newly made undead followed some unheard command and filed out of the room. The lone exception was the strange creature that the Nightmare Weaver had made.

Once the new undead were out of the room the off feeling in the room increased to a palpable level. Suddenly the creature leapt forward and began to devour the leader of the undead that had brought in the offerings.

It leapt around the amphitheater attacking every undead that it could reach. Meterove turned to the Weavers, " *What is the meaning of this? What have we done?"*

"Done? You are all serving the Ashen Soul by having your lesser necromantic energy used by the superior undead we create. You are all going to be of use in the end, but for now you four shall be spared so that we may question you."

The creature had finished killing the other undead in the room and devoured their bodies. As for where the consumed undead went in the creature that was anyone's guess. It looked just the same as before. It was growling from one mouth while wheezing from the other.

The five Weavers descended on them, and the creature eyed them hungrily. Meterove felt the Weavers try and search through his drone and control it.

"What are you? Are you one of those rumored human sympathizers? I can feel you communicating with others far away. Who are they? How many are you?"

Dras suddenly bolted across the room as if trying to escape and the creature jumped onto him and began to devour him. The Weavers chuckled and said, "Not so brave now that you're caught-"

The Nightmare Weaver stopped talking and peered at its new creation, perplexed. The creature began to act strangely, shaking its head around. The Nightmare Weaver moved towards the creature clearly disturbed, "How is that connection still there?" What is it? WHAT ARE YOU!"

It made a move to try and assist the creature, but it jumped at it and attacked. The Weaver dodged out of the way, and it crashed towards the other Weavers. This was enough distraction for the others to abandon their own drones and make their escape from the Cathedral.

They moved as fast as their constructs would allow them to get as far up as they could. After a few minutes Dras managed to join them. They flew them across the city and went through the Gateway. Once through Meterove, opened his eyes and sprinted over to the Gateway. He reached through and pulled the crystal free, and it began to close.

Meterove ran back to the others. They had brought the constructs back and Dras was sitting down on the ground out of breath. He may have been using a drone, but the fear was still real.

In between gasps Dras said, "I managed to read the creature long enough to hear the one Weaver's command. It tracked us. I have no idea how far, but it knows we are in this general direction. They are coming."

CHAPTER 7
AMBUSH

Dras moved quickly through the mountains depositing the Shaping Crystals along the path that he wanted to herd the undead army down. Meterove was across the path mirroring him whenever he placed a crystal. This plan was Dras' idea so for now Meterove and the others were taking orders from him.

They had verified that the Weavers had tracked them to the general area, so they had decided to use this opportunity to put his plan into action. It took them half a day and now all there was to do was wait.

They had set up a number of traps that would help bring the undead the direction that they wanted. That combined with a harrying force would hopefully bring the undead force right where they wanted them.

While they waited for the undead to arrive, they planned their next move. As of right now the plan was to move the Citadel of Time to the location that the undead referred to as "The Blight" although Joleen was angling to have them return to the Empire.

Meterove and Jolson were both personally for heading to this "blight" ever since they had heard about it from Valaas. Not only was there the life energy that was somehow pushing back against the necromantic power but according to Valaas and Syr there was some sort of structure.

Joleen had come over to the Citadel to try and help make her point. "Having the Citadel back in the Empire makes the most sense. If the enemy is able to get through Dras' trap, then we will need all the defense that we can get."

Meterove shook his head, "Even if we had the citadel back in the empire, the amount of undead that we were able to verify would still be able to wash over us."

Jolson added, "The enemy knows that the citadel was in the empire, but they also have some knowledge about it thanks to the Lich. Keeping it away from the undead is also important."

Joleen slapped the table in frustration. "Then why would you want to keep it in enemy territory!"

Terenia tried so make calming gestures while saying, "Think about it Joleen. If this "Blight" were an area that the enemy could easily deal with then it would not exist for us to find."

Jolson took advantage of the opening that Terenia had made and expanded on her point. "The undead clearly have trouble with that location. Furthermore, they are likely expecting that we would have the citadel somewhere that we would view as safe from them. This might draw them away from the empire."

Dras was not particularly paying attention to the conversation. He was going over his plan in his head again and again, trying to find flaws in it.

He could dimly here the argument continue for a little while longer. The original plan had been altered a few times once flaws and better ideas became apparent. Jolson had suggested something that had been rather brutal.

After some time, they were able to convince Joleen that the plan of moving the Citadel to the "blight" was the best thing. She was not pleased but still gave her grudging approval.

After she returned to the empire, they pulled the Crystal out and severed the Gateway. Then Valaas and Syr readied the Citadel to transfer again. Meterove, Dras, Terenia and Jolson would stay behind with the one hundred soldiers. Once they were done with their task, they would make their way across the land to the "Blight" and meet up with Valaas and Syr.

They had rigged some of the traps to set off signal flares when they went off. It was not long before they saw one go off in the distance. The harrying force got ready to head out and once they had left Meterove and the others made their way to their assigned places.

Each of them had a special tent that they had made that would slow the corruption. Had there been more time since the discovery of the "blight" they might have made more progress. Once they had each arrived at their respective locations it only took a moment to set the tents up. They were mostly for concealment anyway.

With nothing to do but wait they occupied their time as best they could. It was during this time that Dras first felt something brush against his mind. He straightened up and glanced around but saw nothing. The feeling was gone as well.

Maybe this place is just getting to me. All that time talking with my mind has me hearing things that are not really there.

Dras shook himself physically and mentally and went back to watching the bleak landscape. It was the strangest thing watching the Citadel slowly fade from solid and imposing to transparent and then it was gone. It was quite a sight, so much so that it almost distracted him from another touch, almost.

This time Dras was sure of it. Something was attempting to touch his mind, but it was weak and kept fading in and out. Suddenly the sound of a horn drifted to his ears, and he put it out of his mind for now. They had a job to do.

Dras had picked this pass to draw the enemy to because it already had the downward slant to it that he wanted. It also went under an enormous arch where a huge stone pillar had fallen. The time of day was perfect for hiding their trap too, just enough to see but not enough to give good perception.

The force could be seen in the distance using their various transports to stay ahead of an impossibly big undead army. Clearly, they had sent at least the bulk of what was left to try and take them out. More than likely, they had discovered that there were humans responsible for what went on in the Capital.

The force looked to be mostly intact. Here and there an arrow or bolt would make its way out from the undead but often fell far short. One or two did find their marks though. The men that went down bursting into searing flames, which burned them to ash.

Every member of that unit had a special spell applied to them that would activate when they died. It would cremate them, preventing them from being turned or eaten. The fire would only burn them or something undead though. The spell was a new one that they had only recently perfected.

Dras watched as another man took an arrow to his chest but stayed up. He was slumped to the side and even at this distance you could see him cough up something that was certainly blood. He turned his vehicle around and charged directly at the army. He maxed out his speed and plowed right into their front ranks.

The impact threw him and the vehicle in separate directions. The crashing vehicle took out dozens of undead before coming to a stop. The soldier died after impacting the first undead, his body going up in an intense blaze. This fire caught onto the nearest undead and after mere moments over a hundred undead were ablaze.

This slowed the advance of the army, and the rest of the force was able to get ahead enough that they were out of range. There was a massive roar of frustration from the undead army, and they pushed around the group that was aflame and redoubled their efforts to catch them. This was what Dras was waiting for.

Once the undead had filled about half of the pass Dras' plan went into effect. This whole plan hinged on two things. First was the harrying force making it through the pass. The second was the constructs. Hovering two hundred feet above the front of the pass was a ring of constructs, each of them holding a tiny gate crystal.

When Valaas has explained that it was the person's mind that activated the crystals not their body and had also explained that multiple crystals could be used to make a larger Gateway it had given him an even better idea than his original.

Dras gave the signal once he saw that the force was past the checkpoint and had equipped the control crystals for the second set of constructs down there. As one Dras, Meterove, Jolson and Terenia activated their crystals and the ground of the pass writhed and flowed.

In no time it had reshaped itself into a long super hard and impossibly smooth slant and a nearly forty-degree angle. The undead that were caught in it slid uncontrollably down the slope. Dras gave the second signal and he and the soldiers activated the Gateway.

Dras watched as a thirty-foot-wide gateway appeared in midair and after a few seconds undead began pouring out of it. They fell the two hundred feet onto the top of the slant. Now crushed and shattered from the impact of falling they tumbled down the slope again, taking others with them.

While this was only about a tenth of the total army that was caught in this it was hardly the whole plan. Those Gateways would hold for about a day. The size of the crystals and Gateway changed how long they would last. Large Gateways with small crystal would break fast. They would last long enough for phase two though.

Dras looked across the way at Meterove and one the count of three they used the next two groups of constructs. A massive flash of light appeared under the feet of the undead near the front of the pass and was gone, along with nearly a quarter of their remaining troops and siege weapons. High above, and behind, where they had been, they could be seen falling right onto the bulk of the army.

The devastation that this wrought was beyond comprehension. With the path ahead still a death trap and a massive blow to their numbers and coordination the enemy was unlikely to mobilize soon. Just to make sure Meterove, Dras, Jolson and Terenia made a point to have themselves and the remaining soldiers very visibly move in the direction of the "blight", Dras even gave them a cheery wave.

Once out of sight though they separated. The soldiers had been through enough and Meterove used the crystal to make a Gateway back to the empire. New soldiers would be sent over to the citadel later. Once they were through Meterove was about to suggest that they head there but noticed that Dras seemed off. Considering how well his plan had just worked you would think that he would be ecstatic. Instead, he just sat there staring back at the area he had been sitting in.

Meterove clapped him on the back. "Is something wrong man? You just pulled off a great operation."

Dras kept his eyes on the direction that he had been looking and said, "While we were waiting, something touched my mind over there." Noticing the alarm on Meterove's face he quickly added, "It was not able to do anything, but I felt it. It was not the same as how it felt while we were using the drones. I think there is something over there that is not undead."

Jolson appeared interested, "You mean you think that there might be something intelligent over there that has somehow avoided the corruption?"

Dras nodded. Terenia looked over in that direction and nodded as well and said, "I can feel something over there. A very small area that has blocked out the corruption. I feel like it is under the ground. Maybe even deep under it."

Meterove asked, "How far away do you think it is? More importantly do you believe we can investigate safely?"

Terenia shook her head, "There is no way to know either of those. If we move quietly and slowly, I think we can avoid the undead."

"If there is something out there that can resist this undeath it is worth looking into," said Jolson after a moment.

Meterove was of the same mind, so they set off keeping to cover whenever possible. They used Terenia's senses to track the location. Eventually they came to an area where they could feel the touch on their minds. They split up With Dras and Jolson and Meterove and Terenia searching around the area.

All around them there were mountains and the occasional tree. They were currently standing on a plateau overlooking a deep ravine. Here the touch was strongest and almost eager.

Terenia touched the ground and said, "Yes, it is below us. Whatever is down there is blocking out the corruption."

Meterove surveyed the area and said, "Dras, go check on the undead. I want to know what they are doing. Once we know that we can decide if we are going to look around anymore than this."

Dras took off in the direction of the undead army. They really were not that far from it. After a few minutes Dras came to the ridge that was just before the one where he had hidden for the ambush. Here he pulled out his spyglass and crawled on his belly up to the top.

Looking through the spyglass Dras first watched the main body of the army. They were still recovering after the ambush from earlier. Looking at the damage from this angle it had truly been devastating. It appeared that they had some Weavers that had deployed with them but there was only so much that could be done. They did not appear to be moving anytime soon.

Dras turned his gaze on the slope now and watched as undead attempted to use rope to slowly descend. Even if they managed to make it down it was slow going. They would not be able to move down that quickly, even once the Gateway was gone. For now, the same bodies kept falling in a loop. He did not look to closely though; he was not interested in what falling hundreds of times had done to their bodies.

Dras crawled back down the slope then went back to the others. "They have not moved since we left, though they are trying to get to the bottom of the slope using some ropes.

Meterove smiled, "Good. Then we will continue to search this area for the time being. This works out well since we needed to be nearby for the final phase of the operation anyway. For now, though it is getting late. Dras and Terenia you guys take first watch, Jolson and I will take second."

Getting rest that night was difficult with the presence brushing their minds but they were so exhausted that eventually they drifted off to sleep regardless. Finally, when it was morning and Dras was shaken awake by Jolson, they made a meager breakfast, checked in on the army again then set about searching the plateau.

They searched every crevice and under every rock but found nothing. It was not until Dras, remembering a weird dream he had the night before, decided to look over the edge that he saw a ledge and what appeared to be a cave.

The fact that he had dreamt this put everyone on guard. They climbed down and confirmed that it was indeed a cave, and it went deep. They could all feel a sense of glee in the area.

It was almost time for the final phase, so Meterove and Dras went back up, while Jolson and Terenia stayed on the ledge. Meterove and Dras crawled up and waited. It took another half an hour, but it finally happened. The Gateway up in the air shattered and the corpses stopped falling.

They had all piled up at the entrance now as planned and the undead were heading down to investigate. Once a good number had made it down and were poking through the remains Meterove fired a single ball of fire down at the corpses.

The fire was the same kind as the spell that the soldiers had cast on them. The ball exploded causing the corpses to catch fire. It burned so fast that it quickly ignited the hundred barrels of explosive powder that they had placed there. The explosion launched the fire and corpses out into the main army, again causing mass disruption and caused the arch to collapse.

Meterove and Dras did not stick around to watch. They hurried to the ledge and quickly made their way down and, after they met up with the others, hid just inside the entrance. Once they were reasonably sure that they were in no danger of being spotted they sat down to discuss what they should do to investigate this place.

Meterove said, "I can see pros and cons to both courses of action. If we go in now and explore, we are not at our best and are also heading off without anyone else knowing where we went. We are also holding onto the Gateway crystal for the empire. I do not like the idea of that getting lost. Looking at it from the other perspective if we wait the undead might very well find this place. The fact that they have not yet is curious."

Dras added, "We did a lot of damage with those ambushes, but I do not think that they will pass up investigating this place if they notice it."

Jolson was looking into the depths of the cave, as though he could see through the darkness. "There is also the possibility that whatever is down here is something that the undead wish to avoid."

Terenia said into the silence that followed, "Well that is a singular unpleasant thought."

Meterove also looked down that dark passage and felt the sense of elation that was floating about them. This place was worrying him because Jolson had a point. What were the odds that what was down here had gone unnoticed? If the undead feared what was in here how bad was it? What was it?

There was a pulse that went through them and Meterove saw images in his mind's eye. It was like watching things happen behind his eyes. Closing his eyes, he was able to see things more clearly.

Falling through the endless dark. Massive orbs of matter scattered between vast distances were seen from time to time. The direction had been decided long ago. The destination may have been anywhere.

Near so near to the destination but something was in the way. One of the orbs of matter was in the way. Now it was pulling. Could not escape. Now all was fire.

A heavy impact and all went dark. Awake and things were fuzzy. All around were strange reptilian creatures with feathers. Time passed and the stars changed.

Then came man. They built the cage and sealed it.

Meterove opened his eyes slightly shook. What was that? He was about to tell the others what he had just seen when he noticed the looks on their faces. They clearly had seen the same thing.

The first one to speak was Dras, "where was that?"

Jolson responded, "I believe that was out there in the stars. While we have never been able to prove it, it is believed that there are more places like our own world out there amongst the stars."

Maybe it was because they had been to Nexus and had seen Creation, but the idea of other worlds was not that hard to believe. The way that had felt though and some of the things that it had shown. They were better off not taking chances with this thing.

Meterove checked the time and said, "It is almost time to attempt the Gateway. I say we wait and use that method to escape from here. We can always return later."

The others agreed and Meterove used the crystal and made a Gateway in a small corner. Without a word they all passed through. They emerged from the Gateway at the new location of the Citadel of Time. All around them there was a lush rainforest filled with fan palms and other exotic plants.

Here and there animals could be seen as well. Living, breathing, NORMAL animals. It felt nice to see that again, but it was also strange to have a sense of confusion as to why this place was even here.

Meterove led the way to the conference room. There as they had expected they found Valaas and Syr.

Valaas looked up questioningly, "You look as though something is off. Did your plan not work as you had hoped?"

Meterove shook his head, "No, it went off better than we had hoped. It was what we found during the operation that has us worried. We discovered...something out there."

Valaas leaned forward, "What do you mean by something? What did you see?"

Jolson took over, "We did not see what was causing them, but we all felt something touching our minds out there. We could also feel a tangible sense of various happy emotions. Lastly, just before we returned, we were given a sort of vison."

Valaas and even Syr seemed a little interested. Jolson decided to go into detail. "It was of drifting through an endless expanse of darkness past worlds and stars. Then it was pulled towards one. It showed weird creatures reptilian creatures with scales and feathers then later men."

Valaas looked at Syr, who shook her head, then said, "I am sorry to say that neither of us have heard of anything like this. While this does sound like it warrants investigation, I personally think that we have enough to be getting on with already."

Meterove said, "I would agree except for one thing."

Valaas said, "And what is that?"

Jolson said, "We were thinking about it and the chances that the undead have never felt that thing suggests that either it can hide itself from them or they do not want to go near it."

Syr widened her eyes, "If the Ashen Empire fears this...!"

Meterove nodded, "Exactly. We could have found something that could be used against them. On the other hand, I am worried about whatever might be able to cause such fear,"

Dras who had been mostly silent said, "As we were leaving, I thought I felt something else. I think that whatever it was thought we were going to come down and was happy. But then we left and as we stepped through the Gateway I swear I felt rage."

Jolson said, "That is also a valid point. I think that we should return home and update Joleen on this matter. We need to have new troops assigned to the Citadel anyway."

Valaas and Meterove both nodded and Meterove said, "There is that too. I agree. We will go talk with Joleen" Meterove stood up and after a moment said, "First though I think we should get cleaned up.

.   .   .

Joleen said, "So there is something else that might be incredibly dangerous over there and you want to go poking at it?"

Meterove thought it was a little unfair to say it like that. It was worth looking into. Jolson looked a little offended by that statement too.

He does not like being lumped in with Dras and I.

Meterove made a mental note to smack Jolson later on. Fortunately, even though he looked offended he still felt the same about this situation and decided that investigating it was important."

Jolson pressed from a different angle, "There is also the area that is free of the corruption. Based on what we saw and felt there is something down there that is not natural that is keeping the corruption from spreading to that area."

Joleen said, "We already have one area like that, and we have done nothing to investigate that."

Dras said, "This thing already exists. Would it not be better to know what it is? If it is a threat, then it will stay a threat no matter what. At least this way we would know more about it before it becomes a problem."

Where Jolson's curiosity was not winning over Joleen, Dras' defensive thinking was having a bit more of an impact. She now seemed pensive. Terenia decided to press the advantage that they had.

"I can guarantee that whatever is holding back the corruption down there is not of nature. I can sense the clean earth but nothing that might be causing it. If this is a threat, then something capable of that might have other tricks that we do not want to learn about at the wrong time."

Joleen said, "I still do not like this. I will agree that it needs to be investigated though. However, if something is sealed down there you are forbidden to impulsively do anything. We are not helping it or hurting it without properly thinking it through. Am I understood?"

Meterove was fairly sure that last part had been meant for himself and Dras. Joleen made direct eye contact with all four of them before continuing. "As far as soldiers go, I was thinking of sending a full legion this time."

This startled Meterove. That was far more than he had been expecting. Seeing his face Joleen went on. "From your report it sounds like the main army of the undead has been thrown into disarray. Additionally, you have led them to believe that the attack was carried out from within their own territory. This will mean a lower chance of an attack on us and higher chance of an attack on you."

Meterove had thought about that but to dedicate a full five thousand men to the citadel was beyond what he had expected. With that many, holding back the full army long enough to move would be easy.

.   .   .

They had returned with the legion that Joleen had promised and after helping the officers get the men settled went to go discuss the plans with Valaas and Syr. The men had all been told that there were two undead that were allies within the Citadel but not their names.

Rumors could easily start and lead to declining morale. For now they were portrayed as having retained their personality and were rebelling against the others.

When they arrived at their usual conference room the only one there was Syr. Quiet and expressionless as always, she explained, "Valaas went to further examine the area around us. He asked that I stay behind to communicate with you. Are you planning to head to the cave and investigate?"

Jolson said, "Yes, that is our current plan."

Meterove added, "Once we are done there, we will move directly to exploring this place. I am very curious about this place as well."

Syr stared back at him. Meterove wondered if he would ever get used to this woman. It amused him a little that he had taken to thinking of her that way and not as just as some undead.

True she looked different than many of the ones he had seen but it was also her nature. She was expressionless, yet it felt like she still held some of her humanity.

Meterove mused over this while they prepared to head into the cave. He could only speculate but perhaps their time seeing into the lives of the undead had also played a part. They had learned a lot about the Ashen Empire.

The Gateway opened in front of them and led to the inky blackness. Once they stepped through, they felt it again. The first thing they noticed was that Dras had been right about it being angry. There was palpable rage in the cave. Once it had touched their minds and noticed that they were heading deeper in it began to abate though.

Meterove paused and looked at the others. Whatever this thing was it had emotions, but they felt different than their own, more primal. When he pointed this out to Jolson his brother said, "I was thinking the same thing. Personally, whatever this thing is I would have preferred that it did not have emotions at all."

Dras asked, "Why is that?"

Jolson said, "Whatever this thing is, it is intelligent and emotional. It also seems to have been alone down here for an extraordinarily long time. It might not think that it is our enemy but that does not mean that we will think the same way. What happens when it gets really mad?"

CHAPTER 8
ELDRITCH

Meterove led the way forward into the dark. Whatever was in here was pleased at their approach. But underneath that feeling was a deep alien void. Whatever was ahead Meterove was uneasy about heading towards it in the dark.

Dras, who was half a step behind him, looked similarly uneasy. Meterove had the feeling that if he looked at Jolson and Terenia, they would also look uneasy. There was something about this place, Meterove just could not figure out what it was.

The walls of the cave were rough at first but after a while they became smooth. The stone was perfectly flat and kneeling to look, Meterove saw that the corners appeared to be perfect ninety-degree angles, also now the floor had a gradual decline. After a while the corridor turned sharply and continued.

It was impossible to know for sure how long they had been walking when they began to smell something off. Terenia was the first to notice it. "That smells almost like that room we found in the labyrinth?"

Meterove thought back to that room and realized he had smelled something similar in that lab he and Dras had found in the manor. No sooner had this thought occurred to him than Dras spoke it aloud. "Hey Meterove. It smelled like this in that manor basement too, right?"

Meterove nodded and Jolson spoke up, "I think it is the solution that was in the tanks that held the specimens."

They continued to move forward and eventually they stepped out of the hallway and into a room. As if it sensed their presence the room began to light up. It was a lab like the kind that they had seen before. Whatever had kept the dust off the other lab clearly was not working here. None of them had ever seen so much dust.

They went around and cleaned off the equipment in the room. None of it looked familiar to any of them. There was a large window on one end of the room, that was also coated in grime. Meterove went over and wiped the glass as clean as he could and looked through.

Dras watched as Meterove shook his head then looked out again then backed away from the window going

pale. Curious and worried he walked over to Meterove.
"Hey! Hey! Are you ok?"

Meterove did not respond and just stared off into
space. Dras looked over at the window and then back at
Meterove and asked, "What was out there?"

Dras walked over to the window and looked out and
understood completely. There was an insanely large cavern
out there. There was a massive chain that could be seen
held taught against the wall. The chain was connected to a
cuff that was clasped around the wrist of some enormous
creature.

That thing was massive. Also, what little light that
they had showed that it had what appeared to be countless
lips with eyes in between them all over the arm and hand. It
was hard to tell but it looked like there might be some more
on the tips of the fingers as well.

Jolson had been looking around the room and had
found a handful of drawings. The language was
indecipherable but combined with everything else it was
clear this place was here to study the creature outside the
window.

The feeling of being pleased had been growing all
this time. However, when Terenia noticed two other doors
the feeling first intensified before plummeting. The reason
was that upon feeling it get happier she had reached for the
other door.

Despite a feeling of rage that felt like it might cause the ground to shake she opened the door and gave a small gasp. Inside there was a small living area with a dozen bunk beds, kitchen, table and chairs and a lot of mummified corpses. The grizzly thing was that they all looked to have killed themselves in various ways.

One had what looked like a candle holder in its hand that was imbedded in the skull through its eye socket. Others looked to have used kitchen implements or other mundane tools. One even looked to have bashed his head against the wall repeatedly until he died. One had worn one of his fingers down scratching some words into the wall.

Dras looked in and muttered, "What the hell happened in here?" before fearfully looking back at the window. Meterove was simply muttering to himself. He looked almost like he saw something that was beyond comprehension, something past the world.

Terenia closed the door and walked over and shook his shoulder. Meterove continued to look at the window though. Finally, after she gave him another few shakes, he snapped out of it. He looked around for a moment before looking at her slightly startled.

He seemed unsure as he spoke, "When did you get over there?"

"What do you mean," Terenia responded?

Meterove pointed where she had been several minutes ago. "You were just there. Actually, everyone moved."

Dras asked, "What did you see when you looked out the window?"

Meterove looked startled at the question then said, "I do not remember looking out the window."

This caused everyone to stop and look at him. Jolson said, "You cleaned off the window then looked out of it. You then backed away from it."

Meterove thought back to when they had entered the lab and followed his memories. When he got to that part, he felt something press on his mind as though trying to keep him out of his own memories.

Suddenly its grip broke, and an image flashed in his mind. He made sure to speak quickly in case it tried to interfere again. "There is the giant creature out there. There are eyes all over the arm that we can see. There are lips around the eyes but there are also lips inside where the pupil should be. I felt a deep terror once I looked into those eyes."

Dras looked out the window again, trying to find one that was open but saw nothing. They were all closed at the moment. He could see something far below though. It looked like there was some kind of chamber that was just off

the big cavern the creature was chained in. The other door
likely led there.

Meterove seemed to be thinking the same thing. "I
am not sure that I really want to, but I think we should see if
this other door leads down to the bottom of that chamber."

He still seemed off, but Jolson could not think of any
other course of action that was left to them. Meterove led
the way and after opening the door they saw that there was a
staircase that went down.

It did not seem too far until the bottom. Once there
they found themselves in a room that ended with a large
stone ledge on the edge of an abyss. Hanging in the center
of room was the most horrifying thing that any of them had
ever seen.

It was absolutely enormous, with grey tinged skin.
Dras had estimated one of the link in the chain to be twenty
feet long and the metal to be over five feet in diameter. The
arm that they had seen the wrist of was not the only place
that had the lips and eyes. They appeared to be all over its
body and there was an immense one at the bottom instead
of legs.

The lips were the whole width of its abdomen and
the eye between them was shocking white. Again, like the
ones all over its body there were lips where the pupil should
be. There was a second arm that was chained to the ceiling

on the other side. What appeared to be a writhing mass of tongues was where a head would normally be.

The eye at the bottom swiveled over and stared at them, and suddenly every eye on the creature shot open and stared at them. Meterove felt a strong urge to approach the creature. It was absolutely manipulating them to try and get them closer.

Meterove said, "You want us to free you huh?"

The feeling of alien pleasure filled the area.

Meterove continued, "Why should we? What reason do we have to let you out of these restraints?"

Now the feeling changed to anger and rage. It threw itself at its bonds with all its strength, but the chains held strong. Whatever they were made of was far beyond this creatures ability to break.

Jolson shouted over the roars, "WHAT ARE YOU? WHAT IS IT THAT YOU ARE AFTER?"

The creature stopped roaring, but dust still fell from above and it now stared so strongly at Jolson he felt as if it were looking at his soul. He felt an insatiable hunger and an all-encompassing desire to go where it was meant to.

Suddenly Dras drew his sword and swung it at Jolson. At the last second, he forced it off to the side. "That thing just forced me to move. It can manipulate us!"

There was a vile feeling of malice, joy and desire all mixed together. Jolson retaliated with a swipe from the dagger at his belt but also forced it off course. The creature was frustrated but turned its eyes to Meterove and Terenia.

After a moment frustration began to overpower the other emotions. Meterove and Terenia were not being manipulated. Meterove shook his head, "You really should have saved this trick until now. Trying to use it earlier helped me know what it felt like so I could block it."

The creature raged again but this time Meterove shouted over the roars. "Go on great beast, roar all you want. I will seal this cavern for all time so that none can ever find it again!"

Fear overtook all the other emotions except for hate. It abandoned all pretense and tried its best to worm its way into their minds and drive them mad. The large eye at the bottom of the creature opened the lips within the pupil and another eye appeared. Over and over, they opened, getting smaller but the increased numbers made it far more disturbing.

There was a series of clicks behind Meterove and something flashed past and hit the creatures eye causing it to close the eyes and gurgle and roar in pain. It threw itself against the chains. The tongues at the top wriggling in their direction as though trying to reach them. The weight on their minds vanished.

Meterove looked over his shoulder to see Dras standing there with his hand crossbow out. Meterove had forgotten that he even had that thing. A bolt to the eye was one way to show this thing that it was not in control. It continued to throw itself forward against the chains but there was no slack in them so there was no effect.

Now that they had been down here for a while their eyes had adjusted to the level of light and they could clearly see that there was something far below in the dark. After a few minutes Meterove finally realized that they were more chains.

Jolson made an orb of light and sent it down there having also seen the chains. Down there was an intricate, if immense system of gears and pulleys that the chains were connected to.

Jolson shouted over the creatures roars, "I CANNOT TELL IF THESE ARE THE SAME CHAINS OR NOT. IT IS POSSIBLE THAT THEY ARE ALL INTERCONNECTED AND THAT IT IS SOME KIND OF SAFEGUARD IF IT WERE TO GET FREE.

Dras looked at the gears and shouted, "IT MIGHT ALSO JUST HAVE TAKEN SOMETHING THAT BIG JUST TO GET IT UP THERE."

Meterove could barely hear them, so he pointed back to the entrance, and they left the creature thrashing in pain and rage. They retreated back to the lab. Meterove said, "I have no idea what that thing is, but I do know that I want it dead. Baring that I want it sealed away forever."

Jolson said, "I also have no idea of what it is, but I might know where we can find out. This thing, whatever it is, came from beyond our world. It would stand to reason that Flare would know what it is or at least know how we can find out what it is."

Dras asked incredulously, "You want to head back to Nexus right now?"

Jolson shook his head, "No. We have to put this to the side for now. I think we can all agree that the undead would be unable to do much about this thing. Letting it loose risks it attacking them."

Terenia said, "Whatever is preventing the corruption from reaching here is coming from that chamber itself so I am willing to guess that they would be incapable of attempting to turn it even if they could find it."

Jolson said, "This is just conjecture but I think that the undead would be even more susceptible to that things control since they actually use a telepathic link. Looking around this lab I see no means of audio communication and those corpses looked vaguely human but were also very different.

I think they also communicated with telepathy. I am not sure what they were, but this place looks different enough and the language different enough that I am wondering if they were not also from some other world."

That was something that had not occurred to Meterove. They had been to Nexus and used the portals there to travel to several other world doing simple jobs for Flare. It was not out of the realm of possibility that other people had come through and explored their world.

Meterove took a deep breath, "Ok. Here is what we are going to do. We will search this lab once more, thoroughly this time. Once we are sure that did not miss anything I will make a wall that looks like the cave wall to help disguise this place in case anyone does try to come look."

Meterove looked at Jolson to see if he agreed with this course. Jolson nodded and they began their search. While were searching they did their best to ignore the pressure that the creature was exuding over the area. There was the feeling of pure murder over them.

After two hours Meterove called the search to a halt, and they retreated down hallway. Once it turned to cave walls Meterove went another ten feet then they used magic to bury the corridor. What they had found had been interesting to say the least. They used the Gateway and returned to the Citadel.

.   .   .

Back at the Citadel they had called Joleen over and were now explaining what they had found. They had retrieved all the records that they could and amongst them had been several detailed pictures of the creature.

Joleen was now holding a copy of one of those pictures, looking at it with disgust. "I knew whatever was down there was going to be bad news. I just felt it."

She looked at the other pictures that they had retrieved as well. One was of one of those feathered reptiles. Another was of some enormous hand rising out of the earth with a proportionally large sword piecing the palm from above. Something that looked like a group of trees with a line to a single tree. There were a few that showed the planets where they had clearly been edited either adding and removing various planets or moons.

Meterove said, "Well no one is likely to go in there other than us anyway and if they do, they will find the remnants of a camp that they will assume was used to hide in before and after the ambush."

Dras said, "It can stay there forever for all I care. That thing was a nightmare."

Terenia shivered and said, "I have no idea what that thing was, but it seemed...old. I have met some old beings and that thing seemed older than almost anything else."

Jolson thought back to how he had felt in that chamber. That pressure it had exerted. That will it had tried to impose. It clearly had thought that they were like insects to it.

Valaas and Syr had quietly been listening to them and Syr was staring hard at the image of the creature. "I think that you will have a hard time finding answers to this. I have never heard of anything like this before."

Valaas who had also looked at the picture said, "If Syr has not heard of anything like this and you have not, then I would hazard a guess that there are none that have. She has read everything in the library at least once and many of them she has read time and again. The only exception would be the sealed section on the second floor of the Library. We still have not been able to gain entry even after all these years."

Everyone else present looked surprised. Meterove looked at them then at Syr.

She is a bookworm huh? I never would have guessed that she was the kind to curl up with a book.

Jolson said, "We were planning to ask Flare back on Nexus what she thought of this. If anyone would know the answer or where to find it is her."

At the mention of Nexus and Flare, Joleen had a complicated expression. Meterove understood. Flare probably would have the answer they were looking for, but the odds were that she was going to want something from them.

"What is this Nexus and who is Flare?"

Meterove and the others turned towards Syr in surprise. They had assumed that Nexus and Flare were part of the knowledge that had been sealed away after Mardelnier's death.

Jolson asked, "You really have no idea what we are talking about do you?"

Valaas and Syr both shook their heads and looked keenly interested. Jolson said, "Have either of you ever heard of Creation?"

Valaas said, "I know of the word and the meaning, but I have the feeling that you mean something else entirely."

Jolson launched into an explanation about everything that they had learned. The Dragon Lord, about Nexus and Flare and about Creation and all the worlds and the Planes attached to it.

Their looks of shock and disbelief were pretty strong at first but as Jolson kept talking their expressions changed to rapt attention. By the end Syr was mumbling something under her breath and Valaas let out a sigh.

"We were never aware of this. From what you have told me there has been others that have crossed between worlds, your father amongst them. It is entirely possible that some of the answers we seek are attainable after all."

Meterove said, "We will have to put that aside for now. The Ashen Empire is a higher priority. We plan to survey the area ourselves. You were out looking around, right? Did you learn anything useful Valaas?"

The change back to their preferred topic usually pleased Syr but this new revelation seemed to leave her torn. It could not be more obvious that Syr really wanted to know more about this strange creature.

Valaas said, "Yes. I have scouted some of the area around the perimeter of the Citadel and I did find something odd in the direction of those buildings that are in the center of the "blight". There were a large number of statues that appeared to be undead of various types all over the place."

Dras said, "So this place was some kind of temple to the Ashen Soul?"

Valaas shook his head, "No, I had thought that at first too, but the details on the statues were too perfect and some of them were in poses that looked to have been fleeing or hiding. I made my way closer to the temple and found some recent tracks. I followed them all the way up to a statue of an undead."

Meterove said, "Are you saying that the statues are moving?"

Valaas sighed, "What I am saying is that this is much worse than that. These were all regular undead and they were turned into stone. There is only one creature that I have ever heard of that can do that. Based on your faces the same thing has dawned on you too. There are gorgons here."

This pronouncement was followed by a ringing silence before Dras said, "I thought those were just one of those stories that parents use to scare their kids into going to bed. Are you saying that they are a real thing?"

Jolson said, "There are no substantiated accounts of a gorgon in the empire for a long time. The accounts that do exist are so old that their validity is questionable based on that alone."

Syr said, "I can vouch for their existence. I personally killed one when I was younger. They are very real and every bit as dangerous as you have likely heard."

Meterove leaned in with interest, "What do they really look like?"

Syr replied, "Not all that different from those monsters that attacked the Citadel a while back. Their lower half is snake-like, and they have human top halves. Where their hair would be there is a mass of venomous snakes. While the stories say their gave turns you to stone that is only partially true. They can paralyze with a glance but in order to turn someone to stone they must gaze upon them

191

for a much longer time. Furthermore, they must make eye contact with the one they are attacking, or the power will not work."

Dras asked, "What about the part where they have three heads?"

Syr nodded, "That is true. Two of the heads will regrow no matter how many times you sever them. In order to kill it you must sever the third head. The stories say that you need to sever the center head, but I had to sever the right head. It might be different for each one however, since I have only ever seen one, I can only guess."

Meterove asked, "Is there anything else that you think we should know about them before we explore this place?"

Syr frowned and after a moment said, "The only other thing that comes to mind is that it held two bows and quivers. One was a short bow made for close range. The other was a monstrosity, as were the arrows that went to it. It did not have any form of mele weapon."

Meterove said, "That makes sense. Anything that would get in close would likely be taken care of by its ability to paralyze."

Dras asked, "So do you have any ideas on how to counteract that? I am not exactly in a rush to get shot or turned to stone."

Meterove shrugged, "No clue. We will just have to wing it like usual."

Jolson groaned a little but Terenia and Dras both grinned. That was much more their style anyway.

CHAPTER 8.5
UNEXPECTED

To think that they would find one of the First Ones! Those that came before me are always hard to keep track of. Not being whole was probably not helping as well. Still one of the First Ones being anywhere was cause for worry for the ones they were near. This particular one, The One that Devours Through Sight, was bad.

Even more interesting is that someone had bound it. The fact that they had done so and that it had gone unnoticed meant that there were only so many that could have done it. Those who existed outside of the influence were rare but not nonexistent.

The other First Ones were mostly missing as well. Some slept in the center of worlds or drifted through the void. There were some few that had been slain but they were notoriously difficult to kill. This one had been sealed away for a while, so it was weakened. Still those chains had to be something special to hold it in place.

What will they find next? Knowing that they were going to be up against gorgons was cause for worry. Those were some of the more dangerous monsters on that world. Perhaps it was time to try and send more help? But what kind of help would be best?

Maybe arranging an encounter with one of the ones that could move around the influence would help them? No that would take too long to pull off. Not a bad idea though. They would undoubtably need more help in the future so beginning to work on that now would be wise.

Perhaps it was time to meet? No...soon, but not yet. There were still a few selves scattered that could be reached. Once that was done then it would be prudent to meet them. Perhaps a special weapon or two would be good? There were some very unique weapons in the Armory. Maybe a little nudge would get them to find them.

Yes, two of them already had something special. The oracle had his Artifact and the other one had the strangest thing, a sword that was another self. It was like an Artifact except that it held no dangers if destroyed. Yes, sending a dream this time should be enough. No need to make the one suffer more than necessary.

CHAPTER 9
BLIGHT

Meterove's eyes snapped open. The dream that he had just had, was so vivid that it startled him. Beside him he felt Terenia stir, she was also awake. He looked down at her and said, "Sorry if I woke you. I had-"

Terenia cut him off, "a strange very vivid dream about weapons down in the armory?"

Meterove froze. Yes, that had been exactly it. Had he been talking in his sleep?

Terenia sat up and let the blankets fall off her. She stretched and said, "I had the same dream. We all went to the Armory and you, and I found weapons."

OK...this was not just a regular dream. There should be no way that we both had the exact same dream, right? There is almost an urge, like something is trying to nudge me to act on this too.

Terenia asked, "Do you feel like something is trying to push you there too?"

Meterove widened his eyes.

That seals it. This was not some accident. Something was telling us to go there.

Meterove nodded and got up and started to get dressed. His coat that he had been wearing was starting to show wear. Pretty soon it would be time to get a new one. He put it one while Terenia used her power to dress herself.

Meterove opened the door to see Jolson and Dras about to knock. The fact that they were there made this even more unnerving. Was there something like that creature around here?

Jolson said, "I take it that it was not just Dras and myself that had that dream then. It felt similar to when I have visions but holds less certainty to it. Whatever sent that wanted to make sure it was not taken as a regular dream."

Meterove said, "So then do we do what it said? After that creature we found underground I am wary of following the instructions of anything, much less something that put thoughts in my head."

Dras grunted, "While I agree with you there, it was directing us to explore the Armory. We were already planning on doing just that. We are already here in the Citadel."

Jolson said, "I agree with Dras. If it wanted to send us somewhere else, I might be against it. We have already been using several different devices and weapons from here."

Meterove agreed. "Alright, but I still say we be cautious. I still do not like something touching my mind like this."

Jolson said, "I understand what you mean, but let me reiterate what I said. This felt like when I get a vison, only a lighter touch. Perhaps my visions come from an entity, and it chose to do things this way for some reason."

They had been acting on Jolson's visons from the beginning so to question them now would be pointless. Meterove did not feel like anything more needed to be said on the topic though. They had agreed to tread carefully but they were still going to do it.

The Armory was one of the few places that they had been to at all in the Citadel. Even then they had barely looked in before deciding to put it off for another day. The reason had been the size. There were racks upon racks of weapons.

How Meterove viewed arming a soldier and how Valaas viewed arming a soldier were two very different things. This place held far more weapons than he had said.

That or maybe he had simply not looked to closely at the Armory. There were also an insane number of unused racks as well.

Their destination was a small room to the side of the entrance. There was an intricate lock on the door that looked like the solar system. They had examined this door before but could not open it. Valaas and Syr had said they had never been inside either.

The dream, though, had shown them how to open the lock. You had to set planets to the exact alignment that they were currently in. After a few minutes the lock clicked, and the door rolled up. Inside was a good-sized room with weapons of all types, though far fewer. These seemed special though, as if there was more to them.

Meterove and Terenia looked at each other then went where their dream had pointed them. Their guidance ended there though since they had all woken up at that point.

Terenia found a small red lacquered case. She opened it and inside was a bracelet. The design was simple at first but once she touched it, she could feel that there was far more to this thing than it just being a bracelet. As she watched, it changed form, and now looked like the branches of a purple maple tree.

Terenia was entranced by the bracelet. It was beautifully made and looked perfectly sized for her as well.

There was the question as to what its purpose as a weapon was, but an inscription carved into the lid answered that. The more she read the higher her eyebrows rose, and further her mouth hung open.

The name of this bracelet was Grace. It would effectively double her abilities that were tied to nature. She could also use it to form a bow out of pure energy that would fire arrows that would turn corporeal upon impact.

Lastly it had a defensive ability that if she were to take an attack would be able to create a duplicate of her body that would take the attack instead. This ability would be very draining though and would deactivate after being triggered twice, until the bracelet detected enough energy in the body for it to be safely used again.

Meterove had been drawn to a different box. This one was far larger than the one Terenia had opened. Inside was a sword with a blade of blue and crimson marbled together. Like Terenia's bracelet Grace, there was also an inscription on the inside of the lid.

This sword was called Oblivion. It could lock a location that the wielder had stood in and transfer itself and its wielder back to that location as long as it was within their line of sight. It could create a small singularity that crushed whatever had been cut into an unimaginably small ball. Last was an ability to nullify any poison or other similar abnormal condition. The inscription made it very clear that it could not stop or heal wounds.

Both of these weapons were insane. True they would only be able to use some of these abilities so much, but compared to not having them at all there was no contest. Meterove could not even begin to place a value on this stuff.

Dras and Jolson had both found simple gold rings that could help their bodies recover from exhaustion at twice the normal rate. Dras had also noticed a hand crossbow that created a new bolt thirty seconds after it was fired. Jolson had found a dagger that when activated would freeze it in that location in space forever. The only way to move it was if you chose to release it or if you destroyed it.

They took their various items out of the room and closed the door. It relocked itself automatically, but that did not matter since they knew the secret to opening it now. Meterove knew that he would have to bring Joleen and Narok here later.

.   .   .

Joleen sat at her desk staring blearily at the documents in front of her. This kind of work was the worst. Requisition forms, recruitment reports, and the like kept piling up. She had also been training daily with Narok to get better at using her Artifacts.

Without noticing it she had drifted off to sleep with her face pressed against the paper that she had been reading. Narok had other duties that he needed to see to, so another guard was in the room with her right now. He barely registered the music before it was too late.

Crouched over Joleen's softly breathing face, its own face cocked to the side and inches from her own was the same child that Jolson and Narok had seen in Orilion's lab. It gently tapped Joleen's nose. It opened its mouth and a jet-black tongue moved as though to lick the lips it did not have. It then gently caressed Joleen's cheek with the back of two fingers.

The sound of the doors opening woke Joleen up and Narok's disgruntled muttering fully awakened her. She lifted her head and looked around. "Is something wrong?"

Narok looked annoyed and said, "The guard that I had stationed here left his post. I did not see any sign of him on my way down the hall on the way here either."

While Narok was muttering under his breath, most likely how severe the punishment was going to be, Joleen stretched. While she did, she heard the sound of something hitting her desk. She looked and saw a single dark drop. She touched it and seeing red, jerked her head up, while jumping back and shouting.

The missing guard was all over the ceiling of the room. In one corner crouched on the top of the bookshelf was the child. Seeing it in person was a whole different experience to seeing a memory. Joleen quickly made a barrier as it jumped at her. It burst into existence and severed the left arm of the child at the elbow.

A horrifying shriek blasted through the room that made her hair stand on end. It looked down at the shoulder where the arm was severed as it bubbled and expanded quickly regrowing. Its eyes and expression never changed from before. Alight with malic, yet joyful and ecstatic with that same horrifying smile in place. It moved so fast that it seemed to teleport around the room. That eerie, jerky movement was the worst.

Her shout earlier had alerted the other guards and they now entered the room. The child swooped down and landed in front of Joleen. Knowing the barrier was around her did not make her feel any less afraid. It watched her, those red eyes that she now noticed held a small amount of green as well and stared into her own. It mimed running a finger down her cheek, laughed erratically as it vanished and was now clinging to the ceiling, licking up the blood.

The sound of a circus could be heard in the room as the shadows grew and swarmed around the child. The blood and bits from the guard almost looked like they melted into the darkness. Faintly, horrifying animals could be seen, far too skinny to be their living counterparts as well as some tents.

The circus faded away slowly then with a few more erratic laughs from the child, it was gone. Narok and the other guards surrounded Joleen. It was a testament to how terrified she was that even surrounded by guards and with Narok at her side she kept her barrier up. Narok was shouting orders, but she was in her own head.

That thing came here for me. I have no idea what it wanted but it clearly had something to do with me. That poor guard. I doubt he even knew what happened. It has shown itself now to Meterove, Jolson and me. I also suspect that those random grisly murders that I have been hearing about have something to do with it as well.

.   .   .

Meterove and the others had been practicing with their new weapons in order to get a good feel for them. They had found some notes in the Library that had given them a clue about Dras' sword and Jolson had finally fully manifested the combat form of his Artifact.

It turns out that Dras' sword had essentially become an Artifact. While holding it he could double his mental processing and kinetic vision for short periods of time. He could also leave a single attack suspended in space for a short duration. Essentially, he could slash the air and then trick the enemy into walking into the area and they would get cut.

Jolson's Artifact was a scythe. It could be of any size from a small hand scythe to a massive two-handed monstrosity that made him look like a reaper. The blade of it looked like a ghostly raven's wing. It could rapidly age whatever was hit by the blade. It worked far faster on organic matter, but it could also work on other things.

Looking at the jungle around them Meterove and Dras had decided that they needed to rethink their coats. They both currently had sleeveless leather chest pieces, thin cloth pants, with calf-high leather boots and thin fingerless gloves. Meterove's were brown and Dras was in all black.

Meterove had both swords crossed over his back. Dras had just the one, but he also had a leather bracer on his left arm where his hand crossbow was. Additionally, he had several throwing knives on his belt.

Jolson was just in cloth, with leather boots. He also had a satchel on his side that held various useful items. He had also grabbed a longbow and a quiver of arrows. While not the greatest archer, Jolson had reasoned he was good enough that having it was a good idea.

Terenia had also decided to change her clothes. She was wearing a black cloth wrap halter top and a forest green skirt that went halfway to her thighs. She kept her knee-high boots but now they had slightly raised heels. Grace rested on her right wrist.

Meterove took one look at her and asked, "What do you plan on doing if we have to fight?"

Terenia who had been admiring how her new outfit looked from different angles using a mirror their room said, "Change."

Meterove asked bewildered, "Change?"

Terenia said, "Yes. Change. Just like this."

Terenia was covered in a slight shimmer and suddenly the cloth was replaced with leather armor that covered most of her torso, though in typical Terenia fashion, there was a gap that showed her cleavage.

It appeared to be a full body suit though it stopped at her hips. Her boots though, were now thigh-high and were connected to the bodysuit with leather ties. Her arms also had elbow length bracers on them, and she had simple finger loop gloves.

The change took less time than usual and Meterove suspected that Grace had something to do with that. Meterove also noticed that Terenia had grabbed a belt that held two large daggers behind her back.

Terenia asked, "Well?"

Meterove said, "That certainly looks much better suited to combat. Twin daggers huh?"

Terenia said, "Yep. I was thinking that it would be best to have some kind of weapon that I can use without magic just in case."

Meterove nodded then asked, "Are you ready to go?"

Terenia shimmered and returned to her former look. "Yep"

She looped her arm through his and after he shook his head Meterove made his way out to the courtyard. Jolson and Dras had already arrived. Once outside Meterove pulled the sunglasses out that he had gotten while on Nexus and put them on. It really helped in bright places like this. Seeing Meterove put his on, Terenia used her power to make a pair of her own.

Dras pointed at Meterove's sunglasses and said, "I wish I thought to grab my own."

There was a shimmer around both Dras' and Jolson's eyes and two pairs of sunglasses appeared. Dras laughed lightly and said, "Thanks Terenia."

Jolson also thanked her then asked, "Are we ready to look around then?"

Meterove nodded and then started walking to the wall. Passing through was still strange to him but he was slowly getting used to it. Stepping out into this place was strange after the time they had spent in the Ashen Empire.

There were plants everywhere. Trees hundreds of feet high with huge leaves towered above them. Closer to the ground were fan palms and other exotic looking trees. The ground was a mass of thick bushes, long snaking vines and countless beautiful flowers.

There were several paths through this forest that appeared to have been made by whomever had made the structures that they were going to investigate. Meterove had been torn about taking these paths at first but after they encountered a massive spiders web just inside the forest, he changed his mind.

They could not see the spider at first but there were several animals the size of a large cat that were stuck in its web. Suddenly a large brightly colored red and blue bird flew into the web and the spider than had been sitting down near a bush shot up the web. It must have had a leg span of two feet.

Dras looked at the thing and loaded his hand crossbow. Meterove heard a single "NOPE" before he shot it. The spider fell to the forest floor and Jolson went up to investigate it. The thing was bright green and black. There was some blood on its fangs from where it had bitten the bird before Dras shot it. The bird had died instantly so clearly the venom was pretty deadly.

They moved down the paths keeping a close watch for not only gorgons but giant spiders as well. They also saw several large snakes that were idly lying about. The one had to be large enough to swallow a man. They had been walking for a short time when they found some of the statues that they had heard about.

There was no mistaking it. They looked like so many of the undead that they had seen in their time in the Ashen Empire. There were regular risen corpses, but also skeletons and even some of the more horrifying things like the ghouls. Some movement in one of the bushes nearby caught Dras' attention and they took cover.

A strange creature popped out of the forest, and it took them a moment to really begin to see it due to the shock. It was about two feet tall and maybe four feet long. Two scaly wings about four times the size of its body protruded from its back, and it was walking around on two legs. There was a long scaly tail, but the majority of its body was covered in feathers.

The creature had a long neck that ended in a small slightly elongated head. The mouth was kind of a mix of birds beak and a reptiles mouth. It looked like someone had crossed a rooster with a dragon. The feathers were bright red and green.

It was walking along and pecking at the rocks in the path. There was a very chicken-like demeaner to how it moved. It walked up to one of the undead statues and began to peck at it. Bits of the stone would flake away, and it would pick them up and eat them.

Jolson opened his satchel and pulled out a book. He quietly flipped through the pages until he found what he was looking for. "Hmmm so that is what they really look like."

Meterove looked back at him and whispered, "Are you going to share?"

Jolson showed him the book. Meterove looked back at the creature then back at the place in the book that Jolson was pointing. There was an artist's rendition of what it might have looked like in there, but it was not quite what they were looking at. Still, it was close enough that it was obviously the same creature. Meterove read the short entry.

Cockatrice: This small creature has the body of a dragon and head of a rooster. There have been legends that being seen by a cockatrice means instant death, but the reality is different. These creatures live in a symbiotic relationship with the actually dangerous gorgons. They eat the stone of the petrified victims. They are immune to the petrification effects of the gorgon's eyes. They have sharp talons and can shoot a congealed acid ball from its mouth if threatened.

OK. That still seems kind of bad but at least the only real weapons it has are its claws and acid spit. We will just leave them alone and hope that they leave us alone.

Dras tapped him on the shoulder and Meterove looked around and he revised that opinion a little. There had been one before. At least another dozen of them had come out of the forest now. Before long, the statue began to break and toppled over. The cockatrices scattered with small squawking roars, only to return and begin pecking a moment later.

Meterove whispered, "We are going to leave them alone and hope they leave us alone. I have no interest in going through the forest if I can help it. These are probably not the only pack out there either. I can only imagine how many there are.

Terenia said, "I can feel through the forest and try and find the larger creatures but smaller ones like these will be impossible. There are too many for me to keep track of."

Meterove said, "Focus on finding anything larger than them. We will have to keep our eyes open for the other ones."

Jolson said, "This probably confirms that there are gorgons here and that these statues really are undead that they petrified."

Dras said, "Not going to lie, I was hoping Valaas and Syr were wrong."

Meterove sighed, "Me too."

Terenia closed her eyes and said, "I can feel at least twenty large creature in the area. One of them appears to be stalking us."

That caught everyone's attention. She pointed to the southwest and said, "That way. It is about twenty feet into the forest. Whatever it is it thinks that we are prey."

Jolson considered putting up a barrier but decided against it. Barriers were too costly to use unless absolutely necessary. Meterove took the opportunity to pick up a rock and throw it ten feet to the right of where Terenia had pointed. This also happened to be in the direction of the pack of cockatrices.

The cockatrices gave that weird squawking roar again and moved to look at the sound only to run away as the creature that had been stalking them barreled towards the sound as well. They could see it through some of the gaps in the forest. It looked like a serpent that was even bigger than the giant snake creature that had attacked the citadel. It also appeared to have at least six heads.

Meterove and Dras both unsheathed their swords while Terenia created her bow. Meterove said, "Jolson did you see anything in that book about this thing?"

Meterove was keeping his eyes on the creature as best he could, but he knew Jolson was searching franticly through that book based on the sound of pages flipping.

The creature knew that they were aware of it now and it decided to attack.

Meterove and Dras spread out while Terenia stayed with Jolson. With that many heads, each with nearly twenty feet of neck, they were going to have to split too far apart to help each other. Luckily, Jolson was able to find the creatures entry fairly quickly.

Jolson yelled out, "IT IS A HYDRA! IT HAS POIONOUS BREATH AND BLOOD! THE HEADS ALL HAVE TO BE SEVERED AT ONCE OR THEY WILL JUST KEEP GROWING BACK!"

Meterove said, "Great...there are six of those. I have no idea how we are going to pull that off."

Dras dodged a snap from one of the heads.

That thing could swallow me whole with ease!

A spray of weird yellow mist came out of one of the other heads and immediately all the plant life in the area began to wilt and die. Dras saw this and took a few extra steps back.

OH! He meant like REALLY poisonous! I am guessing that its fangs have venom too. SHIIIT!

Dras dodged back two more times as two more of the heads went after him. Meanwhile Meterove had decided to test the regeneration part out and went for a slice.

The head fell free and writhed and snapped a little before going still. The blood that soaked the ground and splattered around seemed even more toxic than its spray.

The way it ate through the plants...this stuff is almost as bad as acid!

The head grew back just as Jolson said it would. The speed that it did it though was insane. It was back to having six heads in just a few seconds and the new one seemed to glare at him with new cunning.

Two arrows flew at one of the heads, striking it in the eyes, blinding it. It thrashed around a little then two of the heads turned to it and began to violently attack its neck. Meterove was confused for a second before it clicked. They were biting the head off.

Sure, enough after a moment the head tore free in a spray of blood and a new one grew in its place. Meterove decided that he was going to try magic next. He sent out a couple small blasts towards the heads, but the hydra was a lot more cunning than they had given it credit for and it used one head to take multiple hits.

Where it had been a spray of blood before it was now a shower. A small amount touched Dras' skin and as he watched a splotch of black begin spreading up his arm. He took out his knife and with a quick slice cut the afflicted flesh away from his arm. There was gush of blood, but he quickly wrapped a cloth bandage around it to slow the bleeding.

On the ground the section of flesh that had the splotch disintegrated. Dras dropped back and fired his hand crossbow to give himself some time. The bolt struck inside the mouth of one of the heads. It may not have killed it but at least it closed its mouth instead of breathing out more poison.

Jolson turned his Artifact into a large scythe and took a slice at the hydra. The cut did more than just the physical damage. The area that had been cut rapidly aged. Jolson went in for another attack and after dodging the heads a few times managed to land a solid blow, sinking the scythe to the haft into the hydra's skull.

The head turned to dust over the course of several seconds. It did not stop there as the decay began to spread down its body. The hydra panicked and the five remaining heads all spat out poison then used the cover to all try and bite the neck off that was decaying.

They just managed to do it before it spread to the rest of the body. Angered, the hydra swept its tail across the ground and hit Jolson in the torso, sending him flying back.

"Meterove! Dras! Get back," shouted Terenia!

Meterove and Dras both did instant backsteps and watched as countless tree roots burst out of the ground and impaled the hydra all over its body. The blood was eating through the roots, but Terenia was using Grace, which strengthened roots. She then manipulated the roots to tear away at the body managing to sever all six heads.

There were a few strangled hisses then the heads stopped moving. The body fell to the forest floor and a moment later Terenia sank to one knee. Meterove ran to her while Dras ran over to help a groaning Jolson.

Meterove placed a hand on her shoulder, and she brought a shaking hand across to grip it. She looked up at him with a little bit of exhaustion but mostly triumph. She mumbled, "I did it...I can stand with you guys now...not just behind you."

Meterove pretended that he had not heard her. He figured she would rather not have it known she had been worried about that.

Even though I have never once thought of you as anything less than amazing.

Dras came over supporting a slightly dazed and limping Jolson. Terenia had recovered her energy and used her magic to heal their wounds.

After that they moved a little further down the path and found small clearing that they used to rest. After their rest break was over, they continued on, though they moved more slowly since they were using Terenia's ability to sense through the forest.

There were several more large creatures but they managed to keep their distance. They passed by a large group of giant lizard like creatures in the river, their eyes and snouts just barely breaking the surface. They even found what appeared to be a carnivorous plant. It had a large bulbous end that kind of resembled jaws A small bird landed on it and they snapped closed.

Draw stepped slightly further away and said, "Even the plants can eat us. There is no way I am going in there."

Terenia cocked her head and said, "I agree. I cannot sense a difference between this plant and the others around it. There is no telling if this is full grown or a seedling."

Eventually they reached the area that they had been looking for. Ahead there were about a dozen different stone structures.

While they were all different, they had the same feel of balance and symmetry and they all had lots of large pillars of what looked like white marble. Meterove judged that it was about midday based on the sun. Making sure that he was well in the shade of a tree he pulled out a spyglass and looked around.

The first thing he noticed was that there were far more statues here. Hundreds, maybe even thousands of them. Not all of them appeared to be undead though. The only thing that he did not see statues of were cockatrices.

He did see plenty of them moving around the buildings though.

Meterove lowered his spyglass, "I do not see any gorgons out there. There are a ton of statues though. Oh, and there are a ton more of those cockatrices too. I guess that book was right in that they like to hang out with gorgons."

Dras said, "So what is the plan then?"

Meterove looked at Jolson and asked, "Were you able to find anything more than what we already knew about gorgons?"

Jolson shook his head, "No, I can only assume that Syr is one of the only people that have ever fought a gorgon and lived. Additionally, I think much of what is in books is based in superstition and myth, not fact."

Meterove looked at Terenia, "Are you able to use your abilities to sense what is going on in there?"

Terenia closed her eyes and after a moment frowned and then shook her head, "No there is something over there. Lots of small things, so many that I cannot differentiate between them all."

Meterove sighed, "Yeah, I kind of expected that. There were tons of those cockatrices over there. I can only assume that they make nests where they feel safe. You are probably feeling all of those."

Dras said, "OK, we cannot know for sure what is over there and how many. Could we do that distraction trick from earlier again?"

Meterove gave a noncommittal grunt and pondered it. "The only way that I can think of that working out there would be if it were really big. Back in the forest we were able to make sound that sounded like prey. Here we would be trying to draw who knows what from who knows where. The biggest downside that I can see with this would be that we would have to give away our presence and position to do it."

Dras took out his own spyglass and looked out at the buildings. He saw a cockatrice pecking idly at an enormous statue and he had a flash of inspiration.

"Terenia! Do you see that big statue over by the third building from the right?" he asked

Terenia looked where he was pointing. "Yes, I can. What do you want me to do?"

Dras asked, "Do you think you would be able to weaken the leg on it with your roots like you did with the hydra, so that it would crash down? A crash that big should draw some attention."

He handed the spyglass over to her and she looked through it. For a moment she just looked through it while silently mouthing what Meterove assumed was her thoughts on how to make it work until there was a massive crash.

The other three looked over to see a huge cloud of dust billowing out from where it had landed. Terenia handed the spyglass back and said, "Yep that worked."

Dras took his spyglass back and he and Meterove watched as cockatrices scattered everywhere. That was not the only thing that they saw though. From within several of the buildings several gorgons came slithering out.

True to the stories they were snake on the bottom and humanoid on the top. They all appeared to be women, though they did not know if there even were male gorgons. They all had beautifully proportioned faces that were terrifying because of the eyes, forked tongues and slithering mass of venomous snakes that were where their hair should be. Each one had three heads, and all were scanning for the cause of the disturbance.

As they watched more and more of them emerged from the buildings. As it was now there had to be at least a hundred of them slithering around.

Meterove assumed they were safe, but he still found himself crouching down. He looked at the others who had done the same and whispered, "That is far more than I was expecting. Even if we take the whole legion in there, I cannot be certain that we will be able to kill them all."

Dras said, "Do we even need to? I mean these things are in an area that makes them a problem for the Ashen Empire and not us."

Jolson said, "You are forgetting that we originally came here to find out why this area is not only alive but actually pushing back on the corruption."

Terenia said, "That is one thing that I do know for sure. Whatever it is that is allowing the land to flourish like this is over in that direction. The flow of energy through the ground is almost unbelievably strong here."

Dras looked over at the buildings. There was one that was far larger than the rest of them and it was right in the middle. "Let me guess...the big one that we cannot get near without the gorgons from all the other ones seeing us, right?"

Terenia nodded, "Yes as far as I can tell that is where it is."

Meterove said, "well I think we should look at using some more of the constructs-"

Jolson cut him off, "We damaged most of them when we pulled off the ambush. The few that we do have left I think should be saved for when we have no other options. I did send one off to have it studied but without someone who specialized in magical engineering we cannot make more."

Meterove went quiet for a moment clearly thinking of what other methods they could employ. Finally, he said, "I think we should report back to the Citadel. It is possible that Valaas and Syr or Joleen have some useful input on this."

They took one last look at the buildings before heading back onto the path. They made sure to keep to the path the whole way. After everything that they had seen from this place the danger of being on the path was nothing compared to what was hidden in the undergrowth.

.   .   .

Valaas was highly interested in what they had learned. From the fact that there were hydras in the forest to the number of gorgons he listened with rapt attention. Syr...the only time she showed any signs of hearing them was when they mentioned the hydra and the gorgons. As for how to get inside the building, the only advice they had was to check the Lab.

Later they made a report to Joleen, and she likewise listened to them with rapt attention, though she did not appreciate the description of the spider or the news that there were plants in there that were carnivorous.

Her own report about the child paying her a visit left them shook. Meterove smashed his fist down on the table. "What is that thing? Why is it following us?"

Joleen folded her hands. She was not surprised that her brother had made the same connection that she had. "I do not know but I am taking precautions. As uncomfortable as it is I have taken to sleeping with an entire squadron of guards in my chamber and a mage casting a barrier that is changed on hourly rotations."

Jolson said, "At first, I was worried about that vison where you and Dras were fighting it Meterove. Now I cannot wait until it happens. Perhaps it will be killed then."

Joleen cleared her throat, "For now we need to put that aside. Getting into that building with the gorgons may prove invaluable. I agree with Valaas and Syr. See what can be found inside the Lab."

Meterove and the others returned to the Citadel a short while later. Meterove was ready to go tear the Lab apart right then and there. Jolson was of another mind.

Jolson yawned, "Meterove, I know that you are ready to go all in on this, but some of us got knocked around earlier and would like to take the rest of the night off."

Meterove was going to argue but then he saw that Terenia and Dras were also nodding along with Jolson. He thought about it for a moment and realized that it had been a long day for all of them.

He was the only one that did not expend a ton of energy or get injured. He sighed and realized that he needed to rest too. The rush that came from battle had not had a chance to fade. He rolled his shoulders and said, "Yeah, you have a point. We can go in first thing after breakfast."

The others relaxed a bit. They had clearly been expecting more resistance to the idea of taking some rest. Regardless they were not going to question it and they all returned to their rooms and turned in.

CHAPTER 10
GORGONS

The next morning found the four of them searching through the Lab. Most of what was in here was beyond them, even Jolson.

We really need to find someone that is an expert in this kind of stuff.

They all split up and searched around the Lab examining things that were on shelves or flipping through notes. They found numerous items of varying levels of usefulness.

There were canteens that pulled moisture from the air to make clean drinking water, tools that could sense metals in the ground and small circular objects that could go over one's eye and allow them to see what was sent to it through a magical transmission, just to name a few.

There were also cabinets full of vials of liquids with complex names on them. There were also many small sharp metal instruments that were supposed to be used to administer the contents of those vials. Apparently, they could also be used to take blood from something.

The whole morning, they searched through the lab but with no real idea of what they were looking for it was all a game of chance. Finally, Dras stumbled on something that seemed promising.

Optical camouflage...bends light around a small area... I have no idea what that means but it says camouflage.

Dras called out, "I might have something here."

Jolson came over, "What did you find?"

Dras said, "The name is optical camouflage. Here look. Does that make any sense to you?"

Jolson took a look at the information card that Dras showed him. After reading it and thinking about it for minute he shrugged and said, "I have no idea what it means by "bending light" but the name makes me think it hides things."

"Then we need to just try it out and see what happens." Meterove and Terenia had come over as well. Meterove was holding a small cube with two arrows pointing in opposite directions on it. Jolson asked, "What did you find?"

Meterove lifted the cube up a little and said, "Apparently it can be used once to expand out to fill a large gap and seal it. How I have no idea but there was a bunch of technical writing with it that I did not understand."

Dras looked interested and Jolson felt like putting his head in his hands, but he knew that Meterove was right. There was only one way to be sure what these things did and how they worked. He had a question first. "How many of those were there and how big did its card say that it could get?"

Meterove said, "The case I found held six. As for how big it did not say, but how big could it possibly get?"

Jolson would normally agree but given what that cube was supposed to do he thought it best to check. "We should make sure to test it far away. Common sense did not seem to exist for the ones that made this place."

As they were walking out of the Lab Terenia said, "Have you noticed that the stuff in this place seems kind of cobbled together? Like some of the things use crystals others use metal or stone. Even the designs of the weapons are all vastly different."

Dras said, "What do you mean?"

Terenia held up her wrist, "Grace and Oblivion both came out of the armory, yet their designs are so different that there is no way that the same people made them. Not only are they made from completely different materials, but the aesthetic is totally different."

Jolson said, "You know I have been wondering about that. The rings that Dras and I found are made in a totally different style as well."

Dras said, "so, what are you getting at?"

Terenia said, "well, this place is called the Citadel of Time, right? What if these are objects that have been collected throughout history? Perhaps even from other worlds?"

Meterove suddenly had a small flash of something across his vision, but it was gone before he could register what it was. What Terenia had just said stirred something in his memory for sure.

Jolson said, "That could very well be the case. We know that there was some kind of civilization here before humans came. The ruins that the Acephali live in are proof of that."

Once outside the four of them went outside the walls to an area that was well away from the Citadel. It was a path that led between two small rock outcroppings. Meterove set the cube down on the ground and faced the sides with arrows towards the rocks. He pressed the top and stepped back.

They all watched in shock as the cube stretched and expanded until the whole gap was filled. Meterove climbed up and found that the wall it had made was as wide as the rocks too. There was a smooth metal wall, as thick as any fort's.

Dras pulled a small camp shovel out of his pack and started digging at the ground and found that it went down into the ground as well.

Meterove said, "Well that will be useful. We could station some archers here that could really hurt any enemies that tried to go around this."

Dras said, "I think I saw some stuff in the Lab that they could use to watch for incoming enemies without being seen."

Terenia said, "We should test the other one."

Dras took out his device. His was much larger. Half the reason he still had his pack on was to help carry this thing. It was a metal box with a switch and a dial on it. He placed it on the ground then activated it by flipping the switch. The others backed up about twenty feet to watch.

At first nothing seemed to happen then as he slowly turned the dial, he vanished in front of their eyes...sort of.

There was an area of distorted space around where he was. As they watched the distortion changed to become clearer.

After a moment Dras stepped out of thin air. He looked back and put his hand into the space he had been standing in a moment ago.

WHOA! That is freaky!

Jolson said, "that works pretty well, though the fact that it appears to hide an area will be a problem. It would be hard to miss if something vanished through it."

Terenia said, "We can solve that by using it at night. If any of them sees that they will likely just attribute it to a trick of the light."

"That is true. I think we should try it out on them from a distance first though," agreed Jolson.

.   .   .

The humans had been playing them. There was no other possibility. They had entered the Ashen Empire and through unknown means learned much. There were reports from several different areas of undead entering the Farms and buying stock, only for those undead and the stock to simply vanish.

Then there was the incident in the streets where an officer, Major Klepton, had been killed. That had supposedly been done by human sympathizers, but that just did not sit right. Word had also come in that there was an incident over at the Cathedral.

Lastly the army had suffered such horrendous losses. That ambush had been devastating. Over half of their forces were lost and of that number only a fraction could be reanimated again. The weavers that had been going through the remains were hesitant to give any concrete numbers.

Now here he was, Brigadier General Aleksandr Gorchevka following the tracks that the humans had attempted to hide. He was standing in a cave, whose mouth was out on a ledge. Remains of a small camp were here. He had seen through their foolish attempts to hide there was more past this point.

He was part of the second generation of Ashen Converts. There were only a few bone constructs that were older than he was. His silk officers uniform with the grey and faded blue, two-tone coat adorned with the single Ashen Wing that showed his rank, and matching pants.

He had a full one hundred thralls with him. They would be more than enough to deal with whatever traps the humans had left.

If they wanted to hide this, it must have been something that they really wanted to keep from us.

It did not take too long to clear the "wall" away from the corridor. Now he was walking down the corridor with his thralls behind him. He entered a strange room. His countless years of service still did not give him insight All he knew was that the humans had been here and had likely taken whatever interested them.

"Take everything that is left! If those bags of unused parts left anything important, I want to make sure we have it!"

"SIR"

That is the only useful function of the newly raised like these. I do not understand why someone of my station was sent here with newly raised!

This area had long been restricted, with nothing but whispers and rumors about the reason. That had been the only reason why he had agreed to this search. Alexsandr had long wondered why someone of his level had not been fully briefed. If that had not been the case he would not have agreed to take this assignment.

There were two door off this strange room. He took the first one not even bothering to look out of the window. Humans putting a window underground just prooved their uselessness. He walked for a time and eventually came out to a ledge. At first he did not see much but he soon saw the monstrosity that was infront of him.

What in the Ashen Nightmare is that!

232

The thing looked at him. There were so many eyes. They all focused on him and his thralls that had come down with him. He felt a strange pull as those eyes stayed on him. Those lips around and inside the eyes almost seemed to moisten.

The tounges at the top parted and swirled around. The eyes were lit up with excitement. The pull grew stronger and Alexsandr walked over to the edge and stood there. The thralls that had come down with him followed. They were worthless.

Alexsandr watched as several of them lifted off the groud and were pulled towards the large eye on the bottom. As they floated near it, the lips that had been where the pupils would normally be were now full of teeth.

The thralls were swallowed by the gaint eye.

Why are they so useless! Someone on my level should have been given command of some of the elites! As it stands I will be the only one left!

Alexsandr had failed to notice that he was no longer on the ground. By the time that he was aware of it he was floating into the endless maw of those eyes and it was too late. He and those with him were devoured whole.

·   ·   ·

The test had been a success. They had deployed the camoflauge at the same location that they had watched from previously and had lobbed rocks to catch the attention of various gorgons, none of whom could identify where the rocks had come from. All that was left was to enter the structure later that evening.

Jolson could only shake his head. Meterove and Dras were like two kids. They wanted to see how well this worked out and neither of them seemed to really care about what would happen after they were sealed in that building with who knows how many gorgons.

As the sky darkened they moved their way up towards the buildings and activated the camoflauge. Several times as they walked a cockatrice would look in their direction. When Dras worriedly mentioned that Jolson said, "This device makes us harder to see, but they can still hear and smell us."

Dras mumbled something about not stinkning and Meterove cracked a grin. Banter was good. Banter meant that no one was panicking. They slowly but surley made their way up to the buildings. Only once they were closer did Meterove realize just how big the central building was.

Its distance from the others had given a false sense of its dementions. This building was quite large. Each of the pillars was twice the width of his shoulders and there were hundreds of them on this thing.

The entrance was a huge square flanked by two of the pillars. The doors appeared to be made of bronze and all of one piece. Wheather they were solid bronze or simply encased was anyones guess. There were reliefs of gorgons on the door.

Once they were near the door they stayed near a pillar waiting for one of the gorgons to open the door. Terenia used her power to make another of the larger statues fall over and hopfully draw out some of gorgons. They could feel the ground shake with the impact of the fall.

Even that did not bring a gorgon to the door and Meterove decided that it was time to take the risk and push it open themsElves. They moved over to door and gave it a huge shove. In the silence of the night the squeel of the door sounded far louder than they had expected so they hurried inside and closed the doors.

They were inside an antechamber that had three gorgon statues on each side. There was a large stone cased opening at the other end. Meterove pulled the cube out quick and set it down on the ground between the door and the first statue, the pressed the top.

After a a few moments a massive barrier was in place, sealing the door closed. Meterove led the way forward and once they were through the arch they saw a truly breathtaking sight.

The building was open to the sky with a covered area twice as wide as the antechamber that surrounded the center. In the middle there was a rock outcroping that was spewing water into a pool that had channels that led underground.

Terenia whispered, "The power that is fighting against the corruption is coming up from that spring."

There were four large gorgon statues around the spring and the area around and bewteen them that was not covered in water was worn cobblestone. Scattred across the rest of the building were statues of those souls who had tried and failed to sneak in.

In the fading light the shadows may be helping to hide them but they were also making finding any gorgons difficult. They moved slowly over to one of the streams and Meterove dipped his hand into it and brought some water out.

The water was crytal clear and quite hot. There was something about how it felt that stired a memory in his mind but Meterove could not place it.

A soft hiss and the twang of a bowstring caused him to move without thought. He pushed Terenia down while Dras was getting Jolson. A massive arrow flew through the space they had been in a moment ago and shattered a statue.

From the ground Meterove looked up at the gorgon. This one looked a little different from the ones that they had seen outside. For starters it was almost twice their size.

The snake tail was an emerald green and there were four wings, remeniscent of a dragon's, coming out from its back. The humanoid torso held the three heads as usual but these were less human. They had larger eyes with the left eye looking human while the right eye looking like a snakes.

While the body was large enough to accommodate the heads it was still very slim and snakelike. The chest was barely raised and had scales that ran up the sides and partially down the arms. The faces themsElves looked ageless. A forked tongue was flicking out of each mouth.

Meterove looked back at the others. He saw they all felt the same. This thing knew they were here. Even that little bit of movement somehow caught its attention and it nocked another arrow and drew.

Dras grabbed a rock and threw it over by the edge of the camoflauge and as it clacked against stone and fell into the water the gorgon snapped its aim over to there an loosed its arrow.

As it harmlessly hit the side of a channel the four of them lept to their feet and Meterove fired a blast of magic. The gorgon batted it aside as though it were nothing and its eyes began to glow. Meterove shut his eyes and dove to the side.

SHIT! Magic is off the table I guess.

Meterove yelled, "Terenia can you do the same thing you did to kill that hydra?"

237

Terenia shouted back, "I would but we are not going to have that luxary. Look up!"

Meterove looked up and swore. There were dozens of the things on a second floor over the perimeter that he had missed.

Jolson shouted, "The pillars! At least we can break line of sight and have cover!"

Meterove did not like having blind spots but he could not see any other options. The four of them took off for the pillars. At least they would also have to camoflauge in there.

Arrows flew past and Meterove vaugely registered that even though the ones from above were smaller they were still larger than what humans would normally use.

Taking cover in the pillars they spread out as much as possible while still staying in the camoflauge. Once they were under cover Terenia started focusing her power. While she was doing that Jolson located the way up to the second floor and took up a position where he could watch it from relative safety.

This left Meterove and Dras to deal with the larger gorgon. Meterove picked up one of the arrows it had fired at him before.

This thing is nuts! I think I saw a smaller balista once that used something this size! What is that on the tip? Is that poison?

Meterove was wondering what to do next when Dras did something incredibly brave...and stupid.

"Here I am! Shoot me," Dras shouted while jumping out from cover and running through a maze of petrified victims! The gorgons all took the bait, eager to kill him. The statues exploded as arrows flew at him.

"Everyone! Close your eyes! This is going to be bright," shouted Dras and he raised his sword! Meterove barely had time to react as a bright light flared up from Dras' sword and filled the room along with hisses and shrieks of rage and pain.

Dras ran back while all the gorons were temporarily blinded and for good measure sliced the large gorgons bowstring on the way.

Dras dove back into the pillars as the gorgons started to regain their sight and more arrows rained down. One hit him in his prosthetic arm. As he slumped down to the ground behind a pillar he pulled the arrow out and threw it to the ground.

That little stunt of his had helped some. Now how to handle this situation? They were only really here to look for the source of the power that was cleansing the corruption. If

239

anything the gorgons would be useful in keeping the undead away from here.

A massive hand, with pale skin and dirty nails grabbed the side of the pillar that Meterove was hiding behind. It was focusd on Dras since it had just seen him. This was his chance!

The massive creature heaved itself forward and three heads came into view. Meterove reacted as soon as the first bit of writhing snake hair came into view and swung Oblivion down and severed the head on the right side.

There was a massive shriek and the head fell to the ground its mouth open, hissing and snapping the snakes trying to bite him as well. The hand that had been on the pillar flew in his direction and he swung again and cut off the fingers before sliding back and around another pillar.

From where he was sitting Dras watched as Meterove cut off a head then some fingers before hiding. Unfortuantly the head began to grow back almost instantly.

Roots wrapped around the gorgons body and pinned it down. Jolson and Dras jumped in and cut the other heads off before the first fully regenerated. The heads hit the ground a second before the body, now released from the roots, crashed to the ground.

The roots moved from the body to block the stairway keeping the other gorgons from coming down. While Terenia held the roots in place Dras stayed back to watch her back. Meterove and Jolson went to investigate the water. They moved slowly since the other gorgons were still on the lookout.

The two of them slowly moved up the pile of rocks and examined them. Finally Meterove recognized them. They had the same aura that the Spirit Plane held. This water was too pure to be just from some underground spring.

Jolson had a flash of inspiration. He took a small vial and cork out of his pack and filled it with some of the water. He took another one and placed a small piece of rock in it. Lastly he pulled out a strange tool that Meterove had never seen before.

It was a small box with crystal rectangle on the front. Two small metal probes were attached to it with wires. Jolson moved to the side and placed the probes in the ground. After a few minutes Jolson muttered to himself, "I knew it."

Meterove was about to ask what he had found but Dras shouted, "Meterove! Jolson! Get out of there! The big one is still alive!"

Meterove spun around and looked but the giant body was still laying where it had fallen. Movement to the right caught his eye. The head that he had severed before was still moving. Now a body was starting to form from the severed neck.

HOLY SHIT! That thing can survive in that state! We need to get out of here!

Meterove grabbed Jolson by the shoulder and shoved him over towards the others. "Terenia! Make a barrier of roots around us!"

The roots that were blocking the stairs moved to make a dome around the four of them with one side against the exterior wall. Meterove used a massive magic blast and the wall expoaded outward.

They ran out into the night. Since Terenia was no longer focusing on the roots they faded away. For good measure Dras and Terenia fired a bolt and an arrow back into the opening as they ran. They ran most of the way back.

Once they reached the Citadel they warned the guards and had everyone that was not a scout fall back inside the walls.

They immiediatly went to find Valaas and Syr. Jolson had also sent a message over to Joleen. Once she had arived with Narok, Jolson began his explanation.

"There was no time durring the fight to explain but I believe that the gorgon that we encountered was the original one," He said.

Meterove who had been drinking water set his glass down and asked, "What do you mean the original one?"

Jolson pulled the book out of his pack and showed everyone the section on gorgons. Since they had been believed to be a myth the information was more fiction than fact.

He pointed to the picture that had been drawn and said, "The book says that all gorgons come from the original gorgon. It says that unlike the others the original gorgon can regenerate from one of the severed heads."

Dras asked, "So that thing is immortal?"

Jolson shook his head, "I cannot say for sure but I think that if the others can be killed so can this one."

Terenia said, "Maybe you need to cut off the right head first?"

Meterove asked, "Syr. Did anything like this happen when you fought one?"

Syr gazed at him expressionlessly, "No. It would regrow the heads until I cut off the correct one."

Joleen said, "What I am hearing is that this monster is extreemly dangerous. Are you sure this location is safe?"

Meterove nodded, "We have scouts out there that will be able to warn us if anything is moving this way."

Joleen exhaled, letting go of some of the tension that had built up. Then she asked, "Did you at least learn anything useful while you were in there?"

Jolson said, "Yes. I have a pretty good idea as to what is going on there. There appears to be a small rupture in our world that some of the planes leaked into."

Joleen looked alarmed, "What do you mean rupture?"

Jolson said, "I think that the wound caused by the Ashen Soul was stronger there at one point and that it was such a strain on the world that, like an abcess, ruptured. Once the rupture happened the planes, which make up the world, entered the open wound, and the remnants are so pure that it even washes away the corruption."

There was a moment of silence followed by Dras saying, "Now there is a holy water hot spring..."

Meterove laughed a little and even Jolson smiled. "Yes, I guess you could call it that. If we can find a way to replicate this we might be able to cleanse the whole Ashen Empire."

CHAPTER 11
EMPEROR

Godfrey walked through the halls of the Ashen Keep dreading where he was heading. Godfrey was part of the first generation that was raised by their emperor, whom he was on his way to speak with. The news that he was bringing was a mixed bag.

The halls of this keep, that also served as the palace, were cold. He did not notice though. His flesh had long ago become dry and hard. The only reason he stayed in one piece was the power coursing through his body. There was dust everywhere and a great many spiders, undead all, had made their webs throughout the many rooms.

Brigadier General Aleksandr Gorchevka had been dispatched to track the humans that had attacked the Ashen Empire. The newly turned that had been sent with him had mostly been wiped out and the few survivors claimed that the general himself was slain.

The cause was some monstrous creature that they had found underground. At first Godfrey had thought that the same phenomenon that had afflicted some of their people had taken hold here too but after he had the thralls examined it was confirmed that was not the case.

Godfrey had ordered one of the thralls to lead another team back to the cavern. This team did return, though with a few losses and this time the leader had stayed back in the lab they had found. As much as Gorchevka had been a fool, he had still been a valuable asset. There was no justification for risking another.

According to the report the creature was chained to the walls but was totally resistant to being turned. It was also able to compel those that came near it to become apathetic about it eating them.

That had sealed it in Godfrey's book. Whatever this thing was, it was not something that he wanted to have loose. The humans clearly did not as well, or they would have done it. This news, combined with the massive loss of manpower that the human's ambush had caused, made Godfrey dread this meeting.

Feeling a chill that should not have been possible Godfrey kept thinking about what they had learned. He turned the corner and was at the door to the main hall.

Entering he could see a door on the far end that was guarded by two Nightmare Woven. The one on the right had a dozen arms that came out at strange angles from its body. It had a long furry face. Apparently, this thing had been made from a werewolf.

The one on the left had three eyeless faces. It had once been a feared gorgon, but it was blind. Naturally, it could still use "the sight" that was granted to all undead. It had extra arms as well. The other additions were two scorpion-like tails that came out of its lower back.

As Godfrey approached, they stayed completely still. These two always unnerved him. There was no telling what their orders were, only the emperor knew. Godfrey knocked on the door three times.

"Enter...."

Godfrey did as he was instructed no matter the fear in his heart. He reached out and pushed open the door that was so plain. The room on the other side of the door was the throne room.

There was a long runner of crimson that led to the throne. There were statues of the Ashen Soul everywhere. So many grotesque wall hangings were scattered across the room. The throne was one of the most bizarre things in the room though.

Known as the Undead Throne, it was literally a throne made from undead flesh. It was an undead flesh construct that was made for one purpose. Sitting atop it was one of the most dangerous entities that Godfrey had ever known.

The emperor was the only Lich that existed to his knowledge. The aura that came off of him was on another level compared to first generation undead like Godfrey.

He sat in robes of pure black wearing the Crown of Fingers. His face was that of a skeleton but if you looked closely, you could see that there was skin stretched tightly over the bones. The flesh and blood were gone but the rest remained. He was stirring pus wine with one finger and staring through Godfrey's soul.

Every step that Godfrey took forward the pressure that the emperor exerted increased. He could probably tell that he was not going to like what Godfrey was going to report.

As he drew up to the proper distance, he prostrated himself before the emperor. For several long moments, the emperor was silent.

"What news...Godfrey?"

"I beg your mercy my lord. The news that I bring is ill."

There was a pause and from out of the shadows came a servant that had a pitcher of pus wine and another glass.

"I cannot say that I am surprised. Here drink... let us talk of this news."

Godfrey did not dare refuse the wine, even though he was not sure he would even be able to swallow it. Taking the glass that the servant poured he continued, "Brigadier General Aleksandr Gorchevka has been slain by a creature that we cannot identify."

There was a pause, *"Gorchevka was a fool. It is hardly a bad thing that he is gone. He was foolish enough to allow the humans time to prepare for our attack. As for this creature, what can you tell me of it?"*

Godfrey swallowed some wine with difficulty and relayed the report that he had gotten. Once he was finished the emperor said, "Something like that.... is dangerous. Leave it where it is. The humans would not dare release it and the devastation that it could wreak on the Ashen Empire is beyond reckoning."

Godfrey bowed his head, *"As you command. Next is the damage that the humans ambush has done."*

Godfrey was not thrilled about this report. His tension had been noticed as well. *"For you to worry so, the damage must be great indeed."*

Though the tone had seemed light there as a frightening aura to it. One of murderous rage and endless malice.

Godfrey's telepathic voice seemed to shake as he said, *"Over sixty percent of the army is unfit for combat. The Weavers estimate that nearly a quarter of the force will be lost by the time they finish repurposing parts."*

The emperor's glass shattered. He rose from his throne and Godfrey hurried to place his face on the floor. It did not save him from the emperor's wrath. A mummified hand closed on his throat.

"What did you just say? How could we have lost so many!"

Godfrey was in a panic now. Luckily, he had something that he could use. Hopefully, it was enough to save his neck. He barely managed to focus enough to say, *"There are reports of a battle between some Naga and unknown second party. There were marks left behind that suggest that it might have been the Citadel of Time."*

This caused the emperor to squeeze harder before dropping Godfrey and swinging his arm to the side blasting the wall away. The debris flew out and crashed down into the city below.

The emperor walked back to his throne muttering out loud with a rasp of vocal cords that had not been used in centuries, "Valaas and Syr. Those two must be behind this. I should have hunted them down long ago."

Godfrey was stunned. He had not heard that voice since he had been alive. So long ago...but that was not their way anymore. The emperor did not seem to notice that he had spoken aloud.

The emperor continued, *"I want the Citadel found. If they brought it out from hiding, then they must think they have some kind of plan. I have no interest in losing any more soldiers to them."*

Godfrey said, *"I also believe I have some good news there. The trail left by those that carried out the ambush appears to head towards the Blight."*

The emperor frowned at this, *"That place needs to be destroyed. For too long that afront to the Ashen Soul has been allowed to stand. Burn it all to the ground."*

After he gave this last order, he waved his hand in dismissal and turned and began to walk back to his throne. Godfrey was not foolish enough to wait around and took his leave.

The door closing behind him sounded very loud. The two guards barely seemed to have moved since he entered the throne room. The wall blasting out had barely even registered with them.

How in the hell am I supposed to manage this! He never gave me the opportunity to give the timeline the Weavers had given me about restoring the injured. How am I supposed to organize the destruction of the Blight, hunt down the Citadel and wage war with the living?

The damage that they had caused the army showed that these humans were not to be underestimated. True they are unlikely to be able to pull off another maneuver like the one they did any time soon but there is no guarantee.

Maybe I should talk to the Nightmare Weavers. Perhaps there is something that they can fashion that will serve the needs that I have. Yes, I will call a meeting with the grand council.

.   .   .

Alone in his throne room the emperor sat, the rage and malice pouring off him was unmistakable. To think that two of his own would continue to give him such trouble. He had assumed that they were only working to keep the Citadel away from him. Had he known that they were going to keep working with the humans he would have done things differently.

"WoUlD YoU? WouLD YoU REaLlY"

He shook his head trying to clear away that voice. The other voice kept trying to break into his mind, but he silenced it. What nonsense. Of course, he would have destroyed them if he had known that they would cause problems like these. They had never been a threat.

"ThEY arE StiLl BLOoD. NevER forget WHeRe YoU CAMe FroM."

The emperor nearly used his voice again to tell the voice to leave him alone. Briefly, just for an instant, he remembered not being who he was now. He remembered being a father. Then the shadows and ash covered it all again. After all this time there was no room for anything else.

Pull it together. You must serve the Lord, our maker.

The emperor felt that voice trying to force itself to the surface again but this time he quashed it entirely. He walked over to a door off to the side of his throne and entered his private chambers. He examined an ancient sword that he kept on a rack near the door, the blade of Mardelnier. He felt that voice come back for a second and silenced it again.

Soon those two would be dead and there would be no more reason to think about these things. Valnyr had not died in battle so he could not claim his weapon as a trophy, but he would claim the two-handed sword of Valaas and the twin blades of Syr. "Then I can burry you forever."

.   .   .

Godfrey sat at a large black lacquered table. The grand council consisted of the five Grand Weavers, the Grand Breeder and himself, the Grand General. Their job was to oversee the numerous smaller decisions of the Ashen Empire, freeing the emperor free to commune with the Ashen Soul and make their larger plans.

The Weavers were all wearing what they always did, and Godfrey was wearing his uniform which was standard blue and grey. The only addition to it that was different was the five fingers woven on the shoulder of each arm, signifying his status.

The Grand Breeder favored the clothes of the men of this age and today was no exception. He was wearing a pair of shiny black boots, black pants, a crimson shirt with white ruffles around the neck and a black coat. He had a black high-top hat that was currently on the table with a silver handled walking cane next to it.

"Are you serious!"

"The emperor wants to raze the Blight NOW! NOW! When the majority of our army has been destroyed in battle and that disastrous ambush!"

The other members of the council were clearly just as incensed about this issue as he was. The question was what could they do about it? The answer was nothing.

Godfrey reluctantly asked, *"On the topic of razing the blight and dealing with the massive loss of soldiers from that ambush I would like to ask a question."*

He waited a moment, but no one stopped him so he continued, *"I would like to create something that will be a singular destructive force that the humans cannot fight off so easily. To that end I was thinking that maybe a single entity might be a better choice."*

The five Weavers began to convene while the Grand Breeder was looking down at the table lost in thought. After several minutes of discussion, the Weavers appeared to come to a consensus. The Grand Nightmare Weaver was the one that spoke for them.

"We believe we can accommodate this request by mostly using the parts that are left to be utilized from the soldiers that were slain in the ambush. In addition, we need the parts from some of the lesser beings from around the empire. We also will need some fresh stock."

Here the Grand Nightmare Weaver looked to the Grand Breeder. Otto Bauer was a second-generation blood construct. He was the height and build of an average man, though completely formed from blood. The "skin" of blood constructs like him had the consistency of a clot.

Otto looked down at his hands for a moment before raising his head up and looking around the table. *"There have been some...developments...on some of the Farms.*

There were reports of various individuals coming in and spending far more than would be normal.

Alone this would just be an oddity but combined with the fact that this happened at dozens of different Farms with different individuals makes it suspicious.

The part that makes it certain is that every single one of the individuals is now missing and the people that they claim to have represented say they were missing before the purchases."

Godfrey asked, "How many stock were "lost" during this?"

Otto replied, "If we assume that all accounts are true then one hundred and fifteen stock."

The Weavers looked uninterested by this news. Admittedly the number was not exactly worrisome. Just a drop in the bucket. The problem was that they had no idea who was responsible or why they were doing it. There had been rumors of "human sympathizers" ever since the death of Major Klepton.

Otto continued, "I believe I will be able to supply all necessary stock, but I have conditions. I must have guards assigned to each Farm and I want additional Weavers assigned to each Farm."

Godfrey had no problems with the guards. Pulling enough soldiers from the army to guard each Farm would hardly diminish his force and it would protect their supply of reinforcements. The Weavers were not so kind though.

The Grand Nightmare Weaver was the first to speak, *"You dare demand something of us!"*

The Grand Bone Weaver said, *"We do what we wish!"*

The Grand Blood Weaver said, *"Do not forget who it was that made you!"*

The other two were about to say something as well but another voice cut them off, *"You have quite the ego Weavers."*

Everyone at the table froze. If Godfrey's body were capable of it, he would have goosebumps. The Soul Weaver, who was not even corporeal, seemed to pale.

In the corner of the room stood the only thing in the Ashen Empire that scared them more than the emperor. The Avatar of the Ashen Soul was a horrific entity that would just appear and disappear at will.

The desiccated corpse of a woman of average height and in her middle years stood in a ragged and dirty white dress. Her head was encased in a metal cage, and she had her eyes impaled with spikes that went out the back of her head and were fused with the cage.

Her mouth was sewn shut except for a small bit in the center that allowed her to push her tongue out. Her arms were wrapped in wire that had barbs on it that dug deeply into the flesh so that it bunched up around it. The wire bound her arms across her chest.

Metal restraints held her legs and ankles tightly together. She had two wings coming off her back. One was full of feathers, the other was rotting away and showed bone. She was the one that had turned the emperor to the Ashen Soul to begin with, or so it was said.

Even though he did not need to blink Godfrey felt as though he had, when suddenly the Avatar was face to face with the Grand Nightmare Weaver. *"I recommend that you do what is best for the Ashen Soul...not your own agenda...Marik."*

That sealed it. This thing was far too dangerous for even all of them to try and deal with. Perhaps the emperor could help but he would side with her. Terrified the Grand Weavers began agreeing to do whatever it took to serve the Ashen Soul.

Just as suddenly as she came, she was gone. The tension that she had brought with her lingered though. It was some time before any of them was able to organize their thoughts. Once they did it was decided that a single full Weaver and one apprentice Weaver would be sent to each Farm, along with five guards. They could use the additional Weavers to supplement that number over time until they all had an entire unit.

After the meeting, Godfrey left the palace and went down to the city to look into the damage that the debris had caused. There had been dozens of injuries and the property damage was pretty extensive. The Weavers would be hard at work to heal the injured.

He worked with the crews that were taking care of the repairs, as well as talking to various team leaders. Even when he started to feel hungry, he kept going. The Avatar visiting earlier had unnerved him.

Returning to his office later he slumped into the chair at his desk. He had worked himself ragged between checking on the repairs and putting in inquiries about searching for human sympathizers.

It seemed outrageous that any could exist, but they needed to be sure. There had been various nobles that had attempted to seize control of the empire in the past so perhaps it was not out of the question. Perhaps some held more of their former selves afterwards than they had believed?

As soon as this thought came, memories that had long been buried began to bubble up. There was a time that he had different ambitions. Perhaps the time to act on them was approaching?

Whatever the case there was no doubts about the fact that at least one of the soldiers that killed Major Klepton

had shouted something along the lines of human
sympathizer ideology.

*It was time to enact real change and swiftly.
Rebuilding the army by conscripting soldiers would be a
start. Making an inquisitorial department would also be
helpful. I will pull equally from the army and the magistrate.
I just need to be careful about my picks for those positions.*

Godfrey worked into the night until he felt his mind
become fuzzy. He had a strong outline of what needed to
be done. The Sympathizers needed to be addressed.

CHAPTER 11.5
APPROACH

They were so close now. Soon all of the selves that were within reach would be back and then the portal would have to be opened. What would they do then? Ever since the separation the omniscience was patchy at best.

There were only so many things that were left to do now. What had once seemed like an insurmountable task was nearly complete. Soon it would be time to handle the Darkfire one.

What to do when I meet them? I already know them. I have always known them. They have never known me though. We are going to have a tough time with that one.

The Darkfire one is also approaching. It was still hard to believe that a self had been corrupted. Then there was the question of how it had gotten so powerful.

The Ashen Soul was hiding the Darkfire one's work, or was it the other way around? The Avatar was still beside the Lich. That one was going to be a problem if it was encountered at the wrong moment. Then there was the Child.

The Child had made several appearances. It was outside of coincidence now. It was clearly hunting those of the blood of Valaseri. How would that end?

CHAPTER 12
PREPARATION

Joleen had been working through the night so much lately that she had constant bags under her eyes, and she had lost some weight. She was moving forward towards the future though. Soon the changes that she wanted to enact would begin.

It had been nearly eight months since her ascension, and she had hated every minute of it. There was so much that needed doing that she was forced to delegate. There was so much that was then lost in the red tape along the way.

Who she had been groomed to be her whole life was now fully coming to fruition, but she longed to be elsewhere. The papers in front of her now were some of the drafts for her plans. She had discussed them with her brothers so far but that was it.

Today was the first time that she was going to unveil this plan to the nobles of the empire. She had sent summons off to all members of all ranks. She expected that some would oppose it, but she had hopes that most would support her. There was a knock at the door.

"Enter."

Narok entered the room and closed the door behind him. She had sent for him a short time ago. Now was not his shift to watch her so he was not in armor. The casual look that he had of a minor nobleman was one that she did not get to see often.

Narok gave a small nod, "You went through the trouble of calling me here today "at my earliest convenience" so what is this about?"

Joleen smiled. She had missed this more casual Narok. "Your opinion has always meant a great deal to me. I am going to disclose the topic of the meeting that I am calling later today."

She pushed the document that was on the table in front of her over for him to read. After he read the title of the document his eyes went wide. "Are you truly planning to go through with this?"

Joleen nodded, "Yes. I think that things need to change."

Narok said, "But to this degree?"

Joleen clasped her hands in her lap and looked down at them. "The truth of my family and of how the empire was formed have been catalysts for my decision. However, the different ways that we saw while on our journey have changed my perspective as well as me as whole."

Narok was quiet for a moment but eventually said, "Your father would be proud of this idea."

Joleen felt like everything stopped. Tears rolled down her cheeks before she could stop them. She felt sobs shaking her body. Narok leaned over and embraced her.

After the a few minutes she calmed down enough that they could continue. The tears did not stop completely though. "Thank You for saying that. I am not so certain though."

Narok said, "I am. Your father would often speak of these strange ideas that he had that seemed so foreign. They were not so different from this document that you have drafted. You forget that your father also found his way outside of our world. It is likely that he learned some of what he talked about from those travels."

Joleen's tears continued to fall but the smile she felt growing on her face made it ok. That was right. Her father had seen what was beyond the world. If he had spoken of similar topics in front of Narok in the past, then it must be a sign.

She muttered more to herself than to Narok, "My father wanted the same thing..."

Narok said, "I will obviously support you no matter what you decide to do."

They stayed there for a while before Joleen finally gave a small shift of her arm to tell Narok the moment was over. He withdrew and sat back looking at the document more closely.

After a few minutes Narok pointed out a few details that he thought were worth changing or adding. He stayed with her until it was almost time for the meeting then he left to get ready since he would be there as her guard.

As Joleen was getting ready herself, she got a surprise in the form of Meterove, Terenia Jolson and Dras. They had come back for the meeting that she had called. She had not planned on them being here, but it did make her quite happy. The political advantages aside she was glad to see them with her where they were safe.

They all changed into formal clothes, even Terenia changed her outfit to one that would be considered appropriate. They all trusted her judgement which was worth more than she could say.

In the throne room they stood around her. Narok, Meterove and Dras in burnished plate, Jolson in formal green robes with the family crest on the back and Terenia in an elegant black dress trimmed in silver.

The nobles filed in and took seats. Normally they would have sat according to rank, but Joleen had wanted to set the tone of this meeting immediately, and had arranged for them to sit alphabetically.

There was already some grumbling that could be heard while some voices were raised even higher over towards the door where a few of the older nobles were blustering. She had made her orders firm for the attendants though and they reluctantly submitted.

Once all was quiet Joleen glanced at her brothers one last time and they nodded in encouragement. Joleen stood up ready to address the nobles.

"Welcome one and all. I am delighted that you all were able to attend this meeting. An attendant will bring over the document that I am going to be explaining to each of you."

As Joleen spoke a line of servants, each carrying a stack of documents, walked over to the seated nobles, and began to place them on the tables in front of them.

Joleen continued, "The document that you have in front of you is official and binding. I am restructuring the empire into an imperial republic."

More muttering arose from the assembled nobles, but Joleen ignored them for now. "The intention is to someday transition into a full republic but for now this allows for better, safer governing of the people should anything happen to the imperial family."

"As you will see there will be created two separate bodies of government. One will be the Senate. The Senate will be comprised of one member of each noble house, provided that they are at least of the age of fourteen and are not currently the head of the house. In the event that a suitable candidate cannot be found then a proxy may be used."

The reactions of the nobles were now becoming muddled. Some were angerly muttering, but others were curiously perusing the document. Only one or two seemed to have found the parts that would have the whole room in awe.

"The second body is the Parliament. This body shall be the heads of the houses. Their job, in addition to running their own territory, will be to vote on and determine who amongst them, will be the one to sit upon the imperial throne."

The room had gone dead silent. Joleen was not even sure they were breathing. Joleen took a deep breath and continued, "Additionally the military will no longer be sworn to the emperor or empress or any noble houses. They will be sworn to the people and nation. I am sure that you have many questions, and I will clarify where needed but for now I ask that you read the document through."

．　　　　　．　　　　　．

In the end the meeting lasted well into the night with the nobles fielding hundreds of questions. Some of them had been fair enough, like the baronets asking if their vote counted the same as a dukes. The answer being yes had resulted in a duke demanding to know why his vote should not count more.

Others were so highly specific that it was clear that the political scheming had already begun. She had always known that it would. It was still a shock to see it start that quickly.

In the end they had quickly voted that she would remain on the throne to guide this transition along. Honestly, Joleen assumed that they thought this was a trap and wanted to wait and see. The formation of these new governing bodies would free her up since they could also pick an acting emperor or empress.

This should prevent any further incidents like the one with Vlad.

Joleen had also been busy marshaling an army. Taking down the Ashen Empire and ridding the world of the Ashen Soul were top priorities. She had been hard at work making sure that she and her allies were ready this time.

There were new fortifications set up at the site of the old gate and the wall that Dras had built. There were scouts all along the mountains. Including the new recruits as well as what soldiers their allies were able to send Joleen now had nearly half a million soldiers to send against the Ashen Empire.

Joleen was no fool though. The reports that she had been getting from her brothers about the Ashen Empire made her cautious. They could potentially recoup their losses quickly since they were most certainly going the route of conscription.

We need to strike as soon as possible.

They had to fill the barracks in the Citadel with soldiers, but Joleen was not sure yet about how to go about telling the other nobles and their allies about the Citadel. Its existence was already known but its nature and who currently was in possession of it were entirely different matters.

The news of the Gateways had caused a big enough stir. It turned out that the Elves and Dwarves had known of their existence, though how to make them had never been shared. That Joleen shared the process for making them with her allies helped to smooth over a few ruffled feathers.

Fortunately, her allies had agreed that the Gateways should only be used for emergency travel to avoid damaging the livelihood of small towns. This news had helped to calm some of the lower ranked nobles, whose territories would be most affected.

Today she and Narok were in the Citadel. Meterove had called them over and now the two of them were in a small room in the Armory, which had previously been locked.

The items that they were being showed were beyond what Joleen had expected. She had assumed that Meterove and Terenia's weapons had been the only ones of that caliber, but she was wrong.

She was drawn to a bust with an amulet on it. It had a fat purple stone that almost seemed to transition to pink at different angles. She looked at the inscription with it.

Apparently, it could create something very similar to a Gateway, but it could only do so once before it needed to recharge again. The other interesting thing was that you only had to have seen the locations before. The size of the Gateway was much smaller, as well.

Narok found a shield that could change into anything from a buckler to a tower shield. It would also completely nullify the impact, so long as it was under a certain threshold.

The rest would be given out to various officers or special units. The majority of the weapons in the armory were going to be held for later. They had managed to arm their full force with their own weapons.

The plan was to divide the enemy force by having them attack the Citadel then move it to attack from another angle. They would effectively be able to make the Ashen Empire fight a battle on multiple fronts.

Jolson was currently helping Joleen oversee the establishment of the supply lines. Once those were taken care of, she wanted to see this building that Meterove, and the others had fought a gorgon in. Terenia was practicing with Grace and Meterove wanted to get more practice with Oblivion. The sword that Dras had gotten during their time back on Nexus had yet to repeat the flash of light that it had done during the fight with the gorgons.

Joleen had put in an inquiry with Professor Orthine and the response that she had gotten was not the one that she had expected. It seemed likely that Dras and the sword were linked in a way that went beyond the connection of an Artifact.

She theorized that like an artifact they were joined but she believed that since the sword was made from a second body of his that he might be able to have the sword retake that form.

Dras was currently trying to make that exact thing happen. Professor Orthine had sent along some notes that he would occasionally consult while trying to make it happen. He was currently using a spinning sparing dummy. Just when he was starting to get frustrated something happened.

The moment that the practice sword that was attached to the dummy came around and would have contacted his ribs, he and the sword changed places. To be more exact Dras turned into the sword and the sword he had been holding onto transformed into him. The sudden change in location threw him off but the practice sword was blocked.

Meterove stopped halfway through a swing not sure that he had seen what the thought he had. He looked at Narok who had been practicing nearby and saw the same expression that he knew was on his face.

Dras backed away from the dummy and looked at his sword for a moment puzzled. That was not at all what he had been expecting. "Hey, can someone try and hit me with a practice sword? I want to see if I can do that again."

Meterove sheathed Oblivion and grabbed one of the practice swords that they had brought out to spar with. Unlike the wooden ones that most would use this was metal, though the edges were dull.

Meterove swung and as the blade was about to hit Dras' shoulder there was a metal clang and once again the two of them swapped roles. Meterove tried a few faster attacks, and they too were blocked in the same manner. Dras did look a little nauseous from the constant change in position though.

Interested Meterove picked up a second practice sword and tossed it to Narok. Catching it Narok and Meterove stood on either side of Dras. "We are both going to do a single swing. I will aim for your left leg. Narok aim for his right shoulder."

Narok said, "Sounds good. On the count of three. One. Two. Three!"

They both swung being careful not to put too much force in them. Both of the attacks hit at the same time and Dras once again moved. This time he gave a soft curse of pain as Meterove's blow landed.

Meterove said, "Hmmm...so it works with one attack but not multiple at the same time."

Narok put the practice sword over his shoulder and said, "It also appears that he subconsciously chose to block the blow that he deemed to be of a greater threat."

Dras was rubbing the spot on his thigh where Meterove had hit him while muttering a curse. After a moment he said, "It is such a strange sensation."

Jolson asked, "What do you mean?"

Dras replied, "There is no lost time between locations."

Jolson asked, "You mean you are aware the whole time?"

Dras shook his head, "No, to my mind there is no "whole time" it is just instant."

Meterove said, "You looked a little sick back there."

Dras nodded, "Yes. The sudden shift is really disorientating. After a few times I was getting pretty sick, but I think that I can get used to it."

Joleen asked, "Did you get any insight into that flash of light that you used against the gorgons."

Dras thought for a moment and said, "You know, I think I might now. Cover your eyes."

Everyone did as he asked then he raised his blade to the sky and is sword flashed with a burst of light. Uncovering his eyes Meterove saw that Dras was looking thoughtfully down at his sword.

Joleen asked, "Well? You clearly did it again."

Dras said, "I think it has to do with the magic that makes up my arm."

Jolson asked, "You mean your channeling magic out of your arm?"

Dras shook his head again, "No, I think that the magic of my arm was changed when we went on that job where my double came from. It feels like it's more a part of me than just attached to me. It was for the briefest moment, but I saw the other me and it looked different."

Meterove said, "So you think that the other you coming back through changed you, but changed how?"

Dras looked at his arm, "I can feel a pull. It is so slight that I only notice it now that I have accidentally followed. When I grasp hold of it, I feel as though I could sprint for miles like I-"

""""were struck by lightning and are holding it in your body?""""

Dras stopped talking as Joleen, Jolson and Meterove all finished his sentence. They exchanged glances and Joleen smiled. "It would appear that you need to be retested for magical aptitude."

Dras said, "I was under the impression that aptitude never changed. Our individual strength yes, but whether or not we could channel that power into a spell was fixed at birth."

Jolson said, "Yes that is all true."

Meterove cut in, "But we also do not have any prior examples of someone absorbing another of themselves."

Joleen said, "I will contact the academy and have them send a tester over. I think this is important enough that we know more about it before we move any further."

Joleen went off to contact the academy while the others went back to their training. While she was gone Terenia came over from where she had been practicing in the forest and after seeing Dras sitting down smirked and said, "I thought that you were working on trying to get your sword to change Dras. Did you get frustrated?"

Meterove laughed and filled Terenia in on what Dras had learned so far. She turned to Dras, "You having magic is a little frightening."

Dras glared back, "What do you mean?"

Terenia said, "I get the feeling that you would attack with it in nonsensical ways."

While Meterove choked back a laugh, Dras glared at him, "What do you think is so funny? You are probably the most reckless and unconventional fighter there is!"

Meterove, still laughing, said, "Yes and everyone knows that. Terenia has already told me that I was too unpredictable with how I used magic."

Dras grumbled theatrically to himself, "She creates giant death roots that stab monsters, and she calls me "nonsensical."

Jolson and Narok both chuckled. The five of them continued to joke around for a little while longer. When Joleen returned a short while later, she was accompanied by a middle-aged man with short brown hair and glasses. He was carrying a small hard-shelled case that was about two feet long. After being introduced as Jerven he took Dras over to a nearby table to test him, a look of frustrated resignation on his face.

Before he was even out of earshot Joleen said, "The only reason he even came is because of WHO I am. He thinks that the idea of someone's aptitude changing is preposterous. They all do. They toed the line of calling me a fool."

Jerven was walking away from them and his expression was hidden but the sudden stiffening of his back gave away his feelings. He quickly hurried Dras over to the table and set up his instruments. He now had a smug look on his face. He clearly wanted to prove Joleen wrong now.

Out of a small box in the case Jerven pulled two small crystals. One of them was clear and the other was a very pale blue. Jerven had brought Dras' original test results with him so he could make an instant comparison.

The tester used a needle to prick Dras' finger to take a sample of his blood and put a few drops onto the clear crystal. Next, he had him channel his magic into the crystal. While he as channeling his magic, the tester was mixing two different liquids in a beaker. Once done he placed the crystal into the beaker and waited five minutes.

After five minutes were up, he used some tongs to pull the crystal out and placed it on the table next to the other one. There was a clear difference. The new crystal was almost navy blue.

Jerven said, "There must be some kind of mistake. Did the crystals get mixed up?"

Jerven picked up the syringe and put few drops of blood onto the light blue crystal. The drops stayed on the top, a clear sign of resonance.

Jerven said, "What is this? That is impossible!"

Joleen had a satisfied smirk on her face as she walked over to the table with the others in tow. "I was correct then?"

Jerven's voice was shaking with disbelief, "I cannot explain it. It should not be possible but yes, his records state that he was unable to use magic before. The results of this test are conclusive. For reasons I cannot begin to explain, this man can now use magic."

Meterove clapped Dras on the shoulder while Terenia edged away from him with a grin. For his part Dras looked excited. Meterove and Jolson offered to give him lessons in using magic.

Jerven packed up the equipment, he was still muttering about how this was impossible. He gave Joleen a far more respectful bow than his earlier behavior would have suggested, then Narok escorted him back to the Gateway.

Joleen faced Dras, "There is not enough time to fully train you in how to use magic before we will have to make our move. For now, the best thing we can do is to work on body enhancement and smaller defensive spells."

Meterove said, "I can easily teach you some basic enhancements."

Jolson nodded in agreement, "Meterove would be best for that. I will teach you one or two basic defensive spells, though that blinding light spell you did would also count as one."

Joleen said, "I can teach you a simple healing spell too."

Dras looked a little overwhelmed but determined all the same. He said, "I hope that I am able to do this. It just doesn't seem real."

Meterove placed his hand on Dras' shoulder, "You can do this. I have seen you in battle countless times and you have never given up. That kind of determination is what you need for magic."

Meterove turned to Joleen and asked, "How are the preparations going?"

Joleen sighed, "We have help from everyone except the Leturai and Acephali. Neither of them is responding to attempts at communication. At this point in time, I am not willing to count them as allies."

Meterove said, "What is the total head count of soldiers?"

Joleen took a deep breath, "We are currently looking at a little over a million soldier. While I stopped short of conscription, I did have every willing able-bodied person garbed for war. Additionally, those that were unwilling to march to war are currently getting a crash course in defensive warfare."

Dras asked, "What about the Dragon Lord?"

Joleen shook her head, "No one has seen him since the battle at Yxarion."

Terenia had been silent for most of this conversation, but she finally spoke up, "I think I should try to convince my sisters to join as well."

Everyone stared at her. None of them had even considered asking the other Nymph s for help. The reputation that Nymph 's had was not great. Animatedly they had learned that much of it was wrong or exaggerated but years of hearing about Nymph s had kept the idea from even forming.

Joleen asked, "How many sisters do you think would help?"

Terenia put a finger on her lips and thought for a moment. "Well, there are only a few dozen wood Nymph s in the forest total. But if I include the others then there would be about five hundred or so."

While that was not a very large number it was far higher than Joleen had expected. She gave her blessing for Terenia to act as an ambassador for her. Terenia grabbed Meterove's arm for a moment squeezing herself onto it then she winked and left. Terenia took the Gateways back to the forest.

No one wanted to address how normal that had been for them. For now, they started working on Dras' magic waiting for word from Terenia and the final word from the gathered generals.

.   .   .

Godfrey was looking out over his armies. The Weavers had been working constantly for the last two weeks to restore their numbers. On top of that he had put out the decree for conscription. There was now an army of well over two million that he could field. True most of them barely knew how to use a weapon but fodder was necessary.

Then there was IT. Godfrey had asked this of the Grand Weavers, but even he had to admit that this may have been a mistake. The Grand Weavers had called it the Ashen Colossus . It certainly was large enough and terrifying enough for such a name.

Like more undead its skin was a pale grey color. It was nearly as large as the creature in those reports. It had the same cage and nails through the eyes that the Avatar had on its head. The head resembled those weird creatures that he had seen working with the emperor when they had attacked the human capital.

It had two huge wings that were curled up on its back. It walked on four legs that resembled a human's arms, but one was fused with another on the back side, giving it ten "toes" on each foot. Much of the body was made up of wild animalistic undead. There was fur and scales mixed randomly across its body.

However, throughout the creatures body you could see that many of the parts that had been salvageable from those that had been killed. Bodies that had been fused end on end or side by side. In some cases, the limbs or heads still moved.

According to the Grand Nightmare Weaver, IT had been made to answer only to the emperor and the Avatar. The resentment in their demeanor was outweighed by their fear. The Avatar had scared them into obedience, even if it was grudging. The emperor had ordered IT to take orders from Godfrey in his or the Avatar's absence.

Soon the resistance against us will be gone.

The only thorn left were these rumors of "human sympathizers" that he had thus far failed to either quash or root out. The Inquisitors that he had assigned to the task had found a great many spreading these rumors. So many in fact that they had started to punish those caught. Unfortunately, that had the opposite effect of what they had wanted.

The wind shifted and was now blowing from the south. There was so little time left...he could feel it. He looked out over the marshaled forces one more time before turning and going to his office. He had a few more details to go over yet today.

Soon....

.   .   .

Terenia had returned with news that nearly all the Nymph s would be joining the fight in one way or another.

While some would be joining them directly others were going to act as additional guards for the lands that would be left without most of their protection.

There were five of them with her right now. Meterove had thought that Jolson and Dras were going to faint when they showed up. It had been a shock when the six of them had turned up suddenly, mostly because the other five were essentially naked.

Meterove had thought that he felt a glare from Terenia when he had talked to the new arrivals but after glancing at her and seeing her usual demeanor, he just assumed it was his imagination.

Terenia introduced the girls, "This is Serra, Koleen, Hellana, Casi and Lucille. They are acting as the leaders for the Nymph s."

Serra and Koleen were water Nymph s. They both had mid-length blond hair and ice blue eyes. They were slim with very slight delicate curves. Hellana and Casi were field Nymph s. They both had brown hair, though Hellana's was very short, while Casi had hers down to her waist. They too were very slim.

The last one was Lucille, a Sylph. Fairies of forests were a little different than Nymph s. They had translucent butterfly-like wings and ears that were pointed like an elf's. Lucille's hair, which was chin length, had pearlescent blue and green hair. Her left eye was vivid green while the left was sky blue.

Fairies were also far rarer than the Nymph s. Meterove and the others couldn't help but wonder about her. Sylphs were actually the Plane of Air's equivalent to the Undines and spirit foxes. Fortunately, they did not have to wait long for an explanation.

Lucille said, "I have been acting as the leader of the fairies and Nymph s for many hundreds of years now." her voice was very light and melodic. She continued, "I was surprised to learn that my little Terenia had grown attached to humans...and a particular one at that."

Terenia had gone very red, blushing to her ears. The look on her face said quite plainly that this woman was akin to an older sister or mother to her. For his part Meterove was just bemused.

It seems that Nymph s and fairies think the same.

The others had been gazing hungrily at Jolson, Dras and Narok the whole time. Lucille kept her eyes on whomever she was talking to though. Joleen had subconsciously stood slightly closer and in front of Narok.

Once the opportunity presented itself Joleen said, "It is wonderful to meet you, but I am afraid that I have some urgent matters to attend to back home. Come Narok, we are already late. Good day ladies."

The Nymph s and Fairy giggled as she left, her "ruse" fooling no one. Jolson shot her a look that clearly demanded to know why she was leaving him behind. Dras who had been down for a while now looked both excited and afraid.

Finally, Terenia decided to say something, "Could the five of you please put on some clothes? The humans that are here are not used to such a display. It will make things move far more smoothly."

Her display was a little better than Joleen's had been, though still pretty transparent. The others were eyeing him up now with some of the same interest that he had seen them giving the others.

Meterove sighed at the actions of these women and said, "Let us go inside the Citadel. We can sit down and discuss things in more detail. I will send for some refreshments as well. I am very interested in knowing more about what aid you will be giving."

Again, the Nymph s giggled and looked at Dras and Jolson. Meterove thought to himself that maybe they would behave a little less seductive towards him with the others there.

Sorry guys, but I already have enough to deal with as it is with Terenia.

CHAPTER 12.5
FRAGMENTS

Two more selves had been found but they had refused to rejoin. They had communicated their plan. It was a good one so for now they were going to be left where they were. The enemy had thought that the splitting had been a good plan, but it had not thought about what the others would be able to do.

The truths that had been buried were also preparing to be unearthed. The ramifications of those were going to go beyond what any of them were prepared for. Meterove was...interesting. Now that more selves had been integrated more was understood. The others were just as interesting. Those that were called siblings for sure, but also the others.

The incident with the one that was called Dras was something that was truly remarkable. He was someone else with multiple selves, if only one more. What he had managed to learn to do with that was very interesting. The remaining scattered fragments must know how that is or will be.

The Darkfire one had been on their world for some time now. It was near the Avatar. The Maw of the World was a fitting place for such a thing. Would it still be there when they went there?

Then there was the Child, who was still roaming. How many had it killed now? Such a horrifying creature with such a simple desire. What would happen? Jolson had apparently been given a vision of Meterove and Dras fighting it, but how? Who had sent that vision Was it one of the missing selves or the Darkfire one?

The Ashen Soul itself was still a problem. It had moved its plans on from that world, clearly thinking that its minions there could handle things there now that it had been given a new body. It had been a sad ending to what should have been a great hero. Perhaps that was a truth that they should be given?

Right now, things were escalating outside of their world. There were signs of it in their own world. Things were happening in many different places all over Creation and beyond. Where would they go first?

The Planes were all in danger for sure. There were also a number of worlds that had been severely corrupted and would soon be a massive problem. Would they handle *the Protogods and their legions? What about Damien Winters and his forces? There were also the other forces on their own world. The ones known as the Artificials would play a big part yet.*

Hmmm? What was this? It looks like their next destination had already been decided. It had been harder to notice things since the split but missing this seemed odd. Maybe something was making things change? Hmmm... the Gamemaster...that one had to be responsible. Just who was he though?

CHAPTER 13
WAR

Dras and Jolson both looked more than a little drained the next morning. The Nymph s all looked quite energized. Meterove couldn't help smirking at them. He had gotten used to Terenia, but he remembered that feeling. They had thought it was funny when it was him.

What goes around comes around.

Joleen and Narok had returned and one look at those two had brought a worried glance from Narok and a relieved one from Joleen. Meterove did have a little sympathy for them and passed them the few fruits that he had found helped him.

The last preparations were being made and the war would soon commence. All the magic energy that could be stored in crystals had been carted over and stored near magic cannons in order to minimize the drain on the cannoneers. The same enchantments that had been used to burn the undead before were being placed on as many soldiers as possible.

Joleen led a brief meeting and once it had concluded the Lucille and the Nymph s left to their respective forces. Dras and Jolson both relaxed a little after the Nymph s left, though Dras maybe a little less so.

Joleen looked around, "Everyone here is to rest for the next day. After that...the war begins."

.   .   .

Godfrey stood looking out over the hills at the Blight. That cursed patch of land had cost them thousands of soldiers in the past. Godfrey knew that just sending the Ashen Colossus in would not work. It was going to need something that would keep the gorgons there from swarming it and turning it to stone.

"First Legion! Attack from the south. Second Legion from the north! Third and Fourth legions follow alongside the Ashen Colossus !"

There was an unearthly howling rattle that followed this command. Undead may not communicate verbally very often, but that did not mean that they could not. This battle cry would be heard by the humans for sure.

·   ·   ·

Meterove was standing up in the ramparts of the Citadel of Time. In the distance he could see the army of undead. Their numbers were far greater than he had dared to fear. There had to be at least a two to one ratio to their own troops. The other thing that he saw was the giant monster that they had brought with them.

What the hell is that thing? How are we going to deal with something like that?

Terenia and Dras were up there with him and by their faces they were thinking the same thing about that giant beast. They could also see the legions that were advancing on them from the south and north.

Meterove knew that the enemy was counting on them to focus on the force with the giant then get surprised by these. The next phase of their plan would likely be to have that giant move forward faster while they were distracted.

They know that we can move the Citadel though. They have to have some kind of plan in place knowing that we are going to move once they get close. The question is what? Wait? Does that thing have WINGS! SHIT! IT DOES!

That must have been their play then. Yes, they could move the Citadel, but they couldn't move it too far or they risked the enemy attacking their own nations. If it is close enough to see, then it would be close enough to have that thing fly to.

I had hoped that we would be able to save them for a trump card. Looks like they will be needed to help balance the scales.

Meterove looked over to the side and said, "It looks like you and your kin will have a far more formidable opponent than expected."

Smoke and slight flames were exhaled from the nostrils of the large golden dragon that was currently roosting on the top of the Citadel. She was one of five that had flown in at the last moment and offered her aid. She was the mate of the one that Meterove had mercy killed what felt like so long ago.

"I WILL have my revenge," She snarled.

Down below on the ground four more dragons growled in response. Three were black and red and two were blue. They may be young but even the smallest of them was over thirty feet tall. Individually they were still small compared to the thing out there but together they could hopefully keep it in check.

Meterove said, "I think it is time we said hello."

Dras and Terenia moved to their positions and once Meterove gave the signal they relayed it and all the magic cannons fired at once. A mass of colors fired out in three directions. They had deliberately held longer than necessary to instill panic once the middle ranks were hit.

While the undead would not break ranks like a normal army their officers would still panic and have to adjust their planning. A roar rattled Meterove's ears, and the golden dragon took off and a second later the others joined her. Their eyes all locked onto the massive undead and they gave another roar.

Phase two of the attack was up to Joleen. She had used the amulet that she had gotten out of the Armory to make a portal between the spring that they had found and a point far up in the sky. There was now a fine mist of the purifying water falling from the sky. It would not be enough to kill the undead, but a little testing had found that it would weaken them.

Also, the approaching armies would have to fight their way through the Blight, which would cost them. There were more hydras and other creatures in the jungle. Then there were the gorgons.

The barrages from the cannons continued to pummel the enemy. There was only so long that they could keep this up. Eventually it would be time for them to allow a siege.

.   .   .

Godfrey watched his forces break then regroup over and over from the bombardments. Ahead, just out of range of his main army's archers and mages were five dragons that were attacking the Ashen Colossus . They had been keeping it from moving forward now for several hours.

How long do they think that they can keep that up? What are they going to do once they are exhausted?

Godfrey had reports that there were more enemies stationed on their borders and that there were apparently more dragons and other non-humans that were backing them. The Elves and Dwarves made sense but the Nymph s and others that had been spotted by scouts were surprising.

They have to be running out of energy for those cannons soon. Once that happens then we can move in with the main forces.

Out of the forest burst a large group of gorgons. The sound of battle along with the sight of the Ashen Colossus had alerted them to their presence. Why did they come this way instead of attacking the humans?

The humans must have some defenses set up that the gorgons cannot easily get past. They are pretty mindless and are just going to attack whatever they see.

Godfrey watched as a combination of the dragons attacks and a salvo from the cannons made the Ashen Colossus 's front right leg break and it collapsed. Godfrey wasn't worried though. As he watched the leg began to mend itself and soon it was back on its feet. The reason for this ability was that a number of Weavers had been sacrificed to help make it. This allowed it to heal its own injuries.

So far it had stayed on the ground due to the fact that the dragons would have the advantage of maneuverability in the air. Staying on the ground was not much better but at least its belly was protected.

The blasts from the cannons have lessened significantly. It is time to press them!

"ALL LEGIONS! MOVE FORWARD!"

.   .   .

This was all part of the plan. It was a simple feint, a bluff to make the enemy believe that they were weaker than they actually were. This would lead to a surge in confidence, or rather, overconfidence. There was still a grain of truth to it though.

They had exhausted all the stored magic they had for the cannons after about four hours. Now they only had the strength of the individuals manning them and Meterove wanted to save them for when the enemy brought siege weapons forward. Out over the forest the giant undead was still fighting against the dragons. So far, they were keeping it in check, but they would soon become exhausted.

They had briefly brought it down earlier, but it had healed itself so quickly that the soldier's morale had taken a huge hit. So much effort and it was all in vain. Through his spyglass Meterove could see that their plan of moving the gorgons with Gateways had been successful.

The forces that had entered from the north and south had met with untimely ends in the jaws of hydras or other traps that they had set up in advance.

It might be time for us to start using the archers soon.

Joleen had been overseeing things from a command center that she had set up inside the Citadel. Jolson and Narok were currently with her. Meterove signaled Dras and Terenia who were down in the ward below and they opened Gateways and ranks of archers moved forward and kneeled in front of the Gateway and fired volley after volley through them.

Across the jungle there were two Camouflaged Gateways that were now hitting the undead with arrows from an angle that avoided their shields and barriers. Even with this, the enemy continued to move forward. Sometimes the fallen undead would rise back up on their own. Other times a Weaver would reanimate them if they could.

The enemy forces had fully committed now. A vast sea of dark bodies, as far as the eye could see stretched around them.

We should be terrified of this. They have to outnumber us by at least two to one. That big thing makes that number meaningless though. Once the dragons can no longer fight it will be a slaughter.

The volleys of arrows ceased as the front lines drew closer. Down below the Gateways were taken down and the camouflage set up to hide the exact location of archer units.

Dras and Terenia were taking up positions on the walls now. It was time to head down and join them. Meterove looked out over the sea of undead again. The gorgons were still at it out there.

.　　　.　　　.

DAMNIT! Those gorgons are far more of an issue that I thought they would be!

Who could have guessed that there were so many gorgons here? Then there were those hydras that the flanking forces had run into. Between them and various traps he had still made no real progress into the Blight.

Then there was the Ashen Colossus that had been stalled by the dragons. This whole operation was not going according to the emperor's timetable. Godfrey was not interested in facing the emperor's wrath or that of the Avatar.

Godfrey was so angry that he snarled out loud and gave the Ashen Colossus an order. *"Fall back and help destroy the pests on the ground!"*

The Ashen Colossus took a final swipe at the dragons and went to help destroy the gorgons. The volleys of arrows that had hit his men hard had ceased and there was no trace of the archers. Godfrey could only assume that the humans had been using Gateways.

The battlefield around where the gorgons had appeared was truly a mess. There appeared to be around three hundred gorgons. Given that they could only be killed if the proper head were severed made them deadly. There was now a forest of statues that had once been soldiers outside the perimeter of the jungle.

It was infuriating several of the generals that so many of their soldiers had fallen to so few. The Ashen Colossus was almost to their fortifications though. It should be able to take them down quickly. It opened its mouth and spewed a huge purple cloud that made all in its path rot to nothing.

Fire sprayed down on it. The dragons had sent a parting gift, the golden one seemed to glare at the creature before retreating with the others. Godfrey looked up at the sun.

The battle had started around midday and now the sun was getting close to setting. His soldiers could fight even in the dark but if the enemy had access to Gateways, then there was no reason to believe they had a shortage of reinforcements.

Godfrey looked out over the distance. He could faintly see the Citadel of Time. Inside were Valaas and Syr. They had been the object of obsession for the emperor and himself for so long and now they were so close. A series of shrieks and hisses brought his attention over to where the gorgons were, or rather had been. Nearly a tenth of the Blight was now baren land with nothing but dust.

.   .   .

Meterove was tired. He had not had to personally fight anything yet but coordinating all this was draining. The giant one had gone to clear out the gorgons an hour ago. At first the enemy had thought that they could attack it in the

301

night. Several traps that Meterove had men lay after seeing that thing earlier in the day had caused their commander to reconsider the wisdom of sending them blindly ahead.

Additionally, another dragon had arrived to help. Meterove had never heard of a platinum dragon before today but here she was. Exceptionally old and absurdly large, she had arrived after dark. She was twice the size of the golden dragon that had been in charge earlier.

She gave Meterove a cordial greeting but had been very direct about the fact that she was going to do as she pleased. Apparently, she had been with the Dragon Lord when he made his way into this world. Of the dragons that had been alive back then, most were gone. Meterove was not going to argue. Help was help at this point.

The night consisted of springing traps and ambushes on the approaching armies and making them move slowly. A great stroke of luck for them had come when the large gorgon and a few dozen other gorgons had managed to paralyze the giant one. That would take hours to wear off and by then it would be morning.

The dragons had made a point to capitalize on the large one being paralyzed and rained flames down on it as well as the armies that surrounded it. Despite their numerical advantage at the outset this battle was going well. There were also reports coming in of attacks on several other locations. The Dwarves, Elves and even those stationed at the makeshift gate were all under siege.

Godfrey watched as his generals were nearly pulling their hair out, at least those that still had any. The Ashen Colossus had been immobilized for several hours now. The gorgons had been driven back but the cost... Godfrey did not want to think of the number of fallen soldiers. As the sun rose a massive dragon flew up and out to their lines. It was about half the size of the Ashen Colossus and had glittering silver scales. No...that was something else...platinum scales.

It engaged the Ashen Colossus before it had broken free of its paralysis, breaking legs, and wings. It was clearly trying to wear out the Weavers that were part of its body. Whatever the Grand Weavers had done made sure it kept getting back up.

Once it was free it roared in rage and attacked WITHOUT a command. This threw the army into even greater disarray as the fight between the two shattered the lines over and over. The other dragons had come around for attacks on the rear of the main army. This continued on for an hour before there was finally some good news.

An ear-piercing shriek echoed across the land as one of the dragons fell from the sky, its body pierced by a massive bolt from a ballista. Emboldened by this the archers and other ballista operators renewed their efforts and before long the only dragon left was the gold one. Its wings were tattered, and arrows were lodged in its body.

Clearly knowing that it did not have long left the dragon prepared itself for one last attack then barreled down at the legions of undead. Once in range it let out a ravenous torrent of flame that consumed so many before it too fell from the sky.

There was now just the big one that was currently fighting the Ashen Colossus . His forces moved ahead, making sure to give the two a wide berth. Soon the first soldiers emerged onto an open expanse. What they found was not what they had expected. Instead of the Citadel of Time, they instead found a fairly solid looking fort with fortifications. The humans had somehow built a keep in one night!

Godfrey was so stunned by this news that he dropped the spyglass that he had used to confirm this report. How!?

WAIT! If the Citadel isn't there, then...

Godfrey spun on his heel and looked at the rear of his army. There, just past where the dragons had struck earlier was the Citadel. The crystals were still deploying but there was no chance of catching them before they were all out. All of their siege weapons were in the front half now.

There was the odd ballista but that was not going to do much.

You think you are clever. There is no way that fort can possibly be very sturdy if they built it overnight. Therefore, the few soldiers I can see are the only ones that they would have left there. I can crush them by simply sending in a single legion.

.   .   .

Meterove swung his sword down on the neck of what must have been the thousandth undead since the siege had begun. They had successfully fooled the enemy not once but twice. Jolson had been right in thinking that the enemy would think the fort left behind would be easy to take and so had sent less forces there.

They had discovered to their woe that those walls were quite sturdy, for something made of wood. Also, the number of soldiers inside was far more than it appeared. It had been nearly a week since the battle had started in earnest. They had no way of knowing when that platinum dragon was going to give out, but Meterove had to believe it was coming soon.

Dras and Terenia were nearby, both looking rough and taking ragged breaths. Joleen, Jolson and Narok were currently resting inside the Citadel. They were on a rotation so that there were three of them out fighting at all times.

The area around where the platinum dragon and the giant undead were fighting was completely devastated. There were craters and baren stretches of land. The rot breath from the undead was particularly hard on the landscape. The ground was now hard and cracked.

The platinum dragon attacked the giant undead with claws and teeth to no avail. Wing buffets and kicks did little to slow this thing down. Whatever it was, it was going to take a lot more to destroy it.

Even her blue flames that would have reduced almost anything else to ash would only hurt it for so long. She had taken wounds over the course of this week too. Gashes and small tears in her wings were beginning to add up and slow her down.

.   .   .

Dras was taking a small breather while some soldiers filled in the gap he left. While he gulped down water, he watched the battle between the dragon and the undead.

She must be nearly spent.

Dras sighed and dove back into the battle. He had gotten really good at using his abilities in the last week. His ability to change places with his sword no longer made him feel ill. He had even learned to use it in some very creative ways.

He now flashed through the ranks of the undead destroying one after another. He had barely rejoined the fray when he encountered an officer. This one was a wraith. Fighting these was a pain. You needed to destroy the magic that was keeping the soul chained.

This one had once been a man based on the souls appearance. Its voice was like a chill wind. The only time any of these undead had tried to speak was to instill fear. The strange weapons and armor that wraiths wore were hard to deal with as well.

They had somehow made them in a way that allowed them to be wielded by the wraith and able to hurt humans. The armor on this particular wraith was chain mail that was painted a silvery white that made it blend in with the wraiths own body.

In its hand it held an estoc, its long edgeless blade coated in blood. Dras had donned some mail himself for this battle, but it would be useless against something like that. Still knowing that it did not have a slashing weapon was helpful.

Dras blinked and the point of the estoc was almost in his chest. He barely had time to move to the side so that the point struck his prosthetic instead. The force of the blow pushed him back a few feet. Even though there was no flesh under the mail to pierce, the shock went through his whole body.

The wraith paused for a moment, the only sign of surprise, before it continued to attack. Dras was unable to do any form of attack in that time. He could have switched places with his sword, but he wanted to save that.

The two of them traded blows back and forth for a while with both of them dodging and blocking attacks. Over the sound of the battle, he could occasionally hear the wraith taunting him. Mostly it just kept whispering "death" over and over.

Dras was starting to wear down though. While the undead was unaffected by fatigue, he had been fighting for a week now. A small burst of golden light appeared around his body and his wounds closed. Joleen had just dived back into the battle and gave him a nod as she began to fight some of the undead nearby.

If Joleen is back, then Terenia must be off the battlefield.

Now was not the time to dwell too deeply on it though. With some renewed vigor he continued his fight with the wraith. He had noticed that it would often take the same pose every time that it was about to perform a large thrust.

Just as it performed another large thrust Dras prepared to make his move. He let the attack land and at the last instant swapped places with his sword, parrying the blow. This knocked the wraith off balance and Dras took his right hand off his sword and grabbed his dagger. He drove it through the gap in the armor by its neck to destroy the bonds on the soul of the wraith. There was a flash of white light and a burst of wind, and the armor and estoc fell over the edge of the wall.

.   .   .

Meterove threw the destroyed body of a flesh construct off his sword and over the wall. Nearby Dras had just taken down a wraith. He heard his name and saw Narok coming over. It was time to swap out it seemed.

Once Narok had taken his place he hopped down from the wall and made his way over to the Citadel's entrance. Once he was inside, he found Jolson leaning against one of the pillars, his artifact ready to go at a moment's notice.

Jolson looked up when he heard Meterove enter. Terenia was nearby sitting on the floor, likely waiting for Meterove. She looked up wearily as well.

"How is it going out there?"

Meterove responded, "Dras just defeated another of their officers. This one was a wraith."

Jolson and Terenia shared a happy, if tired, smile. The best part of killing a wraith was that it could not come back again.

Jolson asked, "How is the fight with the giant one going?"

Meterove shrugged looking sad, "No change as far as I could see. She has to be exhausted though. She still will not allow anyone near, so I am assuming that she is planning on fighting it until she is killed."

Jolson and Terenia were quiet as well. Ever since they had lost the dragons there was a tension in the air. The best thing that they could come up with for keeping that giant undead busy was to keep moving the Citadel.

After a few minutes Jolson left to go relieve Dras. Once Dras was back inside he slumped down into a chair. That fight earlier had clearly been draining.

Dras had a thousand-yard stare for a moment before Meterove's voice snapped him back. "Good job with that officer."

Dras nodded, too tired to say anything. Soon a few serving women brought the three of them some food and water. Dras did not even bother to hide the flask that he pulled from his pack. He took a long drink then began to eat. Technically Meterove should reprimand him for that but considering the circumstances...

They ate in silence. There was not much food and in no time, they were done. Meterove was about to head for his room when a massive crash shook the whole Citadel, and a horn was blown outside. The three of them sprinted outside and followed the gaze of the soldiers to the site they already knew they would find.

The massive undead was standing over the body of the platinum dragon. One of its wings had been ripped off and its neck was broken. The giant undead turned towards the citadel and charged towards it bellowing a roar.

.   .   .

Godfrey watched as the platinum dragon fell to the Ashen Colossus . Around him he could hear the elation of the army. Now it was time. They would move in and attack with the Ashen Colossus destroying their precious Citadel!

This battle had been going on for far too long. The emperor was likely growing very impatient. The latest estimates of their losses were also far higher than expected. That strange magic that the humans had that made fire that only burned their bodies and undead flesh was a severe problem.

"Move forward and take the Citadel!"

There was a roar from the Ashen Colossus and it charged towards the Citadel. Now was the moment that the humans would fall. Golden orbs began to appear around the Ashen Colossus .

What is that?

The Ashen Colossus also noticed this new development but seemed to decide that it was not worth its time. It continued to charge at the Citadel. Just when it was about to crash into it the orbs stopped appearing and they all connected with a golden thread of energy.

The Ashen Colossus charged clear through the Citadel, without ever touching it. It quickly faded into nothing then was gone. All around Godfrey there was a stunned silence followed by an uproar.

What had just happened!? WHERE DID IT GO!?

Every officer, aid and foot soldier were asking the same questions! Where and how? What had the human's done! Godfrey knew was not going to let this chance by though. *"ALL FORCES ATTACK!"*

Where the hell did it go?

Meterove looked left and right but saw no trace of it. He looked to Dras and Terenia and saw the same anxiety on their faces. In the aftermath of the platinum dragon's death and the giant undead vanishing, the fighting at the wall had ceased. Joleen managed to rally first and cleared the walls. Then she, Jolson and Narok found Meterove and the others.

Joleen asked, "What just happened?"

Jolson shrugged, "I have no idea either. It was no magic that I recognize. I can only assume that the undead moved it somehow."

Meterove said, "I don't know. We watched them for quite some time before this and we never saw any hint that they could do anything like that."

Dras said, "That is true, but we also never saw any sign that they could make that giant undead either. All indications were that ghouls were as big as they came for amalgamations."

Terenia, who was looking through her spyglass, said, "Hey...everyone...the undead all look confused as well."

Hearing this everyone else took out a spyglass and looked over the massed undead. Sure enough, they all looked unsettled. They were massing though. Meterove shook himself mentally.

What am I doing!? The plan that we had to hold them in check can move on as planned!

Joleen seemed to be thinking along the same lines. She shot a magical red flare into the evening sky, "We need to keep the enemy occupied!"

Exhausted as they were all six now took up their places on the wall. Arrows rained down from both armies. The siege engines had been partially rebuilt began firing rocks and flesh sacks at the Citadel.

.　　　.　　　.

Joleen had never been the most graceful of girls but after her training with Narok and the time that she had invested into learning how to properly use her Artifact, she had transformed. She now danced across the battlefield delivering blow after blow.

Scores of undead fell around her. True she had taken her share of wounds during the fighting, but she had been able to heal all of them so far. She was currently staring down a rather large beast with four arms, each of which held a mace. It had a large helm that went over its face and had no eye holes that could be seen. It was at least three times her size and was only wearing simple leather armor.

This is going to be rough.

Joleen dropped into a low stance and readied her weapons. She did not have much time to plan because the undead let out a loud roar and charged her. Joleen nimbly dodged the maces as they flashed past. Occasionally one would hit the top of the wall and it would flicker.

Joleen dodged around it taking slices at it where she could, but the four arms were making landing a deciding blow impossible. After fighting with it for several minutes it was clear that she was going to have to try something different.

What would Meterove or Dras do?

That thought had barely crossed her mind when she already knew what to do. Images of Dras jumping in to take a blow meant for her father, Meterove charging the same creature. Always the same.

Time to take a risk!

Joleen abandoned her low risk fighting style and chose to charge in, no worrying about having an escape route. Despite the feeling of fear from the battle Joleen also felt some elation.

I can't believe that I am doing this! I am the one that usually yells at Meterove for doing things like this!

Joleen dove forward and one of the maces connected with her arm. She felt the bone break and her one Artifact dropped from her hand. Joleen nearly blacked out, but she pushed through it. She dove under the arm that held the mace that just hit her and inside its guard. Joleen performed a quick forward slice at its elbow then flicked her wrist and sliced the other arm on that side.

Two forearms fell from its body. It was now lopsided, having two arms and the heavy maces in them, on one side of its body. Joleen took advantage of this and, despite wanting to vomit from the pain, she went in for another attack. Just as she was about to land another attack, she felt her world tilt slightly then she felt a heavy impact on her ribs, and she was nearly knocked off the wall.

Joleen coughed up a lot of blood. At the instant of impact Joleen's vison shrank down to two tiny points of light. She managed to grit her teeth through it, and she stayed conscious, but it was a near thing. She pushed herself all the way up and wiped her mouth.

The undead made to finish her off, but Joleen managed to roll out of the way as two maces smashed down onto the wall where her head had been an instant before. Half blinded by the pain Joleen rolled to her feet.

Normally she would wait to heal wounds until she was safer but now was not the time for that. Joleen hit herself with a strong blast of healing magic and she could feel her body growing lighter. She could feel the bones reattaching and becoming whole again. Only now that she had healed did she realize that there were several soldiers that had put themselves between her and the undead.

She scooped up her other weapon and charged the wounded undead. There were too many undead to waste more time on this one. She ran and dropped to her knees sliding for several feet before she popped up under its guard.

The undead seemed surprised for an instant, but she was able to drive her blade up through its jaw and into its skull. There was a small burst of sickly blue light that left its body and then it collapsed. There was no time to celebrate though. Joleen was already fighting another one.

.   .   .

Jolson was battling his own enemy not too far away. His was a Living Shadow, much like the one that had killed his father. This one was wielding a flamberge. Jolson had been using his Artifact in the form of a scythe sword. This would be a rough fight if it blocked any of his attacks.

The best thing I can do is use the men around me to aid in taking this thing down as quickly as possible. Whoever is leading the undead clearly is a good tactician but seems to be making some serious mistakes. Is it just that warfare has changed so much since they had been alive?

Jolson could not wrap his head around why so many of these officers seemed to be attacking them one on one. In regular warfare it was usually anything goes, but with the undead this should have been even more true.

Parry. Parry. Thrust. Slash. Slash. Feint. Thrust. This fight felt like it was taking forever but really only minute or so had passed. There was no real contest once he understood its fighting style. Soon he had severed the bonds that held it to this world. He did not even look long enough to see the flash of light. There were far too many more to deal with.

I really hope they hurry up!

.   .   .

Dras was really getting absorbed into the battle. It was an excellent way to test out his new abilities. He had figured out that he did not have to be holding his sword to change places with it. He only had to be able to see it. He had figured this out when he had been disarmed a little earlier. Once the requirements were confirmed he made a few tweaks to his combat gear. His hand crossbow was now on his right hand.

In a panic he jumped after it and ended up switching places on accident. He had barely been able to react in time to catch his sword that was now flying at him. Now he was flashing across the wall slaughtering undead with near impunity.

A ghoul made to strike one of the crystals, likely hoping that it would bring down the wall. As that seemed likely to happen Dras charged forward and threw his sword so that it stabbed into its shoulder. Then he jumped and switched places with the sword.

He had not thought about what was going to happen once there was nothing holding him to the ghoul, so he slid a bit before he dug is dagger into it. His sword struck at his side, cutting him slightly.

OW! SHIT! I DAMN NEAR SKEWERED MYSELF!

The ghoul tried to brush him off, but he grabbed his sword and stabbed it up higher before changing places with it. He scaled the ghoul using this method until he was on its shoulders.

Now it had abandoned its plan and was giving him its full focus. Dras channeled a bright flash from his sword blinding it for a moment and when its eye was within reach, he thrust his sword in to the hilt. It began to topple and once again Dras threw his sword, this time to the wall.

OH SHIT! I really hope this works!

Dras jumped off the collapsing ghoul and swapped places again. He landed and rolled on the top of the wall the stood and managed to catch his sword with his prosthetic.

.   .   .

This shield is amazing!

Narok was acting as support for this section of the wall. He was not a fan of the order. He was supposed to be beside Joleen. He knew that she could take care of herself, but that did not make him feel better. The walls were littered with the bodies of men and women that had been able to "take care of themselves" and now they were gone.

Narok had taken to running with the shield in buckler form then jumping to intercept blows from foes with large devastating weapons with the tower shield form. He had just blocked the attack from a ghouls mace.

Whatever magic was in this shield was amazing. He had barely felt that hit when that should have left him as paste in his armor. True, he had thought that the wall was actually going to give out, but it was still here.

He kept glancing in Joleen's direction. She had been fighting something nasty for a while now. The way that she was holding her arm...she was hurt!

"You three! Go to the empress! She needs aid!"

The three men that he had shouted to did not hesitate in the slightest. They ran off to aid her, stopping only if engaged.

PLEASE MAKE IT IN TIME!

His lapse in concentration got him an arrow in his right thigh. His armor had taken most of the velocity out of it though and the arrowhead was barely into the muscle. Pulling it out was going to hurt but not too bad.

He ripped it out and quickly pulled a small vial out of a pack and poured it over the wound. It burned and smoked but the wound stopped bleeding and should remain that way for an hour.

I need to find a healer. There is no telling if there was anything on the arrowhead either. Wait! Is that the signal!?

In the distance a handful of red flares were burning in the air. That was the signal!

．　　　　　　．　　　　　　．

Meterove and Terenia had ended up back-to-back fighting on the ground outside the walls. Meterove had jumped in the way of a blood construct that was attempting to overwhelm a section of the wall. The construct was a huge humanoid figure and the blow had knocked the wind out of Meterove.

While he was watching undead figures close in around him, he suddenly saw roots explode out of the ground impaling dozens of undead. A small familiar hand had rested on his shoulder, and he looked up into Terenia's grinning face.

Now here they were facing countless undead. They were doing their best to get back to the wall, but that blood construct had knocked him further than he had thought, and it took a while.

Terenia caught something out of the corner of her eye and shouted, "Look! The signal!"

Meterove looked over and grinned. It was almost time. They just needed to get back. It took another ten grueling minutes before they were able to reach the wall. Unfortunately, something was waiting there.

A Slayer had come and was ready to fight. This one was in light leather armor and had a bastard sword in its hands. Those oversized eyes were glittering with hate. There was a hint of the necromantic energy that coursed through the undead, but it was somehow different.

Meterove did not bother waiting, he just charged in and slashed. A loud metallic clang resounded across the battlefield as the Slayer blocked the attack followed by a screech as its blade slid down and away.

Behind him he could hear Terenia using Grace to keep the undead off him, so he was not overwhelmed. This was no time to hold back.

All I need is to make contact once! Just one cut!

Meterove traded blows with the Slayer for a few minutes. In that time, he received several small cuts but had not managed to even nick the Slayer.

Guess I need to try that...

The next time that the Slayer thrust at him he made his movements just a hair slower so that the blade caught his armor. There were probably some broken ribs from that, but it did what he needed it to do. At least the armor had kept him from being sliced open. Slowed slightly by the armor the Slayer was unable to avoid the slash from Oblivion.

As the blade cut flesh Meterove triggered its singularity ability, and the Slayer was compressed into an impossibly small space. The undead around them backed away. The exhaustion what came with that ability was bad but worth it. They needed to get back inside. Terenia had to half drag him through the wall and back inside.

Around them the soldiers were falling back to the interior fortifications that they had built for this moment. Each one was designed to allow the withdrawal of the one in front of it. Terenia could see Dras and Narok were now working with Joleen to help hold the wall for the last retreating soldiers.

Soon they too followed, and they ran into Jolson at the stairs of the main entrance. The last soldiers fell back into the Citadel, and they transferred again. Their movement was the second signal.

On the outskirts of the undead army a large unit was spread out very thin. These soldiers had been sent out in secret and had not participated in the battle. Their mission had been in jeopardy while that giant undead had been around but now there was no problem. They had sent their signals and had just seen the Citadel move, which was their signal that it was time.

Captain Kierans was leading this mission. There were a thousand men under his command which was far more than he had ever expected to be in charge of. All of his men were in groups of ten. The second that the Citadel vanished they activated the Shaping Crystals just as they were ordered. Around him he could see the other units crystals activating as well.

A wall, thirty feet thick and sixty feet high, rose from the ground forming a large box around the densest part of the undead army. Some scattered undead would be on the outside of it but these ones were trapped now.

It was up to him and whoever was left back at the fort built in the Blight, to make sure that anything that was outside the wall or anything that tried to get over it was as dead as it looked.

Captain Kierans looked to where the Citadel had been a short time ago. He had served the empire for over thirty years. He thought he had done well in his time. He had always known that he was never going higher than a captain and he had been fine with that. Serving had been enough. Now that he had had a chance to see what direction the empire was going, he felt even more honored.

A place where everyone had a chance to be something huh? Go...go and finish this.

.   .   .

Godfrey looked out over the battlefield and just barely kept a look of satisfaction from his face. Everything was going according to his plan. The only hiccup was that matter with the Ashen Colossus.

CHAPTER 14
FAMILY

The Lich stormed through the halls of the keep. Any of the servants and soldiers that had been scattered throughout the halls had fled the moment he came near. The emperor had always been known for being merciless and willing to send someone to the Weavers for the slightest mistakes, almost on a whim.

In his hand he still clutched the remains of the letter that had been delivered to him not twenty minutes ago. He still could not believe that this had happened. The words that had been on the message delivered on behalf of the Grand General were burned into his mind.

Gallanar,

My old friend we have been together since the days of the old empire, but now it is time we parted ways. I agreed to be turned all those years ago in the hope that I might be able to put an end to your depravity. Had I known the true source and reasons behind your actions I would never have tried. I have bided my time until now. The Ashen Empire will fall. I will do all that I can to lead the army to ruin.

Your dear friend,
Godfrey

HOW! How could GODFREY have been a traitor! Their army was going to be led to ruin? HOW? I will have to raise a new army! ...or are there more traitors? The Grand Weavers? They are always scheming...then there was the Grand Breeder. Could they all have been traitors?

There were too many variables now to make a good decision on his own. He would consult the Avatar. Seeing that name on that message had shocked him to the core as well. He had not heard the name Gallanar for so long he had begun to forget it. He had just been "emperor" for centuries.

He was about to open the passage to the Maw when he felt the palace shake and a single sentence was sent out, *"We are under attack!"*

The emperor hurried to the nearest window and looked out to see the last thing he expected. The Citadel of Time was right in the middle of the city. The walls were already up, cutting right through any buildings that happened to be in the way. Soldiers were on the walls and manning the cannons.

The Citadel had appeared in the worst part of the city too. Few of the buildings that the walls went through were tall enough to allow a way in and those were all currently ablaze. The streets there were narrower as well.

I must get to the Avatar!

The thought had barely formed when another followed it. That same voice as before was back.

"YoU KNoW whAT NeEDS TO happen!"

What is this voice? I feel as though I know it...

"GOdFreY IS right. THiS MUSt EnD!"

The Lich shook his head to clear it then ran through the halls to his chamber. As quickly as he could, he donned his ancient armor and hefted his own sword and at the same time took the blade that had been Mardelnier's as well. Eventually he would have to face them. They would come for the Avatar as well.

The city would be lost if there were even a few thousand soldiers in those walls. Too many of their soldiers were gone and the Weavers had spent far too much of their energy making that Ashen Colossus to be able to mass produce soldiers.

Still, they would be useful as cannon fodder. Looking out another window the Lich saw a group of eight leave the proximity of the Citadel and head towards the palace. He could not make out faces at this distance, but he knew that two of them were Valaas and Syr. Perhaps the others were those descended from Mardelnier?

Turning the corner, he walked into an antechamber with a large effigy of the Ashen Soul carved out of stone and an intricately carved stone doorway that led into a long stone tunnel. This tunnel would take him all the way through the mountains to the Maw of the World.

The Lich looked back in the direction that he knew the party that was advancing on the palace was. "Come, those of the shared blood. It shall soon be time for a reunion."

·　　　　·　　　　·

The moment that the Citadel dropped into the middle of the city all hell broke loose. The undead that had been trapped inside the walls had been cut down without exception. They could not risk leaving their backs exposed. Soldiers had been deployed to make sure that all buildings that might allow a path into the Citadel were burned.

Once that was completed Valaas and Syr had led the others into the city to make for the palace. Once inside the plan was to kill the Lich, as well as any of the Grand Weavers they could find and effectively leave the undead with a power vacuum.

Valaas and Syr had planned and waited so long for this that Meterove and the others did not object to them taking the lead. Few of the undead in the streets were willing to come at them. Most ran the other way. Occasionally a small group of guards would attempt to ambush them, but they were no match for them.

The entrance to the palace was guarded much more heavily and it took them several minutes to get through the front gate. Once inside the party moved as quickly as they could.

This place might act as a palace for the Ashen Empire, but the atmosphere was much closer to an abandoned fort that had fallen. Sections of it was full of dust and mold. Most windows that had glass were broken, unless it was stained glass showing the Ashen Soul.

While sprinting through the halls they got into a handful of skirmishes. One involved two undead, one of which had been made with gorgon parts. None of them slowed their advance through the halls for long.

Eventually they came to an antechamber with a massive effigy of the Ashen Soul. There was no doubt in any of their minds that this was where they had to go. The door scraped against the floor and an awful smell wafted up the tunnel that was behind it; sweet and pungent.

Where none of the undead had slowed them, this smell and the long dark tunnel managed to give them a moments pause. Then Valaas strode into the dark with Syr right behind him. Meterove and the others looked at each other and quickly followed.

The tunnel went on for what felt like forever. Their footsteps echoed off the walls and Meterove found himself both cursing the tunnel for making them so easy to hear and grateful that any enemy would be just as noisy.

Eventually the tunnel crossed over a massive stone structure.   The area was lit by some glowing moss around the chamber. The pale green light made the place extra eerie. It was like a massive stone bowl with what looked like blood coating the entire thing However as Dras watched he noticed something.

"Hey...Meterove...I think that blood on there just moved..."

Meterove looked down at the bowl again and after a minute he saw it too. "Yes, it did. I think that is a blood construct. Now that I look at it closer, I think that is where all the "bits" that are collected are deposited."

Joleen asked, "For what purpose?"

Jolson said, "Look over there along the far edge. Do you see those passages? I think those lead to the Necroduct. This thing overflows from being fed and it continuously runs down the Necroduct and poisons the land wherever it leads."

Dras looked at Jolson, "Are you saying that we could stop the spread of the undeath to the land if we torch this?"

Jolson nodded, "Yes, but I would rather we did it when we were near the door. The fumes coming off this room will probably ignite."

Once at the end of the bridge portion they paused so that they could send a few fireballs down into the bowl. The resulting inferno would hopefully torch the whole Necroduct. The continued on for what felt like hours before they saw a bit of light up ahead. The tunnel opened up into a large room with a dozen pillars that were five feet thick on the far end looking out into the sunrise.

They looked at each other the walked over to the pillars and looked out.

Joleen swore, "Holy SHIT!"

Meterove and Jolson just nodded. That was probably about the nicest way to describe the site that was in front of them. There was a hole in the world that was so wide that the other side was hazy. Meterove was quite sure there was no mist either. The hole was lined with countless sharp white stones that jutted out like teeth.

Floating above this hole was a massive black bird, enveloped in dark, black flames. It was only there for an instant then there was a weird popping sound, and it was gone. No one said anything, which was not the most comforting thing.

Now that the bird was gone, they noticed that they were not alone. There were two figures in the room as well. One that they knew to be the Lich but the other was a strange undead with a dirty white dress and a head cage. Closer inspection showed her to have her legs restrained in several places and her arms bound in a barbed type of wire across her chest and her wrists manacled.

There was no sound in the room. Even though there had to be wind out across that hole the room was deadly silent for a moment.

Syr said, "Mother?"

Valaas held his massive sword with one hand while holding Syr's shoulder with the other. "I do not understand. What is the meaning of this?"

The Lich turned and was about to answer when the woman emitted a sort of pressure.. The Lich lowered its head. Now that they could see her closer, they saw that her face was desiccated, and her mouth partially sewn shut except for a small gap where her tongue kept flicking out.

It spoke, "You can call me the Avatar of the Ashen Soul. I was your mother. Once. I have been a mother to others too."

Valaas' grip seemed to strengthen on Syr but Syr herself seemed to have regained some of her former cold self. She readied her short swords and said, "What did you do to her?"

The Avatar laughed, its tongue poking out of its mouth randomly. It cocked its head to the side and said, "Yes, he did do horrible things to me in life. These restraints that he crafted and had me placed in are awful. Unfortunately for him he loved this body, and his seal was incomplete. I was able to turn him, though even he cannot release these bonds."

The creature looked annoyed by that part. Meterove asked, "So what are you? You said you were the Avatar of the Ashen Soul but that does not tell me what you are?"

Meterove blinked and the Avatar was right in his face. He quickly took two steps back. This thing was unsettling.

"I am the Avatar of the Ashen Soul. While I am bound, I am no threat to YOU. That is all you need to know."

Meterove could sense it. It claimed that it was of no threat to them but there was no way that was true. Something about that statement was off.

The air around the room reverberated and once again the Avatar was next to the Lich, who had been strangely quiet. The two of them vanished with another of those strange movements that made the air shake.

Syr fell to her knees and began to sob. Valaas was attempting to comfort her but looked to be in the same state. Meterove and the others went to the other side of the room to give them a moment.

Dras was the first to speak, "OK I have questions. What was the bird? What the HELL was that woman? And last but not least where did they all go?"

Everyone looked at Jolson who shook his head. If Jolson had no idea, then it was unlikely that anyone else besides Valaas and Syr would have any ideas. Meterove knew they all were avoiding the third question for now. They needed the other two to recover before making their move anyway.

.   .   .

The Grand Weavers were scattered across the city trying to aid in the defense of the city as best they could.

They hated that they had to do this personally, but the Avatar was not to be trifled with. She was no threat to the living but the undead were a different matter.

They did their best to raise the fallen as quickly as they could but the difference in numbers was too great. They were going to be overwhelmed soon.

The citizens that were around them had to be cannibalized to make new Nightmare Woven just to keep them in the fight. Just before the attack had begun, word had come through a telepathy chain that the army had been trapped.

Several hours passed and sections of the city were burning. The Grand Nightmare Weaver had fallen not long ago. The Grand Blood Weaver had taken charge and was issuing orders when it saw the Necroduct light up. A massive blast of fire ran along it in all directions.

THE NECROWELL!

That had been a massive achievement in advancing the Ashen Souls will! Now it was gone, the Grand Weaver could feel it. This was pointless, it was time to leave this city to its fate.

.   .   .

Godfrey could not have asked for a better set up than this. They were currently trapped in a massive stone box. He had not seen shaping crystals used in so long that he had almost forgotten about them.

The disappearance of the Ashen Colossus had been very unexpected. He wondered how the humans had pulled that one off. Around him the generals and other officers that were not working with him were franticly attempting to find a way out of this trap.

They had already attempted to scale the walls and those that made it to the top had immediately been riddled with arrows, and in the case of the larger ones, ballista bolts. Often these were just normal weapons, but some had that enchantment on them that burned undead.

As luck would have it none of the other officers seemed to suspect a thing about him. They were all too focused on finding a way out to notice that his own efforts were halfhearted. In order to keep up the illusion that he was still trying to lead them to victory he did make a few legitimate attempts, though he had used officers that he wanted dead.

He did have some soldiers that were more than willing to die for their ideals. Already some had scaled the walls with the intention of getting hit with one of those flame arrows so they could fall onto some scaffolding that was being fashioned out of siege engines.

His letter should have been delivered to Gallanar by now.

I wonder how he took that. No one has called him by his name since before he was turned after all.

At present there were about one million, eight hundred thousand undead inside the walls. Nearly a million of those were either conscripted or newly raised. Most of them were not really interested in fighting anyway. Of the other eight hundred thousand many were soldiers with experience.

Godfrey only really had the support of a few thousand. If his true goals became known there was no way of knowing what would happen but he expected that it would end badly.

.   .   .

It had taken Syr a long time to calm down but once she got there, she was no longer the same apathetic woman. There was cold anger etched into every part of her face. For his part Valaas was not much better.

He had appreciated that the others had given him and Syr space while still remaining close enough to act as protection. He looked down at Syr and she nodded back. The two of them stood and walked over to the rest.

This was not the time or place for sentimental speeches, so he simply nodded his gratitude, which they returned. He was dreading the questions that he knew were coming but was not going to run from them or fault them for asking. This was bigger than his pain.

Joleen glanced at the others and asked, "We have a few questions to ask you. First, do you know what that black bird was earlier?"

Valaas shook his head. At least she was easing into it. "I have never seen or heard of anything like that before."

Joleen nodded then steeled herself before asking, "The A-Avatar. She was your mother?"

Valaas felt his chest tighten, but it was Syr that answered, "Yes, at least she felt like our mother. It is hard to reconcile that face with the one in my memory."

Valaas said, "One thing that was off was when she said that she had many children. Our mother only had four. Mardelnier, then myself, Syr and Valnyr."

Meterove asked, "Is it possible that there were siblings that died at birth that you never knew about?"

Valaas shook his head, "I guess that is a possibility, but I doubt it. Perhaps she was speaking not as my mother but as the one that has birthed countless undead."

Meterove said, "Putting aside whether or not that is your mother for now, what exactly was she? I felt something from her. Like she was incredibly dangerous, but not at the same time."

Valaas said, "Yes, she was dangerous. The whole time she as here I felt like I was in mortal danger. Well to be exact Syr and myself. I had no feeling that any of you were in danger, at least from her."

Syr said, "As for what she is, well I think the title is literal. I think that whatever the Ashen Soul is, it needs to bound to the world through a body."

Dras said, "That might make sense if we had not personally seen the Ashen Soul back in Yxarion. It fused with a man named Vlad."

Valaas said, "Think about what she said earlier though. "I am no threat to YOU." I think that had multiple meanings. First it was a threat towards Syr and I. I think that it was also a threat to you in the form of saying she cannot kill you, but others can. I think she is an anchor for the Ashen Soul."

Jolson asked, "Are you saying that the version of the Ashen Soul that we saw was made by her passing along her power?"

Valaas sighed, "I cannot say for sure. Also, what she had said about my father putting all those restraints on her while she was alive is bothering me."

Syr said in a dangerous voice, "Are you suggesting that there might have been cause for that?"

Valaas said, "IF what she said was true then she was the one that corrupted him. Maybe he knew something that he never told us."

Syr said, "Mom was dead before we left the old empire. She should not even be here."

Meterove cut Valaas off before he could continue, "Enough! Whether she was your mother and how or why she became the way she is no longer matters! What really bothers me is that they did not seem to care that we were here."

Dras said, "Yeah they almost seemed to want us to follow them."

Everyone looked over at the Maw. Those rocks jutting out that looked like teeth were everywhere and the space between them saw so narrow that there was no way they were getting through quickly.

Meterove sighed, "We might as well start making our way down. I would rather we were climbing down in daylight."

.   .   .

The Avatar shuffled along with the Lich are her side. So much had gone wrong but still the will of the Ashen Soul must endure. The Abyssal Catacombs that stretched out under the Maw were filled with dreadful creatures that the Nightmare Weavers would be jealous of.

None of them attacked them, however. To them she was like a wetnurse, only instead of milk they suckled the corruption. This world had held back the Ashen Soul long enough. It was time to accept this loss and move on. Destroying it later was perfectly acceptable.

The next ones to fall needed to be able to grant them armies all across Creation. To that end the Avatar had already been hard at work.

Seeds had been planted and some were already beginning to sprout. While the armies they should have been able to raise from this world would be missed, they would rise above this defeat!

Eventually their army would recover from whatever the traitor Godfrey had done and would continue on with their mission. If they managed to find some of the chambers that the Artificials used, then this would all have been worth it.

She still cursed her luck with that mage from Yxarion. He had been so close to finding out how to transfer her essence out of this body and spawn her true form. The Child had sensed her lingering aura there and had been drawn to it and the mage had likely gone mad from the exposure.

In the end he had failed and that was all that mattered. The two of them soon arrived at their destination. It was a small slit in the side of the cave. Moving through the gap in the rock they found themselves in the heart of an extinct volcano. Laying in the middle of what was once part of the magma chamber was the Ashen Soul, still battered from its fight with the Dragon Lord.

It was not ideal, but it was time to open a path of escape. To do that they needed a power source. This being was a pale imitation of the real thing. That did not mean it was useless. Even though it was sewn closed he mouth moved into a smile.

The Avatar knelt down and looked into the eyes of the Ashen Soul that had once been Vlad. *"You will use all the power that you have left to help make a hole in the world."*

She turned to the Lich. *"You will also be needed shortly. We will establish a new stronghold."*

The Lich bowed to the Avatar. There was no room for argument. He wished he could kill those two, but the Ashen Soul was far more important. Once again that voice broke into his mind.

"ArE YOu SuRE THat YoU REAllY WanT THaT?"

343

Who are you! How are you in my mind when no one else is near and for what purpose?

"I woULD ThINk THAt wAs ObVioUS..."

ANSWER ME DAMNIT! WHO ARE YOU!?

"Is iT ReaLy SO HarD to FIguRe oUt?"

The Lich clutched his head with both hands. This display drew the Avatar's gaze. Any undead, even the Lich should fear that gaze, but he was too preoccupied.

I DEMAND YOU ANSWER ME!

"yOU kNow WhO I Am..."

NO! HOW? THAT SHOULD NOT BE POSSIBLE!

"HeLLo Me..."

THAT PERSON WAS DESTROYED! I GROUND HIM TO DUST!

"Oh, YoU CerTAiNlY DId, BuT EvEN DuST CAn CLuMp ToGetHeR. REmEMbEr WhO wE ARE!"

Memories poured through the Lich's mind. He was back in the old empire. His wife Celaina had just been killed by the rebels assassins. In his grief he had called upon the darkest arts. He would give anything to have her back. What he brought back though...this was not Celaina!

In the secret room where he had used dark magics to resurrect his beloved wife, he now used everything at his disposal, materials and even his own blood, to bind this abomination. He had to make do with some questionable materials but as long as he used his blood they would still hold.

He could feel this...thing breaking into his mind as he worked but he fought as hard as he could against it. He had roughly sewn her mouth shut to slow her, but the last stich was left undone. He had not been fast enough. He fled the room and found some of his most loyal soldiers. They would be tasked with getting her out of here.

.   .   .

The madness that had started when he tried to bring back Celaina was getting worse by the day. He had wanted to lock her away somewhere back in the old empire, but he could not bring himself to do it. He longed to be with her again.

The ship carrying Celaina had arrived and his trusted soldiers, led by Godfrey had taken her to the location that they had found. It was a massive whole in the world with large sharp white rocks jutting out. His scout that had found it had called it the Maw of the World. After seeing it, he had agreed with the name the man had given it.

They had explored its depths and found that near the very back of the caverns underneath it there was a passage to an extinct volcano. Here he would seal this thing away...but perhaps a secret Gateway so he could visit her might be fine?

．　　　　　．　　　　　．

He had been turning some of the recently deceased into undead for Celaina to feed on. He had tried regular food first then at her insistence, had begun bringing her corpses. They had not been enough, and she had begun to deteriorate. In desperation he had brought her a corpse that he raised into an undead.

She had eaten the necrotic flesh and begun to grow stronger again. This continued for some time. Eventually he was careless, and someone saw him raiding a grave. It had not taken long for word to reach Mardelnier's ears. He had then passed down his sentence. His own son had attempted to have him killed! The ungrateful traitor!

No...no he was not the traitor. I committed the atrocities. I should have never tried to bring her back. I should never had brought her with. I never should have made the Gateway to her prison!

That voice was stronger for that small instant but soon the desire to be beside Celaina overcame all else again. Gallanar was no more.

The Lich straightened up and lowered his hands to his sides The blue light that had been in his eyes glowed even brighter. The Avatar said, *"It seems that a fragment of your old self had remained until now. I trust that it is gone now. There can be no room for a weakness like that."*

The Lich took hold of the grip on the two swords that were across his back and unsheathed them. He also released his magic that he usually kept sealed. It was rare for undead to retain magic, beyond a Weaver's ability but he was no ordinary undead. As a Lich he had access to all the powers he had ever had plus what had been granted by his transformation.

He crossed the blades in front of his chest and knelt to the Avatar. *"I swear that any traces of that person are now gone. I live and die for the Ashen Soul."*

CHAPTER 14.5
CONFRONTATION

So, it had finally happened. The Darkfire One had shown itself before the Oracle. The time for a confrontation would soon come. The question was going to be how to deal with it when that time came.

The next path appeared to have been set now. New meetings and crossing paths with an old acquaintance seemed to be in the future.

It was a shame that the Avatar of the Ashen Soul had managed to send out corruption to so many different places. Some of the things that were corrupted though! Now that most of the selves had been reunited, the bulk of what was to come could be seen.

The Planes were all under siege! There were at least a dozen worlds that were already infected. The Protogods and their minions were moving as well. Then there was the Gamemaster. He was a real wild card. It was infuriating not knowing what he was.

There was one of the one from the second race that was traveling and would soon make contact. Since the Second Generation was still outside of the flow, their movements could only be partially seen.

The confrontation had to come and there was no reason to put it off any longer. Pop!

CHAPTER 15
CATACOMBS

The trek down through the Maw had proven to be even harder than it had looked. By the time that they had made it down to the bottom of the Maw the sun had begun to set. Valaas and Syr wanted to press on, but Meterove refused. They might be prepared to enter there after that climb but the rest of them were not. While not happy about it Valaas agreed that entering now was not the best idea.

They made a camp at the mouth of the cave that they found at the bottom of the Maw. It was a little vexing, but once they were at the bottom the path that led back up, that the Lich and Avatar had used, was obvious.

From within the dark of the cave came sounds unlike anything that they had ever heard. They had heard the undead make a multitude of sounds since they first started their journey but these but these were beyond comprehension.

Dras asked, "What the hell do you think that is all about?"

Meterove said, "It sounds bad whatever it is."

Valaas had been silent for a while said, "We have walked the Ashen Empire for a long time hiding and listening. One of the things that I wondered about and only heard fearful whispers referencing, was what happened with their criminals."

Joleen asked, "What do you mean?"

Valaas said, "How are they punished? What happens to them? Where do they go? I could only ever find one word; Catacombs."

Jolson looked into the blackness, "You think that inside there is where the undead that were considered criminals were placed?"

Valaas said, "I think that it is more than that. As you noticed during your time here, the Ashen Empire has obedience as its core. If you remember, the Grand Weavers tore a number of undead apart when you infiltrated the church. They brought in what the Grand Weavers believed were "human sympathizers" and were torn apart and remade for it."

Terenia said, "OH! No one kept looking for those undead that we used as drones after a few days. They just stopped acting like they ever existed, didn't they?"

There was silence for a moment then Syr said, "The other thing that we have never seen was that creature. I have no idea what that thing truly is, but it is wearing my mother's body like clothing, and I hate it."

Valaas patted Syr's back and said, "I know. I do too. I am also very interested in her. What is she that the majority of the populace have no idea about her? Is she simply so feared that none speak of her?"

Meterove said, "I do not think that she was lying to us earlier. There was something about her aura. It was almost like she was trying to frighten us away. There was no mercy or kindness in that creature so I can only assume that it was playing for time."

Dras asked, "How does giving us information help buy time?"

Joleen said, "Its simple. When we had nothing but its existence to go on, we might have acted rather than waited Knowing that little bit made us wary. What more is she hiding?"

Jolson muttered, "Psychological warfare."

Meterove nodded, "I think that thing, the Avatar, just needed to get out of that room. Once she was inside she did not care if we followed or not. I think that was also what she meant about not being a threat. She needed something before she could be a threat."

Dras said, "So she was threatened before, but now that she has this place between us, we are not a threat?"

Terenia said, "No, I think it is much worse than that. I think she believes that by the time we can reach her that it will not matter that we did."

Jolson said, "I agree. The two of them appear to have simply abandoned what they had been building up until now. This tells me that they either have a backup plan, or another motive entirely."

Joleen said, "Flare did mention the Ashen Soul to us. Now that I look back on it, she was avoiding being specific about it. At the time I just put it down to her summarizing rather than fully explaining."

Dras said, "You think she was hiding something from us."

Joleen sighed, "I cannot say for sure. It might not be that simple."

Narok who had been mostly silent besides the sound of ascent here and there asked, "What do you mean simple? This thing is a threat to this whole world!"

Joleen stared at Narok for a moment, and he seemed to realize his outburst and worked to calm himself down.

The fire had not fully left though. Regardless Joleen continued, "To something on the scale of Flare, the death of just this world is nothing. It is part of the cycle of Creation. She watches worlds end from their own hubris all the time. This time she helped."

Dras said, "So this is a much bigger problem than we thought. If that was the case, then why did she not send more help with?"

Joleen said, "I fear that the answer to that question has to do with the reason that Flare was so vague when it came to the Ashen Soul to begin with."

.   .   .

The Lich stood guard at the door. The scattered bones and bits that had been the Ashen Soul the Dragon Lord had fought littered the chamber. The Avatar sat, blood coating the front of her mouth. Now that the full power of the Ashen Soul was back with her, she opened tears in reality and proceeded to prod the seeds she had planted.

The dark of the Abyssal Catacombs, lit only by the numerous natural gas vents stretched out in front of him. He could hear the screaming of those who were sealed within this place. These fools had their connection severed for their transgressions so they needed to rely on their voices if they had one.

There were some in here that were not prisoners. The jailors trudged along throughout the catacombs administrating torture, forcing labor and, when needed, feeding the prisoners.

It would be interesting to see if anyone would make it to them. The Avatar and himself were one thing but fresh meat walking into this place...he did not think for a second that the jailors were going to be able to control them. He was not even sure if the Avatar even wanted them to.

Cracking bones could be heard behind him, but he paid them no mind. It was strange that he had been able to hear them in this place, with the sounds of torment all around. Undead did not feel pain in the same sense that the living did. For undead the physical body getting injured was not what caused the sensation. Instead, it was when the energy that held them in this world was cut that they felt pain.

In here the two in charge were the Warden and the Director. The Warden to lead the jailors and keep the prisoners under control. The Director worked alone but was considered equal to the Warden. He was responsible for experimenting on those here to find their defects.

The Lich tightened his grip on his swords. None of the prisoners had come near while he was with the Avatar, but he had already had to deal with two that had approached him, thinking that they had found food. More had just looked at him from around the corner. Those fools had better hurry in. This was tedious.

.   .   .

The sun's rays were barely visible when Meterove kicked dirt over the remains of their fire. It was time. Each of them took a torch. They had agreed to hold off on using magic to make light. Valaas and Syr took the lead, followed by Meterove. The middle was made up of Joleen, Jolson, and Narok. Dras and Terenia took the rear.

Not long after entering the caves they had encountered the smell of rotting flesh, blood and also burnt flesh. The screams coming out of this place were something else. At least they did not have to worry about something hearing them easily. Of course, the opposite was true too.

The walls in this place were...weird. Meterove could not quite pin what it was about this place that was off, but it was there none the less. Jolson seemed to feel the same. He was examining the walls. He picked at a section a little and a piece came off.

Jolson whispered, "This is similar to stone or mortar but something about the consistency is off. I would like to check it quickly."

He opened the satchel he always carried now and pulled out a tool that even Meterove recognized. It would use a small amount of magic to analyze a sample and tell you what it was made of. They were originally meant for geological studies but could also be used for any number of uses.

After a moment, the device finished, and Jolson looked disgusted. "This IS mortar, but it is made from ash."

Dras said, "You have no idea how badly I am hoping you say it is from a campfire."

Jolson wiped his hand on his coat, "Well, your hopes are dashed."

Valaas said, "I fail to see how this matters. Let us continue to-"

Midsentence the wall that was next to Valaas exploded as an undead burst through the weak mortar and tackled him to the floor. While most undead that Meterove had seen were vicious, this one was feral. It was straddling Valaas trying to claw at him with its bare hands as well as bite him.

Valaas gave it a hard shove and it flew off and hit the wall hard, collapsing in a heap. The impact led five more undead to break through the walls and enter the hall. Instead of attacking them they turned to the one that was on the floor and swarmed it. They were all just shambling rotting zombies, but they tore the first one apart and ate it.

They sat in the shadows, hunched around the fallen, one tearing into fetid meat Soon they noticed there was fresher meat and attacked. Syr was still helping Valaas to his feet when an arrow and a bolt flew forward from Dras and Terenia hitting the two in the front in the heads dropping them instantly. The other three barely took two steps before two more dropped the same way. Syr dropped the last one with a simple slash from one of her short swords.

The party held their breath for a moment, but nothing more came. Meterove relaxed and said, "Nice going Dras. You too Terenia."

In the back Dras nodded and Terenia winked. She and Dras bumped the back of their fists together without looking at each other. Jolson and Joleen were looking at where one of the zombie had come out of the wall.

Joleen said, "This was not meant to be a trap."

Valaas asked, "How can you be sure?"

Joleen said, "There are marks all over the walls in this small chamber. It was clawing in all directions trying to find its way out. I think this was torture, its similar to being buried alive."

While looking into another of the holes Dras said, "Do you smell that?"

Jolson came over to him and said, "Yes, I can. We should be careful not to get close. That is sometimes found underground. The smell is a type of gas. To be exact, what you smell is what happens when the gas mixes with the air. It is very flammable and will ignite if the concentration is high enough."

Dras moved his torch away from the door, "Great so if there is one leak in here then the chances of there being more is high."

Jolson nodded, "Yes, I would say that is a good assumption. It would be a good idea to switch to magic light."

Meterove said, " Agreed. We need to keep moving though. We will just have to make sure we watch the walls."

Meterove, Joleen and Jolson each picked up a small rock and imbued them with some magic to give off some faint light.

Meterove nodded to Valaas who turned and continued to lead the way. Now they kept their voices down. Soon they found a small sturdy wooden door with metal casing and rivets. There was a small, barred window on the top. Valaas looked through then turned the handle and pushed the door in.

The room that they entered looked to Meterove like some kind of guard post. There was a small rack in the corner that held a small assortment of weapons. There was a small table in the corner with four chairs. There were three more doors in the room, one on each wall. One had bars on them, but the other two did not.

In unspoken unity they checked those two doors first. Behind the first was a small office. Inside it was nothing special. Based on the documents that they found it appeared to be the Wardens office. The second room was horrifying.

Those who had been in Orelion's lab recognized a thing or two. This room was far larger than the Warden's office. It also had a very tall ceiling with some alcoves of books. There were many glass tubes holding various undead. There were also several chairs that had bodies that had been undead chained in them.

One chair was covered in tiny spikes. The other had metal restraints holding the limbs to the chair and the head in place. There was a cart with a tray on it next to that one. The tray had series of wicked looking instruments on it. They were all covered in flecks of coagulated blood and hair.

One of the tanks held a body in it along with two metal probes. It was connected to a strange setup of metal leads that were in turn, connected to a crystal. Curious Jolson touched the crystal. Inside the tank an arc of electricity could be seen. The undead in the tank reacted by jerking around and attempting to scream.

Jolson let go horrified and the machine stopped. The undead inside tried to pound on the glass but some force seemed to have it bound in there. There were several large tables, not unlike the one that had been in Orelion's lab, with bodies on them.

One had a blood construct with metal probes imbedded in its head. Another had a regular zombie. It had manacles holding it to the table. Its chest and abdomen were sawn open. There was a section of its skull cut away and the brain was showing. There were several probes set up to be used. The last was a wraith.

This thing looked more horrifying than any wraith any of them had seen yet. The soul that made up its core looked like the other wraith souls they had seen, except he was absolutely beaming, but something seemed feral about that smile as well.

The wraith was watching them. Soon it spoke. "I want to bathe in your eyes. Let me scoop them out. Squish them..."

Dras whispered, "What the fu-"

The wraith started talking over him, "Let me go. I wish to dance through the rotting. I want to find the fire and burn the eyeless."

In another act of unspoken unity everyone left the room. It continued to babble about eyes while they left. Meterove was the first to speak. "What were they doing in there?"

Valaas and Syr even looked unnerved by what they had just seen so they did not protest to holding up here for a moment. Jolson said, "It looked like they were experimenting on the undead that they sent in here. That wraith sounded insane though. I think the undead are also sending any that show signs of mental illness here."

Dras asked, "To what end?"

Jolson shook his head, "I could not even begin to understand what the reasoning would be."

Meterove started to speak then cut off and jerked his head back towards the lab. He was not the only one. Dras, Valaas and Syr were also looking back at the room. As one they moved back to the door and burst back into the room.

Sitting in the middle of the Lab was an undead that looked vaguely like an old man. He was wearing a tattered, dirty white robe under a leather apron. Its eyes were wide in shock. It jumped and for the first time it occurred to Meterove that they had not checked the alcoves. The mad wraith had driven the thought from their minds.

The four of them prepared to kill the undead but the wraith had started to talk again. "Director! I wish to bathe in their eyes! Give me eyes!"

At the mention of "Director", the small undead made a slight jerk. Meterove said, "Wait! Do not kill it. Yet."

He looked coldly down at the undead. It really did just look like a shriveled old man. "That wraith called you "Director" did it not?"

The undead just stared back at him, dead eyes glazed and empty. Meterove prepared to sever its head when a rasp finally came out, "Fine! You win. I am the Director here."

Meterove lowered his blade a fraction, "What does that mean? What are you doing in here?"

The Director said, "I was put in charge of the criminals that are housed here. My duty, given by the emperor and the Avatar herself, is to discover what is wrong with those who are sealed within here. Why they do not obey."

Dras said, "You torture them."

The Director laughed, "They are criminals and the insane. What does it matter?" He narrowed his eyes and sniffed the air, "Some of you are alive." Then he pointed at Valaas and Syr, "I cannot speak with you two. I know that you are turned. Why is that?"

Meterove placed the tip of Oblivion on the Directors eye socket, then said, "You are answering our questions, not the other way around."

From the room Terenia said, "There are some undead heading this way!"

The Director eyes opened wide, "There were more of you!?"

Meterove said, "You thought that you could buy time for backup to get here and save your neck."

Valaas said, "Just kill him. We need to get going."

Meterove shook his head, his face cold, "No I have a better idea."

Meterove walked over to the chair with the restraints and removed the body from it. Then once it was out, he stood over the Director and pulled him over. The Director said, "I would never be so foolish to try and attack you myself. There is no need to restrain me."

Meterove slammed him into the chair. Dras came over and they swiftly locked him in the chair. Meterove looked the Director in the eyes and said, "Dras. When we leave this room, I will put up a barrier that will keep everything inside of it contained. It works on spectral enemies as well. Do me a favor and release that wraith."

Understanding showed on everyone's faces, and horror on the Directors. He said, "N-No! I-I a-am th-the D-Dir-Director! You! NO!"

Everyone else exited the room while Dras opened the restraints on the wraith, noticing vaguely that there were strange runes etched into them. Once they were off the Wraith sat up. Dras quickly exited the room and Meterove sealed the room. Before closing the door Meterove heard the Wraith muttering about "eyeballs" while closing in on the screaming Director.

Out in the room Terenia was sniping one undead after another that was coming from the other door. When Meterove closed the door there were already three of them on the ground with arrows in their skulls. They all looked the same, basic undead. They had simple clubs for weapons. Clearly, they were meant to subjugate, not kill with those.

They fought with the guards for a few minutes. Once a dozen had fallen, they stopped coming. Meterove waited a moment after the last one had fallen before he stepped through the door. On the other side was a large room filled with dozens of torture devices. Giant wheels and racks, pokers, and hot coals, stretching tables, and iron maidens.

The room was currently silent except for the pained gasping and sobbing of the undead that had been in the process of being tortured. Though they had been released they made no move to get up. They looked at Meterove and the others. Meterove wanted to kill them off right away, but he could not bring himself to do it.

Dras seemed to share his thinking, "I wish they would attack us. I do not want them behind me but if I go over there, I am going to feel like a monster."

Joleen and Jolson both looked at him first, then at each other and came to the same conclusion. Valaas and Syr had no such inhibitions and made quick work of the undead. There were two doors out of that room, one on either wall.

Dras opened the door on the left and an enormous hand made of blood pushed through at him and slammed him into the wall. The blood fell down into a puddle and lay still. Everyone else focused on the door while Narok helped Dras to his feet.

Meterove said, "Come out Blood Weaver!"

Dras and Narok were focused on the door as well. It was not until Dras felt the blood moving off his skin that he made the connection. "SHIT! Behind us!"

Everyone spun around to see that the blood that had been the giant hand had risen and made a type of gate that the Weaver had used to enter behind them. This was different to how they had seen Weavers behave up until now. It was blood construct with six legs and two arms on its long body.

Any of the blood that had been inside the undead had also joined with the Weaver now. More and more seemed to bubble up from that Bloodgate that it had entered through. It made countless icicle-like blood spikes that it launched at them.

Everyone scattered. Jolson and Joleen were behind Narok and his shield. Valaas and Syr had tipped a table over and were using it for cover. Terenia was huddled behind a table of her own. Meterove and Dras could only run at the moment. If they came near cover the Weaver would try to catch them ducking into it and skewer them.

Dras yelled, "I have a dumb idea. I will need you to throw me a sword though."

As soon as he said this Dras directed his path so it would connect with Meterove's and threw his sword at the rack that was next to the Weaver. It stuck point first in the rack. The Weaver cackled in a strange, echoing gurgle and went to send a swarm of spikes at him.

Just as it sent out the spikes Dras vanished, and a sword was in his place. The Weaver stopped, clearly taken aback. It missed that where the sword had been on the rack there now stood Dras. Meterove had also thrown a sword but his was two seconds after Dras' and in a higher arc.

Dras caught the sword and cut the surprised Weaver in half right where the second set of legs were. All the blood stopped moving and the construct collapsed into a puddle. Dras jumped back to dodge the blood. Meterove picked up Dras' sword and when Dras came over he handed it back to him.

Joleen said, "I cannot say that I would have done that myself, but I will not call that a dumb idea Dras. That plan was quite brilliant."

Meterove clapped Dras on the back, "I second that. Though I know that I would have done it."

Valaas and Syr were looking down at the Weavers remains, pensive.

Jolson noticed this and said, "Is something the matter?"

Valaas said, "I have never seen or heard of a Weaver that used their abilities like this before. I can only surmise that it was one of those with mental illness. It is good that never became common."

Meterove agreed. Fighting just one had been bad enough. Fighting dozens or even hundreds of those would have been catastrophic. Going through the door that the Weaver had been behind they found themselves in a vast network of tunnels.

More screams emanated from all directions. There were no candles or lamps out here. The only light came from flames jetting out of holes. Jolson looked at them with interest. "Hmm it would appear that the gas that we smelled earlier is stronger down this way. It has actually ignited and now is permanently feeding these flames."

The slight flickering of the flames from above gave off some weird shadows. It was this that allowed them to sneak around the many cells that they passed. While the many undead inside clearly needed to be detained the barbaric methods were hard to look at.

Many were kept in near to total darkness. The Living Shadows that they encountered in cells appeared to have been placed in those with the brightest flames. Cells were all tiny as well, barely enough room for the prisoner to fit behind the door. It took Meterove over an hour of seeing them before he realized that they were modeled after coffins.

The deeper that they went into the Catacombs the more disturbing the undead became. One stretch turned particularly dangerous when six undead came running around the corner on all fours. Two were on the floor but there were two on each wall as well.

They moved with terrifying speed and once they attacked the party, they revealed this weird ability that kept them on the wall was not the only thing they could do. Their faces had a strange vertical scar down the middle which was revealed to be a split in the head that opened to reveal fangs.

It was when Terenia and Dras tried to shoot two of them that they learned another terrifying trait. As the arrow hit, the flesh spread apart and closed after it had passed. Dras suddenly felt a hand seize his arm and followed it to one of the undead that was hanging from the ceiling, its head split wide, ready to take his head off.

Dras changed places with his sword just as it bit him making running his sword through its head easy. "Watch out! They are on the ceiling too!"

What had looked like a pack of six was actually ten, well nine now. Up front Meterove, Valaas and Syr were each engaging two of them Joleen and Terenia were each fighting one while Narok readied himself to take one from Meterove.

Seeing Narok and Dras ready Meterove and Valaas let two of the undead through and the three of them focused on the four that were left. Dras killed his second one a second after Joleen killed hers. She had really improved a lot. Terenia was just a hair slower in finishing her opponent. Up front the others had also finished. The last one to fall was the one Narok was fighting.

Meterove who was panting slightly said, "We are taking a breather after that."

No one complained. Once they had rested, they continued on until they came to a fork in the caves. Valaas chose the right path and they continued. There seemed to be less severe changes in the undead this way. Joleen was the first one to comment on it.

"Is it just me or are these undead less deformed?"

Meterove looked at the undead that they could see here and there through small openings in the cells. "Now that you mention it, yes you are right. They are less deformed."

Terenia asked, "What do you think that means?"

Jolson said, "It could mean that we are in a different section. It was hard to hear over the screaming in this place, but I believe I heard muttering back that way. Perhaps those were the ones with mental illness?"

Joleen said, "That could very well be the case."

After a little while they came to a door that opened into the torture room that they had been in earlier. Seeing this Valaas seemed to relax slightly. Joleen shot him a quizzical look. "Now that I know this connects, I do not have to worry about more surprises coming at us from behind."

That made sense. They were about to leave when Dras stopped, staring at the floor. His hand shot to his sword, "NO! This is a trap!"

Everyone jumped into guarded stances. Meterove said, "What is going on Dras? I don't see anything."

Dras said, "The pool from that Weaver earlier is in the wrong spot. There is no mark from my sword in the rack either."

The color fell away from the world giving it a weird monochrome feel while the air temperature dropped significantly. Everything in the room distorted for a moment flashing into and out of existence while appearing like a mosaic.

Now the room was empty save for them and a single wraith in the corner. It mimed giving them applause before it said, "I am surprised that you were so observant. So be exact this was NOT a trap, just an attempt to escape undetected."

Meterove asked, "Who are you?"

The wraith said, "I am the Warden here. I have been here since the founding of the Ashen Empire."

Valaas was looking at the wraith's spirit when he suddenly murmured, "Edward. Is that you?"

The wraith laughed, "I see you did recognize me Valaas. Yes, it is me."

Valaas said, "I thought that you were lost back in the old empire. You and Godfrey both."

The wraith laughed, "Actually, Godfrey was here too. The Grand General of the Ashen Empire's armies was none other than Godfrey."

Valaas said, "I don't understand. Why are you here?"

The wraith sighed, "Your father. When your mother died, he was destroyed by the grief and went temporarily mad. He used all the forbidden knowledge he could find to try and bring her back. What he made was not her though and he used the last bits of his sanity to forge restraints on the creature."

Syr's face softened, "So that creature IS our mother. His grief at her death is why he turned to the foul magics."

Valaas asked, "But why is she here? Why not leave her back in the old empire?"

The wraith said, "The original plan had been to do just that. Your father still loved her, and our eyes were blinded by loyalty, so when he ordered us to smuggle her across, we did."

Valaas asked, "What happened afterwards?"

The wraith sighed, "Your father convinced us that we were keeping her away from the enemy by bringing her across and then when we arrived, he convinced us he had the perfect place to hide her away. We agreed and brought her down here. What we did not know was that he managed to make a Gateway and that he used it to come see her. Over time she fully corrupted him until the day that he turned."

Syr asked, "What about you and Godfrey?"

The wraith said, "We were taken soon after he turned as "willing" converts. Truth was that Godfrey and I felt responsible for what had happened. We should have seen what was happening."

Valaas asked, "What were you going to accomplish by becoming undead?"

The wraith laughed, "You ask me that? You became Revenants! This allowed us to stay close and perhaps sabotage the Ashen Empire."

Meterove said, "This Godfrey person was leading the army you said? That was why it was so easy to get them into the traps. He was purposely trying to fall into them."

The wraith nodded, "That is true. Before the army left Godfrey sent me a letter. All it said was "It is time." and was marked with a single G."

Syr said, "We are here to put an end to this for good. Where are they?"

The wraith stared at Syr; the intensity of her voice seemed to shake him slightly. "Go back the way you came and take the other tunnel down. Beyond this room is the real experimentation room you were in earlier. Follow the path down to a crack in the wall. If you reach magma pits you have gone too far. Go and end this."

The wraith seemed to almost smile peacefully. Valaas and Syr hesitated a moment before turning and leaving through the door they had come in. No one said anything as they backtracked through the tunnels. Once they reached the fork, they took the other tunnel down. It twisted around a lot but eventually they reached a stretch that was straighter and level.

There was no danger of them missing the crack in the wall. Standing outside the crack was the Lich, carrying two swords, both of which Valaas and Syr recognized. One was their father's and the other their brother's. It watched their approach impassively. Once they were within reach of words the Lich said, "I have long awaited the chance to kill you two. So kind of you to finally come to me."

Valaas said, "I do not care about your words monster. You are not my father, just an abomination using his body."

Syr continued his thought, "And we WILL purge you and the atrocity that is in our mother's body!"

CHAPTER 16
UNSEALED

Valaas and Syr each let out a bestial shout and charged the Lich. Their attacks were aimed to kill. Both of their attacks were parried simultaneously. The Lich was moving at impossible speeds. Not only did it block their attacks ,but it used the shift in their balance and channeled the momentum put onto its blades into slashes.

Seeing that it was outnumbered the Lich stepped backwards into the crack in the wall. Valaas and Syr gave chase with the rest just seconds behind them. The crack was dark, but it was short and soon they found themselves in the center of a massive crater. In the center there were dozens of tears with a toxic blue energy pouring into them from the Avatar.

Dras and Meterove joined Valaas and Syr in attacking the Lich while the others tried to focus on the

Avatar. The Lich did not seem to care that two more had joined the fight. Parry and slash. Parry and slash. Parry, parry, parry, parry, slash, trust, slash.

The four of them darted around the Lich, Valaas and Meterove using magic as well as their swords to try and end the Lich. Syr and Dras used their speed styles to try and get in a hit. For its part, the Lich was using magic along with its swords to hold them at bay.

While this was going on the others were attempting to get to the Avatar. The Avatar looked to be busy, but a sudden burst of blue mist suddenly came out of its mouth and traveled in a line towards them. They dodged it easily but the fact that it was able to attack put them on edge.

The bones that they had only vaguely registered on the ground before rose up and changed form to attack them. Narok used his shield to block while Joleen and Terenia used their agility to dodge around the attacks. Jolson dodged where he could, but he kept near Narok.

Across the chamber Valaas and Meterove had been knocked back and were in the process of getting up and back to the fight. Dras was flashing all around the Lich, desperately trying to make up for the sudden loss of the other two. The Lich looked frustrated that this had not turned into the opening he thought it would.

Blocking another slash from Dras the Lich then used its magic to make a stone pillar burst out of the ground and hit Dras in the ribs, blowing him away. Valaas had made it back though, and he filled the gap before the Lich could capitalize on it. A second behind him Meterove arrived, but just as Syr was parried and kicked in the ribs sending her sprawling.

The Lich imbued a ton of magic into the sword it was holding and did a double slash at the ground causing a massive explosion of rock in front of him. As the dust settled Dras and Meterove were getting to their feet both holding their sides. Valaas was further back, almost to the crater wall.

While they struggled against the Lich, Joleen and Terenia were trying to get in close to attack the Avatar. Terenia had tried to snipe the Avatar, but it moved around too fast to hit. The strange burning smell was thick in the air now.

Jolson and Narok were making their way closer too, but the bones had morphed into two small bone constructs that were attacking them, falling apart when attacked then reanimating once the attack was past.

The Avatar was not making things any easier with the occasional burst of light out of its mouth. There was no telling what that would do. So far none of them had taken anything more than a scratch.

The Lich sent a second massive slash, creating a wave of rock that blew towards them. Jolson and Narok had no choice but to chance the debris. Jolson took a rock square to the left shoulder. Narok seemed to get by unscathed, but Terenia also took a chunk of rock, which entered her forearm.

As Terenia cried out Meterove and Dras made it back to the Lich to reengage it. Meterove was furious and Dras was not far off. A lightning quick slash came from the Lich's blind spot, but it managed to avoid the blow from Syr. While she was off balance the Lich attempted to sever her head with a back slice.

More undead had come down from above but rather than swarm them the Avatar used its power to pull apart their bodies and use their parts. There was a hail of bone and flesh and now the Avatar had two extra arms and the bones had been compressed and reshaped into swords.

Joleen dodged a slice from one of those swords noting that they were barely long enough to be called long swords. Terenia had taken the rock out of her arm and healed the injury. She was firing arrows to try and keep the Avatar on the defensive.

A scream of pain echoed across the chamber as the Lich brought one of its blades down onto Dras' prosthetic arm. The impact of the blow had cracked it and arcs of magic were firing out. This caught the Avatar's attention as well. A disgusting smile spread over its face pulling at the stitches in its mouth.

Valaas and Syr tried to pressure the Lich while Meterove helped Dras to his feet. The Lich blocked the attacks and once they were off balance jumped forward towards Meterove and Dras. It clearly looked like he wanted to finish Dras off now.

The Lich slashed down at Meterove, who caught it with his guard. The Lich used its other sword and blasted it flat into Dras' chest, knocking him all the way back to a wall, near the Avatar. The impact made his arm arc far more violently and the Avatar disappeared from where it was and reappeared next to Dras. It grabbed his left arm and pulled.

The arm came free and Dras screamed. It would have felt the same as having his real arm pulled off. The energy arced more, then the Avatar held it close and snapped the arm, causing it to burst entirely. The energy from the arm shot to the restraints on the Avatar's body.

The Avatar moved gently, and the restraints fell away. She pulled the headage off, ripping the spikes through her skull without any cares. She ripped the stiches from her mouth. The feral grin on her face was terrifying.

It went to grab Dras, but he changed places with his sword and just barely managed to dodge her. He then changed back and rolled away. He grabbed a dagger with his right hand and rolled up next to Joleen panting.

There was another scream and Syr was down to one knee with a blade through her stomach. She still did not give in. Syr grabbed the blade that was in her and held it while using the other sword to try and cut the Lich's hand off.

Valaas shouted, "Syr! NO!"

He and Meterove charged in again. The Lich was now able to fight them easily. With a flick he blasted them both back across the cave. They both had intense magic fortifications but even that was not enough. The force of the attacks had been enough that their bodies had left small cracks in the stone.

This is bad. Dras lost his arm, and it looks like whatever those restraints were, have been released.

Syr had been released when she had tried to take the Lich's hand but the wound to her stomach was bad. She might be undead but based on how she was holding herself this was still bad for her.

The Avatar began to laugh. Its arms were raised wide. The skin on its body seemed to writhe like there were countless worms beneath it. The skin began to split, soaking the front of the dress with blood and something reached out of her body. The dress was already tattered before all this and now it shredded and fell away.

The Avatar's body that had so long been in chains was a horrifying pale puss yellow. There was a gaping hole from her chest to her groin where blood and two hands were emerging. Next came a head and two wings, one bone and one of feathers. Stepping out of the Avatar's body like a discarded piece of clothing the Ashen Soul stood.

The Lich began to laugh, "YES! The true Ashen Soul has been reborn!"

His brief lapse in concentration cost him though. Valaas swung his massive sword down and severed the Lich's left arm. His laughter turned to a scream of pain and in his head, he once again heard that voice.

"YoU FAiLeD HeR! YoU MuSt DiE!"

Syr dove in and rammed both of her blades through the gaps in the Lich's armor. He grunted and pulled free and swung his blade around to kill her, but Valaas took the hit for her. He was knocked to the ground his right leg severed.

Dras came sprinting across the room and jumped at the Lich headfirst. The Lich just laughed and swung but its eyes suddenly showed alarm. It had remembered that this man could change places! It was too late as Dras changed into his sword, which buried itself in his side. With a howl of rage the Lich tore it out and cast it aside.

Meterove stepped around the fallen Valaas and drove Oblivion into the Lich and activated it. A flash of light and it was over. For the Lich it felt far longer. All he could think of was how he wished he could hold her once more, though he could not remember who that person was.

There was no time for celebration. The Ashen Soul was barely awakened so it was still vulnerable. Dras had picked up his sword and Valaas had forced himself up by using his sword as a crutch. He had picked up one of the blades that the Lich had dropped in his other hand.

The Ashen Soul whispered, "Die here. Even I could die here. The end here would not be the end. Make you die here."

That burning smell and the Ashen Soul was gone then a second later it was back, with Syr's head in its hands. Valaas looked to his side and saw Syr's body falling to the ground. He looked back as the Ashen Soul crushed her head causing a flash of white light.

Meterove could not believe what he was seeing. Syr had taken wounds sure, but to be killed so easily. This was no normal enemy. "Everyone! Keep it off me!"

Meterove did a large backstep and began gathering magic. While he did this Valaas finally registered his sister's death and became enraged and limped towards the Ashen Soul. The Ashen Soul held its hand out and that wicked halberd that they had seen before materialized.

It swiped at Valaas, but Narok jumped in and took the hit with his shield. He had to change it to a tower shield to tank the hit, but he managed it. The Ashen Soul vanished again but this time it did not catch them unawares. It appeared next to Jolson, but an arrow flew from Terenia which forced it to vanish again.

Valaas was picked up and thrown tumbling across the room. When he came to a rest on his stomach the Ashen Soul appeared and drove his own sword through him down into the stone. The only thing keeping him alive was that he was undead. The Ashen Soul went for a kill but recoiled with shriek. There was a dagger thrown by Dras stuck in its right hand. It pulled the dagger out and threw it back at Dras, but Narok blocked it.

The halberd swung around and ripped through Dras' side. He screamed and collapsed holding the wound. The Ashen Soul picked up Dras' sword from the ground with its right hand. It used the halberd to rip the shield off Narok's arm then used some of the undead pieces to form two large spikes that impaled him in the shoulders.

Joleen screamed, "NAROK! NOOO!"

The Ashen Soul then picked Dras up by the neck and impaled him against the wall through the stomach. It grinned in his face but an arrow striking it in the back took its attention off of him. It looked at Terenia who was already drawing her bow back to fire again.

"Hey bitch! Don't you look away from me!"

The Ashen Soul snapped its head back towards Dras and found his hand crossbow right in its face. There was a click then a howl of pain as Dras launched a bolt directly into the left eye of the Ashen Soul. Another arrow slammed into the Ashen Souls side, and it flailed around and ripped the arrow and bolt out.

Jolson had cut the bone spears holding Narok up and he crashed to the ground and Joleen began healing him. Jolson ran and transformed his scythe into a massive two handed one and took a swipe at the Ashen Soul. A lightning quick slash with the halberd and Jolson was on the ground with a gash across his chest that was down to the bone.

Meterove poured all of the magic that he had channeled into a single enhancement spell. He glowed with white light and when he pushed off the ground a small crater formed around his feet.

He met the Ashen Soul at the same time that it appeared ready to kill Jolson. The blow blasted the Ashen Soul up into the crater, then Meterove jumped after it. The two of them began a midair battle, Meterove using the walls of the crater to leap around.

Down on the ground Joleen had finished healing Narok's injury and had moved onto Dras. While she was healing Dras Terenia was healing Jolson. Narok scooped up his shield and sword then went over to Valaas. There was no getting that sword out of him alone, so he had no choice but to wait. Valaas grunted to him. "Gather Syr's swords, my blade, and the other sword that I was holding. Please."

Narok had been on the verge of saying something but one look at those eyes and he knew. Valaas was in a different kind of pain. He remembered what Valaas and Syr had said what seemed like years ago. Revenants are undead that will live until their goal is achieved. Their father was destroyed. He was not long for this world.

Narok quickly gathered the weapons and when Joleen came over with the others, he shook his head when she gestured to Valaas. At first, she made to check herself but then she too seemed to remember that conversation. Jolson looked at the weapons that Narok was carrying then at the one still in Valaas and then at the other blade on the ground.

He helped Narok get the blade out of Valaas and then went and picked up the other one. At first Valaas looked at it with anger. Soon that turned to sadness, then acceptance. "I left a letter in the study back in the Citadel. It details everything that we had learned about it since the day we first took it. I can honestly say that I am glad to have met you all. Thank you for helping us get our revenge."

The light began to go out from his body. He looked up at the battle above with fading eyes. "I am truly astounded by what you are all capable of. I hope that this ends in your favor. I truly do."

The glow left his body entirely and it almost seemed to shrink slightly. Above the battle continued to rage on. Narok and Dras both limped their way to the crack in the wall. Both Joleen and Terenia had been forced to be sparing with the healing, so they were far from fully healed.

Meterove slammed the Ashen Soul down into the base of crater and fired a huge blast of magic power at it. The impact bored far down into the ground, punching through layer upon layer of stone. There was a huge rumble from the ground then a few dozen cracks opened up in the ground.

Hot air poured out. Dras looked at the others, "This looks bad."

Jolson said, "I think this was an extinct volcano, but their fighting is rerouting the magma underneath us."

Dras said, "Are you telling me that those two are bringing a dead volcano back to life? I hate this place. Even the damn volcano is undead."

The ground rumbled again. Jolson said, "That would apparently seem to be the case. We had better get out of here. We can watch from the entrance."

As they limped over Narok asked, "How long can he keep that up?"

Terenia looked over her shoulder, worry etched on her face. Joleen was the one who answered, "He is probably already nearing his limit. I think he knows he can't win so he is purposely trying to get the volcano active again."

Dras stopped walking and looked up at his friend. The fight did seem to be leaning further and further in favor of the Ashen Soul every second. Drops of blood were raining down and most of it had to be from Meterove.

There was a loud crack and a small shockwave as Meterove was blasted down to the ground nearby. Almost as one Terenia and Joleen sent what little healing magic, they had the energy for over to him. It was enough that he was able to stand back up, but the ground suddenly gave an ominous rumble and he fell to one knee.

Above the Ashen Soul looked alarmed. It had been so focused on fighting Meterove that it had not noticed that the volcano. Meterove looked over at the others and then back at the Ashen Soul, which had begun to move for the summit.

Meterove said, "No you don't!"

Meterove jumped after the Ashen Soul and swung at it with Oblivion. He activated the singularity ability and tried to hit the Ashen Soul, but the Ashen Soul used its halberd to take the hit and kept flying. An arrow flew past and caught the Ashen Soul in the wing.

Down on the ground Terenia was down on one knee panting for breath. This bought Meterove the time he needed to catch up to it and he managed to cut off the right wing. The Ashen Soul screamed and fell, flailing, into the crater.

As it fell past Meterove its remaining wing clipped him under the chin and he was momentarily dazed while he fell. Jolson used what little energy he had left to reinforce his body to caught him as he fell. The volcano gave another large rumble.

Joleen said, "We need to get out of here."

Dras asked, "What about the Ashen Soul? And are we going to leave Valaas and Syr here?"

Jolson looked back at the bodies in the crater. "There is no time. Ideally, they would be brought back and buried where they belong."

Meterove groaned and opened his eyes. "Jolson is right. I don't like it but there is no other choice. We need to go. NOW!"

Joleen led the way back through the crack in the wall. Once they were through and up the cave a few yards the volcano gave another larger rumble and a burst of hot air blasted through the caves. Meterove sent a blast backwards to cause a small cave in.

They hurried through the caves as much as they could in their injured states. They were no longer worried about the undead. They pushed through as fast as they could, but they could not quite get clear when the pyroclastic blast blasted through the caves. Joleen used her amulet to make a Gateway. She was too drained to go far but she was

389

at least able to get them back to the overlook where they had first seen the Avatar and the Lich.

Once they were through Joleen doubled over and vomited before passing out. There they sat and watched as a blast of ash and hot air exploded out of the Maw and a huge cloud of ash and smoke appeared on the other side of the mountains across the Maw.

Meterove sat down on the ground and he, Jolson Dras and Terenia looked over at the rising cloud of ash while Narok moved Joleen over and placed her head on his lap.

Meterove said, "Goodbye Valaas. Goodbye Syr. I hope that you are able to rest now."

Jolson said, "Now that this is over, I think that we should give them back their proper place in history."

Dras said, "Maybe leave out the part about their father being the leader of the Ashen Empire and their mother being the Avatar of the Ashen Soul."

Meterove said, "From the point of view of politics you are probably right. However, there is an important lesson in what happened to their father. Just because we do not like history does not mean that we have the right to revise it."

Narok said, "Not to change the subject but, how long should we stay here? We may not be in the best shape but there is still likely a battle going on in the city. The sooner we get back and move the Citadel the better."

Meterove shook his head to clear it then stood up. Dras said, "Getting back through the city might be rough."

Jolson said, "If we cover ourselves with robes, we will probably be able to blend in with the civilians."

Meterove looked back out over the Maw one last time then turned to the tunnel entrance, "We better hurry. The sooner we are back home the better."

CHAPTER 17
INHERITANCE

It had been a month since the events in the Ashen Empire. When they had emerged from the tunnel to find the palace deserted and the streets were mostly quiet. They had made their way to the Citadel without incident. Once inside they had moved the Citadel back to where they had left the undead army and gathered the troops that had been left there.

The undead had attacked numerous locations and there were heavy casualties all around. It was hard to believe that they had still been able to put up such a fight when their main army had been trapped. Unfortunately, there were still far more undead left across the mountains. However, with no one to lead them, it was unlikely that they would move again any time soon.

The Citadel had been transported back to the location that it had taken during the siege of Yxarion. They had since spent a great deal of time examining and cataloging everything. There had been two letters, one from Valaas and one from Syr. Just as Valaas had said, they had left them everything that they knew about the Citadel as well as a handful of other lost pieces of knowledge. This was their inheritance.

Joleen was torn on what to do with some of the knowledge. On one hand she felt that she was required to share everything with her allies and the people. On the other she wanted to guard them jealously. Official matters had taken up so much of her time that she had not been able to properly process everything that had happened.

The announcement about Valaas and Syr had been met with serious criticism. Many were skeptical about their origins while others had since demanded further explanation. A few had even had the audacity to demand reparations from Joleen, stating that their family was responsible for their actions.

Those few had mostly been from the older families. Meterove had been about to say something when Joleen had stood and walked up to the duke who had stood as the leader of the families that had asked for reparations. She stared him down for a solid thirty seconds then slapped him across the face.

The man, Duke Edleburn staggered backwards then began blustering before Joleen said, "You demand we pay you for your suffering. You and your family, who have grown exorbitantly wealthy over the centuries have no room to talk of your suffering. All you have done is send others to die in your place. Do not think that I missed the fact that there were no members of your house that joined the fight in the Ashen Empire."

Duke Edleburn bristled, "You dare suggest that we have not done our part! We have helped to support this disastrous plan of yours. What have you brought to show for this? You have refused to let anyone that you do not have direct control over anywhere near that strange building."

Joleen was even more enraged, "You "contributed" you say? To a "disaster" you say? You thought that you were going to get something out of this war? I have heard enough. Duke Edleburn, I am tired. Tired of you. Tired of all the bullshit!"

The assembled nobles gasped. This was far from the decorum that they were used to. Duke Edleburn looked around then back at Joleen and smirked. "The new governing system that YOU proposed has placed you in no higher position than me. In fact, I have the power to call you and your family to task! What other crimes are you hiding?"

As soon as the words left his mouth there was a stunned and awkward silence. He had gone further than any of them had expected he would. Many of the nobles were anxiously looking at Meterove, whose hand was on his sword.

Joleen looked at Duke Edleburn, "Enough. Duke Edleburn, you forget your place. You are correct that I am in no higher position than you. You should know, I did not remove a specific law. I will duel you. Should I win, your life will be forfeit and all assets of your house will become mine."

Duke Edleburn looked taken aback. After a moment he smirked, "The little girl thinks that she can defeat a man. I am going to enjoy putting you in your place. Do not worry, I will not take your life. You should make a perfect OBEDIENT wife for my son."

Joleen saw Meterove out of the corner of her eye. The look in his eyes was murderous. Joleen pulled her Artifact and activated it. Duke Edleburn was shocked. The Edleburn family had mostly contributed monetarily. What few soldiers they had offered had been sent to the border or used to protect cities.

Duke Edleburn looked a little less sure of the situation. He still looked smug, clearly sure he would win. He took up his sword, which Joleen was sure was ornamental. His stance showed that he did know what he was doing though.

Meterove sighed and said, "First blood wins. On my mark. Five. Four. Three. Two. One. BEGIN!"

The duke scoffed as he made to do a slash but found nothing but open air. Next, he felt a twinge of pain on his cheek and after touching it, his hand came away red.

There was a gasp from the assembled nobles. Edleburn had lost so quickly, and Joleen had made the victory conditions clear. Realization seemed to take its time catching up to Edleburn but once it did his face paled and he began to protest.

"This is preposterous! She clearly used some sort of magic to cheat! Yes! That has to be it! All of you saw her!"

One at a time the nobles looked away, even his erstwhile allies. It was clear that they had all abandoned him. Joleen wiped the blade of her Artifact off on Edleburn's coat, "Your execution will take place in the morning."

Edleburn screamed, "YOU CANNOT DO THIS! Then as the guards seized him, "Get your hands off me!"

One of the guards punched Edleburn hard in the stomach and he went limp. As they dragged him away, Joleen said, "Back to the matter of Valaas and Syr. They are the origin of the Valaseri family name. I intend to restore their rightful places in our history. Furthermore, I intend to have an addition to the tombs of Mardelnier and Valnyr.

The weapons of all four siblings along with their father will be buried there. Are there any objections to this?"

Silence followed and Joleen left the nobles to their own devices. Meterove and Narok followed her out. Outside the assembly hall Dras and Terenia were waiting. Dras had gotten a new arm that was upgraded with the knowledge that they were able to get from the Citadel's Library.

Terenia was back to her usual risqué clothes with a revealing halter top and short skirt. Jolson was off to the side at a table reading a book. He had declined to join in this session and had been dealing with other matters for her.

No one had heard from the Acephali or the Leturai in months. It would not have been that strange if they had simply not wanted to fight, but to have fully cut off communication was strange. Joleen had given permission to send a full battalion to investigate the Acephali. They had returned stating that an impassible bank of fog was preventing them from entering.

As far as the Leturai were concerned, they had sent another messenger to try and contact them, but they had found the last message still sitting at the post. The main task that he had been doing for her was preparing to mark the anniversary of her ascension to the throne. This would also mark the anniversary of their father's death.

The decision to mark the occasion was difficult. None of them had really had time to grieve. It had been one thing after another. Now that things were quieter Joleen, Jolson and Meterove had each taken to their own means of grieving.

Terenia was staying glued to Meterove and Dras had stayed around the palace as well. He would often spend time with Meterove but had taken to sitting and talking with Jolson some as well. Joleen had Narok to help her, but Jolson had been mostly alone. Jolson's visions had subsided lately, but they still occurred a few times.

When the morning of the anniversary dawned Joleen spent an hour alone with her thoughts. The celebration was bittersweet like she thought that it would be. While there were gifts from nobles and dignitaries, they were careful to keep them subdued.

The original plan for an addition to the tombs of Valnyr and Mardelnier had not seemed enough so after some discussion it had been improved upon. In addition to the tombs Meterove had also been in favor of building a new structure that would house the weapons only. Joleen had commissioned the Dwarves to sculpt statues of the four siblings and their father.

Once completed, their actual weapons had been placed on them. The statues were then placed in a small building that would be built out in front of the palace.

Joleen had discussed it with her brothers, and they had agreed that the building should be in a public place.

The Dwarves speed and skill had absolutely lived up to the hype. The statues looked so realistic that you almost expected them to come to life. Seeing Valaas and Syr again, even if only in statue form had been more emotional than Joleen had anticipated. She still felt guilty about leaving their bodies behind in the volcano.

The dedication had been small and quiet. Only those who had personally known Valaas and Syr were invited. The soldiers that had been part of the initial exploration of the Ashen Empire were also invited. After the official dedication, the six of them spent some time alone looking quietly at the statues.

While they were there a messenger came running up. The boy looked at the ground panting and said, "There is someone at the gate that the guards are screening right now. My father sent me ahead to tell you."

Dras asked, "Why not send an official messenger?"

The boy looked very awkward and said, "My father just said that we needed to alert you as soon as possible. It was a strange looking lady with horns."

Joleen froze and noticed that the others had stiffened. That sounded like a Leturai. She looked at the boy, "Thank you for your haste young man." Then she turned to the others, "We should get to the audience chamber. Dras, could you head down to the gate with this young man and escort this woman directly to me?"

Dras gave her a crisp nod and motioned the boy to lead the way. While they headed off, the rest of them went to the audience chamber. In no time there was a knock on the door and Dras entered with a ragged looking Leturai woman.

Unlike the Leturai that Joleen had met previously this one was far younger with smaller features. Now that Joleen thought about it, this was the first female Leturai that she had ever met. Her age was hard to guess but Joleen assumed that she was no more than sixteen, at least that was how old she looked.

Her face was only slightly longer than a humans and her hair less wispy. The horns on her head were smaller than on the men that she had met over the years. The skin was still that pale greyish blue, and her fingers were longer. She had bright golden eyes and the robe she was wearing was in tatters. She was currently wearing a cloak that the guards had likely given her.

She looked weak and Dras had an arm ready to catch her should she stumble. She wobbled and made a motion to bow but Joleen raised a hand to stop her.

"You look exhausted. Formalities and pleasantries can be set aside for now. Narok, could you bring a chair over so that she can sit?"

Narok brought a chair up and Dras helped the girl sit down. Once she was seated Joleen asked, "Is there anything that you need?"

The Leturai said, "Some water would be welcome."

Her voice was voice was breathy but still with a thick accent. The r's were rolled, the vowels were long and there was a lack of a w in their native language, so she used a v.

Once she had a drunk some water she said, "My name is Inessa Belyaev, and I am the third princess of the Leturai. I am here to beg you for aid!"

Joleen asked, "Aid? What has happened?"

Joleen had been tempted to confront Inessa about the Leturai's silence but seeing her expression had changed her mind. Something was very wrong here.

Inessa's voice was shaking as she said, "Our home has been terrorized by some massive sea beast. For months now we have been trying desperately to respond to every knew attack. We have lost tens of thousands to this beast. Any attempts to escape to the surface have failed with deadly consequences."

Joleen said, "This news troubles me. I feared that there was something wrong when we had not heard from you, but I did not expect this."

Meterove asked, "What kind of beast is this?"

Inessa said, "It is unclear what kind, but we suspect something that normally lives in the deepest parts of the ocean. It has massive tentacles, similar to that of a squid."

Jolson said, "A Kraken."

Inessa said, "Yes, that is our assumption."

Meterove said, "I had heard that Krakens lived in the very deepest parts of the oceans. What would one be doing so close to your people? Unless I am mistaken your people live under the shallower waters specifically for that reason."

Inessa said, "That is mostly true. We do have some cities in deeper water, but this beast is attacking all of our cities, sometimes simultaneously."

Jolson said, "You mean there are more than one attacking?"

Inessa shook her head, "No. The tentacles are all the same size and pattern. A single tentacle was large enough to seize and destroy one of our battleships."

Meterove stared, Jolson began muttering to himself, likely trying to calculate the size and Joleen sighed and asked, "What aid were you looking for?"

Inessa said, "I do not know. I was able to escape but it cost so many lives. There were two dozen ships that left with me. The lifeboat that I used to escape the ship I was on is the only craft that made it."

Joleen said, "Will you allow me to discuss this with my advisors for a short time? We have only recently returned from the frontlines of our war with the undead. We can accommodate you in a sitting room."

Inessa bowed her head, "I will accept your offer, but I beg you to hurry with your decision. I must find aid if not here then somewhere else."

Inessa stood and Narok walked her out of the audience chamber. A few minutes later he returned, and Joleen said, "Now that Narok is back I would like to hear everyone's thoughts."

Meterove said, "I am all for helping them, provided that the risk to our people is not too high. We risked and lost much in the war with the Ashen Empire so far, and we have still not really recovered ourselves."

Jolson said, "The size of this alleged Kraken is beyond imagination. I have read some accounts of Krakens before, but their size is nothing like what she described."

Dras asked, "Do you think that she is making this story up or perhaps hiding something?"

Jolson said, "I cannot say for sure, but I feel like what she was telling us was the truth. Just because no one has ever seen a Kraken this size does not mean it does not exist. One thing that I do know for certain is that they never do stop growing."

Terenia said, "I'm lost. How big is this Kraken thing supposed to be then?"

Jolson said, "Given the size of the ship princess Inessa described being destroyed by one tentacle I would estimate that this thing would have to be the same size as the Dragon Lord."

Terenia's eyes widened and Narok, who had been about to say something else stopped and said, "We had no idea he existed until recently. I am not saying that I necessarily believe her story but if one giant creature can be hidden from us then why not more?"

Joleen said, "That is a valid point. However, the question is how would we help? It sounds like the Leturai struggled just to get Inessa here to ask for aid."

Meterove said, "That is exactly what I was thinking. I am not opposed to helping, but how do we get them aid? We would have to send ships out to them. Assuming that they are not sunk by this beast, how do we get down to help?"

Dras said, "We could ask Inessa."

Everyone looked at Dras and he shrugged and continued, "She looked worried and saddened but not defeated. She plans to go ask others for aid if we will not help. To me that says that she has some sort of plan."

Joleen said, "That is a good point. Are we agreed then that aid can be given so long as the risk is relatively small?"

Everyone agreed and Joleen said, "Narok, could you go get her please?"

Narok left and returned shortly with Inessa. She looked a little apprehensive. Joleen asked, "Before I give my answer, I would like to ask a few further questions."

Inessa nodded, "Of course I will answer them to the best of my ability."

Joleen said, "I am aware that you cannot guarantee the safety of any of the personal I would send from this "beast" but what about from your own people? It has long been established that outsiders are not welcome in your territory. Does your presence indicate that this is an official request for aid from your government?"

Inessa said, "Yes it does. My eldest brother, Malkom, is now sitting on the throne. My father was killed by the beast in one of the first attacks."

Joleen noticed the pain in the girls voice, "I offer both my official and personal condolences for the loss of your father." Joleen's eyes softened, "I know well the pain you must be feeling."

Inessa nodded, "Thank you. I also extend my belated condolences to you for your loss."

Joleen gave a sad smile and said, "Thank you. Now my second question is how were you planning to return with aid?"

Inessa reached inside her tattered robes and pulled out a small gold pendant with a large pearl set into it. "The pearl in this pendant is called a Recall Pearl. You activate it twice, once to mark the location and the second to return to it. After the second time the pearl breaks."

Jolson said, "I have never heard of these before."

Inessa said, "They are very rarely found from really old Trench Oysters. To my knowledge we only have two others in our possession."

Meterove said, "I can see why you would keep those secret then. If they are that rare it is a good way to protect the royal family."

Dras asked, "How many people can that transport?"

Inessa said, "I can move as many people as can be directly in contact with my body at the time of activation. I know that would not be much, but we are desperate. Can you help us?"

Dras looked at Meterove with a smirk and Meterove could not help grinning himself. Joleen saw them and also smiled herself. The timing of this was fortuitous. Had this happened before they had the Citadel of Time things would have been vastly different.

Joleen said, "It just so happens that we have something called a Gateway, that when used in tandem with your Recall Pearl will allow us to give aid and even evacuate your people."

Inessa gasped and teared up, "You mean...?"

Joleen said, "Yes. We will come to your aid. I will send my brothers and a handful of soldiers ahead with you to establish a safe location to set up the Gateway. Once we have that up and running, we will begin operations immediately. While they prepare, I will have some clothes brought for you."

Terenia left to handle the clothing arrangements and Meterove, Jolson, and Dras prepared to depart. Narok sent another guard with a message to get a platoon of soldiers to come to the audience chamber in full gear and packs.

In less than an hour everyone was back in the audience chamber and Inessa was changed into some new clothing. The human clothes looked strange on her, but they would at least keep the poor girl covered. She seemed to have developed a bit of an attachment to Dras.

Joleen could not help but feel a sense of camaraderie with the girl. Dras had this presence about him that seemed to draw women to him in one of two ways. Either they wanted his body or, like Inessa and herself, they felt like they had found a brother.

In the year that she had known him Dras had settled in as another member of the family. In some ways he was even closer to them than Narok, who had known them far longer. Joleen could only assume that it had to do with his personality.

The soldiers were cramped but still able to squeeze in and once everyone was touching her Inessa activated the pearl. Their bodies slowly became transparent and after about thirty seconds they were gone. Joleen sat down on the throne and said to Narok who was next to her, "I hope they hurry back."

Narok smiled and said, "You just want to join them."

Joleen side eyed him then broke out in a giggle, "You may be right. For now, we just need to have to trust them to have the Gateway up and running at the appointed time. Is the area in front of the Citadel prepared for the Gateway?"

Narok nodded, "Yes, I have a large unit of medics and two dozen mages with skill in healing ready to go. The wall was retracted to give us more room and a supply train is set up."

Joleen said, "I just wish that there was more that we could do right now."

Narok placed his hand on her shoulder, "Every member of that platoon that I sent are not only good soldiers but expert field medics."

Joleen looked wistfully at the spot that they had vanished from, then placed her hand over his and gave it a slight squeeze.

You idiots had better not get yourselves into any trouble while you are there. At least wait until I can find a way to join you first.

Joleen distinctly heard Narok mutter, "You four had better wait for us before getting into anything too dangerous."

She could not help but smile, "I think those two are rubbing off on us."

CHAPTER 17.5
CONNECTIONS

Just when things were starting to get under control, this had to happen. What had been one was now so many. There were dozens of worlds infected. Meterove and the others were going to find out soon enough just what they were getting into.

There were clues that they needed to find to get the real answers though. Finding someone to guide them along to get where they needed to go would be difficult as well.

There were a few that would be ideal to arrange a meeting with. Meterove had already been in contact with one of them. As for the other one, well that meeting was only going to happen if they could reach her.

A vision would only go so far. Given the scope of the problem they would need further guidance. It was still *too soon for them to meet face to face. The best course of action would be to arrange for them to go back to Nexus. Flare would be ideal for the task.*

.   .   .

Floating above the endless water was the massive bird cloaked in black fire. Feathers would fall on occasion and where they landed water, along with any sea life that happened to be near, ceased to exist. Far below the massive beast began another assault.

The Darkfire one continued to flap its wings and stayed for a while longer. It would be interesting to see what would happen now. Its power had been growing for some time now. It had been a near thing when it had first found itself able to have a sense of self.

It had been so sudden. First there had been the sense of self and then the realization that it had a purpose. It had a singular desire now. It needed to assist the Ashen Soul in its endeavors.

The former selves were a problem though. There was nothing that could be done about them for now. Soon enough though that would change. It was time to move now. There were other places and matters that needed its attention.

411

CHAPTER 18

KORLOVOK

The first thing that Meterove noticed after the audience chamber vanished was the smell of salt water. The next thing that he noticed was that he heard the sound of waves. When his vision caught up with him, he could only look around in awe.

The city around him was unlike any other that he had ever seen. The buildings were all made of stone, with the primary colors being earthy. To contrast that the rooves were all brightly colored and in many cases were domed, some of which were bulbous and rose to a point.

There were many narrow windows on the buildings and the tops of them had domed arches. There were lots of columns with more domed arches over them. There were large courtyards with large elaborate fountains in the middle of them. Many of the fountains had multiple statutes around them. Most of them were made of simple stone but here and there statues with gold leaf pressed into them could be seen. All of this was enclosed in a massive dome.

All of this would have been breathtakingly beautiful if much of it had not been in ruins. They were standing on the top of some stairs overlooking the city. There was water just a few feet down the stairs. It looked like much of the city was flooded.

Inessa looked around sadly at the city. Her shoulders slumped and she said, "I wish you could see our capital as it used to be." She shook her head slightly then said, "You had said you needed to find a safe place to set up this Gateway, correct? This is one of our courthouses, though it has been turned into a shelter for those whose homes have been destroyed in the city."

Meterove said, "Lead the way."

Inessa opened the door and the rest followed after her. Inside there were hundreds of Leturai. It was a mark of how despondent they had been left by events that they barely even registered them.

Meterove said, "Lieutenant, please get your men to work here."

The woman in question gave quick orders to the others and they began to disperse around the room. While this was going on Meterove pulled a small pocket watch out and checked the time. It had originally been a fun souvenir that he had brought back from Nexus, but it had turned out to be extremely useful when it came to making Gateways. He put the watch away and said, "We have an hour yet before we can make the Gateway."

Inessa said, "I can bring you to the person in charge of this shelter while we wait. Judge Holkoff is a distant cousin of mine."

Jolson said, "That would be for the best."

Inessa led them deeper into the courthouse. Dras noted as they went that the Leturai were big fans of having their roof supports visible across their ceilings. Large squares were made where there were various materials set into the square, though gold leaf seemed to be the preferred medium.

Inside what looked like a courtroom everything had been hastily pushed to the sides of the room to make something of a command room. There were four Leturai around a table looking at papers and a few dozen guards around the room. Everyone looked up at their entrance.

Three of the Leturai wore black and navy-blue uniforms, with three silver buttons on the chest. One of the Leturai wore ornate robes and smiled and rushed to greet Inessa. This had to be the Judge that Inessa has spoken of.

His voice was deep but there were clear tones of joy as he said, "Inessa! You made it then! The fact that you returned means that you accomplished your mission too!"

Inessa said, "Yes Lord Holkoff, I was able to reach Yxarion, though the cost was the life of everyone else that went with me. They have promised aid. Allow me to introduce the First prince, Jolson Valaseri and the Second prince Meterove Valaseri."

Inessa stepped to the side while Jolson and Meterove stepped in to give their greetings. Jolson took the lead, "Greetings Lord Holkoff. My brother and I are here as official envoys as well as direct aid to your people."

Judge Holkoff shook Jolson's hand first then Meterove's and then said, "I do not mean to sound ungrateful but are you all that came to our aid?"

Jolson shook his head, "No we are not. We have an entire platoon of medics that we brought with us that are currently treating the refugees in this building. We have an item that will establish a connection with Yxarion. Once we have that up and running you will be able to move your people directly to Yxarion where a refugee camp is ready to receive them. We will continue to aid in rescuing your people by sending soldiers in through the Gateway."

Judge Holkoff looked relieved, "I cannot thank you enough. I will contact who I can from here and have word relayed across the city."

Judge Holkoff looked at Inessa and said, "His majesty is still at the palace. If you could go, there personally after this Gateway of yours is set up that would be for the best."

Meterove checked his watch again, "We still have awhile before we can make the Gateway, but I suppose I should ask what the safest place to use is going to be. We do not want refugees flooding your command room."

Judge Holkoff asked, "How big of a space do you need?"

Meterove said, "If you have another room about this size that can be cleared that would be perfect."

Judge Holkoff said, "There are several more courtrooms that are currently packed with refugees but if you are going to be getting them somewhere safe then moving them together for a short time will not be a problem."

He motioned for one of the guards who stepped forward, "This is Sergeant Miilkov. He can take you to one of the rooms and help move the refuges to another location."

Meterove nodded and said to Dras and Terenia, "I want you two to keep an eye out for this Kraken. I have no desire to be caught off guard by this thing."

Dras rolled his eyes and said, "You don't say." He then grinned and returned from where they came from. Terenia gave Meterove's hand a quick squeeze then followed Dras out.

Meterove and Sergeant Miilkov went over to the other courtroom and began to clear it. Once it was the appointed time, he activated the crystal and the Gateway formed. Sergeant Miilkov was shocked. "I had no idea that humans had something like this."

Meterove said, "It was lost knowledge to us until just recently."

After that Meterove stepped through the Gateway and began giving directions to the soldiers in charge of the camp. After that he stepped back through to see that Judge Holkoff had joined Miilkov. He too looked astounded. He said, "Truly a marvel. When can I begin sending my people through?"

Meterove gestured to the gate, "You can begin immediately. We already have a sizable camp set up."

Holkoff turned to Miilkov and said, "Begin sending the people through. I want a handful of our soldiers to go with to help them feel at ease, but I want the bulk to stay and look for more survivors."

Miilkov gave a salute and said, "Sir!" He quickly left the room. Once he was on his way, Holkoff said, "Princess Inessa, I think that you should escort Prince Jolson and

Prince Meterove to the palace to see his majesty. He will have a more comprehensive list of shelters."

Inessa nodded, "Yes, I agree. Now that we have a means of getting our people to safety we need to save as many as we can. Come, I will lead the way."

On the way out Meterove stopped and gave the platoon orders to assist in moving the refugees, then to search the city for more survivors. Once outside they picked up Dras and Terenia and Inessa led them through the flooded streets.

As the waded through the streets Dras said, "Something bothers me. You said that there were lots of casualties. I have not seen any bodies."

Inessa said, "Now that you mention it, you are correct. I know that many of the victims were wrapped up in the tentacles and taken away but so many more were killed by the falling debris from the buildings."

Terenia asked, "Is it not possible that they have been taken away by your people for whatever burial rights you practice?"

Inessa said with a heavy voice, "At the time that I had left to try and reach the surface we had made the decision to leave the dead and focus on saving the living."

They turned the corner and at the end of the street was the largest square that they had seen yet. Six fountains were evenly spaced throughout it and on the opposite end was the palace. Like the rest of the city, it was primarily a brown color and had a number of domes on the roof. They were bulbous and brightly colored. There was also a large number of gaudy decorations.

The sight might have been majestic but there was no ignoring the destruction around them. Halfway up the stairs there was a landing that had a handful of soldiers getting ready to head out.

When they spotted their group at first, they were cautious since it was clear that most of them were not Leturai. Once they saw Inessa their faces changed to one of relief. Once they were up the stairs the soldiers bowed to Inessa. One of them said, "Your highness! You have returned!"

Inessa said, "Yes, I have, and I have brought help. I must see my brother immediately."

The soldier gestured to the palace. "His majesty is inside the palace. He is currently using the majority of the palace as a shelter. We have found over a thousand more survivors since you left."

Inessa looked relieved, "I had not hoped for so many. I assume that you are going out to look for more survivors?"

The soldier said, "Yes, your highness."

Inessa said, "Then take them over to the courthouse where Lord Holkoff is. We have established a path out of the city to a safe location."

The soldier looked slightly confused but refrained from asking any questions. Instead, he saluted and said, "As you say, your highness."

Inessa led them up to the large double doors and two of the guards that were up there looked equally cheered to see her and opened the doors for them. Jolson was impressed with the level of detail that was carved into the doors.

Inside there were ornate rugs and the ceiling was of the same style as the courthouse but even more ornate. There were hundreds of Leturai in the entry chamber, huddled around dozens of braziers that had clearly been set up in a hurry. The same look of defeat pervaded the room and none of the Leturai even looked up.

Inessa resisted the urge to look around and instead led them up the stairs and through several halls. It was clear based on the number of items on the floor that any wooden furniture had been taken to be burned.

The room that Inessa took them to did not have a door, it had clearly been taken for fuel. The weary looking man that was inside sitting simple table had to be the king, though he was wearing a soldiers unform, he also had a crown on his head.

When he saw Inessa, his face lit up. "Inessa! You survived!"

He rushed over and embraced her. Now that he was closer it was easy to see a resemblance. The king looked to be only a handful of years older than Inessa herself.

The king released Inessa and said, "It appears that you succeeded in getting help as well."

He patted her on the head then turned to the others. "My apologies. I am Radomir and I am the current king of the Leturai. I have not met either of you before, though I can see your father in your faces. I was saddened to hear of his death. He was a kind man and the reason that I chose to trust your people. I will miss Aphen's wisdom."

Jolson said, "We thank you for your words. We have come to not only help while we are here but to offer refuge to your people. We have set up a method of transport at the courthouse of Lord Holkoff that will take your people directly back to Yxarion."

Radomir's eyes widened, "Inessa is this true?!"

Inessa said, "Yes, it is true. I have seen it with my own eyes. Some of our people are already there at a refugee camp."

Meterove said, "Once we have the courthouse emptied, we will send in a legion of our soldiers to help with rescue efforts. Do you have any other means to reach the other cities?"

Radomir shook his head, "Unfortunately we do not. I fear for my people that are in the other cities. This beast has been attacking us is relentless."

Dras asked, "I have already asked Inessa, but can you tell me why it is that I have not seen any sign of the dead?"

Radomir did the smallest of double takes at Dras using Inessa's name so casually before saying, "Unfortunately the beast takes as many of the dead off with it as it can. Those that are not often vanish anyway. We have no idea what happens to them."

Terenia said, "I do not like the sound of that. This feels far too familiar."

Radomir asked, "What do you mean by that?"

Jolson said, "While you were trapped down here with this beast, a war against the undead forces began. While the leaders of the undead have been defeated, the majority of the nation, called the Ashen Empire, still exists. It is possible that they are using the Kraken attack to bolster their numbers."

Radomir growled under his breath, "I do not like the idea that my people are being killed but to even think that they may also be getting defiled after death fills me with rage."

Inessa said, "Brother. We need to give the orders to send ships to other cities. I do not like the idea that we will lose more of our people, but we must find out if there is anyone left out there to save."

Radomir shook his head, "Yes, you are right. I will also begin sending our people to the courthouse to evacuate. I must work on saving our people first. I can feel my rage and suffering later."

Radomir called, "Renat!"

A Leturai man about the same age as Radomir stepped in from the hall wearing the same uniform. "Your majesty!?"

Radomir said, "Give the order to begin evacuation to the courthouse."

Renat bowed, "Sire!"

Once he had gone Dras looked at Meterove and said, "I have a question that I have been meaning to ask you. I have heard your father referred to by several different names now. Why is that?"

Meterove cocked his head, "What do you mean?"

Dras said, "I have heard you call him Aphen as well as Corvine."

Meterove looked at Jolson before saying, "I am positive that no one has ever referred to our father by name Corvine."

Dras looked from Meterove to Jolson then back, "I heard you specifically say that when we first met Yuromea. Both of you referred to him as Corvine. I feel like both are right, but that does not make any sense."

Jolson said, "There is something strange about this. As a citizen of Yxarion, you would have been well acquainted with all the names of our family. You remembering another name goes beyond the normal lapse in memory. We should look into this, but it can wait."

Meterove said, "Anyway we should focus on how to help. You had mentioned contacting the other cities, how would you go about that?"

Radomir said, "The only method that we have would be to send some of our smaller ships out and hope that they can make it to the cities. Would you be able to make more of these paths of yours?"

Jolson said, "Yes but not easily. It requires near perfect timing."

Meterove said, "We might be able to make something work but first we need to focus on getting some of those ship ready to launch."

Radomir sighed, "I have some sailors here in the palace, but I am not sure how many of the ships are still seaworthy or how many of the sailors will be willing to risk their lives."

Dras said, "We will only know once we try. For now, it is our best plan."

.   .   .

Outside the Citadel of Time Joleen was overseeing the flood of Leturai that had begun to come through the Gateway. There were so many of them but considering the amount of space in the barracks they could easily house them if they needed to. The soldiers that Joleen had originally stationed in the barracks had been moved back into the city.

The Leturai were mostly civilians but there were also some soldiers. Joleen had mounds of dry clothing brought over to the camp and hot food was being produced as fast as possible from cook fires.

There were dozens of mages, herself included healing the worst of the injured, while medics and doctors that had been conscripted tended to those with minor injuries.

The scope of the project was immense, and Joleen was worried now that they were going to get overwhelmed. Meterove had stepped through the Gateway just after forming it to pass on some information then went right back through.   Based on his report and the state and number of refugees things were really bad on other side.

Narok was by her side for the most part. He would assist with refugees now and then but mostly he stayed and acted as her guard. Right now, Joleen was healing a group of children. She had learned from one of the adult Leturai that had been with them that their parents were all dead or missing.

How terrible to lose your parents at such a young age. Not only that but their homes are destroyed, and they are sitting huddled in a strange place surrounded by a completely foreign people.

Joleen finished healing the young girl that she had been treating and moved to the next. This one was younger still, perhaps only four. Joleen steeled herself and kept herself focused. If she let her emotions take control, then she would not be able to help everyone that she could.

Once she was done with the last child, she asked Narok, "How many Leturai are currently in the camp?"

Narok had gotten the hourly report while she had been focused working on the children. He pulled the report out and handed it over to Joleen. She unfurled the report and the numbers that she read gave her mixed emotions.

She was truly happy that she was able to save so many lives and to give comfort to them. However, the number of survivors that were coming through was far fewer than she had been ready for. She could only imagine how bad things were if these were all that had been able to evacuate.

Joleen looked over at the Gateway, which was currently being used to transport another battalion of soldiers through to help search for survivors. She had been reluctant to risk so many soldiers but seeing so few survivors had made her heart ache.

Please tell me that most of the people are just too scared to come out of hiding.

.   .   .

Jolson was issuing orders to each new group of soldiers that emerged from the Gateway. He was assisting Radomir and Holkoff with coordinating rescue efforts. Meanwhile Meterove, Dras and Terenia had taken Inessa, a group of Leturai soldiers and a company of human soldiers down to the docks.

It was a remarkable sight for sure. The docks appeared to be made of a similar material to what the undead had used for some of their construction. Inessa called it concrete. They then used some other material that Meterove assumed came from the ocean to act as a guard along the edges of the pier to protect the ships.

The Leturai boats were of a strange design. They were all metal and were totally enclosed with a small door on the top. The water in the harbor was interesting as well. It was almost entirely calm.

Just when Meterove was wondering how they kept the water out, Inessa said, "The barriers that we use keeps the water back while letting the oxygen from the water to enter the barrier. Down here the barrier is weaker to allow our ships to pass through and out into the ocean."

While the Leturai were getting onto the ships there was the sound of breaking glass above them. Meterove looked up to see an impossibly large tentacle pummeling the top of the dome. Then a few more appeared, from nowhere. Beside him Dras said, "I may have just shit myself."

Meterove was not sure what he was going to be able to do about that tentacle. That thing was far larger than he had believed it would be. While he was contemplating that, it punched its way through the barrier raining water down on the city.

Terenia yelled, "ITS NOT ALONE!"

This shout broke Meterove out of his reverie. He quickly took stock of their surroundings but did not see anything else that looked like a threat. After a moment he realized that he was overlooking them because they were so much smaller than the tentacles.

CHAPTER 19
KRAKEN

Looking out into the water there were thousands of smaller shapes swimming out of the darkness. The tentacles ravaged the city, destroying buildings and occasionally pulling a Leturai up and out of the barrier. Each time that a tentacle entered or exited the barrier there was a downpour of water.

Down in the harbor the smaller shapes had begun to emerge from the water. Unfortunately, their fears were confirmed, and the smaller figures were undead. If that had been the worst of it, then Meterove would not have minded as much.

There were also numerous creatures that Meterove had never seen before. Their bottom half looked like a fish, but their top half was humanoid. Their faces were truly terrifying. They had extremely long pointed teeth that stuck out of their mouth and sections of their bodies appeared to be giving off a slight glow.

Their bodies were mostly covered in scales but what was not was a deep blue-gray color. Their hair was a ragged and dirty white. The eyes were twice the size of a humans. They had large crescent shaped ears and frilled gills on their faces.

The all appeared to be wielding spears. There were far too many to fight head on, so Meterove and the others took a defensive position. It was strange, even though the undead had clearly seen them they had not attacked. The tentacle continued to feel around the city smashing buildings and grabbing the occasional person.

Meterove said, "This is odd. Why are they not attacking us?"

Dras said, "I know they saw us. One of those weird fish people looked right at me."

Terenia said, "I do not think they are here to attack. I think this is a raid on the dead."

Dras said, "You mean they are just here to harvest the dead?"

Terenia said, "I think so, though I doubt they would object to killing any easy targets they find."

Meterove asked, "What are those other ones? The weird fish people?"

Terenia said, "I have no idea. I have never heard of anything even remotely like them. Inessa, do you know what they are?"

Inessa shook her head, "I have never seen or heard of any creature like those."

Meterove said, "I am do not like any of this. We have no idea what is going on. Those tentacles are far larger than we feared, and they almost look like they are appearing out of nowhere. Our best bet is going to be to fortify the courthouse as best we can and to take cover while those tentacles are here."

Inessa began to weep, "I know that you are right. My heart just breaks knowing that there is nothing that we can do to stop this."

Just then one of the tentacles crashes down near them. Now that he saw it up close it looked horribly familiar. That was tainted with undeath as well. Meterove had not wanted to think about the possibility but there was no question now. The undead were not using the Kraken, the Kraken was one of them. The tentacle made to grab at them.

Meterove unsheathed Oblivion.

I guess I need to try and fight this thing. I have no idea how big of an area the singularity effect will cover but I guess I am going to find out.

As the tentacle crashed towards them it seemed to notice their presence somehow and suddenly it was moving far quicker. Soon there were several around them moving so fast it was hard to track them. Several of the soldiers that Meterove had brought with them were scooped up, screaming as they found themselves pierced by the massive chitinous teeth inside the suckers.

Meterove jumped forward and used Oblivion to cut one of the tentacles. The blade sank all the way to the hilt but given the size of the tentacle it was barely anything at all. The singularity effect however did far more damage. The flesh of the tentacle was ripped apart and pulled to the cut.

The end result was a spherical area of the tentacle with a radius of fifteen feet cut out of the tentacle. This completely severed the section of the tentacle after the cut. Fifty feet of tentacle was currently thrashing around on the square outside the harbor.

The remainder of the tentacle pulled back and the others began smashing the area up, no longer trying to grab anything.

Dras pushed Inessa back, "Now you pissed it off!"

"Did you have a better idea?" Meterove retorted.

Dras said, "Yeah! Run!?"

Ignoring Dras' sarcasm, Terenia shouted, "Those undead are heading this way. That Kraken seems to be regenerating that tentacle too."

Meterove looked up and sure enough, that tentacle looked to be growing back. Even if it was not instantaneously that fact that the regrowth could be seen was frightening.

Meterove shouted, "Fall back! Draw attention onto us!"

Dras fired a bolt at one of the weird fish people and Terenia fired an arrow at another of the tentacles. Several of the soldiers with them had short bows and worked to pick off what undead they could from a distance.

It worked better than Meterove had wanted though. He had expected that if they could draw the undead that weren't Leturai away from the water they would be helpless but as the fish people moved up something inexplicable happened. Their fins slowly split and then changed into legs.

These creatures hissed angrily then charged forward. Once most of them were out of the water Meterove fired a few blasts of magic at the tentacles to keep their attention on them. The ships must have been watching and took this as the signal to depart. They sank down under the barrier and moved out.

Some of the tentacles looked as though they were going to pull out of the city and attack the ships. Meterove sent as large of a volley as he could muster up at them and they returned their attention to them with renewed rage.

Dras looked at Inessa and the few Leturai soldiers that had stayed with them and said, "You need to get out of here. We can handle these things here, but this is no place for noncombatants."

Inessa looked like she wanted to argue but sighed and agreed, "Very well. I will leave here with my people but leaving without doing anything to help is unacceptable."

She pointed over to some large tanks that were by the docks, "Those tanks hold the fuel that we use to power our ships. It is extremely volatile when ignited."

Dras grinned, "You want us to start those tentacles on fire?"

Inessa said, "Yes that is exactly what I am saying. We have had few encounters with Krakens but one thing that we have found is that burning them has better results than anything else. We used boiling water but this should work better."

Meterove mirrored Dras' grin, "Sounds like a good plan to me. Dras and Terenia, I want you two to head down there and find a way to get that fuel onto its tentacles."

Inessa said, "I wish you luck. Please stay safe my friends."

The Leturai soldiers escorted Inessa away while the human soldiers held back the waves of undead. Since most of these undead were unarmed, it was really just a battle of endurance. The few fish people that did make their way up to them seemed reluctant to expose themselves.

Their biggest threat was the tentacles. Dras and Terenia had gone down and around the back. It would take them a few minutes before they would be able to reach the square again.

.   .   .

Dras and Terenia were staying low hiding behind various crates and retaining walls. The undead continued to pour out of the water and up to where Meterove was.

Dras looked out over the top of the wall they were currently crouched behind and saw their destination across the harbor. It must have been a good couple hundred yards to their target. He had no doubt that they would be able to reach it if they ran but they would be seen and they had no idea how they were going to accomplish their mission.

Dras sighed, "I wish we had that camouflage device from then citadel."

Terenia said, "Well, we don't. We had better start thinking up a way to get across this."

Dras looked around the pier and noticed that there was a small drainage ditch along the length of it. "Hey Terenia, do you think we would be able to over ourselves with some of these cargo bags and move slowly down that drainage ditch?"

Terenia looked at the ditch, "Can and want to are two very different things."

Dras shrugged, "I know that it is not going to smell great, but it should be easier to move across this gap below their field of vision."

Terenia sighed in exasperation, "Fine. You are going first though."

Dras rolled his eyes. He dug through a nearby cart and emptied out a few bags of most of their contents then stuffed them with more bags, then secured them to his body. Once he crawled down into the ditch and crouched down, he really did look like a floating pile of trash.

Terenia was true to her word and followed suit, though not without grumbling about the smell. It took them the better part of an hour to make their way through the ditch over to the fuel.

Twice along the way they had been forced to stop and wait with bated breath when they had been scrutinized more thoroughly. Once they were able to get out of the ditch the first thing that they found was an open door that they ducked into. Much to their relief there were no undead in here.

Dras muttered, "I do not know what Meterove expects us to do. I have no idea how any of this works."

Terenia said, "We have to try and figure something out. They are depending on us."

Dras looked around the room and saw a strange wheel with a long hose connected nearby. Dras tried turning the wheel and after a moment a strange liquid came out of the hose that had a very pungent odor. He quickly turned the wheel and the liquid stopped coming out.

Terenia said, "I think that this must be the fuel that Inessa talked about."

Dras said, "I think you are correct. Also, I barely turned that wheel, and that stuff came pouring out. If I had to take a guess that nozzle on the end is supposed to lock into place during the fueling process. That hose is really long too. I think it is meant to directly fuel some of the ships. If we can get the tentacles over here, we can hose them down then Meterove can roast them."

Terenia asked, "How are you going to aim it?"

Dras looked around the room that they were in and found something that looked vaguely familiar. He pushed a large wide jawed contraption that was on wheels out of a corner.

Panting he said, "This thing should be heavy enough, especially if we chock the wheels."

Terenia raised her eyebrow at it, "And exactly what is that?"

Dras said, "I have no idea what it actually is, or what it is for, but it looks similar to a clamp. I can use this to lock the hose in position then I can aim by rolling it."

Terenia said, "You know that we are going to need to get those tentacles really close for this to work."

Dras grunted as he connected the hose to the clamp, "Yes, I know that. Other than trying to draw it over here and then blowing the whole facility I have no idea how we are going to pull this off."

Terenia looked at the tanks around them, "How big of an explosion would that be?"

Dras shrugged, "No idea. I am willing to bet that we would get burned to a crisp trying it though."

Terenia said, "I guess there is no other option than to try your idea. How do you plan to get the tentacles in range?"

Dras looked at her and smiled, "I think a few projectiles will do the trick."

Terenia looked out of the door at the tentacles thrashing. Hitting them at this range was not out of the question.

Terenia sighed and prepared Grace to fire an arrow. She stepped outside and took cover while Dras wheeled the hose outside. He aimed it in the general direction of the tentacles then went back inside to turn the valve once Terenia had lured them over.

Outside Terenia stood up just far enough to have a clear shot and released the arrow. The first one missed but the second and third shots hit tentacles. The undead noticed where the shots were coming from, and they likely told the Kraken.

Soon enough there were three tentacles crashing around them. Dras turned the wheel as far as he could and soon a spray of fuel blasted out of the hose. Dras ran out and aimed the spray at the tentacles. For good measure he also sprayed some of the undead. The reach of the spray was truly impressive. True they were near the edge of the dome where the top was closer, but the spray still went halfway to the barrier.

The tentacles were well and truly soaked. Once all three were covered, a ball of fire flew at each of them. Apparently, the fumes from the fuel were also flammable. There was a massive flare and suddenly everywhere that the fuel had been sprayed was aflame.

Undead were flailing around screaming while burning to ash. Whatever that stuff was, it clearly burned really hot. The flames were burning blue, and the tentacles were flailing around but they could not put out the flames. Even submerging themselves in the water did not help since the surface was full of burning fuel and they would just reignite.

Meanwhile Dras was continuing to spray the tentacles with more fuel. While this was playing out the undead had started towards them and Terenia had begun picking them off using Grace. With no defense against the torrent of flames the tentacles withdrew and a massive roar could be heard in the distance.

The undead ceased entering the city and the ones that were already in began to retreat. Dras shut off the valve and the spray died off. Luckily, there was little in the city that could burn so the fire did not spread far and soon burnt itself out, though there was a massive cloud of smoke that had filled a portion of the dome.

Dras looked at Terenia, "I would say that is a mission accomplished. I think it is time to get back to Meterove."

Terenia said, "I could not agree more. I do not want to be anywhere near here if those tentacles decide to come back. I am pretty sure we really pissed that Kraken off."

Getting back to Meterove was going to be a trick. It took Dras and Terenia twice as long to get back as it took to sneak their way over. Once they were back, Meterove said, "I did not expect it to go quite like that but whatever works I guess."

Dras asked, "You heard that roar, right? Do you think that it is retreating for now?"

Meterove nodded, "It looks that way. I think that we should head back to the palace and discuss what to do with the king."

Dras looked back at the water and noticed something odd in the water. ""What is that?""

Meterove looked down at the water too and spotted the thing that had caught Dras' attention. It was an extremely ugly fish. Dras hopped down before Meterove could stop him and wadded slightly into the water and grabbed the clearly dead fish.

It was about half his size, so he had to struggle to carry it back. Once he was back and plopped the thing on the ground Meterove got a better look at it. It had several characteristics in common with those fish people that had been here.

It had large silvery eyes and huge fangs that jutted out of its mouth. There was a strange appendage that hung near its head with a small glowing ball on the end. Dras looked at Meterove, "I think that we need to show this to the Leturai ."

442

Meterove said, "I agree. There is something off about that thing. Speaking of off, what is that smell?"

Terenia went pale and Dras chuckled lightly, "That would be us. I think we should take the opportunity to dunk ourselves in the water when we can, so we don't stink you guys out."

.   .   .

Joleen was currently lost in thought. Some of the soldiers had returned from the Leturai city with tales of horror about an attack from a Kraken and undead coming to claim the dead. There had been casualties but thankfully very few.

The better news had been that the Kraken had been driven off and that the Leturai had been able to send several ships off to their other cities carrying Gateway Crystals. The Leturai had their own synchronized system of measuring time. They had instructions to attempt to use the crystals at the same time each day.

A few of the soldiers had also spoke of strange creatures that were a combination of a human and a fish. Dras had also apparently found some strange sea creature that none of the Leturai had ever seen before.

Joleen had wanted to join them, but the attack had highlighted that things were still too dangerous for that. Another company of soldiers was currently being swapped out. The commander from the returning unit came over to make a report. Joleen was in the middle of healing some injured soldiers, so the man spoke to Narok.

That had become the procedure since Joleen was spending so much of her waking time right now either healing or handling administrative affairs. It was nearly twenty minutes before she was finished. It was time for her to take a break, so she went and sat at one of the tables set up for the relief personnel.

Once she was seated Narok said, "You will be pleased to know that two of the other Leturai cities have made Gateways. According to the Leturai the other cities will require another one or two days to reach."

Joleen closed her eyes and exhaled. That was a weight off her mind.

The people from the capital were not the only survivors.

Joleen opened her eyes and smiled at Narok. After a moment she said, "I wish to meet their king in the near future."

.   .   .

It had been three days since they had driven the Kraken and the undead back. In that time seven cities had made Gateways to Yxarion. According to Inessa there were only three cities that they had not heard from. Whether or not that was because they were destroyed, or the ships sent to them had been was unknown.

Jolson was currently sitting in the corner of his room. He had returned to Yxarion after he had a vison. Luckily, he had been alone at the time it happened. He hated having others see him in that state.

The vision had shown a world where there was water everywhere. It had also shown him Nexus. They were showing Flare images of the strange fish that Dras had found.

While Jolson recovered, the others continued their humanitarian work. He had informed Joleen of his vison and she had called a meeting with the others after she had met the Leturai king. The consensus was that they return to Nexus and ask Flare for further guidance.

Jolson was feeling uneasy about what he had seen. It had seemed like the visons were getting harder to decipher lately. Where once they have been very clear and full of details now, they were getting vague and fragmented.

He closed his eyes and felt weariness wash over him.

Perhaps I will just sleep for the next day or so. Joleen and Meterove can take care of the rest for now.

CHAPTER 20
MERMAIDS

Ever since she had been a little girl Laticin had known that she was different from her peers. She saw life itself in a totally different light than almost anyone else that she had ever met. As the eldest of the Reifke clan's children it would one day be her duty to lead her people. In her heart though Laticin knew that she could not be what it was that everyone else wanted her to be.

Her people had long made the practice of entering the worlds of Creation to draw men down into the water and use them for their seed. Many of these men would then be returned to where they had come from. In the past they cared less about the survival of these men and had simply shoved them back where they had been taken from.

Laticin had seen some of these men at a distance and had certainly felt some of the urges that all the other Mermaids felt. Her problem was that she also felt these same urges when she saw some of the other women and this led her to be confused. She was already an adult by the standards of her people, but she had yet to mate once.

She currently spent her days avoiding her mother and sisters. When she could manage it, she would try and explore beyond the edges of the Mermaid territory. Her people lived in the shallow, tropical waters off the Benoral Shoals. More specifically they lived in a large lagoon.

The Benoral Shoals were some of the shallowest water on the entire Plane. Only the Undine territory was shallower. The shoals were named after her people's ancient ancestor that was said to have been the first of their kind.

Today Laticin was out swimming as fast as she could go. Her two-toned hair of deep purple and light blue trailing behind her. All Mermaids had heterochromia that matched their hair and scale colors. Her long slim tail had two large fins that stuck out just below her waist that would allow her to glide through the air.

Unlike their deep-water cousins, the Sirens, her humanoid half was very similar to that of humans, though with some differences. Her skin was paler, and her ears were slightly crescent shaped. There were almost no scales on the humanoid portion of her body, which was bare. She had knew some of the other races that dwelled on the plane, and some of them covered their bodies but that was not something that the Mermaids did.

Laticin went even faster and rose to the surface and glided through the air looking out over the plane around her. All around her was the only sight that she had ever known. Endless water in all directions, even above her.

Connecting the top and bottom were hundreds of spiraling pillars of water. Every one of them spun at a different speed. Some were small and slow, but others were huge and moved with such speed that only the largest of creatures would dare to enter them.

Laticin was beautiful and was full to the brim with curiosity. Learning new things was almost an obsession with her. Once she started on a topic, she would be relentless about it until she had exhausted her resources. She was also fond of pushing her boundaries.

Today she was supposed to be attending a meeting with her mother and the other elders, but she had chosen to go for a swim instead. All they were going to do was recite the same scripture that they always followed. None of them ever questioned the words that had been passed down, they simply treated them as absolute.

Laticin had once brought up a question that contradicted the scripture and her mother had practically lost her mind with rage. There was no thinking amongst them only following the scripture and doing what all Mermaids had done before them.

She had heard tales of other worlds, but she wanted to see more than just a small section of ocean long enough to kidnap a man. She had heard that there was actually stone that was above the water on some of them. What a sight that would be!

Laticin dove back under the water. Once she was down a little ways Laticin looked around. Fish of all types swam around her. In the distance she could see larger shapes that were likely some kind of shark.

Right now, she was swimming through a small coral reef. The abundant sea life darted around and off to one side she could see a small kelp forest. She swam along the edge of it for a little while. She would frequently meet her friend Claire here, but she would be busy today.

Claire was an Undine and the daughter of the Undine matriarch. The Undines and Mermaids were two of the three governing races of the plane. The third was the Snow Women. All three races got along quite well but while Laticin was adventurous, Claire tended to do as her mother told her.

Laticin swam around the kelp rather than through it and found herself at her destination. She was looking down over the vast drop-off that marked the border of Mermaid territory. Past here it was a kind of neutral zone for thousands of feet, until she reached the territory of the Sirens.

She would come here from time to time hoping to see one. They were said to be ferocious, and she had no desire to get up close with one, but she still wanted to see one just once. Of course, the Sirens were not the only site worth seeing. There were tons of deep-water creatures that were never seen close to the surface down there.

All Mermaids and Sirens could adjust their bodies to handle the water pressure at different depths and she had on two other occasions dove down a little ways to try and see something of interest.

Something felt off today though. She had this sense that if she went down there, she might find more than she wanted. She thought about going anyway and nearly started down when she saw something move down there in the blackness. Whatever that was, it was one of the larger creatures of the plane.

Laticin watched the depths for more signs of movement for several minutes but did not see anything more. She still had a vague sense of danger and decided that it was time to leave.

Once her back was turned she felt the sense of danger magnify so she swam through the kelp this time, instead of around it. Once inside she slowed down and soon felt the sense of danger vanish.

451

She waited there for several minutes just to be sure and then slowly made her way through the kelp to the shallow side. Once she emerged the sense of danger returned, and she ducked back into the kelp.

Something is hunting me...!

She stayed low and moved through kelp until she found a small rock outcropping that she and Claire had found years ago. There was a small cave that was more of a ledge she could hide in. It also had a small stone knife that she had hid there.

She quickly used the knife to cut some kelp free and fashioned a decoy. It would not fool most creatures, but the plan was to attract the sharks she had seen earlier. For a finishing touch she dug up and stabbed a crab, which she tied to the kelp.

She threw her decoy out over the kelp bed and soon the sharks that she had seen earlier had come over to attack it. Several large tentacles that were at least thirty feet long shot up and wrapped up one of the sharks.

WOW! A colossal squid!

The other sharks scattered while the squid began to feed on the shark that it had caught. Laticin waited a moment to make sure that the squid was focused on its meal then she slowly moved away. When she exited the kelp, it took everything she had to not try and dart away.

Once she had gotten about thirty feet past the kelp her nerve failed her, and she swam as fast as she could back to water that she knew was too shallow for the squid to enter.

Now that she was no longer in danger, she was giddy with excitement. She did not know anyone that had actually seen a colossal squid before. True there were larger creatures in the plane than those, but it was still an impressive creature.

Soon she had made it back to the lagoon. She knew she was going to get an earful from her mother. Though she longed to argue back the number of times that her mother had shouted in her face as a result had shown her that reason was not something that her mother possessed.

She swam over a large rock outcropping that nearly reached the surface and she was home. This massive area was the lagoon that the Mermaids lived in. The reefs around this area made a huge area that was safe from the larger predators.

All around her were tens of thousands of caves. Some of them were natural but others had been made with tools that they brought back on occasion from their raids into the worlds. That was also where the weapons that the Mermaids used came from.

Most of the weapons and tools were simply left stored in a special cave that they had found that held a pocket of air. Eventually they would decay and those would be thrown out. The only things they had found that would last were items that were made of gold, silver, and platinum.

Laticin swam over to the cave that was where she should have been hours ago. Inside was empty, which did not surprise her. The elders would have lost patience and finished their rituals long ago.

She continued on and came to the small cave that she used to sleep in. Her mother was there waiting for her. She had her arms crossed over her chest and she was frowning. She was quite different in appearance from Laticin. The only thing that she had in common was their colors.

Her hair was chin length and mostly grey and her eyes rarely held kindness. Her face frequently looked as if she were displeased by something, which she often was. She was also a bit larger built than Laticin.

Once Laticin was close enough to hear she said, *"I do not understand how you can be so selfish! What we do is important! You must follow the teachings!"*

The lecture went one for what seemed like several cycles. Laticin just let it wash over her. She knew that her mom was a zealot and would never listen to her, so she chose to not listen to her too.

Once the tirade was over her mother put her hands on her hips and said, *"Well, I hope that someday you come back to the teachings."*

"You know Elise, you have the temper of a shark."

Laticin and her mother looked over to see her mother's friend, and fellow elder Moira, smiling at them. Her colors were deep green and black, though both her and her mother's hair held streaks of gray. Laticin liked Moira.

While most of the elders were like her mother Moira would at least listen to Laticin when she brought up her questions and would admit that perhaps she had a point sometimes.

Moira said, *"So Laticin, what was so important that you chose to skip your lessons today?"*

Laticin grimaced. Just because she was more tolerant did not mean that she would let everything just slide. That smile had no real mirth in it. She wanted a good answer. Laticin decided to tell them what happened earlier.

I will just embellish on how long I was hiding a little bit.

Laticin said, *"I went for a swim earlier over by the ridge on the border."*

Both her mother and Moira nodded. This was not news to them. Laticin continued, *"While I was on the top of the ridge looking down, I saw something move in the depths. I watched for a while, but I did not see any more movement, so I went to leave but when I turned my back, I suddenly felt danger and swam into the kelp. I tried to leave out the* shallow side but felt that I was in danger again, so a ducked back into the kelp."

Moira said, "That was a good decision."

Laticin nodded, "I realized that I was being hunted so I moved slowly through the kelp and made bait out of kelp and a crab to lure some sharks I had seen earlier over by me."

Moira looked confused, "What made you so sure that the sharks were not what was hunting you?"

Laticin said, "I could just feel that whatever I had seen earlier was down there stalking me. The sharks took the bait, and so did the colossal squid."

At the mention of the colossal squid both Moira and her mother looked skeptical. Her mother said, "There is no way that a colossal squid was that far up. You had me going along with you, but you really should have chosen something more believable than that if you wanted to get out of trouble."

Laticin clenched her fists and her jaw. She was so sick of this attitude. Her mother always did this. She made her feel stupid or like she was crazy or making up stories.

Moira said, "Yes that is pretty unbelievable. What would make a colossal squid come so far up from the deep?"

Elise said, *"Oh please Moira. Do not encourage her imagination."*

Laticin was about to blow when Moira said, *"If she was going to make up a story, would she not have chosen something more believable?"*

Laticin and Elise both looked at Moira as she continued, *"If I wanted to get out of lessons, I would have embellished on the sharks not gone for something that would sound made up. In my experience truth can be stranger than fiction."*

Laticin said, *"Then you believe me Moira?"*

Moira said, *"I am willing to believe you enough to ask that you take me to see it. What I know of colossal squid, it is unlikely to leave in the near future."*

Laticin asked, *"How do plan on luring it out? I doubt something small like that crab would attract it on its own."*

Moira said, *"Simple. We will bring one of the large Tuna that we have caught and will gut it and throw it over the edge."*

Elise scoffed, *"I still do not see why you are bothering. It is a waste of a tuna. Even if she really saw something down there it would not have come up. It is just her imagination."*

457

Moira said, *"Then this will prove that there is nothing to worry about."*

Elise threw her hands up, *"I have important matters to attend to. If you want to indulge her fine. I tell you that it is either an overactive imagination or a dumb lie!"*

Elise swam off, leaving Laticin fuming. Moira patted her on the shoulder, *"She always has had a hard time accepting things that were not what she wanted. Come. We will go get that tuna and you can show me what it is you saw."*

Laticin was so grateful that Moira was listening to her that she was able to brush her anger at her mother off. They collected the tuna and used a net to carry it back to the kelp. Once they were in the kelp Laticin used the stone knife that she dug out of the rocks to slice open the tuna and then the two of them threw the tuna out over the chasm.

It floated there for a few minutes and just when Laticin was beginning to despair that she was going to have to listen to her mother gloat about how she was right a pair of tentacles shot up and grabbed the tuna. These were far smaller than the ones that she had seen earlier, perhaps only fifteen feet long.

Laticin looked at them confused.

Did I just think that they were bigger because I was so frightened?

At that moment, another pair of far larger tentacles reached up and wrapped up the squid that was eating the tuna. Moira and Laticin both huddled back close to the rocks and Moira gestured for them to move back.

Once on the other side of the kelp they could not stop themselves from swimming as fast as they could. Laticin looked back over her shoulder but saw nothing. They did not stop though until they were back in the lagoon.

Moira was exhausted, but she still managed to say, *"I would say that is proof. What concerns me is why there was two of them. Why are they so close to the surface?"*

Laticin hated saying it, but Moira needed to know, *"It was three, not two."*

Moira looked at her alarmed, *"What do you mean?"*

Laticin looked back in the direction that they had come from. *"The one that I saw earlier was not as big as that second one. There are at least three of them out there."*

Moira looked back at the way that they had come as well. *"I have no idea what this means but it cannot be a good sign. The colossal squid may not be the largest predator in the depths, but they are still quite large. I have never heard of them moving closer to the surface. If there is something down there that is forcing them to the surface in large numbers I fear what else might follow them up."*

Despite the seriousness of the situation, Laticin could not help but be interested. *"What other creatures are on the bottom that are even larger than that? The only other one that I am aware of down there are the Leviathans."*

Moira said, "It is true that Leviathans are amongst the largest creatures on the Plane there are several other creatures that are down there that are also quite large. There is something called an Ichthyosaur that can grow to immense size. Then there are the Krakens. Krakens never stop growing but rarely reproduce because they are highly hostile to everything, including others of their own kind."

Laticin said, *"I have never heard of either of those before."*

Moira said, *"If you would stop skipping your lessons you might have. The Krakens are extremely dangerous. There is only one thing that is mightier than the Krakens, and that is the Great Lord."*

Laticin would normally roll her eyes at this kind of talk. The great serpent that circled the entire plane and slept deep beneath the water. Something of that size was simply impossible. After seeing the colossal squids and seeing how scared that Moira looked, she was feeling a little more open to the teachings of the elders. Perhaps there was a grain of truth in it.

Moira said, *"We need to gather the other elders and contact the Undines and Snow Women. A full Planer*

Council meeting must be called. If nothing else, the others need to be made aware of the threat of these colossal squids coming to surface."

There was something about this day that Laticin could not put her finger on. Something about this day almost seemed like it had been meant to be. Why had she chosen to swim there today? She knew that Claire was not going to be meeting her there and that was the only reason that she ever went over to that area.

While Moira was swimming in front of her Laticin kept looking around. She could not shake the feeling that she was being watched.

CHAPTER 20.5
CONCERNS

Well, that was an interesting development. This one could sense being watched, even if it were only in instances where she was the direct focus. The nudge of pushing her being noticed was also a surprise. It was rare indeed for anything to notice that. She was certainly going to be useful.

The corruption was bad there. One could only hope that the denizens of that plane would be able to survive until help arrived. Fortunately, there were many large predators around where the corruption was, and this had slowed the spread.

Then there was the matter of the one named Dras. What he had noticed was beyond troubling, He was the only person, perhaps the only entity, in the whole of Creation, that could have noticed it. Now that I am aware of it, I must work to contain this. So many problems to deal with.

There was no doubt though that Mia had been corrupted and was now the source of chaos for countless worlds. The governing members of the Plane of Water would have to awaken its guardian to deal with her. The problem was that he would not be interested in any collateral damage from dealing with Mia.

The nudge that had been given to Jolson had worked but every time a new vision went through the degradation became more and more severe. There was not much more that could be done now. Help was on its way, that was all that could be done for now.

CHAPTER 21
DIRECTION

Joleen sat at her desk staring at the document in front of her. It would officially put power into the nobles hands. She had removed most of the troublesome nobles so there was no real concern about abuse of power. Really the only thing that was holding her back right now was that once she signed over the responsibilities of the throne, she would no longer have an excuse to keep her from having to go see Flare.

Jolson is right, but what I would not give for him to be wrong. I am not looking forward to dealing with her again. This time though we need to demand a few more answers.

Meterove already had the Citadel of Time ready to move. That was one perk this time around, at least they could cut out the long trip and just go to the tear. There should be an actual entrance to Creation but since they had not used it before they had no choice but to go the same way they did before. Joleen made a mental note to learn the location of the entrance.

Joleen sighed and signed the document, then walked over to her bed, where the clothes that she had picked were laid out. Knee-high brown boots A one piece leather armor bodysuit that went halfway down her thighs but left her shoulders bare.

An identical padded garment went under it. An asymmetrical black wrap skirt with ties on the left hip went over that. She also had brown leather bracers that went over her forearms. The final piece was a simple brown cloak with a black clasp.

It took her a little while to get dressed but that was half her wanting to avoid going back to Nexus. While she was getting dressed, she thought of the last time that she had been to Nexus. In no time her mind snapped to her walking around Nexus with Narok.

That really was a nice time. Even though we were worried about what was happening back here for that short time there felt like there was nothing more pressing than to walk around and enjoy his company.

As soon as she thought about that, the memory of the people around Nexus gossiping about how they were a couple surfaced and she got a little embarrassed. She was about to shake away the thoughts but then she realized that while it embarrassed her, she really did not mind people thinking that.

I am not really the empress anymore, not at the moment and I changed the standing of the family with that change to our government. Eventually there won't even be an imperial family anymore, as long as everything goes the way I want it to. Maybe it is time that I stopped denying what I want...

Once she was dressed Joleen looked around her room one last time. This room hardly felt like it belonged to her anymore. This was where her other life, where another Joleen had lived. Closing the door felt very final even though she knew that she would still be able to return here.

.   .   .

Meterove was sitting down at a table near the refugee camp. There were tens of thousands of Leturai that had been evacuated once access to the other cities had been established. There had not been any further attacks since the day that they drove the beast back.

They were using the Citadel's walls to act as a safety buffer for the refuges. The plan was to use the Citadel to move to the tear in order to get to Nexus. They had a few soldiers that were trained to move the Citadel. Once they had dropped Meterove and the others off near the tear they would return and then they would establish a Gateway.

Once the Gateway had been established there were three platoons of soldiers that had been chose to operate as guards. They had instructions to open the Gateway the same time every day.

Once this was done, they would enter the tear and go to Nexus. None of them were really all that eager to deal with Flare again. Once Joleen arrived with Narok they would be ready to leave.   The changes that Joleen had made to Yxarion were starting to bear fruit. Already it was far easier for her to take action herself.

Terenia was sitting on the ground leaning against the trunk of a small tree. Meterove worried about her being away from the forests for so long, but she had waved away his concerns saying that she was fine.

While Meterove was worrying about Terenia, Joleen and Narok arrived. Jolson and Dras were inside already so it was just a matter of the four of them going up the steps. Just before going inside Joleen stopped to look out over towards the city one last time. Meterove did the same. The land still bore the scars of the battle that had been fought there.

Joleen inhaled deeply, as if to make sure she would not forget the smell of home, then turned, and entered the

Citadel. Narok followed suit while Meterove and Terenia took slightly longer. She looked into his eyes as if to say, "I will be fine." Meterove sighed and the two of them entered the Citadel as well.

Inside Jolson was going over how to operate the Citadel with the soldiers in charge of moving it back. Once everyone was ready Jolson pulled the miniature model of the world down and activated it. There was a small humming sound and then Jolson touched near where the tear would be. An image of that area was projected out and Jolson used his hands to move and zoom in on exactly where the Citadel would go.

Once he had picked his location, he pressed his hand against the top of the model and the Citadel moved. The view on the projection changed to show the Citadel was now there. The six of them did not want to waste time so they grabbed their equipment and exited the Citadel.

Once they gave the signal the soldiers inside moved the Citadel back to where it had been before. They waited for a short time before activating their Gateway crystal. Now they would have a fast way here that did not involve using the Citadel.

Dras and Meterove were once again the first to enter the tear. This time the others followed pretty quickly, Narok was carrying a sack that held the fish Dras had found. Soon the familiar sight of Nexus and Creation greeted them.

Instead of wandering around this time, they knew exactly where to go.

They entered the office of Ricaran Zircalago and when he looked up, there was a mixture of confusion and apprehension in his eyes. As far as anyone had been aware they would not be returning when they had left the last time. Yet here they were. Also, the last time that they had been here they had done some work for Flare.

That work had been full of complications that had meant an insane amount of paperwork for Ricaran. Then there was the unknown malfunction with the portal that had resulted in Dras' sword.

Meterove took the lead, "We need to see Flare."

Ricaran flinched, "I can only imagine."

Meterove let his impatience show slightly, "This is important."

Ricaran rolled his eyes, "Oh I am sure it is. To you."

Dras leaned onto Ricaran's desk, "Oh it will be important to you as well. That aside, just think of how much paperwork you had last time we were here. What do you think will happen if I were to TRY and make a mess?"

The smile that Dras punctuated that statement with made Ricaran go pale. He glared around at them, "I will go let LADY Flare know that you are waiting."

Ricaran left the room for a few minutes and when he returned, he looked a little smug. He said, "LADY Flare says that she cannot see you right now."

Joleen grabbed the sack that Narok had been carrying and dumped the dead fish onto Ricaran's desk. The smell was atrocious and there was a layer of slime that coated everything.

Ricaran looked horrified, though whether it was from the fish's appearance or that it was on his desk was up for debate. Joleen dropped the sack on the ground and crossed her arms in front of her. She imitated the smug look Ricaran had just given them, "I think you will find that she had better make time."

Ricaran could not take his eyes off the fish, but he was still defiant, "Why would this disgusting thing make any kind of point?"

Joleen said, "Because it was found alongside another creature. Neither of them had ever been seen by any race of our world."

Ricaran shrugged, "I still do not see how this of anyone else's problem other than yours."

Meterove finally snapped, "I am sick of your attitude Ricaran. Go tell FLARE that she better get her ass down here now, or I am going to drag this thing there myself."

Ricaran looked like he was going to argue further but he saw Meterove and Dras reach for the fish. He scurried back out of the room and after a few minutes he returned with a furious-looking Flare.

She looked much the same as the last time, though today she was wearing far more reserved clothing than the first time that they had met her. She was wearing a simple black dress with a woven gray sweater over it and her ever-present high heels.

Flare glared at them, "What is the meaning of this? I am busy with far more important matter than-"

It was at this point that she actually looked at the fish that was on Ricaran's desk. Her face went from furious to confused in an instant. She looked back at Meterove and asked, "What is this about?"

Joleen stepped forward and said, "Much has happened since last we spoke Flare. If you are expecting a short and simple explanation, then you are going to be disappointed."

Flare registered a bit of shock but mostly hid her reaction. She was likely confused since the last time that they had been here Meterove had been the one in charge, yet here was Joleen taking the lead.

She glanced at Meterove one last time then turned her attention to Joleen, "You have one minute to make your case."

Joleen wasted no time, "We fought the Ashen Soul and defeated it but something else has been happening. Giant tentacles are attacking the Leturai, they live under the ocean. Additionally, this fish and strange creatures that are a combination of fish and people were attacking them. Neither the creatures nor this fish have ever been seen before."

Flare placed her hand over her eyes and groaned, "Why is it never quick with you people? Ricaran, get someone up here that can identify that fish. The rest of you come with me."

They followed Flare back to her office, where they found the room already full of people, two of which they were familiar with. Yuromea and Koetsu looked just as surprised to see them. The others were unfamiliar but had the appearance of Flare's agents.

Flare said, "We are going to have to end here for today. Something has come up that requires my immediate attention. For now, Dobson, continue to observe Winters. Kole you are to investigate that stranger. Yuromea, you look into these inconsistencies. Are there any questions? Then get to work!"

As the others filed out of the room Yuromea came over to talk. "Were you able to avenge Corvine?"

The moment he said that a shiver went through the group. Everyone looked at Dras. Meterove slowly said, "Alright Dras, you might be onto something after all."

Yuromea looked confused and Meterove said, "Dras had mentioned something odd recently. He had heard our father being called several different names. We had no recollection of this before. Every one of us, except Dras and now you, calls him Aphen."

Yuromea looked at Koetsu, who took out a journal and began writing. Yuromea said, "This phenomenon is not isolated. There have been a lot of reports of "inconsistencies" like this. Lady Flare has asked that Koetsu and I look into this."

Meterove said, "This is the only one that we know of. If we find anything we will let you know. To answer your question though, yes, we did. The whole story is rather long so we will save it for another time."

Yuromea looked at Joleen and Jolson, "Yes, I suppose you must have something very urgent. There is something more that I too need to discuss with you. It can wait for a more convenient time, but I do think that it should be soon. Farewell."

Yuromea and Koetsu left the room and once they closed the door Flare said, "Please take some seats. The fish that you so kindly left downstairs is a smaller matter. The creatures that you mentioned make me nervous.

Would you be able to elaborate on their appearance, or perhaps show an image?"

Jolson had anticipated the need for this and pulled out a crystal that showed a detailed image of the creature.

Flare sighed, "I was afraid that was what you encountered. That is called a Siren. They are a creature that rarely leaves the Plane of Water. When they do it is solely for sake of gathering "seed" for propagation."

Joleen went slightly red, "Are you telling me that these things just invade worlds to make babies?"

Flare said, "That is exactly what they do. There are no men amongst the sapient races of the Plane of Water. The other races are, their cousins the Mermaids, the Undines who are the Plane of Water's equivalent of Yuromea's people, and then there are the Snow Women."

At the mention of Snow Women, Meterove gave a small twitch that Flare did not miss. She looked at him with an inquiring look.

Meterove said, "I have met Snow Women before. I wandered into a group of them before my father's death."

Flare said, "I think we need to have a more in-depth conversation about who you are in the near future. You have met some exceedingly rare beings in such a short time."

Flare said, "Next, I need to address the part that worries me the most. You said something about tentacles? This sounds like the Kraken."

Jolson said, "I have seen the tentacles personally. They were impossibly big. We have information on Krakens and none of it mentions anything as big as these."

Flare said, "I misspoke. I mean a specific Kraken, the first Kraken Mia to be precise."

Dras asked, "The first Kraken!? That sounds ominous."

Flare said, "Mia has been around for a very long time. She and her mate were made to manage the depths of the oceans. The vicious nature of her species was necessary to keep them from spreading too far."

Joleen asked, "So this Mia is on our world?"

Flare said, "No, Mia is on the Plane of Water. Occasionally holes are opened for various reasons, but they are all in extremely deep water. I have no idea why holes would be opening in such shallow water."

Meterove said, "I might have the answer to that question. The tentacles that we encountered clearly belonged to an undead."

Flare, who had been about to pour herself a drink from a decanter on her desk, knocked over the glass which shattered. She disregarded this entirely, "They were WHAT?!"

Meterove said, "After we left here, we began a war on the undead that are in our world. We fought several battles starting with a siege of our home. The Dragon Lord fought against a massive version of the Ashen Soul. The battle ended mostly in our victory, though the leaders and the Ashen Soul fled. Over the past months we have been fighting a war against the undead of the Ashen Empire."

Flare was now fully focused on them, "Are you telling me that you saw the actual Ashen Soul?"

Dras said, "The naked decaying angel girl with the freaky looking halberd? We saw a lot more of her than we wanted to."

Joleen said, "We fought it, the leaders of the Ashen Empire, which were our ancestors in the form of a Lich and a woman that called herself the Avatar of the Ashen Soul."

Flare put her head in her hands, "So the Ashen Soul has revived."

Dras said, "And died."

Flare looked up, "Died?"

Meterove said, "We fought the Lich and the Avatar, and later the Ashen Soul in a volcano. The last we saw of the Ashen Soul; I had sent it crashing into the volcano just as it began to erupt."

Flare said, "So long as an undead exists, the Ashen Soul can return. Usually, it only comes into a world by chance."

Joleen said, "From what we know, the first emperor of Yxarion lost his wife to assassins. He was mad with grief and tried to use necromancy to bring her back. Once he had performed the ritual, he realized that it was not her and tried to seal it but was not able to complete it before it had corrupted him."

Flare looked sad, "So that was how it was reborn on your world. The Ashen Soul is attracted to suffering. While your world is not the only one with undeath the suffering attached to that particular reanimation would have helped draw it to your world. However, we went off topic slightly there. This news that Mia might be corrupted is bad."

Joleen asked, "What exactly is happening?"

Flare said, "If Mia has been corrupted, then it will not be something as simple as just "an undead" but something worse. It will be some higher form of undead, one capable of acting as a surrogate to the Ashen Soul."

Jolson asked, "Are you saying that this Mia can do everything that the Ashen Soul could?"

Flare shook her head, "Not quite. If it has kept its form as a Kraken, then the Ashen Soul is clearly not trying to manifest there. That being said, it can spread its corruption to every world in Creation from there."

Dras asked, "If you already knew all this, then why did you need that fish examined?"

Flare said, "I might have knowledge of a great many things but not everything. I have no idea if that fish is from your world or the Plane of Water. If it is from the Plane of Water, there is no telling the damage that might be caused by introducing it to a new world."

Jolson said, "This is all very interesting, but I feel like there is a lot more that you have not told us yet. It seems like you are telling us only as much as you feel we need to know to solve any given crisis. I would like to know the whole story now."

Meterove said, "Jolson makes a good point. When we were last here you gave us tasks to help you and we carried them out without complaint. In return we were given minimal information and access to a chance of learning what we needed to know to save our people."

Flare glared at them, "What makes you think that I need to answer to you?"

Joleen responded, "That is a fair point. Who DO you answer to?"

Flare narrowed her eyes even further, "I do what I was made to do. I do not need to explain more than that."

Joleen said, "What I am hearing is that you have no oversight. You could be causing many of these problems yourself for all we know. You keep too many secrets Flare. For instance why have you been so vague about the Ashen Soul?"

Flare was bristling now, "You dare to question me child! I have been holding the barriers between the worlds as I was made to do since long before your world even existed!"

Joleen stood up and walked over to Flare and slapped her across the face, hard. Saliva and even a little bit of blood hit the floor to the side of her. Flare was stunned, she had clearly expected her posturing to have intimidated them.

Joleen went back to her seat. After she sat, she said, "Now that you have ceased that insufferably arrogant babble of yours, you can answer our questions."

Flare wanted to glare back at her, but the watering of her eyes just made it look like she was a pouting child. Her anger had far from abated, but she was wary of getting another slap.

She straightened herself in her chair and said, "Very well. You wanted answers. Here you go. The Protogods and their minions are mobilizing all across the planes and various worlds. The Ashen Soul had been strangely absent for a thousand years but thanks to you we know why."

Meterove said, "I have seen one of them, I believe it was Gluttony. I think a second one, Envy took it away."

Flare shrugged, "It is entirely possible; however, I will treat sightings by humans with a grain of salt. Many of your legends and records of Protogods are incomplete or incorrect. In some instances, they have become juxtaposed with other legends and creatures."

Meterove said, "The one that I saw had the seven-pointed star, which my people call the hell star, on it."

Flare grimaced, "Then that one is likely the genuine article. Regardless there are more concerns. I have several worlds that are showing unusual changes as well. This matter in the Plane of Water is what is currently a problem for your world, but it is not the only one."

Joleen nodded, "What else are you referring to?"

Flare said, "Something has happened to Time."

There was a loud silence that followed this statement. Finally, Dras said, "Come again?"

Flare did not seem frustrated as she said, "Something has happened that has changed Time. I heard you talking to Yuromea about your own inconsistency. There have been other instances that have been just as alarming and a handful that were even more so. There have also been reports of enormous birds on countless worlds, but their origins are as of yet, unknown.

Everyone glanced at each other uncomfortably. Meterove said, "We have seen a large bird as well. It was a massive bird with black feathers and wreathed in black flames. Wherever its feathers fell the world would vanish around them."

Flare sat back in her chair, "It has to be because of who you are. I really need to have a chat with you soon, but I know that Yuromea has a similar revelation that needs to be made so I will have him here so they can be made together."

Joleen said, "Why should you wait? If it is something that we should know then you should tell us."

Flare shook her head, "This is one secret that is not mine to share. You will learn it soon enough."

Joleen had opened her mouth to argue further but Meterove shook his head. He asked Flare, "How unusual is it that the Protogods are active?"

Flare said, "They are always fighting amongst themselves, but for them to make a large scale move anywhere else is practically unprecedented. The other rarity is that ALL of them are currently active."

Meterove asked, "Is there some reason that you can think of that might explain this?"

Flare lowered her eyes, which were now full of worry and said, "The news about Mia might hold a clue there. If the Ashen Soul has managed to corrupt the Protogods then things are about to escalate dramatically."

Jolson asked, "Escalate how exactly?"

Flare said, "We will have to begin preparing for a higher form of war."

Dras asked, "What does that even mean?"

Flare said, "We might be looking at the sort of thing that has never been seen. I am talking about entire worlds being weaponized, people fighting across countless worlds, perhaps even directing forces on countless worlds simultaneously."

Meterove said, "I feel like you are manipulating us again. You want us to take care of more of your problems. The only difference is that instead of vague promises you are using a common threat to get our help."

Flare said, "Even if I am manipulating you does it really matter? You know there is a threat, and you know that I am your best lead on how to handle that threat. Follow my instructions and you will be able to save your home."

Dras said, "For someone that just got slapped by someone that you called a child you are awfully full of yourself."

Flare went bright red, even her ears went red. Joleen on the other hand appeared quite pleased with herself. Apparently, the memory of getting slapped had little effect on Flare because she continued to attempt to bully them.

"You can either do what I tell you or you can watch your world die. You know that I have no need to save your world in particular. I am doing this as a kindness. I could just as easily-"

Joleen had shifted in her seat as though she were planning on getting up to slap her again and Flare's nerve failed her, and her voice faded to nothing. After a few awkward seconds Jolson said, "I understand that this enemy is coming from the Plane of Water. My question is what we are going to be able to do about it. If it is the Plane of Water, then shouldn't everything be water there?"

Meterove had not thought of that.

How are we going to breath while there?

Flare shook her head, "While the Planes are all primarily composed of their own element there are small amounts of the others that are in each."

Here Flare picked up a pen and a blank piece of paper and drew a circle on it. She then drew a handful of other bits then turned it around for them to look at. She continued, "This is a rudimentary map of a plane. The outside is a shell of stone. Inside is the element that makes up the plane itself. Mixed in are bits of the other elements. For example, there is a massive bubble of air in the middle of the Plane of Water."

Meterove said, "So there is some air for us to breath then."

Flare said, "Yes, but that will not be enough for you to traverse the Plane of Water. I will have an enchantment placed on you that will give you gills for when you are submerged in water. The enchantment is permanent, but it will only trigger under water and if you yourself intend to."

Joleen asked, "When do you intend to do this?"

Flare said, "I should be able to get someone here by tomorrow morning. We can also arrange for that chat with Yuromea then as well. It is not the sort of thing that I would want to put off any longer. I need to get working on this now. If you let me work I can get you on your way in the morning, so until tomorrow."

Joleen knew that she was not alone in thinking that sounded ominous. As the rest of them got up to leave she realized that both Narok and Terenia had been silent the entire time. When she commented on it the two of them looked at each other, then back at her and Terenia said, "We just watched you slap Flare across the face. She is supposed to be this super powerful dragon lady, right? We were stunned speechless!"

Joleen had not really thought about it much, but now that Terenia brought it up, her slap had actually been absurdly dangerous!

She side eyed the other three and saw that they were deliberately not looking at her. The slight smirks on their faces said just what they thought of her outburst. This was going to come back to haunt her.

CHAPTER 22

KIN

They had gotten rooms back at the same inn that they had stayed in the last time. They arrived back at Flare's office first thing the next morning. Flare looked like she had not slept. She was wearing the same clothes and there were bags under her eyes. With her was a small pale skinned woman with blue eyes and hair. She seemed to almost give off a mist around her. The other person in the room was Yuromea.

Flare said, "This is Cora. She is an Undine and has kindly agreed to help with both placing the enchantments on you and giving you some background information on the Plane of Water."

Meterove said, "It is a pleasure to meet you, Cora."

Joleen followed up with, "Thank you for your help. We truly appreciate it."

Yuromea said, "I can vouch for Cora personally. I have known her for many years. She is very knowledgeable about many things."

Flare nodded to Yuromea, "Now there is the other matter that we need to discuss with you. Specifically, the three of you."

As she pointed at Joleen, Jolson and Meterove, none of them really looked surprised. Meterove said, "What exactly do you have to tell us? You mentioned something about what I was yesterday. What did you mean by that?"

Joleen said, "I want straight answers. What did you mean about Meterove and why did you also want to see Jolson and I?"

Yuromea smiled sadly, "You truly do remind me of her."

Joleen asked, "I remind you of who?"

Yuromea said, "My daughter, Yue."

Joleen said, "I do not understand."

Yuromea said, "You knew her as Cassandra, or more specifically, your mother."

Time seemed to stop for Joleen.

What is this man saying? Why is he saying that his daughter was my mother? Is this another way that Flare is trying to manipu-

Her thoughts cut off as memories of her mother bubbled up to the surface, one after the other. One of the common things that she remembered were those eyes, the same eyes that were now looking back at her from the face of an older man.

Joleen gasped and seconds later she heard Jolson gasp as well. He had likely just remembered the same thing.

Jolson said, "Are you saying that you are our grandfather? That our mother was a fox spirit?"

Yuromea nodded, "Indeed I am young one. I went to your world years ago out of curiosity. Some among our people had been there in the distant past but it had been a long time and I was curious. I took my son and daughter with because they were just as curious as I about your world."

Joleen said, "I still do not understand. How could she be our mother?"

Yuromea chuckled, "I met your father when he was just a young man. We were in the city, though we were keeping our identities a secret at the time when Yue happened to run into your father."

Their first meeting was not anything special, just your father bumping into Yue and apologizing, but they remembered each other's faces. It was not until some days later that there was an assassination attempt on your father in the streets that they really met.

We happened to be on that very street at the time and Yue moved the second she saw trouble. My son Akio and I followed quickly and the four of us along with his guards foiled the attempt. It was once the fighting was over that they recognized each other."

Jolson asked, "What happened after that?"

Yuromea said, "Corvine, or is it Aphen? For the sake of telling this story I will use Corvine. Corvine invited us to the palace to thank us for our assistance. It was there that we learned more about the tensions with Vorthain and the impending war."

Joleen asked, "Why did we never hear about this?"

Yuromea looked at them sadly then glanced at Flare, "I suspect that has to do with another secret. I have not been told what it is, but I have my suspicions."

Jolson said, "Father did mention you some to us, but he was always very vague."

Yuromea said, "That was the promise he made once we revealed our nature to him. I came to view him as a good companion and friend. I did not see the growing affection between Yue and Corvine at first but once I did, I chose to allow her to make her own choice. She chose to stay after the war and married Corvine and eventually gave birth to you two."

Meterove said, "You know."

Yuromea looked a little surprised, "I am honestly shocked that you know. Did Corvine tell you?"

Meterove shook his head, "I never knew the whole story, but I just sort of knew and said as much to him when I was five."

Joleen asked, "What are you two talking about? I am totally lost."

Jolson looked similarly perplexed. Meterove said, "We do not share the same mother. I do not know who my mother is, but I know that much. Once I asked father about it and finally got him to answer me, he still kept that from me."

There was a stunned silence in the room. Dras, Narok and Terenia were sitting there with their eyes wide and faces mostly blank. Joleen and Jolson were openmouthed trying to say something.

Yuromea said, "Yue's health degraded substantially after giving birth to you two and eventually she caught ill and passed. Corvine brought her body home to have our rights performed and to have her buried with us, as Yue had asked.

While he was in the Planes, he like you, needed to earn his passage and performed a number of tasks for Flare. As both my son-in-law and my friend I chose to help him. During one particular task we found ourselves in a tight spot that meant that Corvine was held up here for several months."

Here Yuromea nodded to Flare, who cleared her throat and said, "One of my daughters had vanished on a mission that I had sent her on. Corvine and Yuromea were tasked with finding her. It turns out that an extremely powerful man, named Damien Winters, had captured her."

Meterove said, "You had mentioned something about a Winters earlier when we first arrived."

Flare said, "That is the same man. The whole story would leave us still sitting here tomorrow morning, but I will say that during the search your father was captured by Winters as well. While on the inside he tracked down my daughter, who had taken on a human form and the two planned to escape."

Joleen said, "But I remember my mother holding Meterove."

Jolson said, "I do as well."

Flare said, "It could simply be that you were too young to remember clearly or perhaps your memory was altered."

Jolson said, "No. I think it is a lot more complicated than that. You said something has happened to Time. Perhaps this is another of those inconsistencies?"

Flare said, "That is another possibility. Regardless, once they were in captivity it was a few weeks on that world before they were able to get free. In that time, they had made a child. Unfortunately, your mother was killed in the escape and your father and Yuromea were forced to flee."

Meterove was silent while he digested this. Joleen and Jolson were both looking at him. Finally, Dras spoke. "So, Joleen and Jolson are half spirit foxes and Meterove is a half dragon?"

Flare said, "No. Meterove is indeed a half-dragon but the others appear to be human. If I had to take a guess, Yue had chosen to "become" human to be closer to your father."

Narok said, "I guess that explains why all three of them have such prodigious skills and power in magic."

Dras asked, "Are half-dragons really rare or are there tons of them walking around this place?"

Flare said, "To the best of my knowledge there are no other half dragons that are currently alive."

Meterove finally broke his silence, "So we have no idea what sort of path is ahead of me. I do have a question though. You said daughter earlier. Did you mean-?"

Flare smiled, "No. She was not my direct daughter. I consider all dragons to be my children, even if they are dozens of generations removed from me."

Dras whistled, "For a second there, I was like OH SHIT! Joleen just slapped Meterove's grandma!"

The tension of the moment broke and everyone but Dras, Flare and Yuromea laughed. Joleen wiped her eyes and said, "Thank You Dras. We needed that."

Jolson nodded also wiping his eyes. He turned to Meterove, "So you knew that you had a different mother, but you never told us!"

Meterove shrugged, "As far as father and I were concerned, it did not matter. You are still my brother and Joleen is still my sister."

Joleen leaned over and embraced Meterove and mumbled, "Damn right you are our brother. There is no half, just brother."

Jolson embraced the both of them. After a minute Flare cleared her throat and Joleen and Jolson retook their seats. Once they had sat back down Flare looked at Yuromea.

Yuromea said, "I do have some items that belonged to Yue that I would like to pass on to you. First this bracelet which was a gift to Yue from Corvine." He handed the bracelet over to Joleen. "Second this tome was a rare find of hers that I think you would benefit from Jolson. Place your hand on the cover, channel magic and state the topic you are looking for. Everything that you know about it, no matter how deeply it is buried will fill the pages until you change them."

Yuromea turned to Meterove, "You may not be blood but being Corvine's son makes you family. This dagger was Yue's. She kept it on her at all times."

Yuromea passed over a small single edged dagger with an eight-inch blade. Meterove took it with reverence. He too felt the same notion that Cassandra, or rather Yue, had held him as a baby. Whatever the case he was not going to refuse Yuromea's gift. The design of the blade and sheath allowed it to fit inside of a coat sleeve without being noticed.

Flare said, "I think that should be everything. The matter on the Plane of Water is rather urgent and I think we have kept Cora waiting long enough. She will explain everything else that you need to know before you go. I pray you succeed."

The Child sat in its strange circus home that it had built for itself. All around were bits and pieces that it had been hoarding. A dagger here, a necklace there. It was a large collection that was scattered around the giant tent that it used as its home.

There were horrifying creatures that looked as though they should be dead all around. It grabbed the skin that it had found in the volcano just before it had erupted and curled up underneath it.

It had been unable to recover any of the others that had been there. The wings on the one would have been a nice addition to the collection here. Whimpering in the corner disturbed its rest. It angrily pushed off the skin and glared at the cage that was nearby.

The cage in question was made from various human bones, sometimes held together by tendons. Inside there were four humans: two adults and two children. The whimpering was coming from the younger of the two children. The mother was currently trying to silence the child while weeping silently herself.

The Child continued to glare at the cage but eventually it decided that there was nothing for it and left the tent. Those ones were for later. What to do though?

The others that it wanted to see were nowhere to be found. They had been easy to find for a short time, but something was keeping it away from them. That had been very aggravating. It had snatched a few hundred people since then to put it in a better mood.

It could feel them again but wherever they were, it was not able to get there. Maybe it should look further into where they were? No, it really needed to rest. It had been a long time since it had been injured and the burns it had suffered from the volcano were still healing.

It decided that it would watch some of the animals for a while in the hope that the child would be silenced. The mother had another one that was inside it. It brought back the memories of when it had first been born.

As an unborn child there was little that it registered from the outside world. Some vague sounds were all that it knew. From its world there was the constant pounding that it heard, the rhythmic comforting pounding. One day when the warm place was really tight, the pounding stopped.

As it had begun to fade away itself sometime later it felt something else. It was a strange feeling, one that it would later come to know as cold. Sometime later it felt pressure behind it and with a burst it found itself immersed in the cold.

There was something else in the dark with it. It was hard and cold, yet softer than the rest of the new place. The smell of that place was somehow comforting. It had instinctively opened a hole to where it was now, though there had been nothing here at the time.

It had gone back after some time, but it did not know what it was that it was looking for. It only knew that it longed for something that was no longer there. It could sense the ones that it wanted to get to and followed the feeling for some time. However, while it wanted to find them, it also sensed that it would be extremely dangerous to get too close.

So, it had watched from a distance for many years, only rarely coming out for more than a few hours at a time. It had on occasion returned to that first place of cold. The smell that had been there at first had long since faded though.

All it wanted was to try and recreate that smell, that feeling that it had back then. It was on an endless search to feel that again. What that feeling was back then, it did not understand. It did know that it yearned to feel it again.

The Child had no idea how long it sat there. It went back to its tent and the child was silent now. It would be silent forever soon. As would the others. The two parents sat between the children and the Child as if they thought they could protect them. Soon it would be time for fun. The Child crawled into the corner and covered itself up with the skin. The smell was soothing, and it soon drifted off to sleep.

．　　　　　．　　　　　．

The explanation of the Plane of Water had taken almost two hours and then another hour to use the enchantment on them to allow them to breath. They had been instructed to be careful of entering the water immediately after entering the Plane.

They took the lift down like they had before, but this time they entered the portal for the Plane of Water. Touching the portal felt wet but no moisture came away. Meterove looked at Joleen who nodded. She knew he was asking if it was ok to take the lead. She was not going to be foolish enough to let her new confidence get them killed.

Meterove said, "I am going to go over the plan one more time just to be sure. Once we go through, we are to try and meet up with one of the leaders of the Principal Races. They need to be alerted to the danger and we need to get them to awaken the guardian of the Plane of Water. Once awakened the guardian will purge the corruption from the Plane of Water."

Dras asked, "Have we actually figured out how we are going to do that?"

Meterove said, "We will have to make that judgment based on how things are going when we get there."

Dras nodded, "So make it up as we go along like usual."

Meterove knew that was true, but he still did not want to admit it. Instead, he just said, "Ok it is time to go." and entered the portal.

CHAPTER 23
WATER

They stepped through the portal and out through a stone arch onto an island of ice. The sight in front of them was something else. All around them was water. As far as they could see was water. Far above there was water. Meterove looked through his spyglass and he could see waves rolling.

Then there were the countless spiraling towers of water that connected what Meterove assumed were the top and bottom. The water right now was rather violent with waves nearly twenty feet high smashing around them.

The island that held the portal was also protected with a barrier. They had been warned that if the waves were too violent that it would be best to wait to try and enter the water. To that end they had brought a large tent that they could use to wait in until the seas calmed.

Waiting inside the tent they left the flap open to look out at the scenery. Meterove was not sure, but he thought that he had seen something in the water. Cora had not been very specific about how it worked but there was some kind of magical light that created a day and night cycle.

While they were looking out of the flap Dras noticed something. "Hey, is that some kind of sea creature?"

Meterove had seen it too and sure enough after a moment an elongated head rose out of the water on a very long neck.

Jolson watched it with interest, "That thing's neck has to be twenty feet long!"

It raised itself slightly out of the water and they could that instead of legs it had large oar like flippers. It extended its head stealthily towards the tent.

Meterove said, "Oh, it thinks that we are prey."

Just as Meterove was preparing to attack the creature, it gave a frightened screech as it slipped, and its body moved back into the water with a large splash. It resurfaced and as it was preparing to make another attempt at hunting them a humungous shark leapt completely out of the water and tackled the creature with its jaws open.

Meterove and the others ran out to look where the creature had vanished and saw a large patch of the water was dyed red.

Dras said, "Did you see the size of that thing!? That shark had to be at least fifty feet long!"

There was a rumble that shook the entire island they were on, and the shark reappeared, speared on an enormous, spiraled horn. The horn itself was the size of the shark. The lifeless shark was pulled back into the water, the dead creature that now looked so small still held in its jaws.

Dras said, "I am going to start bringing extra small clothes when I go somewhere with you guys."

They had been warned that every creature that lived in the water of every world was here, but the actual danger level had gone over their heads. Not anymore. They had just watched something that would be a predator to them get picked off by another predator only for that one to be killed as well. They had no doubt that there were even larger creatures here as well.

They watched the water for some time after that until finally the cold drove them back into the tent. The ice island that they were on was not very large but there was a large section of ice nearby that made the air very chilly.

The instructions they had been given by Cora were to head towards the Core and once at the Core they would find the meeting place of the Principal Races.

They waited on the island for the better part of three days before the seas calmed down enough to enter them. All of them were reluctant even though they had been told that the enchantment would also help them adapt quickly to different water temperatures and pressures. The scene that they had all witnessed on the first day was also still fresh in their minds.

As usual Meterove went first. Once in the water he felt a surge of instinctual panic as he went under the water. The sensation of gills opening behind his ears was strange but the rush of oxygen that came was a relief.

Once under the water he found that he could see quite a ways. Since they were on an island of ice and larger masses of ice could be seen in the distance Meterove had assumed that there would be minimal marine life, but he was wrong.

He could see schools of fish swimming around him. For the most part they were a combination of black and silver but on occasion he would see shocks of color in their scales. In the distance he could even see some larger shapes swimming along in small groups.

A series of splashes announced the others. They spent a short time getting used to moving around under water then they set off. It was unnerving knowing that there were tons of predators in the water. Everyone kept their eyes open looking all over. It did not help that there was sea life everywhere.

Narok had packed his shield into his bag to lower his drag in the water. Knowing where they were going, they had all bought a spear, but they saw so many large creatures that they felt like nothing more than a twig. These became abundantly clear when Joleen spotted something moving down in the blackness of the deep and a preposterously huge creature swooped up and swallowed a nearby whale whole.

The creature was built like a snake but had the head of a dragon. There were some long tendril like spines coming off the back of its head. Along the ridge of its back there were a dozen or so large spines. The tail ended in a point but there was a large fin that was connected to the top of the last spine and the tip of the tail.

It hunted the rest of the whale pod before heading back to the deeper water. Joleen kept her eyes on the water below them now.

Dras has a point. Extra underwear might be a good idea.

Every so often one of them would head to the surface to check that they were still heading towards the core. They were still in the colder waters so they could use the presence of icebergs to help them navigate. They had been told that once they stopped seeing icebergs that they should be able to see the core, the largest of the water pillars.

Jolson suddenly felt a sense of danger. Looking around he could tell that he was not the only one. Meterove was urgently signaling them to head to the surface towards a nearby iceberg. It was too late. The creature that was hunting them moved through the water at lightning speed.

It made to snap up Dras, but he released one of those flashes of light and it swerved off. Dras had used his body to shield their eyes from the flash as much as possible, so Jolson was able to get a good look at the creature.

It was about twenty feet long with a long thin body. It had two sets of mandibles. One set on the sides of its head and one on the top and bottom. It had a horrible circular mouth that was open with rows of teeth filling all of it. Its body kind of reminded Jolson of a millipede but instead of legs to walk on it had flippers. There were four rows, two on the top and two on the bottom. On the back was a long, pointed tail that looked like it was made for stabbing.

This creature was certainly intimidating. There were tons of other things it could be hunting, but the fact that it chose them probably meant that this was less an apex predator and more of a hybrid that was more of a scavenger, perhaps even a parasite.

Once it came back around for another attack it went for Dras again.

***This is good news. It is not a very intelligent
creature.***

While it was going for Dras he brought up his spear
up and managed to bury the head into the creatures mouth.
It released a strange rattling roar and dove to the side nearly
ripping the spear out of Dras' hands. The trail of blood that
it left behind made a large ribbon in the water.

As it swam away a memory hit Jolson with the force
of a bolt of lightning. He franticly motioned for everyone to
get to the iceberg. Once they had reached the iceberg there
was no way to get on, but it was the cover that Jolson had
wanted. He began using magic to make a hole in the
iceberg. He motioned for Joleen to help while the others
kept the creature at bay.

As soon as there was room for the six of them Jolson
began shoving the others in. He was the second to last to
enter followed by Dras. Meterove tapped him on the
shoulder and looked at him questioningly, but Jolson just
pointed out into the water. Meterove got his answer within
minutes.

The creature had continued to try and reach them.
When it failed with its mouth it attempted to use the stinger.
Jolson had expected this and had placed a barrier to block it.
While it was focused so completely on them the blood that
had leaked into the water had done what he had feared it
would.

Several of those giant sharks that they had seen when they first arrived had shown up and the blood combined with the creature's thrashing put them into a feeding frenzy. One of them snatched the creature off of the iceberg and soon all three were tearing it apart. The frenzy did not stop there as they began to attack each other as well.

Blood filled the water. Behind him Meterove and Joleen were doing their best to dig their way up. Eventually they broke through to an air pocket and the six of them climbed up and into it. Once inside they melted smaller holes the rest of the way out to give them an air supply.

While they were doing that Jolson used his magic to dry them off. He also pulled the blanket out of his pack to sit on. The others did the same thing. Once their shelter was finished, they all collapsed.

Meterove sounded exhausted as he said, "Is everyone having a nice trip?"

Joleen grabbed a small chunk of ice and threw it at where his voice had come from, at the same time that Narok and Dras chuckled. Terenia huddled close to him. Jolson looked down into the whole that they had come from, but they either did not have enough light to see, or it was so full of blood that it was opaque.

After they caught their breath Joleen said, "Why is it that there are some many large predators here?"

Jolson replied, "It just feels like that because we are prey here. If you think about it, we have seen a few large creatures back on our world. The difference is that all of the creatures that live in water on every single world live on this plane. No matter how long we search we will still only see the smallest percentage of what lives here."

Dras asked, "How far do you think we have traveled?"

Meterove said, "I plan on tunneling up soon and looking to see if I can still see the portal yet. I am hoping that we have made decent progress, but my hopes are not high."

Joleen asked, "We need to find a way to make better time. Even if the portal is out of sight, we will need to spend weeks getting to the core."

Terenia looked back at the hole they had climbed out of then at Meterove, "Weeks of getting chased by things like that. You sure know how to show a girl a good time."

Meterove gave a small grunt of amusement then said, "I suppose. That tunnel is not going to make itself."

He began to use his magic to shape the ice around him rather than melt or break it. He had to make the cuts rough to give himself traction on the way up. He was gone for several minutes but when he returned, he looked down.

Meterove sighed, "We have traveled a much shorter distance than I feared. Joleen is right, we need to find some way to make better time."

Narok asked, "Do you have any plans?"

Meterove shook his head, "Not at the moment."

Joleen said, "I know Cora thought that we would meet someone from either the Snow Women or the Undines soon after we entered the Plane, but I am not so sure."

Terenia asked, "Would it be possible to use magic to propel us?"

Jolson shook his head, "Not for the kind of distances we need. We might be able to move an extra half a day's travel, but we would be exhausted."

Dras asked, "So what is the plan then?"

Meterove thought for a moment then said. "We should rest. We have no idea how long that feeding frenzy is going to last out there anyway. We can rest for a few hours then I will take a look to see if it is safe to continue on."

Two hours later Meterove went down the hole they had come up. There was no sign of the sharks when Meterove poked his head out of the hole at the bottom. The water was completely quiet. Meterove chose to swim out a little ways, Oblivion in hand to see if anything came for him.

He stayed out for a few minutes without incident, so he returned to get the others. They were all reluctant to leave the safety of their den, but they had no choice. They moved through the water as fast as they could.

They felt safer after an hour when they found themselves surrounded by a huge school of fish. They were about the size of a man and there were thousands of them. They showed no interest in anything other than chasing around the massive cloud of mackerel they were hunting.

If these fish were here, then the chances of anything dangerous in the area was significantly lower. It also meant that they would have plenty of warning if something did come along. As they continued to swim along the size of both the school of mackerel and the fish that were eating them continued to grow.

It felt like they had been swimming forever when Meterove saw a landmark that Cora had told them to look out for. He pointed off to their left at the rock formation. The three rock pillars had been set up by the Principal Races to act as a marker. Past here was a large reef.

Being in shallower water would be both a blessing and a curse. While they would be far less likely to encounter the large predators that they had seen so far, it was not impossible. Also, now they would have to beware of the smaller but faster predators.

Moving out onto the reef they could see abundant life. There were tons of fish of all shapes, sizes, and colors. There were nearly as many coral formations. Then there were the sea anemones, star fish, sea horses, sponges and a huge assortment of shellfish and mollusks.

The water was far warmer here. Their bodies adapted to it quickly but for a moment it felt almost like they had swum into a bathtub. A large stingray swam past hunting some shrimp that were also swimming past.

Considering the foggy blue and deep black that had been most of their experience thus far with the Plane of Water, the coral reef here almost hurt their eyes it was so bright. Dras could not help but look everywhere like a child. Everywhere you looked there was something new that was bright and a new combination of colors.

Meterove had to admit that this was a beautiful sight. They might be here on a serious mission but that did not mean they were not allowed to enjoy themselves some.

Jolson pointed off to their right and when Meterove looked he saw a fish as long as he was swimming past. It almost felt like it was eyeing them nervously. The light of the Plane was beginning to wane now though. Meterove pointed up and everyone swam up to the surface.

Once everyone had surfaced, he said, "I know we want to make better time, but I am not about to ignore Cora's warning about swimming at night. I think we should use this reef as a resting point. A simple barrier in the right spot down there will keep us safe."

Joleen asked, "Can we at least force the water out of it and make a vent to the surface? I really do not want to sleep IN the water."

Meterove weighed the cost of magic against the moral dip that would come from all of them sleeping in the water. They might not even be ABLE to sleep. Meterove nodded, "Yes that makes more sense. I honestly don't know if we COULD sleep in the water."

Dras said, "Even though we will have a barrier I will sleep better if we have watches set."

Meterove said, "I agree. I will take the first watch."

Terenia chimed right in, "And I will join him!"

Dras gave a small smile and said, "I will take the second watch with Jolson."

Jolson nodded at him. Joleen looked at Narok and said, "That leaves us for the third watch."

Narok gave a smile and said, "We had better get back down there then and get this camp set."

CHAPTER 23.5
HELP

They had gone to the Plane of Water but were a long way from where they needed to be. What kind of help could be given? They were far from any of the Principal Races and there was no time that they would ever be in that area other than passing through from or to the portal.

Wait!? What was this? When did this get here? It was something that would work perfectly! It was a gamble due to the dangers involved but if it was them then the risk was negligible.

The prods that would be needed to make them encounter this were some of the easiest manipulation that had been needed so far. Now for the few other nudges that were needed to make this work.

Those that were needed were nearly in place. All that was left was to arrange the meetings. The one was going to be easier than the other. They were already heading to where that one was. The question was what to do about the second one. She had already noticed meddling once before.

The easier option was going to be to manipulate Meterove into meeting them. The means of doing this would be fairly straightforward. Might as well get started.

CHAPTER 24
MAIDENS

There is something coming. Some kind of change that will be cataclysmic. I can also feel that HE is involved.

Rakira had been intrigued by the events that had been happening for some time. Ever since they had returned to the Plane of Water, she had been working hard to make sure that should the need ever arise that she would be ready.

They had cut their stay in his world short after they had sensed the corruption. None of them had wanted to risk their people getting exposed when they could simply go to another world. Still Rakira was drawn to this man. She knew that he was important to all of Creation but also to her in a more personal sense.

She had liked him, and his nature had been so pure towards her. His desire to protect had also been something of an inspiration to her. Now that she had returned, she was focusing on her studies with renewed effort.

She looked around their village. The igloos that made it up had been built after visiting a world where they were used. She was looking for her mother, the leader of the village. There were quite a few Snow Women on the Plane of Water, but they were scattered around a dozen or so other villages.

Today the leaders of every village were meeting to discuss a topic that had been brought to their attention by the Mermaids. Rakira was to attend alongside her mother as the next leader. From her understanding the Undines and Mermaids were holding similar meetings in their territories.

She spotted her mother and walked over to her. The meeting was still a little ways off, but she wanted to make sure she was not a cause for delay. Her mother looked her over and smiled with approval.

They went around the village checking in on serval smaller matters until it was time for the meeting. There was a large section of the glacier that the village was built on that was hollowed out into a large chamber. Every village had something similar, and each village took turns hosting the meetings.

The leader of each village would attend along with their successor. Rakira could only speculate on the topic of this meeting since the finer details were still only known to a handful of women. Once it was time for the meeting Rakira could sense nervous energy from her mother as well. That worried Rakira, since she had rarely seen her mother rattled.

The two of them walked along the path marked with small shrines that were carved from ice. These shrines were to honor those that came before. The passage that led into the glacier was lit with some lanterns. The main chamber was exposed to the light of the plane through the mostly clear ice of the glacier giving it a soft light.

Being Snow Women, none of them were bothered by the cold so there was no source of heat inside. The seats were carved from ice and each one had a small side table with it. There was a large podium on a raised dais in the middle of the room that the seats all faced.

After several minutes, the seats were as filled as they were going to get. Rakira did a fast count and found that including her own village, there were ten villages that were represented.

This is odd. I have been to dozens of meetings like this and there has never been less than twelve of the villages there. Where are the others?

Rakira glanced at her mother and saw that her worry was reflected on her face. The protocol was to utilize a sand

517

timer once those present had all been seated and once it ran out the meeting would begin. Her mother as the host would be the one at the podium. Rakira would stand behind her to the right.

Once everyone had been seated her mother took the timer out and flipped it over. The grains of sand all fell without another woman entering the chamber. Her mother began the meeting. She had not even opened her mouth to speak when one of the other women quietly voiced the same worry that Rakira had.

Flykra's voice carried despite not being loud. She had clearly not meant to interrupt. "So, few have come. Something is wrong."

Her mother looked at Flykra who blushed a little, "I apologize Demetria, I did not realize I had spoken aloud."

Demetria nodded, "It is alright Flykra. I think we are all thinking the same thing anyway."

There was a small murmur of agreement from the assembled women. Demetria formed a gavel of ice with magic and banged it on the podium. After the murmurs went silent, she said, "We have much to discuss. This just adds to our topics."

Rakira had been looking around the room the whole time noting who had come. She could see Eira with her long silver hair in a braid. Her face was round and her features were more girlish than womanly.

Gwen was one of the oldest living amongst them. Her hair that went halfway down her back was grey and she wore it loose. Her eyes were steel grey and held a sharpness that made everyone that she looked at sit up a little straighter.

Then there was Icyln. She was widely regarded as the most beautiful of the Snow Women. Her hair was a deep black and her eyes were large and green. She had high cheekbones and soft pink lips.

Janara and Lumi looked alike enough that they could have been sisters, despite there being no relation. Both had long light brown hair and were on the shorter side. Both women were average in appearance.

Neve and Nivia actually were related. They were twins, which were exceedingly rare amongst Snow Women. They had shoulder length blond hair and brown eyes. They too had more girlish looks than womanly.

Skadi was the last one there. She was an average looking woman with black hair that was starting to grey. Her eyes were brown, and she wore her hair in a short bob.

All of them were wearing the simple white dresses that were traditionally worn by leaders. Additionally, some of them were wearing various pieces of jewelry that they had brought back from the worlds that they had visited.

Demetria said, "As the concern has already been voiced let us start with the absence of the other representatives. Has anyone heard from any of the villages that did not send representatives?"

Silence met Demetria's question. Around the room everyone glanced at each other. The tension grew with each passing second as they realized that none of them had heard from any of the other villages.

Demetria tried not to let the tension show on her own face but was not entirely successful. "We will send someone to each village. I will now ask for volunteers. I will send someone from my own village.

Gwen was the first to raise her hand, "I will volunteer."

Neve raised her hand, "I volunteer."

Nivia said, "I will as well."

Eira said, "I will volunteer."

Icyln raised her hand, "I will volunteer."

Demetria said, "The volunteers are noted. Is there anything else that someone would like to address before we close the matter of the other villages for now?

The other women shook their heads. Demetria banged her gavel and said, "The matter is now closed. Next is the matter that was brought to my attention via a messenger from the Mermaids."

There was a murmur around the room at this. While they were not hostile to each other the other two principal races rarely contacted them outside of the once per cycle meeting that they held. Apparently, Demetria was the only one to receive a messenger, which added to her worry.

Demetria exhaled softly, "The messenger said that they were seeing changes in the movements of deep-water creatures. Specifically, they have observed several large species, one of which was Colossal squid."

Eira asked, "What kind of changes?"

Demetria said, "They have seen them close enough to their own territory that they may become a direct threat. It is my understanding that several of the squid were observed from a kelp bed."

More murmuring followed this. Colossal squid lived in very cold and very deep waters. For even one to have moved so far indicated something was off.

Skadi voiced that very thought, "For something like a Colossal squid to move into waters so far from its habitat..."

Demetria said, "The report indicated that no fewer than three were seen in the same area at the same time. Additionally, there have also been sightings of Ichthyosaurs.

This time there were audible gasps. This made no sense. The squids alone were unbelievable, but for there to be other massive creatures like the Ichthyosaurs moving had left them flabbergasted.

Flykra said, "Surely the sightings were just younger ones that had gone up by chance."

Demetria said, "The report stated that the initial sighting was of a lone squid that had been hunting one of the Mermaids. After she managed to draw its attention to a shark she escaped. She later returned with one of the elders. The two of them lured a smaller squid out that was soon ambushed and eaten by another squid that was far larger than the first."

Flykra eyes began to show some wariness. Janara cleared her throat and asked, "And what of the Ichthyosaurs?"

Demetria looked grave, "The report estimates that the Ichthyosaurs that have been spotted were all similar to blue whales in terms of size."

Janara looked down at her lap with a frown. Rakira was standing behind her mother looking very alarmed. She glanced at the other successors present and noted that they had similar looks on their faces.

Lumi said, "I am sorry, but did you say "Ichthyosaurs" plural? As in more than one was seen?"

Demetria said, "Yes, as of the time the messenger was dispatched there has been five individual sightings in different areas."

Icyln asked, "Why were only you given this information? I am not questioning its validity, but I have to wonder why the rest of us were not told of this before."

Of course, you are not questioning it. You would not want to insult the Mermaids at all. You would just rather make it seem as though they were favoring me. Even now while there is evidence of a major crisis you are playing politics!

Demetria said, "Unfortunately if what I am telling you is new information, it means that the messengers dispatched to your villages either had not arrived yet, or that something has happened to them."

The slight smile that had been on Icyln's face froze and then vanished. This news sent a new wave of murmurs through the room. For Demetria to shut down Icyln like that was unheard of.

Demetria continued, "On this matter the Mermaids have asked for an emergency meeting of the Principal Races."

The women in the room gave their agreements almost as one. Demetria looked around the room. Then she asked, "Are there any further questions on this matter?"

Around the room the various women all looked like they had plenty of questions that they wanted to ask. Demetria knew they were keeping them to themselves because they knew there were no answers anyway. After a reasonable pause she banged the gavel, "The matter is now closed."

After this the meeting went to more normal matters for the majority of the time. Demetria knew that she had one more major matter that needed to be addressed. She decided that she would save that for the end of the meeting.

As was tradition two of the least serious matters were handled by the successors. This would give them experience with speaking, negotiating and most importantly political maneuvering.

Watching the young ones making their reports would be helpful in getting the leaders back into the proper mindset. Demetria proudly watched Rakira handle the next two matters. Fishing grounds rotation and educational reports were simple enough to get through. Once Rakira was finished it was time for the remaining six topics. Once those were done it was time.

Demetria said, "There is one additional report that I would like to make. On our most recent reproduction expedition we encountered a few problems."

This caught the attention of the women. Snow Women were just that, women. Without men they could not continue as a species. They made a practice of visiting various worlds that had several things in common but the most important was that it had humanoid life. Encountering problems was not unheard of but if it were serious then it might mean that they would have to find a new world to replace it.

Gwen asked, "How serious were these problems?"

Demetria said, "First the more serious problem was that we encountered a large number of undead. The humanoid races there were currently banding together to fight against them, but I do not know how serious the threat is."

Skadi asked, "Which world was this?"

Demetria said, "Aural."

The other women were not surprised, even if they were disturbed. Eira asked, "What else happened? You implied that there was more."

Demetria took a steadying breath and said, "We encountered one of the Valaseri."

Even those who had not been to Aural knew that name. There had been several encounters with that bloodline over the centuries. She personally had known the boy's father. She had once bargained with him. In exchange for promising not to hurt any men and obtaining consent of the men involved they would be safe to enter those lands searching for men.

Icyln asked, "Exactly how is that a problem? I had thought you negotiated a truce with one of their leaders?"

Demetria felt a prick of annoyance now. That woman did not wait long before going back on the attack. Demetria had never liked her much, but she had expected better from her.

Demetria said, "I certainly did. However, given that we are not of that world, that deal would only last as long as he was alive. I will need to approach his eldest now that he has been killed. The one that we met was his youngest. I could tell from just the short time that saw him that he was not truly human."

Gwen cocked her head, "What do you mean?"

Demetria said, "He has the aura of a Planer Dragon."

Gwen said, "So the rumors that we heard were true."

Eira said, "Wait. Backup. Did you say the man that fought his way out of Damien Winters' slave camps was killed?"

Demetria said, "Unfortunately yes. From what I understand he was killed in an attack from another nation that was under the influence of the Ashen Soul. We left before I could learn anything more."

Icyln laughed, "Undead are one thing Demetria but now you are trying to convince us that the Ashen Soul is real? That is just a legend and even those scripture obsessed Mermaids would be hesitant to claim they had encountered it."

Demetria glared at Icyln, "I never claimed to have encountered it. This is what I was able to glean without arousing suspicion. The nation was called Vorthain, and it used necromancy. They were betrayed by the ones that they thought were helping them and both leaders were slain."

Icyln said, "Undead exist all over the place. To believe that it had something to do with the "Ashen Soul" is childish."

A few of the other women seemed to agree with her but Gwen shook her head. "It is not ridiculous. The Ashen Soul is real Icyln."

Gwen's comment made Icyln sneer, "Please. I know that you have been around for a long time Gwen and that you are a little more into the scriptures than the rest of us but how can you make that claim?"

Gwen sat up straight, "I know because as you so kindly phrased it "have been around a long time" and I was alive the last time that the Ashen Soul incarnated."

Eira asked, "How long ago was that?"

There was palpable tension to the room. Age was something that you did not bring up so casually. Those that had lived long lives had seen as much suffering as joy and in many cases more. To ask Gwen that was something that only Eira who's own grandmother had been friends with Gwen, could do.

Gwen said, "It was over a thousand years ago. I was a young girl at the time, but I remember it clearly. It was on a small world that ended up being fully consumed by it. The Dragon Lord was forced to burn it from Creation. There were rumors that it had incarnated again somewhere but no sign of it ever appeared. At the time, the hope was that it was finally gone but the belief was that it was just temporarily trapped somewhere."

Icyln rolled her eyes, "That sounds like hearsay to me."

Gwen sniffed and stared down Icyln, "Would the Lady Flare giving the order to sever the connection between that world and the Plane also be hearsay?"

Icyln's mouth hung open for a second. None of them doubted that anything short of a cataclysmic threat would require that order for a newer world. Those that had begun to die were another story.

Gwen continued to stare at Icyln for a moment. Once satisfied she had been put in her place she returned her attention to Demetria, "I have a bad feeling about this."

Demetria closed her eyes and took a long breath before letting it out and telling them the last part. "There is one more thing. I am unsure as to the nature, but I could sense a thread of fate connecting the young man that we met and Rakira."

Gwen looked curious, "What makes you think that the two of them are connected?"

Demetria said, "I could feel the boys aura as I already said. I could also sense that he had a particularly rare trait. He has his story etched into his body and soul."

Gwen whispered, "Soul Ink."

Demetria gave a single nod, "Yes. From their encounter I sensed the magic activate on him."

Gwen looked at Rakira, taking in the young girl. After a minute she asked, "What did you think of this man, young lady?"

Rakira's throat went a little dry. This was not something that she was ready for. She was still nervous talking about the simpler matters. This was not simple. Still, she had a duty and she needed to fulfill it.

Rakira took a steadying breath and then shakily said, "When he first saw us, he was afraid. His head was full of old tales about our kind. When I appeared behind him, he turned to attack but held himself from striking. He had no malice in his heart. He simply had a singular goal that he needed to accomplish at all costs."

Gwen nodded, "You say he had no malice at all in his heart?"

Rakira giggled, "He thought of me as an adorable little girl."

Gwen looked amused, "I have one more question. Do you believe that he could be dangerous to our people?"

Rakira could sense that there was far more weight to this question than she could understand. An answer came from her heart before her head could even begin to think of one and she blurted it out.

"Is there a reason that we would make an enemy out of someone that bore us no ill will?"

.   .   .

Gwen had been both satisfied and impressed with her answer. The meeting had wrapped up and the leaders had just finished saying their farewells. Her mother came up to her and smiled. She said, "I am so proud of you."

Rakira was confused. She had another question to ask anyway so she said, "I do not understand. What did I do that you are so proud of? Also, what was miss Icyln talking about with the Mermaids messengers and why did she look so angry after you spoke?"

Demetria looked around the room and after seeing that it was clear said, "When I spoke about the messengers not arriving yet, it implied that perhaps she was not considered as important as myself to the Mermaids. It also cast doubt on anything that she would claim to know. Lastly it put focus back on the topic making her appear insignificant."

Rakira looked puzzled. Adults were so hard to understand. She lamented that it would be years before she could be able to maneuver at that level.

Demetria continued, "The reason I am so proud of you was the answer that you gave to Gwen. You helped her and I out by placing the thought in everyone's minds that we would have to be the aggressors for him to be an enemy."

Rakira bit her lip, "I did not really think about what I was going to say. It was just how I felt. I did not use any kind of reasoning at all. How can that be good?"

Demetria knelt down and place her hands on Rakira's shoulders and said, "Rakira, you met that young man for only few minutes. I could tell that the two of you are connected to each other, but I do not know how or for what reason. You do not have information that you could have used to make a rational judgement. In instances where that is the case then you need to pass judgement based on feelings."

Rakira still was not quite sure what her mother meant but she nodded anyway. She would commit those words to memory. Perhaps they would make sense to her someday. Suddenly she felt a familiar odd tingle in her mind, and she gasped, "He is here."

Demetria looked startled, "How do you know that?"

Rakira closed her eyes, "I feel a tingle in my mind. I felt it when we met him before." She turned to her left and pointed out over the endless water, "He is there."

CHAPTER 25
SHIP

It had been two days since they had left the portal to Nexus, and they had made almost no progress towards the core. After they had been at the reef, they had encountered several large creatures that they had taken pains to avoid. There was just no knowing what a predator was here.

They had actually been forced to return to the reef once when another of those fifty-foot sharks swam by. They were currently near the edge of an underwater cliff. There was no telling how far down it went but none of them were interested in finding out. They had already seen enough of the strange deep-sea monsters.

The six of them were resting before crossing this wide expanse when a shadow passed over them and they took cover. Looking out from some rocks they could see that whatever it was, it was not moving normally. It was drifting sideways across the waves. Another of those large sharks was following it and tried a few times to take a bite out of it.

Wait a minute... That sound when the shark tried to bite down on it was metallic. Is that some form of ship?

No sooner had that thought passed through Joleen's mind then Meterove and Dras recognized the shape they were looking at. It was one of the Leturai ships! The shark appeared to lose interest in the ship and swam off. Once it was out of sight, they all looked at one another then Meterove pointed up and began swimming towards the ship.

Everyone kept their eyes on their surroundings while swimming up. The ship appeared to be drifting so there was little chance that it would move away too fast. Once they broke the surface, they could see the ship was about fifty feet wide and hundreds of feet long. They quickly swam to it and managed to climb on top of it.

Joleen said, "Leturai ships are strange. How are you meant to get inside?"

Meterove said, "That raised area down there has a door on the top of it that allows you to get in."

They moved carefully over the wet surface. When they came to the raised portion, they found a ladder that was built into the side and used it to climb the ten feet or so up. Once Meterove saw that the hatch was open, but also that there was blood on it.

Meterove held a finger to his lips and pointed to it. Dras nodded and handed Meterove his sword. "I will go first. If something bad is down there I can just pop back up."

Dras climbed down the ladder that was inside the hatch as quietly as he could manage. Going down it was lit with glowing red gemstones. Once he was at the bottom, he found that the gemstones changed to a soft white light. There was more blood down here.

The blood up there was so dry it was cracking, but this looks fresher. I doubt that it is older than a day. This place smells like death too. I wish I knew what sounds were normal on one of these. It looks safe enough right here though. I better get the others.

Dras went back to the ladder and looked up at Meterove and waved him down. Once everyone was down the ladder Meterove sealed the hatch. Joleen raised an eyebrow at him.

Meterove shrugged, "If there is something on board here, I would rather not add to their number or sink because this thing gets tipped over."

Now that everyone was here, they began to search the room, which appeared to be the control room. The various devices around the room were all foreign to them. The writing was all using Leturai language and alphabet. Joleen, Jolson and Meterove knew a little of the language but

535

not enough to be able to understand what they were looking at.

A soft hiss alerted them that they were not alone, and they all ducked down. There was a door at either end of the room and out of the one that faced the bow came a familiar figure. The large glassy eyes and huge sharp fangs over a female humanoid figure that was almost entirely covered in scales. It was carrying a short spear.

Joleen watched as Meterove used several hand gestures to Dras that made no sense to her but clearly Dras understood. Meterove knocked on the console next to him once, just loudly enough to hear in the room. The second he did that Dras popped up and fired his crossbow.

The bolt hit the creature right between the eyes and it fell to the floor. The sound of the spear hitting the floor was louder than the sound the creature made hitting the floor.

Meterove and Dras led the way over to the creature. Narok averted his eyes when he realized that it had no clothes. The rest of them examined the creature.

Meterove said, "So there are Sirens on the ship. This one does not appear to be undead though. I thought Flare said they lived in very deep water though. What are they doing up here?"

Joleen asked, "What is this ship doing here?"

Jolson said, "It must have either been pulled through or simply went through the tears that the Kraken made. That would also potentially explain the Sirens then. This ship would have come through in very deep water. Perhaps they followed it to the surface?"

Meterove said, "I guess that makes sense. Regardless of how they are here, we need to deal with them. This is a large ship we should split up to search. Based on the size of this thing there must be more than on deck. I say that we split up and one pair checks the bow on this level while the other four check the lower deck."

Jolson asked, "What about the stern of this deck?"

Dras said, "The little that I heard from the Leturai makes it sound like the room that powers these things is called the engine room and they sound like they take up a lot of room."

Meterove said, "Exactly. I am only guessing here but I think that the stern is mostly the engine room. Joleen, you and Narok check the rest of this deck. Dras, you and Jolson take the lower-level stern, Terenia and I will take the bow."

Joleen watched the others walk over to the ladder and descended to the lower deck. Narok picked up the dead Siren's spear and handed it to Joleen. She looked at him curiously.

Narok said, "In tight quarters like this that spear will be useful for attacking around me."

Joleen knew that her own weapons would require even less space than this spear, but Narok must have a specific plan in mind, so she took the spear and tied a length of leather to it to make a strap. Throwing it over her back she took up her other spear again and said, "Ok I am ready."

Narok lead the way with a curious shield. It had a slot that allowed him to balance and use his spear. The two of them moved through the door that the Siren had come through.

Joleen noted the design of the ship as they moved through it. Each room had heavy doors with a wheel on both sides of them. When they closed one and turned the wheel it locked the door tight.

Narok said, "It must be in case the hull gets breached. They can seal the room that is flooding and keep the rest of the ship safe."

Joleen looked impressed. She had already seen several marvels while inside this ship.

Perhaps we should consider putting similar construction to use on our own ships.

They stepped through a door and into their third room and they saw a flash of movement and heard a low hiss. Two clangs on Narok's shield gave him a sense of where they were, and he pivoted his spear slightly and thrust it forward. Narok felt resistance and heard a pained hiss.

There was another clang on his shield, quickly followed by another. Joleen realized that it was too cramped in this compartment to properly use the larger spear up front. However, she was not up front. She watched over Narok's shoulder and when she saw a slight glow and thrust her spear over Narok. There was a shriek, and the spear was almost pulled out of her hands.

There were no further strikes on Narok's shield so he lowered it slightly to look over the top. After a quick glance told him that the rest of the room was clear he lowered it the rest of the way and gave Joleen a proud smile.

Narok said, "You did really well."

Joleen tried not to look too pleased with herself. Something caught her eye that made that easy though. There was another door on the other side of the room, but unlike the others that they had seen thus far, it was closed.

Narok had noticed it as well. The two of them looked at each other then walked carefully over towards it. It was only now that they were inside that she noticed a few other details. This was a significantly smaller room, which meant that the light from the gems better lit the room. There was some sort of object on the ceiling.

Joleen took a moment to examine it. She had heard of things like these before. She looked over by the door and found what she was looking for. She flicked the switch up and the room was suddenly much brighter.

Narok blinked, "What did you do?"

Joleen blinked as well, "I have been wondering for a while why this ship was so dark, and I suddenly figured it out. Those gems that are scattered are only by doors. They are meant for emergencies. There should be more of these in every room near the doors to light the rooms."

Narok said, "Why were they turned off?"

Joleen said, "Those Sirens are supposed to be from the deepest parts of the Plane of Water. They are probably not good with bright light, so they figured out how to turn the lights off."

The door across the room gave a creak as it opened. Joleen and Narok both raised their weapons but lowered them when they saw a Leturai face looking through the gap in the door.

The Leturai saw them, and then saw the dead Sirens on the floor and said something back to the others in Leturai . The door opened the rest of the way and showed a room full of Leturai. They all looked a little worse for wear, but they were at least alive.

Joleen asked, "Can any of you understand me?"

One of the older looking Leturai stepped forward, "I can. I am Anton, the Chief Navigator. We have many questions, but I suppose I should start with thanking you for killing those beasts."

Joleen said, "You are welcome, Anton. I am Joleen Valaseri." Joleen saw his eyes widen a bit at the name then continued, "We can answer a number of your questions, but it is going to take a while. Are there any officers amongst you?"

Anton shook his head, "No. Most of the officers and combat trained personnel tried to fight back against the creatures that invaded the ship when we went up for air."

Narok asked, "How many Sirens were there?"

Anton said, "I do not know for sure. The captain and other officers ordered us to seal ourselves in the galley. Once the door was closed the only sounds were what was coming through the air vents."

Joleen asked, "How long have you been here?"

Anton said, "We have been holed up in here for five days now. We only heard sounds of fighting on the first day. We have been lost for several months."

Narok said, "From the look of things the soldiers did not fare well. I am assuming that there are not too many weapons on board."

Anton asked, "Where are we that humans were the ones that found us? Our mission had been to explore uncharted waters. Also, you seem unconcerned about our presence here. Puzzled sure but not alarmed."

Joleen said, "We are aware of and have already assisted your people with their crisis."

Anton froze, "What crisis? What are you talking about?"

Joleen rubbed her temples, "You must have been deployed before the attacks. Your people were under attack by a massive Kraken. The majority of the surviving Leturai are currently in refugee camps. We are here to try and deal with the Kraken."

Anton laughed, "Surely you jest. Krakens can get quite large but for one to attack our cities is ridiculous!"

Narok shook his head, "No, it is very real. You are not even on the same world anymore. Once this ship is secure, we can show you outside. That should convince you."

Anton looked suspicious, "I am not sure what to think of these claims."

Joleen said, "I think the best thing that you can do is to seal yourselves back in the galley for now. We will come back once we know the ship is secure."

Anton looked all too happy to comply with that suggestion. It was clear that he did not trust them. Joleen was happy to have them sealed back in the room. Having scared and distrustful people around in this situation sounded like a bad idea.

All across the deck were the scattered remains of both Sirens and many more Leturai. While they were only armed with spears or rapiers the Sirens had been able to quickly overpower the Leturai, who mostly had improvised weapons.

Meterove and Terenia picked their way through the bodies slowly. They had encountered a few living Sirens and had killed them along the way. They were currently slowly moving through the crews quarters. Meterove had also discovered the lights, which had been used to blind the Sirens.

A makeshift barrier made up of everything that they could find that was not secured to the ship was in the middle of the room. It looked like they had tried to make a stand here. There were several dozen corpses behind the barrier.

It would help if we had any idea how many of the Sirens were even on the ship. As it is we have no idea if there is one or one hundred more.

Other similar thoughts plagued Meterove as they walked amongst the dead. The bodies were stiff and there was the stench of death that indicated they had been here for days.

After the crews quarters there was a door that was locked and had various warning signs on it. Meterove assumed that this had something to do with the ships weapons.

Terenia asked, "What now?"

Meterove said, "We return to the control room. I hope the others has better luck than we did."

Terenia looked at the dead as they walked past. "Do you think there will be a way that we can get them back to our world?"

Meterove asked, "I have no idea. I do not even know what the Leturai do with their dead."

.   .   .

Jolson and Dras cut their way through their tenth Siren. For some reason they were all over the engine room. They had not encountered any of them in the other rooms. Jolson did not understand this room in the slightest but at least nothing looked as though it had been broken.

They thoroughly searched every corner and crevice looking for survivors and more Sirens. They had found another room along the way that had piqued their interest. It had warning signs on the door and was locked. The door was really sturdy so they had made the decision to try and find whatever key it was that would open it.

Once they were done searching the engine room, they returned to the control room. Joleen and Narok were already there. They only had to wait a few more minutes for Meterove and Terenia.

Once they were all there Joleen said, "We found survivors. There are about two dozen of them that have locked themselves in the galley."

Meterove and the others looked relieved. Meterove asked, "Were you able to ask them any questions?"

Joleen said, "Yes, but they did not have much in the way of information. Apparently, they had no idea that the attacks on their people were happening. There was one amongst them named Anton, who understood our language.

The way he tells it they have been lost for some time. I think they might have fallen through one of the openings that were made and had no idea. He said that the Sirens came aboard when they went up to refill their air. About the only other useful thing he said was that most of the officers and military personnel had them hide while they attempted to fight the Sirens."

Meterove said, "I think we found where they made their final stand. I think we should have another talk with this Anton and see what more we can learn."

Narok led the way back to the galley and after assuring Anton that it was safe the door opened. The Leturai that were inside did look pretty rough. Anton stepped to the front again.

Meterove said, "You must be Anton?"

Anton nodded, "And you are?"

Meterove said, "My name is Meterove Valaseri. We need your help."

Anton's eyes widened again but were also suspicious. Meterove could not exactly blame him. What were the odds of meeting not one but all of the human imperial family?

Meterove continued, "I think the first place to start is to show you what it is like outside. Once you see that I think you will begin to understand the situation that we are all in."

Anton motioned to the other Leturai and spoke lowly in their language. Joleen was sure that he was telling them to lock the door behind him. Sure enough, once he was out of the door one of the men inside reached and closed the door.

Anton followed them to the control room. Along the way Meterove explained that they had searched the ship and had found no more survivors and had killed all the remaining Sirens that they had found. Meterove went up the ladder first and Anton followed.

Anton almost fell back down the ladder once he saw the view from the top. He could only fearfully mumble, "Where are we?"

Meterove said, "This place is called the Plane of Water. It feeds all the bodies of water in every world. There are also sea creatures of every conceivable size and shape here too. Many are not in every world."

Anton looked at Meterove with dead eyes, "Worlds? I do not understand."

Meterove put a hand on his shoulder and gestured with the other at the ladder. Let's go back inside and talk where it is safe. You may have heard a banging on the ship earlier. That was a fifty-foot shark."

Anton hurried back down the ladder. Once they were back in the control room and Anton had taken a drink from a flask they found, Meterove asked, "I know this is a lot to process right now but there are a few more questions that I need to ask you."

Anton said, "Ask what you will. I will answer if I am able."

Meterove said gently, "What do your people do with your dead?"

Anton looked blankly at him for a moment before saying, "Oh right, the fallen. We do not worship deities.

We believe in sending the dead back to the world to continue the cycle."

Jolson asked, "Continue the cycle?"

Anton took another drink then said, "We release their bodies into the water and the ocean claims them."

Dras said, "OH! It is kind of like what sailors do for us. We call it burial at sea."

Meterove asked, "Is there any special procedure that we need to follow?"

Anton shook his head, "Not particularly. The nearest thing is having someone who knew them take part."

Meterove said, "Alright. We will help you and the rest of your people move them up to the surface. The next question I have is, can this ship still be used?"

Anton thought for a moment, "The crewmen necessary for operations are all in the galley. I have no idea as to the current state of our fuel supply though."

Joleen said, "We can worry about that part later. For now, we need to focus on getting the Sirens off the ship and giving the dead Leturai their burial."

Meterove, Jolson, Dras and Terenia split up to begin moving the dead Sirens. Joleen and Narok went with Anton back to the galley. It took the several hours, but they finally managed to get all the dead up to the surface. The Sirens they dumped over the side, but the Leturai laid on the top of the ship.

There were only about thirty Sirens, but they had managed to kill almost a hundred Leturai. Once all were up on the surface Anton came to them with news.

Anton said, "It appears that our fuel levels are approximately around one fourth."

Jolson asked, "How long will that run the ship?"

Anton said, "That depends on a lot of things. If we are going against the current or with. Are we under the water or on the surface?"

Jolson put up a hand, "I get it."

Anton said, "According to our chief engineer, the best-case scenario is a week."

Meterove looked pensive, "That still helps. We need to get to the core of the Plane of Water."

Anton said, "With all due respect, this is a Leturai ship. We need to get what is left of this crew back home."

Meterove said, "If we do not get to the core then at the very least your people will likely lose your home entirely. Last we were there your capital was mostly flooded and large sections had been leveled. There was reason to believe that several of your cities have been destroyed."

Anton paled, "I still maintain that I need to get my people home."

Dras was leaning on one of the consoles with his legs crossed at the ankles. He had been looking silently down at his feet over his crossed arms. He said, "Where do you think that you are going to find a way home?"

Anton said, "You found your way here."

Meterove said, "Yes, with permission. The person that gave it to us has no reason to give it to you."

Anton bristled, "Was that a threat?"

Meterove stared him down, "No, it is a fact We had to do a lot of favors for her before she would allow us to have access to the Planes. As it is, I am expecting her to make some demands of us once this is all over."

Anton was quiet for several minutes. Finally, he said, "How is helping you going to help us?"

Joleen said, "If we can resolve what is happening here on the Plane of Water, then we will take you home. From what I understand, the Principal Races of the Plane of Water are capable of moving between worlds. We might be able to get you home through them."

Anton looked puzzled, "What about the six of you?"

Joleen said, "Like I said, we have something here that we need to do. We are here to resolve the matter of the Kraken."

Anton asked, "I just do not understand. Why would a Kraken from here be attacking our home?"

Joleen glanced at her brothers uneasily, something that was not lost on Anton. Finally, she said, "We believe that the undead from our world may have found their way here somehow and infected this Kraken. This is one of the tasks that I mentioned before."

That is true, but it still seems kind of obvious that you are leaving something out. Looking at Meterove and I before saying that only makes it more obvious.

Fortunately, Anton either did not notice or care enough to comment. While he was thinking a panicked Leturai came running into the room and quickly began spewing something out in Leturai. The harsh sounds of the language combined with his rapid speech made it unintelligible to them, but they knew something was wrong.

Anton looked fear on his face, "We have picked something up on our long-range sonar. Something that is much larger than the Stoicheskiy is heading towards us."

Dras said, "We have seen several insanely large sea creatures since we came here. There was this dragon looking thing with a really long body that swallowed a whale whole."

Anton said gravely, "So then this might be a real reading and not a sensor ghost. We do not really have a leader. The only reason that I have been the one speaking with you is that I am the only one that knows your language."

Meterove said, "What kind of weapons does this ship have?"

Anton said, "To the best of my knowledge we have two different weapons. One is called torpedoes and fire from the front. They are designed to travel forward in the water and explode on impact. The other weapon is called a depth charge. These are designed to explode once they reach a certain depth."

Meterove asked, "Which direction is it coming from and how long until it reaches the ship?"

Anton spoke rapidly to the Leturai, who responded back even faster. Anton turned back to Meterove and said, "It is coming from our port side and at the rate it was moving it will be here in minutes. It appears to be moving under the water at a depth of one hundred meters."

Meterove did the mental math to convert the measurement and asked, "So if we monitor where it is and use those depth charge things at the right time it should be hurt pretty bad right?"

Anton shrugged, "Perhaps. I know nothing of warfare. I am just the navigator."

Joleen said, "It sounds like as good of a plan as we are going to come up with in this time crunch. Deploy the weapons!"

Anton shouted in Leturai and one of the other Leturai pressed a button on the console that he was sitting at and spoke rapidly into it. A Siren went off in the ship and a light began to rapidly blink on the ceiling with bright flashes.

Anton said, "You may want to brace yourselves."

Joleen and the others took his advice and Jolson added, "Once the depth charges blow, initiate a dive as fast as we can."

Anton nodded and took his seat next to the helmsmen. Once seated he relayed Jolson's order. A Leutari spoke and Anton relayed, "Thirty seconds. Twenty seconds. Ten seconds. Five. Four. Three. Two. One!"

On one several things happened at once. There was the sound of several explosions that seemed strangely muffled. There was also a massive roar that came from whatever had been coming up to them. A few moments after the charges went off the shockwave hit them some and rocked the Stoicheskiy.

As soon as the shockwave had hit the Leturai began scrambling with controls. There was a gauge that Anton pointed to while doing his work. It was clearly measuring their current depth.

Jolson said, "Once we get to four hundred meters get us back to the surface as fast as possible, while dropping more of those charges."

Anton said, "Yes, Sir!" Afterwards he relayed the commands to the other Leturai.

Meterove looked at Jolson, "What are you doing?"

Jolson said, "This creature is very large. I doubt that those blasts were enough to kill it or drive it off. I think that we are going to need more. The reason it is a threat is because of its size. That is also a weakness since it will not be able to change direction as fast as us."

No sooner had Jolson said this then Anton said, "We have reached four hundred meters. Initiating emergency surfacing and dropping charges!"

Again, there were the muffled explosions and angry roar. One of the Leturai shouted and Anton said, "The creature has passed us and is turning around to attack from the front now."

Joleen said, "Try the torpedoes!"

Anton shouted their order out and after a moment there were several more explosions that could be heard before they reached the surface. Meterove had spotted the periscope and guessed its purpose. He looked through it before saying, "It is still out there. I have an idea. I can use my magic to injure it further and draw it away."

Terenia looked alarmed, but Meterove said, "We do not have time to debate this. That thing is going to sink this ship. We need to get to the core. I will be fine. Dras come with me and close the hatch behind me."

Dras looked less than enthused but nodded solemnly. They quickly went up the ladder and once Meterove was outside Dras hesitated for a moment but closed the hatch with a simple, "Good luck."

Meterove powered up his magic the same instant that he dove into the water. He sent several volleys over at the creature. It was one of the dragon-like creatures that Dras had mentioned before. It did look hurt but nowhere near fatally. The blasts hit it in the left eye and certainly drew its attention.

Meterove was still near the surface and could see that one of the spirals of water that connected the top and bottom were nearby. This one was spinning extremely fast. An insane idea occurred to him.

Meterove dove back under the water and sent more volleys to hurt the creature. Once he knew that its attention was on him, and not the Stoicheskiy, he set out swimming as fast as he could towards the spiral.

He could hear the monster behind him but there was no way that it was going to get to him before they reached that spiral.

I just hope that this does what I think it will do.

Once he was in the current of the spiral, he felt the satisfactory tug of a strong current. The only problem was that seconds later it increased exponentially and instead of being able to employ Jolson's trick he had done with the ship, both he and the creature were pulled into and up the spiral.

Inside the Stoicheskiy Joleen had been watching through the periscope. She saw Meterove and the creature get sucked up the spiral and vanish.

At first her hands tightened on the handle of the periscope, but after a moment she relaxed. She stepped back and said, "We need to get going. Meterove is out of our reach for the moment."

Terenia looked panicked, "What do you mean out of our reach?"

Joleen put a hand to her temple, "He swam into that spiraling water pillar to draw the creature into it and both of them were sucked up it."

Around the room four more hands went to temples and a low groan came from all five. Anton looked from one to the next nonplused. He could not understand how they were so calm. They had just lost a comrade!

Joleen said, "I am sure the next time we see him he is going to be grinning like an idiot too, as though this was all part of his plan and not at all like he accidently got pulled in too."

The others laughed. Dras said, "The least he could have done was take me with."

Terenia rolled her eyes, "You really are just as bad as he is."

Joleen looked at Anton, "There is a massive spiral of water, which is far larger than the others. That is the core and our destination. We need to get moving."

CHAPTER 26
LAGOON

Laticin swam through the Mermaid's lagoon looking for various specks of gems. She had a small pouch that was made from shark skin that she was placing them in as she swam along. She found all kinds of stones, crystals, and metallic flakes.

She collected them until the bag, which was a little smaller than her hands, was full. She then swam through the lagoon until she was near a familiar weed bed. She looked around and made sure that no one was looking then she swam through and into the crevice behind them.

She had found the cave that was beyond when she was younger and there had been a need to excavate new caves to accommodate their increased numbers. This place was where she kept her art. Her mother was always critical and judgmental of her art, so she moved her collection there.

After a moment she surfaced inside her sanctuary. She had found some glowing crystals to put inside to light it, otherwise it was pitch black. It was a large cave, big enough to have fit an adolescent whale. The air that had been in here originally had begun to grow stale and Laticin had needed to use her magic to replenish it.

Scattered around the room were dozens of rock slabs that had various materials attached to them using glue she had made from fish. Some were simply patterns that she liked but most were pictures that she had meticulously put pieces together to form.

She preferred her art to be unique, where her mother believed in trying to copy the work she had seen done before. For years she had struggled believing that her art was bad until one of the elders had said something in one of her lessons about how all art should be unique.

It was at that moment that she had started to rebel against her mother. She had decided that she was not going let her mother mold her in her own image. Laticin pulled herself up into her cave and looked to where she had her two unfinished pieces. One was a scene from the surface with its many spirals and the Core in the distance. The other was of a nude woman.

She was not sure who the person was yet. She had yet to complete the face. She looked over the pictures and decided to finish the first one. Once out of the water her fins were replaced with legs. She sat there meticulously placing the tiny gems and crystals in place for hours.

Eventually it was time for the elders to meet and after the matter with the deep-sea creatures coming to the surface, she had less chances to sneak off from them. She also wanted to go today since today was less lectures and more of a debate on what to do about several different matters.

Laticin put away her materials and slipped back into the water and swam out of the crevice, taking care to see if anyone was looking. She quickly swam over to the Meeting Stone. It was a large round rock that was almost perfectly flat. The Mermaids kept it clear by cleaning it daily.

While she was not the last one there, she was one of the later arrivals. Looking around the cove Laticin could see that a great many of the Mermaids from the cove were nearby to listen in. While not forbidden it was frowned upon, which proved how worried everyone was.

There had been a lot of disappearances lately. Far more in fact than the answers that they had been given thus far explained. Just last night, several had gone missing from their caves, while they slept.

After several minutes, the rest of the elders arrived. Laticin was surprised that her mother was amongst them.

Usually, she was the first one at a meeting like this. The look on her face was unnaturally serious.

Something new has happened! What could it be now?

Soon the meeting began with Moira taking the lead today. Her mother seemed oddly distracted. Whatever it was that was wrong it was serious enough that she was passing on protocol.

Moira said, *"We will be bypassing many traditions and procedures today. There are far too many important matters that need to be discussed. We will be starting with why several of the elders, me included, just arrived."*

Moira seemed to take a moment to collect herself before saying, *"The body of a Siren was washed into the fishing grounds this morning."*

Laticin's mind went blank for a moment. Once she had recovered from the shock, she became confused. While it was not exactly common to find a Siren it did happen from time to time.

What is so worrisome about finding a Siren? Sure, we have a strained relationship but not so much that we need to be worried about them attacking.

Moira continued, *"There was evidence that the Siren had been killed using some sort of bladed weapon, and that this had occurred on the surface."*

561

NEVERMIND! Why were the Sirens up on the surface! What could have killed it? Wait..just one? or...

Moira looked around at the rest of the assembled Mermaids and said, *"We have no idea what the Sirens were doing up on the surface or who killed it. We have no doubt that there were or are more. Additionally, while we do not know for sure, we believe that this is tied to whatever is causing the creatures of the deep to rise to the surface."*

There was an outbreak of scared babbling as dozens of Mermaids began to talk over each other. Moira held her hands up for silence and said, *"At this point in time we do not have any further information on this matter. We will disperse anything that we learn as it becomes available. Next is the matter of messengers that we sent out to the Undines and the Snow Women. At this point none of them have returned."*

Instead of increasing the babbling from before this was met is total silence. You could feel the fear from every one of them. The paths that they had established for messengers to run to the other races had long been amongst the safest on the Plane. Various wards and even guard posts were scattered along the routes.

One of the other elders, Alara said, *"We are currently investigating one post at a time, but it will take some time to find out what, if anything has happened."*

Alara was an imposing woman. She was the elder in charge of training Mermaids as guards and was rumored to have actual experience in warfare from one of her trips to a world. She was very muscular and had her hair cut very short. Her jet black and robust gold scales added to her look.

While she showed this face to the rest Laticin knew a secret about her. She would sneak off to her own secret place to sing. Laticin had stumbled across it once and had kept it a secret, even though Alara had not asked her too.

Laticin glanced at her mother again who still had not taken part in the meeting. What was going on with her? This was too strange for her to let it go.

Moira said, *"As you know there have also been disappearances around and even inside the Lagoon. It is possible that these matters are all connected. At this time, we do not have any leads."*

Alara picked up right where she left off, *"To address the safety concerns we have decided to post additional guards around the Lagoon. I will be needing a dozen volunteers. If I do not get them then I will be selecting as many as I need."*

Moira said, *"To help address the matter we will also be restricting access to some of the fishing grounds that are further out. Our food supply will suffer as a result, so we will have to make adjustments."*

Alara said, *"Before we move to far away from the topic, there is more on the matter of the messengers. We as we are unsure if they delivered their messages, we are unsure at this point if we will attempt to travel to the Core for a meeting."*

At this point Laticin was not surprised. There were plenty of problems here already. Risking the lives of some of the elders to send them to a meeting that may not even be happening would be a bad idea.

Suddenly her mother looked alive. Elise raised her head and said, *"We must look to the scriptures! The Great Lord will protect us! The Great Lord who resides around us shall make sure that all that belongs here shall remain!"*

Laticin rolled her eyes. Of course, her mother would start spouting that nonsense now. This was not the time for promises, but tangible safety. The majority of the assembled Mermaids seemed to agree.

Elise persisted, *"We must stay the course that has been given to us. We must live as we were told. This may be our punishment for not being true to our purpose!"*

Laticin noticed that as she said that her mother's eyes drifted towards her for a moment. Anger boiled up in her heart. Her mother was actually suggesting that she was to blame for this. She did not say it out loud, but Laticin knew. Normally she held her tongue when she was involved but this time she lost her temper.

Laticin said, *"If the scriptures and living to our purpose protected us then why were Adriana and Fiora taken? We all know that they were amongst the most devoted to the scriptures."*

There was the mental equivalent of a collected gasp from the gathered Mermaids. The elders did not look impressed either. This was unsurprising given that most of them were devoted to the scriptures, though not as much as her mother.

Elise shouted, *"How dare you speak here! You-"*

Laticin cut her off, *"We already established that we were not following protocol today. If we were then you would have been leading this meeting instead of Moira. Instead, you have been brooding."*

There was a collected grimace from the elders while Elise looked stricken. There was no denying that she had been brooding while Moira had taken charge. Additionally, Moira had stated directly that protocol would be ignored today.

Elise rallied herself and glared at Laticin and almost shouted, *"You have no authority. You do not know what we know. We know the facts! We know the truth! Something that you would know if you attended your lessons!"*

Laticin shouted back, *"You are no leader! You suggest that we do nothing while something takes our people in the night! You say to stick to the scriptures yet cannot* produce even the flimsiest argument that it will help. You dodged the matter of Adriana and Fiora. Do you know what happened to them? Staying here, doing nothing but praying is not going to resolve this matter."

Elise shouted, "How dare you! I already said you do not know what you speak of! Praying WILL help. We must be faithful and follow the scriptures of the Great Lord!"

Laticin shook her head, "You are useless. You have done nothing here today but to cling to your beliefs while everything else crumbles around you. You are cowering in fear while we need someone strong. I am done speaking to you."

Laticin turned to Moira, "Since Elise is clearly unfit for her duty, I suggest that we look to Moira for leadership right now."

Elise looked like she wanted to argue but there was a strong push from the assembled Mermaids. The exchange between Laticin and Elise had shaken their faith in her. She had made no arguments for her point at all. Moira looked troubled by this turn of events but seemed to realize that things had gone too far to go back now.

Moira hung her head slightly, "Now that you two are done can we get back to business? As much as I loathe to admit it there is nothing in the scriptures that is going to help with these matters."

The onlookers appeared to calm down slightly as Moira spoke. Elise looked scandalized and appeared ready to launch into another tirade when Alara cut her off, *"This is neither the time nor the place for that kind of behavior. You are excused Elise."*

Elise's eyes went wide as she realized that had just happened. She puffed herself up and swam off shouting, *"and the Great Lord of the Plane of Water will make all as it was. All will be remade and be as it should be. That which does not belong will be removed and those that follow him shall be used by him and shall preserve the purity!"*

There was a silence after Elise left that lasted for a very long moment. Once it was over Moira continued, *"As I was saying. There is nothing in the scriptures that can help us with these matters. As of now, the plan of increasing our guards and limiting the distance that we travel outside of the lagoon will be our starting points. That is all."*

Laticin stayed around after the meeting was ended because she knew that the other elders were not done with her yet. Her outburst would be commented on. Sure, enough after conferring with the other elders Moira and Alara swam over to her.

They looked over her impassively until Alara said in a voice full of mirth, *"I should not be amused by this, but I truly enjoyed watching you put Elise in her place earlier. Beliefs aside, she was disconnecting herself from reality and* latching onto her faith. *You were absolutely right when you said she was not acting like a leader."*

Moira said, *"I wish you could have done that with more tact though. Now our people are shaken. Seeing her own daughter pull her down and then place me up in her stead will help keep the peace for now."*

Laticin said defiantly, *"I do not see how I could have done anything differently. She was not acting in her right mind. I knew that she was obsessed with the scriptures, but it has never been this bad before."*

Moira said, *"The scriptures ARE important though-"*

Laticin cut her off, *"All of you are entitled to believe whatever you want to believe. You are NOT allowed to force others to believe it or to get others killed because of them."*

Alara gave her an approving nod, *"I have to agree with Laticin. The words of the scriptures may be comforting but they are doing nothing to keep us safe. There have been more than fifty disappearances. Adriana and Fiora were both as devout as Elise and that did not save them."*

Moira looked saddened, *"I know that you are right."*

Alara said, *"Now onto the matter of the extra guards. Considering the scene that you made, I hope you know that you have officially volunteered yourself."*

Damnit! I cannot argue that point either.

Laticin tried not to look particularly upset about this and nodded. *"What do you need from me?"*

Alara smiled, *"I will take you to the armory and we will get you a weapon."*

They bid Moira farewell and the two of them began to swim in the direction of the armory. There were half a dozen volunteers that had waited around that joined them. They swam over to the wall of the lagoon where the armory was.

The cave that housed their weapons was similar to the one that Laticin used for her art, though smaller. Unlike her cave, the entrance was out in the open. The eight of them swam into the cave and up into the armory.

While Laticin had never seen a real armory before she knew that this was one in name only. There were only around fifty weapons in the cave and most Mermaids, herself included had little to no idea on how to use them. All of these had been taken from other worlds. Most were spears but there were several swords there as well.

The Mermaids had used their meager knowledge of magic to attempt to keep the weapons from corroding. Despite their best efforts some of them would rust from time to time and would get replaced.

Alara passed the rest of the girls spears. Laticin though, she gave a special looking spear as well as a sword. When Laticin raised her eyebrow at her Alara shrugged,

"You may have stated that we should look to Moira for leadership, but you are still Elise's daughter."

Laticin noticed the other girls were treating her with deference.   She tried not to look as though she had noticed. She kept her gaze on Alara, "That should not make any difference."

Alara said, "We need to have a chain of command. I need someone that the others will listen to. That person is you."

Laticin resigned herself to her fate. She asked, "How exactly do you want this command structure to work?"

Alara said, "I will go around and find more guards. I will have you in charge of these six. You will arrange their patrol times as well as your own."

Laticin looked down at the weapons she had been given. The sword she knew was called a rapier. It had a long narrow blade with a sharp point that was made for thrusting. There was an intricate basket of wire that acted as a guard. There was also a type of loop made of leather that was attached to the pommel that could go around her wrist. There was a sheath and belt for it as well.

The spear had a common spear head on it, but a little ways down from the head was a pair of blades that protruded out. They curved down in a "v" shape that would trap another weapon if used right.

Laticin spent the rest of that day working with the other girls. The area of the lagoon that they were going to be watching was from the main entrance to the fishing grounds. The seven of them worked out a rotation so that there was always two of them on guard at any time. Laticin decided that she was going to rotate if she was going to take the morning and night watches.

Over the next dozen cycles there was little of consequence that happened, at least in their area. There were several more disappearances, including a few of the guards. Tensions were beginning to run high throughout the lagoon.

Then there was the increased presence of deep-water creatures. There had nearly been an incident with an Ichthyosaur. The creature had chased some tuna over towards the lagoon and only turned away at the last moment. Had that thing entered the lagoon there would have been heavy casualties.

Even more unnerving were the Megalodons. The sharks had also moved up from their normal habitat and were eating the tuna that the Mermaids had relied on for food. Fighting them off would be difficult with the weapons that they had.

Alara had spent several sleepless nights trying to come up with a solution. By chance one of the sharks had gotten themselves entangled in one of the nets that were used to catch tuna and had died. This had given her the idea of setting up the now unused nets to help protect the lagoon. The meat from the shark had also been useful.

Finally, after several attempts had been made to get answers about their messengers and outposts, one of them returned. She was exhausted and looked half starved. Her name was Risa. She had been sent to the snow woman village of Demetria. After Risa had rested a short while and had eaten, she made her report.

Risa said, *"There are predators everywhere. The Varity Trench outpost looked like it had been attacked by a colossal squid or perhaps even a Kraken. There were still some...parts... of those who had been there."*

Alara gritted her teeth, *"What make you suspect a squid or Kraken?"*

Risa said, *"What little was left of them were inside the outpost and had marks on them that look similar to those made by the octopi around here."*

Alara closed her eyes for a moment then asked, *"What of the others?"*

Risa shook her head, *"The outposts at the Azure Reef and the Great Shelf were both completely deserted. There was no sign of an attack or struggle."*

Alara looked grave. This sounded too much like the situation they were having where women were vanishing in the night. If it were not just localized to the lagoon that would be bad news.

Moira asked, *"Did Demetria mention anything about these events while you were there?"*

Risa shook her head, *"This was all news to her. Additionally, the Azure Reef and The Great Shelf outposts were intact on the way there. Whatever happened occurred between the time I passed through and when I went back."*

Moira and Alara shared a look. While they were still silent Laticin swam in from her patrol. She said, *"I apologize for my tardiness. We had another megalodon that was near the lagoon. We monitored it until it moved off."*

Moira waved a hand, *"So long as it moved away then all is well. Risa has informed us that the outposts at Varity Trench, the Azure Reef and The Great Shelf were either wiped out or abandoned."*

Laticin's face took on the same serious, grave expression as Moira's, *"Is there any- No I can ask about that later."*

Moira asked, *"Risa what did Demetria have to say about the meeting?"*

Risa said, *"The only thing that she had said was that they would discuss it and let us know. Considering how dangerous the trip was for me, I have no idea how they plan to contact us."*

Alara asked, *"What do you mean dangerous? What else happened that you have not yet told us?"*

Risa shuddered, *"I mentioned the predators before. There were far more than usual. There were some that just looked...wrong. I have no other words that I can use to describe them. Their eyes were glassy, and they were far more persistent than usual when they were hunting me. I spent four cycles in a cave while a shark stayed outside the entrance."*

Alara looked very disturbed and struggled to ask, *"Did the water around you seem different?"*

Risa thought about it for a moment then said, *"You know, now that you mention it, there was something that was off with the water. When that shark was near, the water had a strange smell to it. It was like..."*

Alara fearfully supplied, *"like water around something that has been dead for a while?"*

Risa nodded emphatically, *"YES! That is exactly what it was like!"*

Alara's eyes were now filed with worry. She asked, *"At any point, did you get injured by or even near one of these strange predators?"*

Risa shook her head, *"No. That was part of the reason that it took me so long to get back. I was too scared to take any chances."*

Alara looked a little relieved but still said, *"That was a wise choice. If this is what I think it is, then we have a very big problem here."*

Moira looked concerned and asked, *"What is going on Alara?"*

Alara said slowly, *"This sounds like the plague of undeath. I do not understand how it is here. The Plane of Water is very pure, to the point that it is normally damaging to undead. For undeath to exist here is troubling."*

Laticin asked, *"Have you ever seen anything like this before or is this just what you have heard?"*

Alara glared at her for a moment but then realized there was no attitude behind her question. She said, *"I have seen it before but only a single undead. I remember the smell quite clearly. While I cannot be sure that this is what we are dealing with, I believe that the possibility warrants a lot more caution as well as us sending someone to the Core to meet with the other Principal Races."*

Laticin could not help herself, she was interested. She did her best to make sure that she did not accidentally come off as excited, but it was hard. Something big was happening and she wanted to know what it was.

Moira said, *"Risa, how about you head back to your cave and rest? We will talk some more after you have recovered from your ordeal a little."*

Risa nodded wearily, *"That sounds lovely. I will be resting, but if you have need of me, then do not hesitate to call."*

Risa swam off to her cave and as soon she was gone Alara said, *"I want multiple guards around her cave for the next several cycles. If this is undeath then we need to be extra cautious."*

Moira said, *"Surely there is no need to watch the poor girl?"*

Alara said, *I have no idea how the plague of undeath works. I have no way of knowing if she is telling the truth about getting injured or not. I think we all can agree that we do not need someone attacking us from the inside while we are dealing with everything else."*

Laticin asked, *"Do you think this has anything to do with that Siren body that was found?"*

Alara asked, *"What would make you think that?"*

Laticin said, *"Well, first we sighted the colossal squid that were normally in the deepest parts of the plane. Then we started seeing all these other deepwater predators. The Sirens may be our cousins, but they could still be considered a "deep water predator" themselves. Maybe whatever is causing all these larger creatures to leave the depths is also forcing the Sirens out."*

Alara nodded while frowning, *"If there was something down in the depths like you say that had been corrupted that would explain why the other creatures left. Self-preservation is an extremely strong instinct that would certainly drive them out. From what I remember, animals tended to avoid the undead that I encountered."*

Laticin said, *"I was kind of hoping that you were going to disagree."*

Alara said, *"I can understand your feelings. This whole situation is quite frankly terrifying."*

Laticin asked, *"Where do we go from here?"*

Alara said, *"There is only one route that is left to us. We must get the other Principal Races involved. Once we have their support, we can come up with further measures to counter whatever is going on."*

Laticin asked, *"Does that mean that we are going to the Core?"*

Moira sighed, *"I see no other option. We will have to send a large group to make sure that they arrive."*

There was the sound of someone clearing their throat and the three of them looked over to see Elise. She glared at the three of them. Her face hardened most when she looked at Laticin.

Elise said, *"You cannot deal with something like this. It is beyond our means. We must look to the Great Lord! The scriptures will lead to our salvation!"*

Laticin tied to act as though she had not heard her, *"How many do you think that we need to send?"*

Elise bristled, *"You need to stop pretending that you know what you are talking about. I do not know why Moira and Alara are playing along with you. This childish display of yours needs to stop!"*

Laticin gripped the spear that was in her hand hard. She hated this. Once again, her mother was treating her as if she were inconsequential. What she thought was wrong or unimportant. She thought that she had snapped before when she spoke out against her in front of the others.

Laticin glared back, *"You are unfit to be here. You have NOTHING of value to contribute here. You are not WANTED here...Elise. If I must, I will have you removed by force, even if I am the one that has to do it."*

There was a small gasp from Moira and Alara. The fact that she had threatened to have Elise removed was nothing compared to her using her name. Laticin disowning her mother in the presence of elders and publicly stating that she was unfit, again in front of elders meant that there would now have to be formal proceedings.

Elise looked stricken. She knew how this played out as well as any of them. Moira glanced at Alara and then said heavily, *"The matter of Elise Reifke's competency and whether she has shown herself unfit for duty will be discussed amongst the elders and her potential replacement."*

A vein pounded on Elise's forehead. Her eyes went wide, and she lost it. She swam over and made to grab at Moira, her eyes wide with indignation. Alara got between them and after a short tussle Elise gave up and she backed off.

Her eyes were wide with rage as she shouted, *"You think that I am unfit! I am not the one entertaining a foolish child. I think that you are the ones whose competency is questionable! I should have YOU put on trial!"*

She had finally hit a nerve with the other two. Alara and Moira's faces became hard as stone. She may have been friends with Moira but that had not stopped her from venting her vitriol on her and trying to deflect her failings onto her.

Moira looked at Laticin, *"I am sorry, but I cannot have you attend the meeting with the other elders."*

Elise looked smugly at Laticin until Moira continued, *"I am formally requesting you to keep her under guard while the other elders discuss this matter."*

Elise looked like she was about ready to blow but this time Laticin had orders on top of her anger. She held the spear pointed at Elise. Moira and Alara swam off. It was a long wait. Laticin had no idea how long exactly, but the tension made it feel like an eternity.

When Moira and Alara returned they looked solemn. Moira was the first to speak, *"The elders have met, and a decision has been made. Elise Reifke has been removed from our ranks and stripped of all her authority and entitlements. Laticin Reifke has been accepted as the successor."*

Elise looked from Moira to Alara as though not understanding what they had just said. Finally, her comprehension caught up with the present and she paled.

Moira continued, *"I took absolutely no pleasure in this. I have defended you time and again, but no more. Laticin was absolutely within her rights to question you at that meeting. She was also absolutely correct to state that you were unfit to continue and that you should be disowned."*

Alara picked up here as Moira seemed to be getting chocked up. "Today you showed nothing of the woman we have always believed you to be. You have always been severely devoted to the scriptures but this! What you did today, dismissing Laticin, who has done the most to secure the lagoon, as well as accusing US who have been doing YOUR work as an elder, of being incompetent, are both beyond recompense. You have done NOTHING. You are to be formally removed from your position and be thankful that is the worst of it."

Laticin and Elise both flinched at this. Elise was beginning to realize that she had gone too far, that there was no way back. Laticin felt odd. On the outside she was calm but inside she was conflicted. She hated her mother for what she had done for years and what she was doing now. However, she also loved her. She was her mother, how could she not?

She knew though that there would be no going back now. She had brought up the claim of being unfit, but she had been angry at the time and had not really believed that the other two would agree to it. In the end her mother had done this to herself. This was probably for the best for the Mermaids as a whole, but if it was best for Laticin she did not know.

Elise looked around at the other three for a second longer, then she swam off. Moira looked away and Alara said quietly, *"We need you to go to her cave and retrieve several items that were in her care."*

Laticin did not need to ask what items. She had seen them every day since the day she had been born. One was a large chest that held the Tomes of the Great Lord. While she did not agree with her mother's zealotry, she knew that those tomes were still an important part of their peoples culture.

The other item that she was to get was a ceremonial object. It was a strangely shaped dagger. It had two blades. One was where the blade of a dagger should be while the other came out at an angle from where the guard should have been. Both blades were only sharp on the sides that were facing each other. It was also a cerulean blue color, while the blades were polished silver.

Getting those two things out of her mother's cave should not have taken long but she was slower than normal. The longer she had to stew on this the more the ache in her heart felt as though it might burst and kill her.

Several cycles later something happened that shook her out of this depression. While she was out doing her patrol near the fishing grounds, she felt that odd feeling again, like something was watching or directing her actions. This time though she was too curious because instead of directing her down it was telling her to go up.

Laticin broke the surface of the water and looked around. After a few moments she decided that she was just being jumpy and went to dive back under the water. That was when she saw it.

Nearby there was a rip current spiral. These were known by the Principal Races to be extremely dangerous and only the largest of creatures ever used them and even then, only the ones that were in much deeper water. There was most certainly something in that spiral.

Laticin dove back under the water and shouted, *"Take cover! Something is coming through the spiral!"*

The other two took cover immediately and Laticin was not far behind them. Seconds later Laticin was privy to one of the strangest sights of her life. At first, she could not believe what she was seeing and then after she was forced to accept that it was true, she said, *"That is a Leviathan! And it is CHASING a person!"*

Out from the spiral shot a small figure. It was swimming as fast as it could doing everything in its power to maintain the speed that it had gotten from the spiral. It was heading towards the bottom at a breakneck pace. It fired a blast of magic energy over its shoulder, hitting the Leviathan in the face.

Only now did Laticin notice two details. One, this person had legs and two, that the Leviathan was already hurt. None of those wounds were fatal but they were nasty. It was easy to see why it was after this person if they had inflicted those wounds.

The Leviathan chased after this person who continued to swim towards the floor. The Leviathan was so close now. Just another body length of the person and it would have them. Unfortunately for the Leviathan that was too much.

As they neared the floor the person pulled up sharply, using magic to help propel them at an even sharper angle than they would normally be able to achieve. They narrowly avoided the bottom of the plane. The Leviathan was not so lucky.

It was far larger and less maneuverable than the person had been and crashed, headfirst at incredible speed into the bottom. Laticin and the others could feel the impact through the stone as well as through the water. The impact likely shattered bones all throughout its body.

If it had survived that part, it soon had its life ended as it slid across the bottom and a large outcropping ripped open its belly. After a moment Laticin noticed that there was a section of stone poking out of its left eye. It must have been impaled through the mouth.

One of the greatest and most dangerous creatures on the plane had been slain by a single person. Laticin looked around to find them. She wanted to see what kind of person was crazy enough to try a stunt like that. After a moment, her eyes found them...no...him!

CHAPTER 27
SIRENS

The depths of the Plane of Water were a bleak place. None of the light from the surface came anywhere near here. The only light down here came from the glow of bioluminescence. Down here survival was the name of the game. Either you were good at hiding, or you died, whether it was from starvation or being eaten made no difference.

Down here there were a few apex predators. One of them was the Sirens. They were the smallest in size, but their intelligence made up for that several times over. There were few creatures down here that were a threat to them.

A lone halibut moved across the bottom, stirring up the silt. It took notice of a small ,wriggling and glowing object and swooped over to strike. A spear leapt up from underneath it and caught it right in its mouth. The halibut convulsed and a cloud began to spread from its body. The only light came from the small object that had drawn it in. A form rose from the silt and the glow increased.

Amélie had been waiting for something to swim past for hours. This would help the food shortage that had been plaguing her people since they had been driven from their original homes. The ancestral home of the Sirens was an evil place now.

They had long lived in the shadow of Mia. The first Kraken was a voracious eater and very territorial. The chasm that had served as their home had been left alone for generations. Suddenly Mia had begun forcing her way in and snatching whomever she could.

If that had been the worst of it, then they could have hunkered down in their caves and waited it out. However, not only did Mia continue to attack long after she would have normally given up, but those that she killed returned to prey upon their sisters.

It was not always the whole body either. The skeletal remains of some had pulled themselves out of the flesh. There were even roving clouds of blood that attacked as if they had minds of their own.

At first the matriarch had insisted that they reclaim the fallen and fight back Mia. That had been three matriarchs ago. Each successive one had declared their intent to fight back and hold their home. The current matriarch had decided that the time to fall back had finally come.

Amélie was one of the youngest of the warrior cast. She had only been allowed on one mating raid. Her mother had been the second matriarch and the only one to have been killed before being ousted.

With any luck several others had the same or better luck collecting food. The halibut was only a midsize one, but it should still be able to feed a few hundred. She made herself glow all over then flashed it twice before letting the glow fade.

After a moment two more flashes of light came from nearby. Soon two more Sirens, Celine and Marie came to help haul her catch back. It would be hard work to haul back, especially since they were weighed down by their own catches. Vampire squid were common around here and they had harvested nearly a dozen of them.

Between them they managed to move their catches across the bottom, sticking as close to the rocks as they could. There were other large predators down here, though it appeared that Mia had either killed or driven off most of them.

The chasm that they had retreated to was deeper than the one that they were accustomed to, and they had to adjust themselves to the pressure as they went. The gap to enter it was small, barely large enough for them to fit through.

There were a dozen guards outside the entrance. There were four small rocks that were equidistant from each other that were being used as a butchering ground. Once they had their catch harvested, they brought it inside. It was a short swim until it opened up into a larger area.

There was a large line already waiting for the food to be rationed out. From the look of things, they were the first ones back. Luckily, what they had brought would allow those in charge of the line to get to work.

After they dropped the meat off, they received their portions and retreated to their respective alcoves. There they ate and rested. Amélie devoured her rations and fumed over their predicament.

We are the warrior queens of the seas! Yet here we are, hiding in a hole! Why has fate chosen us to suffer so! We should move to other waters, take the territory of the softer ones or travel to a world, and stay there!

She suddenly noticed that the alcove was lit. She had been so distressed that she had begun glowing as brightly as she could without realizing it. She immediately dimmed her light and set about calming herself.

What am I doing? Getting carried away like that is not going to help! My mother is proof enough of that. Pride should come after all else right now.

It took a while, but Amélie drifted off into an uneasy sleep where she dreamt, she was being attacked by her dead mother. After what felt like no time at all she was awakened to once again go out in search of food. She was groggy for mere seconds, then she was off swimming to meet up with Marie and Celine.

She immediately knew something was wrong when she reached their meeting point and found Celine along with two others. Ines and Lya were part of the security force. They all looked very serious.

Where is Marie? NO!

Amélie swam faster panicking. As she drew up to them, Celine looked away. It was true then; something had happened to Marie.

Amélie asked, *"What has happened?"*

Ines relied, *"Marie was killed. The spirit of one of our sisters appeared earlier and attacked her."*

Amélie clenched her jaw and closed her eyes. Another one of her sisters was gone. What had they done to deserve this? Why was this happening?

Amélie asked, *"What do you mean by spirit?"*

Ines chose her words with care as she said, *"It was in the shape of one of our sisters, yet it had a body clear like a jellyfish. I could faintly see something that looked like a sister bound inside."*

Celine finally showed some signs of life. Her eyes glittered with anger. *"Whatever it was, it is taken care of now."*

"Taken care of?" asked Amélie.

Lya said, *"It died."*

Amélie was taken aback at the ferocity in her voice. Lya was normally more subdued. Amélie looked at Celine and Celine answered her unspoken question.

"Noémie and Renée were both killed as well."

There it is.! No wonder Lya was so angry. Her twin sister and her lover have both been killed as well. I can only imagine your grief Lya!

While Amélie was lost in her thoughts Celine continued the conversation. Amélie barely managed to catch her saying, *"There was going to be a meeting to discuss the options that we have left but unfortunately this is not the worst news."*

Amélie tilted her head to the side, *"What else is happening?"*

Celine said, *"The forward scouts have informed us that many of our sisters that have fallen or gone missing are massing together. Additionally, there are other creatures; sharks, squid and even Mermaids."*

Amélie could feel the fear in her. This was not something to be taken lightly. *"What does the matriarch say?"*

Lya said, *"All of the young including those that have not yet gone on a mating raid are to be sent through to the first world that we can connect to. Even the weak that we would normally leave to die after birth are to be saved and sent through."*

Amélie bristled, *"Why send the weak ones?"*

Ines said, *"It is simple Amélie. The matriarch is worried about preserving our kind. Any one of those that are not strong enough to survive down here, could very well be strong enough to survive where they are going."*

Amélie bared her fangs and Ines, *"We cannot let ourselves be weakened!"*

Ines held her spear up to Amélie's throat and she backed off. Lowering the spear Ines said, *"We face extinction Amélie. I have no time to argue with you. We are to get all able sisters ready for battle."*

Celine asked, *"What about food?"*

Lya said, *"There is little time before they will reach here. Do you think that you could possibly find a decent amount of food before they get here?"*

Amélie said, *"There is a trench nearby that is FULL of mollusks."*

The other three all looked at her in surprise. Ines asked, *"Why have you not mentioned this before?"*

Amélie shrugged, *"They taste terrible and can make you sick if eaten too often, but they will at least give us a good supply of food while we fight."*

Ines said, *"Very well. I will get as many sisters as I can, and we will bring all that we can carry back from this trench."*

Amélie grumbled in her mind over the next several hours. She was not a fan of eating these things. They tasted terrible and if you ate too much of them at a time you would become ill. She was also still grumbling about the matriarchs plans.

No matter how dire the situation she just could not see a reason to weaken themselves by letting the young that were born frail live. Better that they be left to die, like they had always done.

Then there was the matter of the defense plan. The matriarch had decided that they were going to fight inside the chasm; make the enemy come to them This was no way to fight! Where was the glory of slaughtering those you were superior to!

Still, she did as she was told. If you wanted to survive amongst the Sirens, then you did one of two things. Either you led or you listened. Amélie knew that she was not a leader.

More weapons than she had ever seen had been pulled out from their stores. One of the worst was a trap that they had encountered on a raid. It involved running lengths of incredibly thin, sharp metal wire across an area and forming something of a web out of them.

Swimming through those areas would mean almost instant death. Still Amélie wondered how effective this was going to be. Getting cut to bits was only scarry if you were a living thing. She had heard tell that these risen sisters were fearless. How did you fight an enemy that was unafraid of getting injured?

She was in a group of six right now. They were receiving the weapons that they would be using when the fighting started. Amélie was still a little skeptical that there was going to be any fighting that was worth the name battle.

The majority of the weapons were simple spears made with stone used for the spearheads. Amélie held her own spear in her hand. She had taken this off of the corpse of a warrior on the previous mating raid. Its blade reflected the light given off by the Sirens making it stand out.

She had taken the lives of many men on her excursion and had taken no wounds. She expected that this was going to be a similar experience. After the others had gotten their spears, they were sent out to be on the watch at the entrance.

When they arrived the guards that were normally outside the gate had already refreshed, but they were not going to be joining them. Their job was to do short patrols around the area outside.

Amélie wanted to take the lead but knew better than to challenge Camille. Camille was far more experienced than her. She had been on more than thirty mating raids. Amélie followed behind a half body length.

As they swam through the depths, they kept their glow down. They were meant to find the enemy not the other way around, another aspect of this that Amélie disagreed with.

Amélie noticed movement up above and hastily said, *"Camille! Up!"*

Camille reacted instantly looking up then diving towards the floor, motioning for the others to follow. As they reached the bottom, the water lit up a brilliant blue.

Above was an endless school of jellyfish. Their long transparent bodies were beginning to glow. With so many of them all doing it at once it lit the blackness as bright as the surface.

The new light hurt Amélie's eyes, and she was forced to both shield them and squint. While blinded by the sudden light the Sirens laid as still as possible. Once Amélie's eyes had adjusted some, allowing her to see again she looked out over the area that was illuminated.

There was a horde of shapes out there in the water. Some were clearly the fallen sisters, but others were there as well. Those shapes looked to be part of the so called "Principal Races" as well as many of the other aquatic lifeforms that dwelled all over the Plane of Water.

In the background she could see the tentacles that belonged to Mia moving. Their sheer size made the other creatures that were around them seem almost tiny by comparison, even the Leviathans.

One of those was swimming along the outskirts of the mass. Amélie noticed that there was a massive whole through the side of it, yet no blood was pouring out. She should have been able to scent blood at this distance and yet there was no trace.

Suddenly a smaller tentacle around twice the size of her wrapped itself around Amélie's tail. She felt hooks inside the suckers dig into her flesh. She began jabbing at them with her spear. Looking around for help she saw that the others were also engaged with tentacles.

Two of her sisters Colette and Lili managed to break free and initially went to aid Camille. Once they had her free, they split up help the other two that were nearby, leaving Amélie for last.

The others are free. They will soon be here to lend me aid as well and then we will need to fall back to report this. Dying in an ambush like this is not a fitting death!

The tentacles pulled her over to a nearby ledge and once she saw what was on the other side of it, she felt true terror. It had clearly once been one of her sisters but now!

While the body and basic form were still like that of a Siren much had been changed. Instead of a dorsal fin on its back it had four tentacles with another four sprouting up from the front. Where the eyes should have been there was a small patch of scales. The mouth had been enlarged to twice its former size.

Amélie panicked and thrust her spear repeatedly at the body of the creature. As thoughts about how she looked to others vanished from her mind their place was taken with a singular desire, to survive. Her spear sank into the flesh of the creature over and over, but it did not react.

It must be true then. These really were the sisters that had fallen. Amélie had not wanted to believe it when she had heard the stories but now, she was confronted with the truth. These things had to have been made with the corpses of her sisters.

Several more spears joined her own and the grip on her finally broke. Amélie swam away from that nightmare as fast as her wounded body would let her. She knew the others were around her and assumed they were in no better shape. Their only chance was to make it back to the chasm entrance.

It was not a far swim but, in their terror, it seemed to take an eternity. Once the entrance and its guards were in sight Amélie felt her heart lighten with hope. The reaction of the guards made her feel more relaxed. They looked alarmed but did not immediately ready their weapons.

It was only once they had reached them and one of the guards asked, *"What happened? Where are the other members of your patrol?"*, that Amélie realized that something was wrong.

She looked behind her for the first time and saw that there were only four of them. Two of them had not made it out of that. She had not even learned what their names were. Two more had joined the dead, and most likely the enemy.

Camille gave a report to the guards, then led them inside and over to the area that had been designated for treating wounds. Once there the group was immediately separated and treated. Amélie was able to get a quick look at the others.

Camille and herself had a number of slashes and puncture wounds. The other two, Chloé and Eléa were in worse shape. From the sound of it Chloé had lost half of her tail and she might lose her left arm. Eléa would be lucky to survive.

Once her wounds were treated, Amélie forced her way over to Camille to get answers. When she got there, she found Camille staring ahead with dead eyes. It took saying her name three times to get a response. Finally getting her attention Amélie asked, *"What exactly happened down there? I know about the creature that had ahold of me but what about the rest of you?"*

Camille's eyes still showed no life as she said, *"Similar creatures to what attacked you had ahold of us. Once we broke away from them and freed you it was not too difficult to outpace them. I think those tentacles slow them down a lot. Unfortunately, those were not the only things out there.* Valérie was snatched from right next to me by a shark. I felt its body graze my tail as it took her in its jaws." Amélie looked down and clenched her fists.

We should have been more aware of our surroundings. Of course, there were other threats.

Camille continued, *"Léa was taken by another of those tentacled abominations moments before we made it back."*

Amélie felt defeated. They had been aware that there was an enemy but even so, they had been torn apart. Two dead. Two severely injured and the one that looked to have lost the will to live. If she was honest with herself Amélie was probably no better off than Camille.

As she floated beside the now silent Camille, Amélie heard the sound of fighting. The creatures from earlier had begun to attack. Luckily, the guards were informed. At least that was what Amélie originally thought. Then she remembered the state that Camille was in and began to worry about how coherent her report had been.

She sped out of the medical ward over towards the entrance, her spear in hand. When she arrived, she found that there were dozens of those malformed Sirens attacking the guards. She used her spear to rattle the piece of metal that had been set up as an alarm, calling her sisters to battle.

She waited only until she could see more of her sisters heading towards them before swimming as fast as she could towards the nearest abomination. It was busy strangling one of the guards and never saw her coming. Her spear caught it right in the mouth and went out the back of its head.

Unlike before when she had stabbed at the tentacles and body to no effect this had worked instantly. She cried out, *"Aim for their heads!"*

She then turned and swam headlong into the fray ready to fight them until the last one was dead. As she fought with another one, she vaguely noticed that Camille had also come. While her spirits had appeared broken before she was clearly ready to fight these creatures to the death.

Soon over a hundred of her sisters were there and though the cost was steep, they managed to kill the last of the abominations. Amélie was exhausted but even so, she stayed to help ensure that all of the creatures were dead. The final tally of the dead was higher than she had feared. While they had killed twenty-three of the abominations, they had lost twenty-eight and twice that number were injured.

Amélie had to admit it now. The matriarch was right to save even the week ones and to send them someplace where they could perhaps survive. She was forced to rest, even though she wanted to be back at the entrance.

Once the medics had used their healing on her she was mostly back to fighting shape. The fighting continued for days on end. The number of small creatures that came through the entrance was smaller now. Clearly the enemy had expected them to be defeated by the initial wave.

The matriarch had sent those unable to fight through to a few different worlds. They could at least take solace knowing that their people would survive this if they fell. For Amélie and many of those still fighting they had two reasons to keep going.

The first was their pride as a warrior race. None of them would ever be able to live with themselves if they fled. The second was revenge. The Sirens had a long history of going to extraordinary lengths to settle a score.

Amélie awoke for her shift at the entrance. It was impossible to tell how long the fighting had been going on at this point. She took up her spear and swam off and in no time was engaged in combat with another abomination.

This one was different than those that they had seen thus far. Its face was unaltered and after dodging several attacks from it Amélie realized to her horror that it was Valérie. The shock that she was fighting someone that she very well might owe her life to caused her to hesitate for an instant.

This mistake cost her. She felt her spear leave her hands and then felt the tip punch through her abdomen. As the abomination pulled the spear back out Amélie felt some of her insides leave her with it. Amélie knew that she was dead but when she saw her spearhead, she felt a deep sadness and rage well up.

With everything that had been going on she had not noticed the signs, but she had been with child. She could see the faint outline of a miniscule tail and hand mixed in with the entrails that were now billowing around her in a cloud.

She was dead. Her child was dead. The least that she could do was make sure that this thing would join her in death. She owed it to herself, her child and to Valérie, whose body had been taken to make this horrible thing.

Amélie grasped the haft of her spear with her hands then suddenly forced the brightest glow out of her body she could manage. This stunned the abomination long enough for her to get her spear back and to plant it in the skull of her enemy.

Her struggle was over now. Her anger fear and grief were all gone. Amélie's world faded to black. Her last thought was a request. Not of anyone in particular just a general plea.

Someone please destroy those things. Avenge us...

CHAPTER 28
UNDINES

Claire had not heard from Laticin in some time. This news that there was something wrong in the Mermaid's Lagoon was troubling to say the least. There were other reports from all across the Plane of strange happenings. This latest news that came with the Mermaid messenger was just the tip of the iceberg.

The Undines territory was one of the most unusual on the plane. It was a large section of the Plane that was very shallow by comparison. It was also fresh water and all the freshwater creatures that lived on the plane lived there as well.

The barrier islands that were around this part of the Plane were surrounded with brackish water. Inside the Shallows many smaller creatures dwelled. There were many small currents that ran through that simulated the river habitats that some species lived in.

Some of Claire's favorites to watch were Glass Catfish. These small fish thrived in the small overhangs and cover provided by aquatic plants. Their bodies were almost completely transparent, and they often schooled together like a cloud.

Claire had always been far gentler than most, even amongst the dovish Undines. She got along well with Laticin from the Mermaids since they were little. She had always supported Laticin's passion for her art.

She was currently knee-deep in a small pool off of a small underwater creek. Like most on the Plane of Water the Undines did not often wear clothes. She had her cerulean blue hair down and it currently hung in front of her chest.

Undines as a whole did not have the largest breasts but hers were at least average. She had never envied the ones that Laticin had to carry around. The strain they had to cause must have been tough, though they were in the water most of the time.

She watched the various fish for a bit longer. It was going to be time soon for the meeting of the Undine elders. Her mother would attend but even though she was to take her place some day she was not allowed to.

She was not overly bitter about that fact. It would be her time soon enough. The few details that had leaked so far were worrisome. There was apparently talk of meeting with the other Principal Races at the Core. Claire had also seen her mother with the strange dagger that the Undines had been handing down for generations.

The dagger had two blades, one of which went out at an angle from where the guard would be on most daggers. The left side of both blades was sharp, while the right side were dull. It was mostly a dark blue, with polished silver on the blades.

She had heard whispers that there were others like it that the other Principal Races had but she had never tried to confirm it. The Undines did not discuss the dagger with others and so Claire knew it would be wrong to ask.

Some movement caught Claire's eye and she watched as a school of minnows swam past her feet. Out from under one of the rocks a large blue shelled crayfish caught a straggler in its pincers and drug it back to the hole that it had come from.

Life had a set cycle, and everything had to adhere to it. You were born and you died. If you lived long enough to produce offspring then you had fulfilled your purpose, objectively speaking. Claire shook her head to clear her thoughts.

She had found herself thinking more and more about things like that now that she was of age. She was currently carrying her first daughter. The pregnancy was new, only a few weeks old. She was excited to tell Laticin about it.

In some of the larger streams Claire could see the larger fish swimming along hunting for food. The trout and pike darted around, while the massive sturgeon moved across the bottoms. The reeds, cattails, lily pads and other brightly colored plants in the area made for a very beautiful view.

Claire looked around feeling at peace until something strange caught her eye. She watched as a clam attempted to bait and trap a minnow. Clams ate small creatures called plankton and the algae that grew. They were not capable of eating something as large as a minnow.

Claire watched as the clam continued to attempt to get any other nearby creatures into its shell. Finally, it did manage to snap closed on a minnow. The minnows tail twitched a few times after it was trapped then went still. Shockingly after a few moments the clam opened up and the minnow swam away. Only now it too was acting weird.

The minnow began picking at other minnows. Claire walked over slowly to both the clam and the minnow, and she scooped them up. She had anticipated a harder time with the minnow, but the thing attempted to nibble on her.

Something is very wrong here. This minnow it seriously trying to bite me, and the clam feels like it is trying to do something similar.

Claire looked around to see if there were any other signs of creatures acting odd, but nothing stood out at the moment. She turned and began walking back to her home. It was not a far walk, but it took her a decent amount of time due to a unique feature of the Shallows. The Falls were a series of waterfalls that ran along the entire perimeter of the Undine city.

The raised rock was still fully covered in water, even though it was many times higher than herself. The four small spirals that connected the area to the water across the plane kept it fed with fresh water. Testing the water had found that while the water contained salt up to the halfway point of the spiral the water after was salt free.

As an Undine traveling across and through the water was a simple task and Claire was soon gliding up the path that had been marked out for generations. The vertical path was the only thing that slowed her down as she was fighting against the flow of the water. Once she came to the top, she could see the Undines city before her.

It was not a city in the same way that other races outside the Plane would think. The Undines used their skill in water manipulation to shape and control the water. Walls of water formed the buildings, and any of them that wished for privacy would simply add some silt and create a current to make the walls opaque.

The streets had one current on each side flowing in opposite directions. The currents of main roads were given priority over side streets so you would have to step across the current to continue on your way. Claire used the currents to get to the Great Hall.

The Great Hall was the large domed building in the exact center of the city. Here was where the high council sat and today was expected to be a long meeting. Normally they were not to be disturbed but Claire felt that this was too important to leave for later.

She could have just ridden the current but instead she ran as fast as she could. Many passersby stared as she ran. Claire barely even noticed; all of her focus was on getting to the Great Hall. Claire ran through the large open doorway and down the hall to the main chamber. Two guards were on duty to keep the councilors from being disturbed.

The guards knew who she was but that did not mean that they lowered their spears. The guard on the left said, "You know the code. No one is to disturb the councilors until they break."

Claire simply said, "I believe that I have found something that the councilors will want to know about immediately."

The guards still did not lower their spears. The second guard said, "Tell us what you found that you believe to be so important?"

Claire held out her hands and showed the guards. At first the two women laughed at her. "What about a clam and minnow is so important that you believe that you are allowed to disrupt the meeting?"

Claire was unfazed, she simply said, "Hold out your hands and hold them and you shall see."

Still looking amused the two guards each took one. Claire knew they were humoring her partially out of her station and partially out of boredom, but it did not matter as long as they listened in the end.

After a moment Claire asked, "What are they doing?"

The guards looked confused then looked down at their hands then noticed. The first guard said. "This is strange. They appear to be attempting to BITE us."

The second guard added, "Also they are so dry. How long have they been out of the water?"

Claire said, "Both of those are the reasons I want to see the council. I caught those down in the far end of the Lower Shallows."

The first guard looked at her alarmed, "That is impossible! They should have died by now unless you had been dipping them in water almost constantly since you caught them."

Claire shook her head, "I have not done that even once. Both of those should have died long ago and yet they are still moving."

As one the guards handed her the minnow and clam then the second guard slipped into the room that they had been assigned to. Claire could hear the council talking to her then after a moment she returned and waved Claire in.

Inside the chamber there was a circle of nine chairs that were made out of shaped water. A woman sat in each one. In the closest one to the door sat her mother. She and Claire were practically mirror images of each other.

Her mother Olivia wasted no time in asking, "We were told that you found something that was highly disturbing? So disturbing that it warranted our immediate attention?"

Her mother's tone was the same as always. Strict and firm but never disrespectful. Her no-nonsense attitude was one of the reason that she was chosen to be on the council. She had been training Claire for the same position in the future.

Claire presented her story and the evidence that she had brought back with her without preamble. Once she had finished, one of the councilors, Amelia asked, "Could you place it here so that we may examine it?"

As Amelia gestured to the center of the chairs the floor rose up, like a controlled geyser and formed a table. Claire placed the clam and the minnow down on the surface and watched.

The clam attempted to move off the table pulling itself along, despite being exceptionally dry now. The minnow flopped around despite being just as dry. Now that she looked even closer, she noticed something else that was off. The eyes of the minnow were glassy. This thing was flopping around despite looking very dead.

Another councilor named Brea said, "Just to verify, you said you found these in the far end of the Lower Shallows? You also said that this clam had captured this minnow and afterwards it was attacking other minnows?"

Claire nodded and said, "Yes. The behavior was so odd to me that it drew my attention."

Olivia said, "I am glad that you brought this to our attention Claire. You did exactly what needed to be done."

Hearing the approval in her mother's voice was nice. Her mother was not a negative person, but she rarely praised anyone so hearing it brought a flood of joy. The joy was short lived however when she heard another councilor Fayre speak.

Fayre was one of the oldest of the Undines. Her body may have appeared old, but her voice was still strong and firm. She looked afraid as she said, "I fear that this proof that of what we have been hearing. While I wish it were not so, at least you have saved us many hours of debate."

Claire looked confused but that quickly vanished as Courtney, the youngest member of the council said, "There is no reason to believe that yet. Just because the girl makes these claims does not make them true."

Claire rarely let anger take hold of her but here she could not help herself. She had known Courtney before she became a councilor. This was nothing more than an attempt to secure her position above Claire once she joined the council in the future. Her mother had been on the point of saying something when Fayre took the matter out of everyone's hands.

There was the sound of something cutting through the air and a loud thunk. She had made a water cleaver and chopped the clam in two followed by the minnow. Both halves of both creatures continued to move to everyone's horror.

Fayre slowly said, "This is no time for your foolishness girl. Claire had brought us proof of what we had heard and guessed. Somehow, the curse of undeath is here in the Plane of Water and it is spreading."

The last four councilors were Alice, Sophia, Evelyn, and Charlotte. They were now murmuring amongst themselves. This whole matter had them really spooked.

Claire had heard of undeath before but had no real understanding of what it really was. Seeing this was shocking to say the least.

Looking at the minnow Claire was suddenly struck by a sense of fear. She could not really explain it, but it had to be some primordial fear. Whatever was behind those eyes was something terrifying. At this moment she wanted nothing more than to run as far away form that thing as she could.

The clam was just as frightening, even though it did not have eyes to look into. The now split shell laying pieces but the clam itself was moving, both halves. The two halves seemed to be working together. Their goal appeared to be to kill something else.

There was nothing around that it would be able to harm, at least that was what she thought. The two halves worked together to grip onto smaller shell fragments and used the sharp edges to try and cut Sophia's wrist who was examining it. There was nowhere near enough force to accomplish anything, but the intent was clear.

Fayre said, "This is a truly grave thing. For the curse of undeath to be here, in one of the planes, something drastic must have occurred."

"Indeed." Olivia agreed, "We must meet with the other Principal Races at the core and formulate a plan."

Fayre said, "Claire, I want you to take me to exactly where you found these two. After that, you will need to get ready."

Claire cocked her head to the side, "What am I getting ready for?"

Fayre said, "I will have you travel to the core with us. I think that your firsthand account is too important to leave out."

Claire was slightly surprised but made no further comments other than to say, "Very well."

Fayre turned back to the clam and minnow pieces and changed the water into table from its solid form. It was now so hot that it was instantly turning to steam and breaking down into gases. Fayre kept it up until she was satisfied that the two had been thoroughly destroyed.

Claire led Fayre and four other councilors down the way that she had come. Fayre had only had her stop long enough to gather a few dozen volunteers to help search the shallows and to also have others search the waters in the city.

She still did not really understand what was going on and that frustrated her. She knew better than to ask questions right now though. There would be plenty of time to ask questions on the way to the core. She knew the situation was serious, but she still could not help but be excited that she was going to get to see the core.

Upon reaching the Lower Shallows and taking the group to exactly where she had been before Fayre took over. She looked around at the women and said, "I want you searching in groups of three. You are looking for anything that is acting out of the ordinary. You must be warry of anything that might have the capacity to harm you in any way."

Claire was not entirely sure what Fayre was worried about, but she joined Fayre in searching around the shallows. To her displeasure Courtney also joined them. Just as Claire suspected, Courtney began to undermine their reason for being there.

Between her halfhearted searching and her constant dialogue about how this was a waste of time, Claire was getting really fed up with her attitude. Fortunately, Fayre was also frustrated with the woman and after enduring her for as long as she could finally asked, "Are you questioning MY knowledge and judgement girl?"

The sharpness of the tone and directness of the words left Courtney no room to deflect to question. She was forced to answer directly, something that she hated. "I just do not see the cause for worry. What does it matter if something small like a minnow or clam-"

She stopped dead as she noticed what was around her. She was waste deep in the water, and she noticed that at least a dozen pikes had been gathering around her. Fish would sometimes come near a person in the water but never like this.

Suddenly she let out a shriek as one of the pike bit into the back of her leg. As blood leaked from the wound more of the creatures swarmed her and she panicked. As she tried to get into shallower water she slipped and went under the water.

As one Fayre and Claire took control of the water and forced the water away from Courtney. Without the water around them the pikes lost much of their strength and mobility and Courtney was able to break free. Though she was covered in wounds none of them were too terrible.

Fayre wasted no time in superheating the water to destroy the fish. After the fish were destroyed, they placed the water back where it had been and returned it to the temperature that it had been before.

A quick check in the surrounding water found no other creatures acting odd. Fayre and Claire helped Courtney back to the area they had started in and forced the water away, making a large area that had no water in it.

Other teams returned and though most reported nothing out of the ordinary, there were some who had similar reports of their own experience. One group did not report back though. Fayre and Claire left Courtney in the safe zone that they had created and took two other groups with them to search.

The area that they had been searching was one of the deeper parts of the Shallows and was also one of the furthest away. When they approached the area that they should have been searching they encountered a horrible sight.

There were dozens of bull sharks that were swarming the women. If these had been normal sharks, they would have swarmed them once they were bleeding, which at least one of them was. The blood seemed to have no effect on them, however.

The new arrivals used their combined power to make a corridor from where they stood to the space the three women had made down in the water. Two of them dropped into it and began to run to safety but a shark dove through the wall that they had created and caught hold of her leg. As it thrashed around it pulled her back and bit her again and again. The other two looked back as she screamed.

This mistake cost them as dozens more of the sharks threw themselves at the walls causing them to break through. Two of the sharks landed on one of them and the third fled, shrieking in terror as the monsters pursued her. When she was finally out of the tunnel, she collapsed sobbing on the edge.

Her relief was short lived as she heard more splashes and looked to see more of the sharks bursting out of the deeper water to attempt to get to them. Claire felt terror take hold and acted on instinct, creating a thin but incredibly sharp, band of water that neatly cut the nearest shark in half.

Luckily, she was not the only one to act as several others began to fight back the sharks that were now coming for them. Many of the sharks were slain, but they lost some more from their group as well. When the sharks finally stopped coming there were only five of them left.

Fayre looked around, her breath ragged. This battle had taken a lot out of her. She began looking around more franticly.

Claire asked, "Fayre what is wrong? Do you see more sharks?"

Fayre shook her head gravely and said, "I do not see and of the dead."

Claire was confused, "What do you mean? There are several of those sharks right over there. Sure, they are still moving some but superheating the water will take care of that, right?"

Fayre sounded panicked as she said, "Not the sharks girl. I so not see any of OUR dead. All of their bodies are gone. I fear that this was a trap."

CHAPTER 29
MEETINGS

Laticin had seen men before but there was something different about the one that was in front of her now. He looked like any other human that she had seen but the aura that he gave off said that was far from true. It was hidden now but she could tell that this man had great power.

She felt conflicted about him. On one hand he was handsome, and the aura about him added to his alure. On the other hand, he had just done something incredibly stupid and dangerous. Had one thing not gone perfectly back there and he would have been killed.

He was currently gazing down at the ruined body of the Leviathan with a small half smirk on his face. While he continued to stare at him, he was completely unaware of his surroundings, or so she thought.

No. That is not the case. He has not noticed us yet because we are not a threat to him. He is focused on things that he perceives as threats and is tuning out all others.

Laticin stared at this man for a moment longer before she returned to her senses. She looked to the others that were with her and said, *"Report back to the lagoon! Let them know what has happened."*

At first the others looked as though they would argue with her but finally, they nodded to her and swam off leaving her alone. The others had not sensed this man's powers and Laticin was not interested in getting them all killed if he was hostile.

There was something about him though that made her believe that she was not in any danger. She would never be able to explain this feeling, but she knew that she was not in any danger. When his eyes finally found her after the others had left, she felt a sense of authenticity and kindness.

The next thing that she noticed was that he looked initially alarmed then confused upon seeing her. The knee jerk reaction that he had of reaching for the swords that he carried told her that he needed to be approached carefully.

Laticin felt nervous as she slowly swam over, making sure to look as peaceful as she could. Keeping the spear out in front of her while swimming proved to be a challenge, so she was forced to swim carrying it at the ready.

Fortunately, something about her demeanor showed her true intention of being peaceful and he did not attack. Once she was a reasonable distance away, she stopped.

Laticin said, *"Hello. I am Laticin. I am a friend. What is your name?"*

He did not respond and Laticin realized that he must not have the telepathic abilities that most of the denizens of the Plane of Water could use. She pointed up to the surface, then pointed at her mouth. The man appeared to understand, and they both swam for the surface.

Once they broke the surface, Laticin noticed his smile first. He looked so happy and relaxed now that he was out of the water. His eyes were a beautiful green color and now that they were closer Laticin noticed that this man was well muscled.

Now on the surface, Laticin repeated herself, "Hello, my name is Laticin, I am a friend."

I am so glad that I got a second chance at that. I cannot believe that I asked what his name was that way before! It sounded so childish!

Laticin hid the embarrassment that she felt and waited for him to answer. His voice sounded strange to her.

I wonder where he came from?

Meterove said, "Greetings to you. I am Meterove and I am also a friend. I hope you will pardon the question but what exactly are you?"

Laticin said, "Based on your reactions earlier, I had anticipated that you might not know of my kind. I am a Mermaid."

Meterove said, "Ah so you are a Mermaid and not one of the Sirens then."

This man was getting more mysterious. He had never heard of Mermaids but had heard of Sirens. Based on his tone he had a negative encounter with them as well. Just to verify her suspicions Laticin asked, "How do you know of the Sirens?"

Meterove replied, "I came through the portal from Nexus along with my kin and some friends to speak to the Principal Races of the Plane of Water. I was told of the different members of the Principal Races, though I have only ever met an Undine before. The reason that we came through is because our world has been attacked and all signs point to the Plane of Water as the origin of the attacks."

Laticin almost dropped back below the water in shock. That was a lot to take in. Whoever this Meterove was he clearly had connections. She had heard of Nexus before but only in vague conversation with Undines.

Still, that did not answer the question she had asked and so she put it to him again, "But how do you know of the Sirens?"

Meterove shrugged and said, "I have now had several run ins with them. Some were regular Sirens, but others were undead."

This sealed it, this man needed to come with her back to the lagoon. Before she could articulate her request, he took the matter out of her hands.

Meterove said, "I need to get back to my group. The plan had been to head for the core and to use whoever that we found there to help us contact whoever else we needed to talk to. As you are a Mermaid, I guess that means that I am at least close to the Mermaid territory."

Laticin said, "Yes. What exactly do you plan on doing now?"

Meterove replied, "I already told you that I need to find my friends. I came here with a mission, and I intend to see it done. Can you take me to the leaders of your people?"

Laticin felt a small surge of annoyance that she quickly squashed. How was a stranger to know that he was speaking to one of the elders? She hardly looked the part, given her youth. She calmed herself quickly then said, "I am actually the most recently inducted member of our elders. I can take you to the others if you are willing to follow me."

Why did I just say that? What does it matter to him if I am a recent inductee? Why is my heart racing right now?

While she was lost in her thoughts she led the way back to the lagoon, the whole time she swam in such a way that she could shield her chest from his view. She was confused at her actions but did not have the time to review them.

As they approached the lagoon, she noticed some of the sentries that were in sight. A strange fear took over her now. She knew full well that there were going to be tons of women in the lagoon before. For some reason, the thought of him going in and seeing all these women bothered her.

This is ridiculous. What do care about this man seeing the others back at the lagoon?

Laticin mentally shook off her confusion and continued to swim back to the lagoon. The same thoughts tried to resurface a few times, but she managed to force them out. Approaching the lagoon entrance Laticin could see that the others she had sent back were there with additional support.

Two dozen Mermaids were waiting for them with spears and rapiers at the ready. For an instant Laticin was worried that this stranger might perceive them as a threat. Then she remembered the Leviathan and dismissed the idea. He also had the look of a man that knew fighting. He

624

would likely know at a glance that the women ahead were not used to holding those weapons.

I really hope this does not go in a bad direction.

Laticin said *"This man means us no harm. He has come to the Plane of Water to speak with the Principal Races. He should be let through to the elders immediately."*

.   .   .

The strange woman...Mermaid that he had met was currently staring at the large group of Mermaids that were standing by with weapons. They were clearly frightened and not just of him. The way that they held those weapons said that they were not soldiers but had no shortage of recent experience in using them.

The hand gestures helped confirm Meterove's assumption that there was a discussion going on. The look on Laticin's face was similar to when she had first approached him.

They must use some form of telepathy to communicate. That makes sense, since they are under water.

As the conversation went on Meterove did his best to not stare at them as well as pretend that he did not notice the way some of them were staring at him. Those eyes were like a predator that had spotted prey. If they realized that his eyes had slipped off their own, he would be hunted, he was sure of it.

Terenia and Dras would love this. They would probably already be over there trying to cop a feel.

Some sense of his thoughts must have made its way through to them because the smiles that began to spread across their lips and the way that they began to push their chests forward was very suspicious.

Trying to ignore it was difficult, after all they were the reason, he was there to begin with. Meterove decided to try and focus on comparing them to the Sirens. Where the Sirens had been vaguely human in appearance, the Mermaids would be easy to mistake for a human if you only saw their upper halves.

Laticin finished her conversation with the other Mermaids and waved him through. He thought that he might have seen an irritated look on her face when she looked at him, but she had turned to fast to be sure.

Meterove followed Laticin until they reached a rock in the middle of the lagoon. She signaled for him to stay there and swam off to a nearby group of Mermaids that had started to approach. She began a very animated discussion with one of them.

After a few tense minutes they appeared to agree with whatever it was that she was suggesting. She accompanied them back to the rock and she pointed up to the surface. Meterove swam for the surface with the Mermaids all around him.

Breaking the surface Meterove brushed the water out of his eyes and looked around him. There was a dozen or so Mermaids around him including Laticin. Meterove did his best to keep his eyes from wandering but it was not easy.

Laticin said "Everyone this is Meterove. Meterove this is Moira and Alara. They along with myself and others are the elders that make up our leadership."

Meterove cleared his voice, "I am Meterove Valaseri. I am the second prince of the empire of Yxarion. I have come here along with others, with instructions to head to the Core."

Moira asked, "Who exactly gave you such instructions and why?"

Meterove replied, "The Lady Flare, who presides over Nexus said that we would need the help of the Principal Races to end the threat that is currently endangering our world as well as others."

Alara asked, "What threat is that exactly? I find it hard to believe that something from the Plane of Water would be a danger to your world."

Meterove shook his head, "That is where you would be wrong. The threat is not from the Plane of Water but has come here. The first Kraken, Mia has been attacking our world through holes that she had made. We believe that she had been infected by the Ashen Soul."

Moira asked, "What exactly is this Ashen Soul that you speak of? We have heard those words before but our own knowledge of it is vague at best."

Meterove took a deep breath, "The details that I have on what the Ashen Soul is are sparse. However, I will tell you everything that I know. The Ashen Soul is an undead force of unimaginable power."

Moira asked, "What makes you believe that this Ashen Soul is here?"

Meterove said, "We have observed hordes of undead arise from this thing. Some of them are from races that we had never seen before including Sirens. The size of the tentacles that attacked our world convinced Flare that it must have been Mia. I saw them up close, and they were not from a living thing."

Moira and Alara looked at each other then over at Laticin. Meterove saw something in their eyes that he wished he had not. There was something about his story that was ringing true to them. Meterove thought back to the armed group he had seen earlier. Had they perhaps been under siege by the undead with no clue as to where they were coming from?

Laticin watched as this man, Meterove explained who he was and where he had come from. The why that followed was more upsetting, but the first part was equally of interest to her. This man was a prince! Laticin had learned some of the cultures of the worlds during her lessons and that was one part that she remembered clearly.

The other stuff about the source of the undead in the Plane of Water was distressing but also relieving. Hearing someone else state that there was something down in the deepest reaches of the Plane that was a threat made her feel vindicated.

Moira looked at her and said, "Now we have an explanation for why the larger predators are making their way up from deeper water."

Laticin nodded, "Larger predators for sure. Meterove here killed a Leviathan that had chased him through a spiral."

The Mermaids stared at her in disbelief then when she did not recant her story looked at Meterove in awe. For his part Meterove had no idea how impressive killing the Leviathan had been. In this particular case since he was not privy to the conversation all he saw was a group of naked half fish women suddenly staring at him.

Meterove noticed that certain parts of the women that he could see had grown excited. This was not the outcome that he had been hoping for. He needed these women to take him seriously. Laticin was also showing this reaction, but she was at least speaking on his behalf.

As soon as Meterove had that thought he glanced at her chest. She was currently pushing her chest towards him. The look in her eye told him a lot.

I need to tread carefully here. Otherwise, things might go in the wrong direction.

Meterove had suddenly noticed that things had gone quiet and looking at the women around him he feared that his wandering gaze had offended them. Another thought occurred to him as well, but he did not want to dwell on it.

Laticin said a little stiffly "We are familiar with some of these undead. They have been an ongoing problem for our people."

Moira coughed and said "We deviated from the topic slightly. We were talking about the creatures of the deep. You believe that Mia the first Kraken is involved. What exactly did the Lady Flare have to say about a course of action?"

Meterove shrugged, "Flare is not exactly what you would call the most forthcoming with information. She only told us that we needed to contact the Principal Races. I am assuming that she believed that you had the answers to what needed to be done."

Moira said, "The only thing that I can tell you is that something on this scale is dealt with at the Core. We have been told for eons that whenever we might find ourselves in danger that the Great Lord would protect us."

Meterove noticed that Laticin rolled her eyes while Moira continued, "The Great Lord is the protector of the Plane of Water. We have been praying to him since the early days of our race."

Meterove asked "So this Great Lord of yours is some kind of deity?"

Moira made to speak but Laticin cut her off, "That is essentially what older members of our people believe. I personally as well as a large portion of the younger generations do not believe it to be so."

Moira said sharply "That is enough child! You may have gotten away with that behavior when Elise was acting so irrational but that does not give you the right to insult the rest of the elders."

Laticin rolled her eyes at Moira "Yet you retain the right to insult those of us that do not believe in the Great Lord? That is hypocrisy!"

Moira looked like she wanted to argue the point but also knew that Laticin had a valid point of her own. While the two of them appeared to be preoccupied, Alara spoke, "You speak of these undead as if they were something out of the past. You have defeated them before?"

These lines caught the attention of both Laticin and Moira. While Meterove would not call it an argument, the term discussion was too light as well. Meterove decided that telling this story might be the best way to get the conversation back on track.

Meterove took a deep breath, then said, "I have faced thousands of the undead in my life. I had always believed them to be horrible and monstrous in nature. Recently I have learned that not only do some fragments of the original person survive in even the most basic of undead but that the higher level the Weaver that raises the dead the more of the person that they were that remains."

One of the other Mermaids that had been floating nearby suddenly spoke up, "Does that mean that the ones that have been turned are still themselves? Can they come back to us?"

Meterove looked into her eyes. They were a deep blue and green. They were so full of hope. Whoever this woman had lost, they had meant the world to her. Meterove hated himself for having to give the answer that he knew he had to.

He sighed, "They retain some of who they were, but they can never again be who they were. They are dead and no magic can fix that. No matter how much they may seem like the person that they used to be, the truth is that they are not the same person anymore."

The woman, whose face had briefly lit up with hope had sunk far lower into the depths of despair. Meterove could only assume that she had lost someone very dear to her.

Moira asked, "What is this Weaver that you spoke of?"

Meterove said, "Weavers are undead that have the power to create more of their kind."

Laticin asked, "What does this Ashen Soul look like?"

Meterove said, "The Ashen Soul is a monstrous creature that looks like a female angel, except that its body is rotting."

Meterove noticed that they all seemed confused by his explanation. This was the Plane of Water after all. It made sense that they would not have a concept of winged creatures.

Meterove asked, "Have any of you ever seen a winged creature before?"

Alara and Moira both nodded, "Yes, we have encountered them on occasion when we go outside the Plane."

Meterove said, "The Ashen Soul has two wings, though one is little more than bone. The other is mostly like a wing of a bird, though there are sections of it that are rotting away."

Moira asked, "What exactly do you think has happened to Mia?"

Meterove shook his head, "I honestly do not know. It could be that it is just a simple Weaver, but I have my doubts. Back on my world we found a spring that was actually directly connected to both the Plane of Water and Plane of Spirit. This water was able to push back the curse of undeath in the surrounding landscape."

Alara said, "That has been bothering me as well. I have only once encountered an undead but to the best of my knowledge the Planes are supposed to be safe from them."

Meterove said, "I worry that the Ashen Soul may have found a way to change the undeath to be resistant to the power of the Planes. It clearly intends to assault the Plane of Water. From here if it controls the Plane, it has access to every world out there. This would allow it to spread unchecked."

Laticin asked, "Do you know of somewhere that is safe? Somewhere we would be safe?"

Meterove wanted to tell her that there was some place they could go to, but he knew that it would be a lie. He looked at her sadly and said, "To the best of my knowledge there is no place that would be safe. If you want your people to be safe, then we need to meet with the other Principal Races at the core."

Moira looked pensive while Alara said, "Very well. We will hold a meeting to decide what our plan of action will be. Laticin I would like to ask you to look after our guest while we hold the meeting."

Laticin looked like she was torn for a moment, but Alara added, "Naturally we will take your vote now to ensure that your voice is heard."

Laticin's face cleared, and she said, "I vote in favor of going to the core. Additionally, I want to personally go with to the core."

Moira said "Your vote is tallied. We shall finish a soon as we can. For now, I suggest continuing this conversation so as to get as much information as possible."

The rest of the Mermaids ducked under the water, leaving just Meterove and Laticin. Meterove said "What I would not give for some place that was dry right now."

Laticin giggled, "I suppose. Humans are not meant to be in the water this much. I can only assume that you have some sort of magic which has allowed you to travel the Plane."

Meterove said, "Yes, we were given the ability to breath underwater, but I would still like to be dry."

Laticin got a small glint in her eyes and said, "Come with me. I know a place."

She dove under the water and Meterove did not hesitate to follow. If she knew some place that was dry, he was all for it. She took him down to a weed bed and after she looked around, she swam inside. Meterove followed after her and found that it was a tunnel.

After following it for a bit he broke the surface and found himself in a large cave with an air pocket. Inside he found tons of pieces of art. Clearly this was Laticin's private sanctuary. He turned to thank her, and his jaw dropped.

Laticin had come out of the water and her tail and fins had all vanished. She now looked completely human, and she was totally naked. Meterove stared, there was no way he could not. This woman was breathtakingly beautiful, and she was standing right in front of him wearing nothing.

Laticin noticed the look on his face and made to cover herself in mild embarrassment. To help hide her body she brought her hair around her front and after sitting down on the floor covered her lap with her hands.

Meterove sat down as well. He tried just looking at her face, but the shape of her body drew his gaze as much as the beauty of her face. Now that she was covered up some, Laticin looked less embarrassed and even began giving him teasing looks and would occasionally let a little more of her curves slip into view.

Meterove had grown used to this kind of behavior with Terenia though. Meterove looked into Laticin's eyes. She looked slightly surprised at his response and cocked her head. Meterove looked at the art that was around the room and decided to ask about it.

Meterove pointed to one with lots of spirals on it and asked, "Is the large spiral in the back of that one the Core?"

Laticin pouted at the change of subject but said, "Yes, the large one is the core. The place that I used for reference is actually over in the Shallows. My friend Claire showed it to me."

Meterove asked, "What are the Shallows?"

Laticin responded, "Just as the name implies it is an area that is far shallower than the rest of the Plane. It is freshwater there and many of the species that inhabit it can only be found there. It is also the Undine territory. Claire is the daughter of one of their councilors."

Meterove did his best not to smile as Laticin continued to pout. She was willing to talk but was disappointed that her efforts to seduce appeared to be falling flat.

Meterove asked, "How do you make them?"

Laticin gave him a short explanation of the process. The fact that he seemed genuinely interested, if only out of curiosity made her happy.

This man is interesting. I have heard others talk about the men that they have met before, but they never mentioned anything like this. He is kind and strong. Wait! I have only been talking about myself! I need to ask about him!

Laticin questioned Meterove about himself for a while after that. It was a nice exchange, with the two of them asking and answering questions. After a short while Laticin decided that it was best that they go find out if the meeting had finished.

Laticin stood up and halfway through the action realized that Meterove was looking. She decided that she might as well try and make the action as seductive as possible and moved her hair behind her back.

She was nowhere near as graceful on legs as she was swimming through the water, but she remembered what some of the older women had taught her and swayed her hips as she walked away and stepped down into the water.

I cannot believe I just did that! This is so embarrassing! What did he think? I really hope it did not look bad! What do I do if he didn't like what he saw?

She smiled try and cover her anxiety then went under the water with Meterove following after her. Back out in the lagoon they swam back over to the rock and found that the other elders were there. Laticin paused a moment to confer with them before signaling to Meterove that they were still in discussion.

She looked pensive for a moment before she motioned for him to follow. She led him up to the surface. Once they were both above water she said, "They are finishing up the meeting now. There were a few of the older members that were hesitant to trust a human."

Meterove was frustrated by this, but he knew that it was probably to be expected. His people had never encountered Mermaids before, but it was quite possible that they had bad experiences with humans before.

Next to Laticin a Mermaid surfaced briefly and said, "We have finished. You must come for the final vote."

Laticin looked at Meterove and said, "You can come with if you like."

Meterove nodded and they ducked under the water. Laticin made a point to swim more slowly so that Meterove did not fall behind. Once they reached the rock Meterove stayed slightly back while Laticin took her place.

The final vote did not take long. From what Meterove could tell there were only two dissenting votes. Once the vote was over there was a brief discussion and then the assembled Mermaids went their separate ways.

Moira and Alara had a quick word with Laticin before they too left. At first Laticin appeared slightly panicked by whatever they were saying. Whatever it was Moira appeared to be slightly amused by it. Once they shot him some glances, he realized that it had to do with him.

Meterove had an odd sense of foreboding. He was pretty sure that he had a vague idea of what it might be about. Laticin motioned for him to follow her again.

Back in her cave Meterove used magic to dry himself off and then he waited for Laticin to say something about the conversation. After a moment she said, "The decision was made to head to the Core. Additionally, I have been told to stay with you at all times until we leave."

Ah! That would explain their expressions as well as Laticin being awkward.

Meterove asked, "What exactly are they worried about?"

Laticin said, "It is a combination of things. You are a guest here and, as hosts, it is our obligation to make sure that you have every curtesy that we can offer. Also, there is the matter of you being a man."

Meterove asked, "Are the others concerned what I might do while I am here?"

Laticin laughed lightly "Actually they are concerned what might happen to you once word spreads that a man is here. There are nearly one thousand Mermaids here. The number that are looking to make children is nearly equal to that."

Meterove suddenly realized his situation. He looked at Laticin and asked, "So why exactly did Moira and Alara want you to watch over me?"

Laticin went a little red, "Well, you and I have already started getting to know each other."

Meterove asked, "And what is the other reason?"

Laticin began playing with her hair, "I have worked really hard to keep this cave secret, but it appears that Moira knew about it. Keeping you somewhere that only a handful of us knew the location seemed to be the best idea."

Meterove was pretty sure that this was an evasion but decided to let the matter drop for now. He also had a bigger problem. He had a bedroll that he could use as a pillow in this cave but there was the matter of Laticin. He decided to roll it the long way to make it large enough for two people to use. It was not going to help much with the rocky floor anyway.

The real problem was getting sleep next to a woman as beautiful as her who was completely naked. For all that she talked about what the other women might be after she had not exactly been subtle about her own interest.

Now that his mind was not split in so many different directions, he noticed just how small she really was. She was shorter than Terenia by at least half a head. Her chest was much bigger, though. Meterove shook his head, then he dug through his pack and found an extra shirt.

He tossed it to Laticin, "Here use this to cover yourself. I can use my magic to keep a small area warm, but I can only make it large enough for two people."

At first Laticin appeared confused by the offer but then she realized how close she would have to be in order to take advantage of the warmth. Her body would have to be very close to his own in order to stay warm. As she was now, her breasts would surely press against him.

The thought was embarrassing and exciting at the same time. She took the shirt. While she would rather sleep in the water like normal, she knew that she needed to stay close to him. She also had no plans on being cold, so refusing to be inside that warm area was out of the question.

It felt odd having fabric touching her body. The thought that it belonged to the Meterove was exciting. She laid her head down on the bedroll. At first, she was tense and faced away from Meterove but after a little time had passed, she turned over and looked him in the eyes.

Meterove looked at the woman who was little more than a foot away from him. The thoughts that were going through his head at the moment were far from pure. In his mind Meterove wondered what Terenia would say.

He already knew that she would be fine with whatever he chose to do. Maybe he could have both of them? No...that would never work...would it?

Realizing what he was thinking of doing made him pause. Would Laticin be ok with this? What would she think if she knew about Terenia? With a start Meterove realized he had actually not spoken of her all that much in the context of them being together.

Meterove cleared his throat and said, "I miss my friends and siblings. I worry about their safety. I have been so busy since we separated that I have not really been thinking straight. My brother and sisters, two good friends and my lover Terenia."

Laticin felt her heart grow tight. She had suspected as much but had held onto the hope that it was not so. Of course, he had someone that he called a lover. Just as Laticin's heart felt was being crushed he continued talking.

Meterove's voice was not very loud, but it was firm as he said, "Terenia would like you. I know that for sure. I can say without a doubt that she would have already tried to touch your body."

Laticin felt the pressure suddenly stop. She looked at Meterove and whispered, "Are you telling me that she likes other women?"

Meterove laughed and said ""Likes" might not be a strong enough of a word. She is just as attracted to women as she is men."

Laticin asked slowly, "And you are not troubled by this?"

Meterove laughed, "Troubled? No. I have awoken in the same bed as Terenia and a woman that I had little memory of meeting."

Laticin was scared to ask lest she get her hopes up for nothing but in the end, she could not stop herself. She asked quietly, "Are you fine with that? Does that not bother you?"

Meterove shook his head, "No. She loves me. I know this without a doubt. Just because she loves me does not mean that she cannot love another. If she chooses to also love a woman than that is for her to decide."

Whereas she had moments ago felt ice, Laticin now felt the heat of joy explode in her heart. This man was who she truly needed to meet. He was pleasant to look at sure, but more importantly, he was accepting of something that she had personally hidden for so long. Her kind had no romantic relationships with their own kind. They would sometimes have one with humans long enough to produce several children.

Those who were caught having anything other than a friendship amongst their own kind were shunned at the very least. This man was not like that. He not only accepted this, but he even encouraged it!

As far as Laticin was concerned now was not the time to be shy. Now was the time to be bold! Laticin sat up and took the shirt off, fully exposing her body. She straddled Meterove before he could move and looked into his eyes from mere inches away.

Laticin smiled and said, "I also like other women. I think I need to meet this Terenia of yours. I am sure that we can come to an arrangement that will be to everyone's liking."

Meterove felt a burning on his back and in that moment, he knew that this decision had already been made. Laticin's lips overlapped with his own and everything fell away. All he could hope for was that he really knew Terenia as well as he thought that he did.

CHAPTER 30
CORE

Meterove and Laticin awoke after a time. Meterove felt a strange combination of apprehension and happiness. He knew that he had made a rash decision, but it felt right.

I just hope that Terenia agrees with me.

Meterove looked over at Laticin who still appeared to be asleep, though he was sure she was at least partially awake. She truly was beautiful her blue and purple hair fell over her back. She was facing him at the moment and Meterove had to work to keep his eyes from drifting down too much.

Meterove wondered vaguely just how heavy those things were. After a moment he realized his gaze had slipped again and he refocused. He set to work studying the shape of her face.

After several minutes she began to stir in earnest, and she opened her eyes. The sight of those eyes, one blue and the other purple was very enticing. The small smile that she gave him warmed him beyond what his magic could have ever achieved.

Underneath his comfort, Meterove felt a trill of fear. What would Terenia think about this? He had been so confident that she would accept this earlier but now he was not so sure. He decided to worry about it later. What had happened could not be undone.

The first thing that Meterove did was to eat something. Afterwards he gathered up the few things of his that he had taken out and once everything was secured, they left the cave.

Out in the Lagoon there was activity everywhere. Laticin took him over to an area that held the Mermaids food stores. There she received some fish for her own meal. If Meterove had not already experienced raw fish, this might have shocked him.

Laticin took her meal over to a nearby rock and leaned on it while she ate. Once she was done, they went to go look for Moira. They found her with a group of Mermaids. They each were carrying a pack made of seagrass.

Meterove assumed that the packs were for supplies. Laticin motioned for him to wait there and swam off. She returned shortly after with a pack of her own.

She was also carrying the spear and wearing the rapier that she had when he had first met her. She reported to Moira and when she came back, she looked annoyed. Meterove noticed that there was a woman nearby that bore a resemblance to Laticin. She and Laticin refused to look at each other.

Moira looked at the woman first before swimming up to Alara. After a moment Moira and Alara grasped each other's forearms and nodded. After that Moira turned and set off, the rest of the assembled Mermaids following after. Laticin and Meterove were at the rear.

At first Meterove struggled to keep up with the Mermaids and knew that they were moving far more slowly than normal to account for him. He did his best, but he could tell that they were also frustrated.

Meterove reviewed what he knew about magic to see if there was some solution. His strong points were in the areas of reinforcement magic and utilizing it as a weapon. Utility use of magic were not something that came easy to him.

Strengthening his body was the only option that he could think of. As he swam Meterove slowly began drawing out and utilizing the power. There would be the problem of creating turbulent water in his wake, but as long as he stayed at the back this would not be an issue.

Laticin noticed his magic and increased speed and said, *"Moira, he has found a way to increase his speed. We can pick up the pace!"*

Moira said, *"That is good! We need to reach an outpost before dark!"*

Once Meterove was able to keep up with them he realized just how much they had been holding back just so that he had not been left behind. As he swam through the endless expanse of water, he would often see various sea creatures. Sometimes he would see pods of whales or huge schools of fish.

Once he saw a huge shape that the Mermaids also seemed wary of. It had an elongated head and a thick body that had four flippers, the back two of which were significantly larger than the front. It also had a short tail.

Given the distance that he was looking at the creature its size was impossible to gauge. The only indicator of size was that when its mouth was opened the teeth could not be seen.

They swam on and occasionally they would see other huge sea creatures but mostly it was fish. Most of them were small but there were still plenty that were larger than a man.

As it was growing dark Meterove spotted a series of strange rock formations ahead. There were hundreds of stone pillars. Some were closer together than others, but none were wide enough for more than one Mermaid to swim through at once.

Meterove followed them in and looked around. There were other smaller stone structures scattered around the interior of the pillars as well as a half a dozen natural caves. He could understand why they chose this place to stop.

Laticin went to speak with Moira then waved for him to follow her. She led him to one of the stone structures. Inside was three separate alcoves and it was lit with what appeared to be glowing algae. Meterove assumed that this was meant to house three Mermaids. Soon enough Moira joined them.

Meterove made a small barrier to move the water out of his alcove. Once he had done so he noticed that Laticin looked surprised. She moved herself over to it cautiously. Meterove adjusted the barrier to allow her through.

Laticin said, "I did not know you could do that."

Meterove said, "It is not as simple as it looks and the number of times that I can do it in a day is very limited, especially if I want to be able to do anything else. My brother can make a far more effective barrier than I can."

Laticin looked interested in asking more but instead said, "Moira would like you to help stand guard on the first watch. The krono that we saw earlier was not the largest of its kind. There is a good chance that the large varieties are also in the area."

Meterove felt a little anxiety at that. He decided to ask, "What kind of threats are there out here that I need to be aware of?

Laticin said, "You have already seen a krono. There are more that are in the same family that are far larger. They can be as large as the Megalodons."

Meterove looked at her blankly. "The WHAT?"

Laticin shook her head and said "OK, it looks like this is going to take a while. I will give you the short versions for now and after your watch is over, I will give you the detailed version."

Meterove nodded. That would have to do for now. As long as he knew that there were large predators and what he needed to watch out for everything would be fine. Laticin spent about five minutes giving him the descriptions of the most likely threats.

Once that was done, he found himself out near the perimeter of the stone pillars. He was staying low to the rocks and staying within reach of one of the Mermaid guards.

Moira must expect something to happen if she wanted me to assist . They had made a point to mention the krono and that there were more in the same family that were even bigger.

Meterove kept watch with the guard until their relief came. As they were changing out Meterove felt a chill down his spine. Before he even had the chance to think about it, he had drawn Oblivion.

From out of the darkness hurtled fifty feet of reptilian nightmare. Laticin had meant it when she said there were bigger ones out there. Those jaws were large enough to swallow him whole with ease.

It paid no heed to the pillars and crashed into four of them before Meterove was able to reach it. Upon getting close to it, Meterove saw that its eyes were glassy and lifeless.

This thing is undead!

Meterove knew that now was no time to hold back, so he struck the beast with Oblivion and was about to trigger the singularity effect when it shook him off. The wound left no blood in the water, as if he needed more proof that it was undead.

Meterove dove after the creature, which turned and was attempting to get to some of the other Mermaids that had scattered when it had crashed into the pillars. Luckily Meterove was fast enough to catch up to it before it could get to anyone and this time, he was ready.

The second that Oblivion contacted the creature's head he triggered the effect, and the front half was compressed into nothingness. The world started to go dark and Meterove barely held onto consciousness. He slowly swam over to where the other Mermaids were now congregating.

Moira was there, taking a head count by the looks of it. She seemed pleased and relieved when she saw him. She nodded over to her left and he saw Laticin looking around worriedly, her back to him. Meterove swam over and tapped her shoulder.

Laticin turned around and when she saw Meterove she instantly embraced him. She had been so worried that something had happened to him. It took some time for everyone to calm down and for Moira to send them back to their caves.

Back inside the stone building in his air pocket Meterove used magic to dry himself off. Moments later Laticin and Moira entered. With the three of them in there it was pretty cramped, so Meterove made a point of leaning towards Laticin.

Moira said, "I am glad that you are alright. It seems that having you join the guards was the right choice. Thank You for saving us!"

Laticin asked, "How did you destroy its head like that?"

Meterove tapped Oblivion and said "My sword can create a small and short-lived singularity on whatever I cut with it. Basically, that beast's was compressed down to an infinitely small space. It drains me to use it though. The larger the object the greater the toll that it takes on me."

Best not to tell them that I had no idea I could increase the radius by pouring more magic into it until I tried it.

Moira looked him in the eyes, "Well regardless of whether it is you or your weapon that saved us, I thank you. No one was seriously hurt. You have the gratitude of us all."

Meterove brushed off the thanks and said, "Would it be possible to ask a question?"

Moira said, "Of course! If it is something that I know the answer to I shall gladly give it."

Meterove asked, "Who was that woman that looks so much like Laticin and why were things so awkward with her there?"

Both women froze but Laticin was the first to speak, "As for the first part that is simple. She is my mother. As for the second part, things are more complicated. It should suffice to say that she and I are not getting along."

Moira said, "Laticin and Elise have different ideologies. Elise believes deeply in the scriptures of our people while Laticin does not."

Meterove asked, "Scriptures?"

Laticin rolled her eyes, "Many of the older generations believe in something called the "Great Lord" that they view as a god like being."

Laticin opened her pack and pulled out a strange set of tablets with runes carved into them. Laticin said, "These are the so-called scriptures that Moira was referring to."

Meterove looked at them and thanks to the magic that Flare had put on him he was able to read them.

The keys shall open the path to commune with the greatest entity of the Plane of Water.

The first key rests with the daughters of the sea.

The second key lies with those that tend to those that are lost.

The third key is with those that have the closest bond with the Plane.

The fourth key can only be obtained by those who are true to their nature.

These four keys will restore the Plane to a state of balance.

Meterove looked up and saw both Laticin and Moira looking at him openmouthed. Unaware of the fact that he had been reading aloud Meterove was confused at first. After a moment he realized that he had read aloud. He looked back at the tablets and said, "Sorry I did not mean to offend you."

Moira shakily said, "What did you mean by all that? We knew some of the contents of the tablets, but you have translated more of it in mere moments than we have in generations. Everything that you have read so far is similar to what we believe them to say."

Laticin said, "Are you telling me that my mother was right?"

Meterove explained, "Flare has magic that allows those that do work for her to read and understand the languages they will be exposed to. This does not refer to some kind of deity if that is what you are thinking."

Moira blanched slightly and asked, "How can you be sure that it does not?"

Meterove took a moment to consider the wisdom of what he was about to say but, in the end, her decided that telling them was the right thing to do.

Meterove took a deep breath before saying, "Flare left no room for doubt when she told us that there was no such thing as gods or other divine beings."

Moira looked stricken. Laticin felt triumph in her heart but masked it while placing a consoling hand on Moira's shoulder. Meterove decided that since he had started, he might as well finish now.

"Flare likes to be cryptic and refuses to share more than she absolutely must. For instance, all she told us was that we needed to go to the Core and speak with the leaders of the three Principal Races. She appeared to believe that you would just know what I needed."

Laticin asked, "Why would she think that? The Mermaids have believed that these were religious texts for as far back as our people know."

Meterove shook his head, "Flare is a dragon, one of the first two dragons, to be more precise. I doubt that the thought of how long it had been since these were written even occurred to her. Even a regular dragon has a different perspective on the passage of time."

Laticin asked, "What do you think that the texts are referring to?"

Meterove looked back at the texts and read them again then said, "I think that there is some form of guardian here that Flare knows about. Probably something that she personally placed here to act as insurance if something were to ever happen."

Moira seemed to come back a little bit at hearing this. She asked, "What do you mean by guardian?"

Meterove tilted his head to the side and shrugged, "There is no way to know for sure. If I had to guess, I would say that there is some being that is supposed to be kept secret and locked away so each of the Principal Races only has part of the story to keep it that way."

Moira looked sad, "What you are saying is that you believe there is some kind of being here that our ancestors mistook for a god."

Laticin shook her head, "We cannot let mother hear this. She threw enough of a fit before. She might actually attack him if she heard this. Why did you bring her along?"

Moira was still slightly in shock but said, "I thought that it would be best to keep her close while we were away. Who knows what she might stir up while we were gone."

Laticin could not argue that point. Once they reached the Core and Meterove spoke with the other leaders that would be there, she would find out. Things might get ugly, but Moira was right, at least she did not have as many willing ears at the Core.

.   .   .

It had been several days since Meterove had vanished into the spiral and Terenia had been insufferable. Joleen had grown quite fond of the woman, but this was too much. She had not left her alone at all, not even when she was relieving herself!

Narok had found the situation funny, though of course he was not the one having their personal space violated. Dras had tried to help but for reasons that she would never understand, Terenia had glued herself to Joleen.

The trip to the Core was going smoothly. They would be there soon based on the measurements they had taken. After Meterove had drawn the beast off they had not encountered anything else that had attacked them.

Dras had been drinking again. He tried to hide it, but they all knew. He tried to put up a front that he was unconcerned about Meterove but when he thought no one was looking he would pick at himself.

At present everyone was on the bridge and Narok was looking through the periscope checking on their progress. After a moment he returned it to the stowed position and said, "We are very close, now would be a good time to surface. You are going to want to see this for yourself."

Joleen nodded and said, "Everyone take your seats! We are surfacing now!"

The alarm blared for a few minutes and after a time they could feel the shift as they now rolled slightly with the waves on the surface. After confirming they were in fact on the surface Joleen led the way up. Opening the hatch, she climbed out and instantly saw what Narok had been talking about.

The Core was directly ahead of them. It was a spiral hundreds of times the size of the one Meterove had gone into. Around the Core was what looked like a structure made of glass that was more ornate and delicate than anything she had ever seen in her life.

Behind her she heard Dras whisper, "Holy shit..."

Joleen could only nod. This structure appeared to reach all the way across to the other side of the Plane. There were three pillars and hundreds of platforms connecting them. At the base of the towers there was a dome that looked tiny next to the Core, but Joleen was fairly sure was larger than their ship.

Drawing closer she was able to see figures near the front of the dome on what looked like stairs. They had long since noticed them and were reacting with alarm. Joleen had anticipated this and had the Leturai close the hatch just to be safe.

Soon a group of them were heading over to investigate them. Several beautiful women swam up to the side of the ship and climbed aboard. Joleen side eyed Narok before returning her attention to the women. Narok had made a point to keep his eyes up as much as he could.

Those that had come aboard were clearly Undines. There were six of them and they were all armed with weapons that looked like the same material as the structure they had come from. The one that looked to be their leader stepped forward.

She called, "Who are you? What business do you have here on this strange object?"

Joleen was a tad peeved by her manners. She responded, "I was always taught that one should introduce themselves before asking the name of others."

The woman stiffened for a moment then said, "I am Ava. I am the regent of the Core. Now answer my questions!"

Joleen still did not like this woman's tone. She decided that if this woman were going to speak down to her, she would return the favor.

Joleen cleared her throat, "I am Joleen Valaseri, empress of Yxarion and I am here on an urgent matter on behalf of Lady Flare, she who presides over Nexus."

Ava's jaw clenched. It was clear that this woman was out of her depth. She decided that teaching them a lesson was in order. She signaled and the other five Undines forced the water up and around Joleen and the others. For good measure she had them disarm them as well, depositing them next to her.

She walked up to Joleen and glared haughtily into her eyes and said, "I have no idea who you people truly are, but I will not tolerate being spoken to in such-"

She stopped talking as a dagger pressed against her throat. She looked back and saw with shock that one of them was now behind her. She could see the shock on the others faces as they prepared to make a move Dras growled, "Try it and I will separate her head from her shoulders."

The other women froze and Dras continued, "Good. Now release my friends."

Ava was terrified and confused. Undines were masters of the water. They had captured this person and he had somehow escaped and turned the situation around where they were the captives!

Once the water had released them Joleen and the others gathered their weapons and after they had restrained the six of them Joleen said, "Let's try this again. I am Joleen and I am here on an urgent matter. We were sent by Lady Flare herself. Now is there someone that actually has authority that we can talk to?"

The insult dug deep but Ava did not have a choice. She and her sisters were captive but had not yet been killed. She had to trust that this woman was who she said she was.

Ava said, "There is soon to be a meeting of the three Principal Races here. You will be able to speak to the leaders that come here. Is that good enough for you?"

Joleen did not like this woman, but she would trust that she was telling the truth. "Very well, we will join you until the meeting so that we can be sure to speak to them as soon as possible."

CHAPTER 31
TRIAD

Meterove could see the Core ahead of him. Laticin had spent the last several days telling him all about it, so he already knew the details. The Undines watched over the Core because it used the same kind of magic that they did in terms of controlling water.

Laticin had also talked at length about the other races and the ones that she knew. She had mostly talked about her friend Claire. She had also grudgingly talked about her mother, after Meterove had pushed hard enough.

These conversations were always interesting, but she never let him go for long without asking her own questions. She had asked many questions about the Ashen Soul and the undead that he had seen. She also made a point of asking about his personal life.

664

Meterove had surfaced once to get a good look at what the Core looked like and had been pleased to see a long black object sitting near it.

Excellent! Joleen and the others have already arrived!

The Mermaids led the way over to some steps. It was truly a sight to behold. The entire structure was made out of water that was held in place. None of it was frozen, it was simply held in place by various barriers.

Meterove could not help but marvel at the beauty of it all. With structural strength a non-issue, the architects had been able to build this place with the only concerns being beauty and functionality. Everything was so intricate.

Meterove noticed that the pillars were not connected all the way around. The tower furthest from him was thinner than the other two but had bridges passing to both of the other towers. Meanwhile the two thicker towers were not connected together.

The banisters that were along the steps held various rocks and shells. As Meterove stepped onto the first step he felt as though it shifted from being water to suddenly being solid and supporting his weight.

As Moira began talking with an Undine that had come over to receive them Laticin asked Meterove, "Is that large black object over there the "ship" that you were telling me about?"

Meterove nodded, "Yes! That means that the others are here. Hopefully, Joleen has not caused too much of a scene. I also hope that Terenia has been able to contain herself given the...sights."

Meterove nodded over to the dozens of Undines that were visible. As with the Mermaids, every one of them were unclothed. Meterove noticed that Laticin was slightly annoyed. She tossed a glance at the Undines and Meterove understood.

Meterove asked, "when would be a good time to ask about my friends?"

Laticin shook her head to clear her mind then said, "Given the circumstances, I would say we should go ask now."

Meterove let Laticin lead the way over to Moira. Once there the woman that was talking to Moira noticed Meterove and her mouth tightened. Meterove would gauge that she was probably in her mid-forties.

Ava said, "Another...human. You must be Meterove then."

It was not a question. Meterove started to laugh, "You clearly ran afoul of Joleen. She is the only one that I know that can cause someone to make that face. I suggest you try and relax, or you will give yourself even more wrinkles."

Ava's eyes shot wide with fury but before she could say anything Meterove had continued, "Exactly where can I find them then?"

Ava took a moment to calm herself then said, "I will have someone come by shortly to guide you to them."

As Ava walked away, Laticin said, "I think you were mistaken about your sister being the only one that can get her to make that face."

Meterove wanted to argue but knew he did not have a leg to stand on. He had just casually riled the woman up. He looked at Moira, "Who was she anyway?"

Moira placed the heel of her left palm on her forehead, "That was Ava. She is the current Regent of the Core."

Meterove did his best to no look perturbed. On the outside he kept up a stoic and calm look and just shrugged off her station. On the inside though it was slightly different.

Oops. To think that Jol and I both managed to piss of the leader of the Core. HA!

Soon another Undine named Elaine came to escort him. Laticin looked distressed for a moment, but Moira shook her head, "Foolish girl, there is plenty of time before a meeting can occur. The only Undines here are the Regent and the other caretakers. Additionally, it appears that the

Snow Women have yet to arrive as well. Go with him and be our representative."

Laticin smiled at Moira and then she and Meterove followed Elaine. She guided them over to one of the larger towers. There was a sharply pointed arched doorway that led to a huge high-ceilinged room with a staircase on one side. This room was mostly empty, except for a large stone obelisk in the middle of the room.

This caught Meterove's attention since he had not seen anything other than the air above the water. In the middle of the obelisk there was a symbol that he swore that he had seen before but just could not put his finger on where.

It kind of looked like a dagger, only it had a second blade coming off where the guard would normally be. Meterove thought for a moment but could not place it, so he just continued to follow Elaine. At the top of the stairs there was what resembled a lounge. It was empty except for five people.

Dras walked over and punched him on the shoulder, "Hey! You lived!"

Joleen and Jolson both visibly untensed now that they knew that their brother was safe. Joleen was the first to speak, "You had us worried. I am glad to see that you are in one piece."

Jolson followed up with, "We really need to reign in some of this risky behavior of yours. You are going to make me grey before my time!"

Meterove chuckled while Narok clapped him on the back, "It is really good to see you well. I did what I could to fill the void you left, but I just do not have your special skills when it comes to the others. Someday, you must tell me how you get Joleen riled up so easily."

While Joleen swatted Narok and Jolson chuckled Meterove was looking at Terenia. The moment that they had walked in her eyes had lit up with so much emotion. However, they had also found and begun analyzing Laticin.

This was the part that he was worried about. Terenia had already noticed the way Laticin was positioning herself. She was also very aware of the fact that Laticin is not wearing clothes.

When he had made that decision several days ago it had been because it had just felt right. At the time he had felt the choice being tattooed onto his back and had thought of it as a good thing. Only afterwards did it occur to him that bad decisions could also be recorded.

Joleen asked, "What happened after you went into the spiral?"

Meterove looked away from Terenia and told them the whole story. How he had managed to kill the beast. How he had met the Mermaids soon after. Here he said,

"On that topic, allow me to introduce Laticin Reifke. She is one of the elders of the Mermaids."

Joleen raised her chin slightly, "I am Joleen Valaseri. I am Meterove's elder sister. It is a pleasure to meet you."

One by one the others introduced themselves to Laticin. The last one to do so was Terenia. She and Laticin stared at each other for a few minutes before Terenia said, "I am Terenia, a Nymph of the forest. It is a pleasure to meet you and I welcome you to our group."

Laticin looked puzzled, "You make it sound as though I am going to be staying with you."

Terenia smiled, perhaps a little stiffly, "Am I mistaken that you plan to stay with us, or more specifically Meterove?

Narok and Jolson walked over to a nearby dispenser to get some water. The conversation between Terenia and Laticin kept going with Laticin saying, "What would give you the idea that I was planning on staying with Meterove specifically?"

Terenia said, "You are just standing so close to him at the moment that I just kind of assumed."

Dras' eyes went a little wide, "You know I think I could use some water as well."

While Dras was walking over to Jolson and Narok, Joleen had begun looking back and forth between Meterove,

Terenia and Laticin. Finally, she seemed to accept the reality of the situation and walked quickly over to the others.

Meterove decided that he need to try and head this off before things got bad, so he said, "Terenia I need to talk to you."

Terenia shook her head, "There is no need. I can tell already."

The calmness of her voice was almost enough to break his nerve. Still, he had to see this through to the end. Meterove cleared his throat, "Terenia, it is as you are thinking. I cannot explain or excuse my actions. I can only do this."

Meterove stepped forward and took her hand and whispered to her. The words were so soft that none but the two of them knew what was said. Once he had finished, she looked at him, her eyes glistening with emotion.

Terenia said, "I am not angry about what you did. I love you and as you pointed out this is the way that we are."

Terenia kissed Meterove then walked over and after walking once around Laticin stopped right in front of her and they stared at one another for several moments. Terenia asked, "How do you feel about Meterove?"

Laticin's eyes widened, "You do not pull your punches do you? I have only known him for several days, but I can say this for certain. From the moment we first started talking I felt a connection to him. Most of my kind use men solely for procreation. That is not what I want."

Terenia asked, "I can tell by observing you that you are not only interested in men. What then do you think of me?"

Laticin looked uncomfortable at first about her orientation being spoken of out loud, but she still replied, "I find that you are quite beautiful, and I would have to say that I am also attracted to you, though I have only just met you."

Terenia asked, "Would you be comfortable with us not just sharing him but all three of us sharing each other?"

Meterove realized this question was also meant for him after Terenia gave him a side-eyed glance. While Laticin seemed taken aback by Terenia's boldness, Meterove simply said, "I could do that."

Laticin took a deep breath through her nose and said, "Yes. I can do that as well."

Terenia grabbed her by the hand and cheerily waved at the others with the other as she said, "I need to take these two somewhere private for a little while. We will see you in a bit."

Terenia grabbed Meterove by the hand a began to pull the two of them after her. Meterove was not entirely sure what she was planning but he knew that the two of them had no choice but to find out when it happened.

Two hours later the three of them returned to the lounge. Joleen looked closely at their faces, but she found no signs of what had happened. If it was what Dras had suggested, then she really did not want to think about it too much. The only thing that she could see on their faces was that Terenia had a smirk and that the other two appeared to be more relaxed.

Joleen decided that she did not need to know the answer. She looked at Meterove and asked, "So, what exactly are we supposed to do next? I have not had the chance to learn anything new, but you have. Have you learned anything that might indicate where we are supposed to go from here?"

Meterove glanced at Laticin and after she nodded, he said, "I had a chance to look over what the Mermaids had been treating as a scripture. It mentions four keys, and something about a "great one" that is supposed to be the lord of the Plane. Thing is these are so old that the actual meaning and purpose of them are long lost."

Joleen looked frustrated, while Jolson looked to be deep in thought. Laticin was picking at herself slightly before she stammered, "You might be best served asking the leaders of the Snow Women."

Joleen turned to her with a raised eyebrow. Laticin went a little red, but Joleen asked, "Why do you think that the Snow Women would have a better idea that you?"

Laticin steadied herself then said, "Unlike the Mermaids the Snow Women have no religious texts. They function on what can be proven through observation."

Jolson clapped his fist onto his open palm, "Since they would not have any religion to pervert the text, any knowledge would retain its authenticity."

Laticin nodded, "Exactly. Asking the Undines would not hurt either. One of my best friends Claire is an Undine. I am sure if we ask her that she will gladly tell us anything that she knows."

Narok asked, "So where does that leave us for right now?"

Dras clapped him on the back, "I am afraid that we both know the answer to that question. We wait."

Once he finished that pronouncement, he plopped himself down on what appeared to be some kind of chair, though it too was made of water.

Meterove looked at Laticin, "Do you need to head back to your people?"

Laticin shook her head, "Moira will have asked where they were guiding us so that she could come get me when needed. For now, I think I would like to stay and get to know all of you better."

For the next several hours Laticin stayed in the company of the humans. Asking questions and answering them. Listening to stories and telling them. After she heard a few of the stories that they told involving the Ashen Soul, she could not help but wonder why such incredible people were interested in talking to her.

They had traveled worlds, fought ancient evils, dueled some of the worst and ghastliest creatures to have ever existed and yet they found her, a simple Mermaid interesting. It just seemed so odd to her. At first, she wondered if perhaps it was some kind of cruel joke.

After telling her third story and seeing that they were all listening to her with rapt attention she began to realize that this was no joke. For whatever reason, these people found what she had to tell them just as amazing as what they had told her.

Eventually a messenger came from the Mermaids and Laticin rose and after a moment's hesitation embraced and lightly kissed Meterove. She left promptly afterwards, and Joleen noticed that her ears were very red. Out of the corner of her eye she saw Terenia smiling at the Mermaids back.

Meterove asked Joleen, "Where have you been sleeping?"

Joleen said, "We have been using the ship. The Undines that reside here were able to provide the crew of the ship with a gate back home, so they took it. Anton made sure to leave detailed instructions on how certain parts of the ship worked so that we could use it if we needed to."

Meterove said, "We could not possibly operate that ship with the six of us."

Joleen shook her head, "No, but we would be able to with twelve. If we can get some help from the Principal Races, we would be able to fully utilize it. As it is we can only limp along at best right now."

Dras chimed in, "He made sure that we knew where everything in kitchen was though. You should see Joleen cook!"

Joleen elbowed Dras in the stomach, "Forget what he said!"

It was too late. Meterove latched onto it right away. He looked at her like she had two heads, "You were cooking? You have always avoided going into the kitchens. Even Jolson joined me a time or two stealing snacks from the kitchen."

Jolson laughed fondly at the memory while Joleen lifted her chin in the air and said, "I am nothing more than Joleen out here. There are going to be times that if I want to eat, I will have to be the one that cooks it. Besides, while I may not be great at it, I have a least found some enjoyment in it."

Hours turned into days and finally when almost a week had passes word came of the Undines arrival. Laticin had been back several times since the first day and this was one of those times. She was pulling Meterove along by the hand practically tripping over herself in her excitement.

Out on the landing near the steps Meterove could see a large group of Undines. He could sense the excitement of Laticin. She had been anxiously awaiting their arrival, no doubt worried about her friend.

One of the Undines saw Laticin and said something inaudible to one of the others then met Laticin halfway and they embraced.

Laticin said, "Claire! I am so happy to see you and thankful that you are safe!"

Claire looked saddened, "Then you know of the dangers that lurk in our waters these days. Things are as bad as we feared then..."

Laticin was about to ask her what she had experienced but thought better of it. There would be time enough for that later. She noticed that Claire's eyes had drifted to Meterove, so she cleared her throat and said "This is Meterove. He and six others are here as envoys of the Lady Flare as well as advocates of their own world."

Claire looked at Meterove and then back at Laticin. In her eyes Laticin could see her making deductions so she decided to head her off and said, "He and I are together."

Claire's eyes lit up even more as she once again hugged Laticin. She then said, "Since we are sharing good news right now..."

She placed her right hand over her stomach and looked at Laticin with a peaceful smile. Laticin now got nearly as excited as she shouted, "That's right! Your reproduction cycles were starting soon! Oh, Claire! This is great news!"

Meterove watched the two women squeal in excitement and joy for a while. There was enough darkness coming, no need to kill off their joy. Once they had calmed down Laticin introduced them. "Meterove this is Claire. She is my best friend. Now I should finish introducing him. He is one of the most reckless people I have ever met in my life. I first met him as he was being chased out of a spiral by a Leviathan."

Claire looked at this man Meterove, "What kind of accident led to that?"

Laticin rolled her eyes, "He did so willingly and used the speed and size of the creature to kill it. Once he was close enough to the rocky bottom he turned away and the Leviathan was skewered."

Claire returned her gaze to Meterove, now with redoubled interest. "You are an odd person. I admit that I do not have experience with men, however I would like to know you better."

At first her words made Meterove and Laticin tense up, but Meterove relaxed once he saw Laticin relax. He made a mental note to ask about it later. In his mind though he was thinking about how Dras would love to meet her.

Claire asked him lots of questions and answered any that Meterove thought to ask. Based on the nature of her questions Meterove concluded that she was a very intelligent woman. She also had a sense of strength about her that Meterove could not help but be impressed with.

Two days later the Snow Women arrived and just as Meterove had thought would be the case there were some among their number that he already knew. While he had not had a chance to speak with them directly yet, there was the young girl and the woman he had spoken to back in the forest.

The meeting was announced to be the following morning. Meterove and the others were all anxious. They had been through a lot since coming here and they knew that there was still a long path ahead of them. Sleeping that night was almost impossible.

The next day, just after the light cycle had begun the meeting began to get underway. In an audience hall the width of an entire pillar they now sat and waited for their time to speak.

Ava was the one to start the proceedings. She cleared her throat then said, "It is time for the Council of the Three Principal Races to begin. Representing the Undines are Fayre Thalassa and Olivia Potami. Representing the Snow Women, we have Gwen Wokensalf and Demetria Dilzzarb. Representing the Mermaids, we have Moira Wels and Laticin Reifke. We also have in attendance the Lady Joleen Valaseri and Lords Jolson Valaseri and Meterove Valaseri who are here at the bequest of Lady Flare of Nexus."

While there were far more members of every race present, they were off in a separate section of the chamber and were forbidden from speaking during the meeting, Dras, Narok and Terenia were allowed to stay with Joleen and the others but were not to speak unless asked to.

The mention of Lady Flare had the room buzzing. Whispers were allowed, so long as they were not disruptive. Hearing Flare's name and seeing that there were humans here had caused enough of a stir that Ava cleared her throat loudly then glared around the room.

Once the room had quieted, she continued, "Lady Joleen has requested she be allowed to address you all and considering the nature of what she wishes to say I believe it is prudent to have her speak first. If you will Lady Joleen."

Joleen stepped forward and after looking each of the six representatives in the eyes said, "While it is true that I have come here with Lady Flare's blessings I would like to stress that I am also here for personal reasons."

Meterove looked around at the representatives and was pleased to see that all of them were giving Joleen their full attention. He had been worried that they might be ignored.

Joleen continued, "There have been attacks on our world that have are likely originating from the Plane of Water. Lady Flare believes that the first Kraken Mia has been corrupted by undeath and is now spreading the curse on the Plane."

There was a gasp from the Undine and Snow Women representatives, as well as a collective gasp from the others that were assembled.

Joleen waited a moment then said, "This undeath is something that we have fought before, and we would like to help end it. We were only told that we needed to seek the Three Principal Races and that they would know what we would need to do. We have since learned that there are four keys that are needed to release something, possibly a guardian of the Plane."

"We must ask the Great Lord for help!"

Laticin cringed as she heard these words shouted out from the onlookers. There was no mistaking that voice and there was no other person that would have shouted that out. She sighed but the damage was already done.

The shout had caused chaos in the chamber. It took the better part of an hour to get the chamber calmed down. Out of the corner of her eyes she saw two of Ava's subordinates escorting her mother out of the chamber.

Laticin said, "So much for her not causing a scene."

Moira did not say anything. Elise had indeed caused them some embarrassment. Once everything was calmed down, Ava said, "Moving on, the Mermaids will be the first to speak. Moira if you will."

Moira said, "We have encountered various deep-sea creatures over the last several months. Some of these include colossal squid, Ichthyosaurs and even a Leviathan. Additionally, we have had many of our people either vanish in the night or being killed then vanishing."

Laticin went next, "While enroute here we encountered one of the mosasaurs that was acting out of character. Not least in that it was out of its usual habitat. This creature attacked our group at the Black Chasm outpost. It destroyed many of the pillars that have long protected that place from larger predators. Had Meterove not been with us, we might have all been killed."

The two women spoke their bits, then stepped back. Once they did so, Ava said, "Next the Undine representatives shall speak, Fayre whenever you are ready."

Meterove noticed the respect that Ava had for this woman, and he looked closer. She did not look terribly old until you looked into her eyes. Physically she looked to be no older than Ava, but those eyes told a different and far longer story.

Fayre said, "We have also experienced our share of loss and strangeness. What started as a discovery of two extremely small undead in the Lower Shallows has quickly become a cancer that is spreading nearly unchecked. We have lost hundreds of our sisters now trying to keep the undead back. Unfortunately, every sister that falls adds to their numbers."

Olivia said, "We have observed undeath in everything from minnows and mollusks to bull sharks and now a great number of our sisters."

Ava looked extremely upset about this news and appeared to want to ask questions, but she kept her composure. Meterove could understand, she was probably worried about someone specific.

Ava said, "Lastly we will have the representatives of the Snow Women speak."

Gwen said, "We have not had the same direct experiences as the Undines and Mermaids. Since we live in separate villages scattered around the Great Ice Shelf our experience has been one of uncertainty. We have lost many of our sisters now as well."

Demetria said, "We had sent out messengers to the villages that did not show at our last meeting. They reported that the villages were completely empty and there were no signs of what had happened. These reports that we have heard now may explain what has happened."

Ava said, "We have now heard from each representative. The matter is now open for debate and questions."

This was the part that Laticin had told Meterove to wait for. During this portion of the meeting the onlookers could address the representatives with questions.

Meterove was about to ask a question when one of the Undines from the crowd asked, "I thought that undeath was just a myth before now. Why has it suddenly come here?"

Meterove had hoped that particular question would not come up. While they had done nothing wrong, there was a good chance that the denizens of the Plane of Water would blame them if they found out this had come from their world.

Joleen cleared her throat and said, "Undeath as a whole is the work of the being known as the Ashen Soul. It has been spreading its curse since the early days of Creation. So long as a single undead exists then the Ashen Soul cannot be destroyed. We thought that we had killed it on our world, but we have learned that is not the case."

Another member of the crowd asked, "Are you saying this Ashen Soul has come here?"

Joleen shook her head, "I cannot be certain, but I do not think that it is here. I believe that it killed and reanimated the Kraken, Mia. It may have made Mia into something more powerful than a standard undead, which is called a Weaver."

Gwen said, "But this is just your speculation, correct?"

Joleen nodded, "That is true, however it is backed up with significant evidence. Our world was under attack by undead creatures in the form of Sirens, which had never been seen on our world before as well as tentacles belonging to something far larger than anything we have ever seen."

Jolson said, "Since arriving here we have encountered things that should not be here. The ship that we arrived on was not something that we brought through. That ship is from our world and arrived some time before us."

Gwen was shocked, "A whole of that size would take immeasurable power! I cannot even comprehend it!"

Meterove said, "Additionally I can say with confidence that the Mosasaur that I killed was undead."

Jolson said, "Another point I would like to make is that I do not believe our world is the only one under attack.

From what Lady Flare has told us, very few know how to reach Nexus and therefore the Planes to investigate. The enemy is likely building an army."

Fayre asked, "If what you say is true, what action do we take?"

Joleen said, "We are not entirely sure. We are hoping that you have some sort of answer for us. My brother Meterove has a potential clue."

Meterove said, "I translated the texts of the Mermaids on the way here and they speak of four keys. One key is held by each of the Principal Races, while the fourth key's location was more cryptic. Are there any objects that you can think of that might be these keys?"

The room went silent for a long moment and then the assembled women began murmuring. After a moment Claire spoke up, "I know that there is at least one thing that both the Mermaids and Undines possess."

Claire vaguely noticed her mother glaring at her, but she ignored her. Laticin knew what she was talking about, so she pulled the dagger out and once the other representatives saw it, they looked around apprehensively before each pulling out their own.

Three different daggers that all looked the same but had slight differences. Mostly it was what sides were bladed and the color. All had polished silver blades, but each had a different secondary color. One was green, one was a very dark blue and the other was cerulean blue.

Once Meterove saw them all together he suddenly remembered where he had seen something like them before.

Meterove's voice was shaking as he said, "I have seen something like those before. It was back on our world. I saw a vision of a wooden shack on the water and an object floating in the air in the middle of it."

The room went quiet as everyone stared at him. Meterove continued, "The object looked just like those except that it was crimson and silver. I also vaguely remember being attacked by something in the water after taking the key."

Gwen said, "You said this was a vison that you had. Are you gifted with the ability to look into the future?"

Jolson said, "No, but I am. It makes some sense that, as my brother, he would also have some sensitivity to it."

Since when? That is one hell of a lie Jolson!

Fortunately, it appeared that this bit of knowledge was not known, and the lie passed without being challenged. Joleen asked, "How are the keys supposed to be used?"

Silence greeted her. Jolson asked, "What is the purpose of the stones that are on the bottom level of each pillar?"

Gwen said, "We do not know. The language on them is difficult to decipher. While we do know some sections, others are a total mystery. The texts of the Mermaids are one of the few parts that are translated, and those are only partially. You say you have translated the Mermaid's texts? What proof do you have?"

Laticin said, "He read the texts and in minutes knew as much as we have translated in generations."

Gwen looked appeased and said, "Then you should attempt to get answers from the obelisks."

The meeting went on for hours after that as the races shared information and asked questions. Once it had concluded Joleen had them split off and check each of the obelisks.

Meterove, Laticin and Terenia went to one. Dras and Jolson went to another and Joleen and Narok took the last.

Joleen and Narok looked up at the large white stone obelisk and found that they could read the writing with ease. Most of it was warnings and an elaborate description of the purpose of the structure around the core. The part that Joleen was interested in was near the end.

Use the key to sever the second seal., then follow with the third.

After examining the obelisk further, they found a slot that looked as though it would fit the dagger. They went back and found that the others had predictably learned the same, except that Jolson's had mentioned that a path to the trial would open and that it would shape itself to the one that entered.

While they were discussing this Joleen got a weird feeling. She looked over towards a side room and saw a single Undine standing there. That on its own was not that strange, but she was just staring at them. Meterove seemed to have followed her gaze and after a moment charged over.

Several Undines that were nearby cried out in outrage as Meterove pinned the Undine to the floor while she flailed about. They ran over to protest but as soon as they reached him and saw her, they backed away in horror. Meterove planted his dagger in one of her eyes and she went still.

As Meterove moved out of the way her glassy eyes and a puncture mark in her neck marked her as undead. The realization of what that implied hit them and Meterove turned to Laticin, "We need to get those keys and use them, NOW!"

Laticin was not as experienced as they were with undead, but she knew that she needed to trust their judgement. They ran to the other representatives, who were still talking about minor things.

Meterove shouted, "No time to explain! We need the keys now and you need to prepare for an attack!"

He had expected questions, but Gwen simply handed her key over followed by Demetria. Meterove took the keys and handed one to Narok and another to Dras and said, "Narok you have the first one, Dras you have the second. If this trial is what I think it is I should be the one to do it. Joleen you should take the rest and have them help with whatever is coming."

Laticin wanted to argue but she had a gut feeling that she was going to be of more use here. Terenia patted her arm and gave her a wane smile of sympathy. Joleen wanted to go with but knew now was not the time to argue. She took the others and began giving instructions as they walked away.

Meterove gave Dras and Narok several minutes to get to their obelisks. Meterove placed the key in the slot and pushed it in. After a moment he heard a click and soon an opening appeared in the wall.

Suddenly everything started to shake and Meterove could see some figures falling from above and screaming coming from all directions. Meterove could see tentacles coming from below while another set attacked from far above.

Dras skidded to a stop outside the corridor. He glanced at Meterove then shouted, "GO! Get through while you can. We will help evacuate everyone! GO!"

Soon dozens of undead of all kinds began to swarm him. Dras began fighting them off and soon was joined by Narok and several Undines.

Meterove ran the rest of the way through it and found that it led to the Core. A small door was on the outside of the Core. Meterove had a gut feeling about what was through that door. He stepped up to the simple wooden door and turned the basic iron knob and stepped through.

CHAPTER 32
MIA

Deep under the surface of the Plane of Water Mia kept herself positioned so that she was out of reach of the Undines magic. Her tentacles battered at the surface grabbing at anyone that it felt move. She could also feel the presence of her most recent mate above.

Once this is done, I must make sure to devour him, lest he take my prey!

When that strange being that called itself, the Ashen Soul had offered her the power to devour everything that she wanted she gladly accepted. It had been a surprise to find out that it meant dying, however since she was still herself and she could now eat even more, that was a trivial matter.

The only part that had chaffed at all was that she had to do what the Ashen Soul told her to do. If the chance came by in the future, perhaps she could eat it as well.

She occasionally felt spikes of pain from her tentacles but mostly the pests up above could do nothing to hurt her. In life, she would never have been able to come this close to the surface. Unlike the Sirens, Krakens did not have the ability to rapidly adjust their bodies for different pressures and would die going outside their normal zone.

She had killed her former mate, then raised him so that he could assist in the attack. In the end though, the two of them were still slow to get within reach of the Undines. Hordes of her undead minions that she had gathered from dozens of worlds swarmed to the surface.

Soon I shall feast on all that lives!

.   .   .

Dras was running along the lowest platform with Laticin and Terenia cutting down whoever they came across. While her power was limited here on the Plane of Water, Terenia had still been able to use her power to make Laticin a similar set of light armor to her own.

Laticin was distracted and uncomfortable with the armor on but twice now it had saved her from injury, so she was damn sure not taking it off. She watched in wonder as Dras flew through the enemies.

I cannot even begin to compare to that. That trick that he does with switching places with his sword is almost unfair! For every one enemy I take down, Terenia takes two and Dras takes five!

Laticin had thrown her spear over her shoulder and had drawn her rapier. It was a good thing that she had Terenia and Dras by her side because she had very little experience fighting and none fighting outside of the water.

Terenia was using Grace as a bow and was picking off undead at long range while Dras fought whatever came near. He was clearly letting only enough through to Laticin so that she would have to deal with one at a time.

Around them dozens of Undines, Mermaids and Snow Women were also fighting against undead. Where Dras and Terenia were experienced in battle, almost none of the other defenders had any combat experience.

Narok and Dras had taken command of the defense and had split the front into three. Dras, Narok and Ava each had a section they were responsible for. The defense was only a short-term measure while everyone else evacuated. Once everyone was clear, the plan was to attempt to leave using the ship.

Dras was currently flashing between a group of undead that were all different types. He was pretty sure that some of the undead that he had seen had been altered by a Weaver.

Meterove, I really hope you know what you are doing. This shit is crazy!

A large shark jumped completely out of the water and attempted to take a bite out of him. Dras calmly changed places and easily planted his blade in the creature's eye before continuing on.

During the course of the battle injuries and losses built up. Laticin screamed when she saw Dras take a spear to his shoulder, then watched in amazement as he spun around and decapitated the Siren that had been responsible.

She looked at his now ruined coat and stared in a mixture of horror and amazement at his arm. Beautiful magical energy made up his arm with an area of rough, ridged scarring where it ended.

The pain he must have felt from the wound that caused that must have been terrible. These people keep fighting even after taking wounds that would have left most Mermaids dead. I will have to ask about this magic for my people.

Terenia shouted, "Latic! On your right!"

Laticin did not process what Terenia had called her until after she had run an Undine through the eye with her

695

rapier. Once she had dropped the would-be ambusher she
realized.

*Did she call me Latic? WHOA!!! OK! I can worry
about that later when I do not have a horde of undead rising
from the depths!*

.   .   .

Mia continued to press the attack. She knew that
there was supposedly something in this place that could be a
threat to her. The only recourse then, was to eat everything
that lived there and fill it with the undead servants she had
been collecting. If she could destroy this place altogether
that would be best.

As she was pressing her attack, she suddenly felt
stabs from near the top of her head. She swiveled her eyes
around and looked behind her. There were several dozen
Sirens that were attacking her head. Mia had thought she
had killed them all off, but apparently these had survived.

This was annoying but there was nothing for it. She
pulled back some of her tentacles and proceeded to attack
them. They were fast though and the tentacles that she used
were the ones that had been injured by those vermin when
attacking that underwater city. She had to try several times
before she was able to swat even one of them.

Enraged by this she pulled all of her tentacles back and prepared to destroy them all.

.   .   .

Narok noticed that the tentacles had retreated from part of the structure. He was using his shield to act as a bulwark for Joleen and several Undines that were with them.

I need to get them to the ship. It is likely that Dras and the others will notice and attempt the same thing. Right now, I have to worry about getting Joleen to safety!

Joleen was spinning around using all four blades of her Artifact in rapid succession. Gone were the clumsy movements that had once plagued her before she had trained so hard. She was grateful, if not for the reason.

Joleen killed six undead in rapid succession. She too had noticed the tenacles withdrawing. As battle raged on around them Joleen knew that the time for retreating to the ship was drawing near. She could also see it in Narok's eyes; he wanted to get her out of there.

Joleen tried to speak to him through her eyes. She wanted to tell him that they would leave soon but that they needed to help save as many people as possible. She hoped that she was able to communicate that. There was far too much noise to hear anything right now.

All around Undines were using their ability to shape water to make all forms of attacks. Some were forcing the water to boil or were shaping it into spears and launching them in barrages. Others were creating large crescent shaped blades that they would launch out.

One of the Undines was Laticin's friend Claire. She may not have been a warrior, but she was intelligent as well as a quick thinker. She almost looked like a dancer, as she glided around this battle. Laticin had asked that Claire be with Joleen after she heard that Joleen was a skilled healer. She whispered to Joleen about the pregnancy and Joleen agreed instantly.

Watching Claire decapitate three undead with one attack, Joleen was actually glad to have the woman with her. The Snow Women were also useful. Their aptitude for freezing water and shaping the ice made them perfect for a siege like this. They were the ones that were in charge of getting everyone else to safety.

Joleen glanced at the Core as she fought another undead. All of their hopes were resting on Meterove now. She decapitated this undead and immediately went after another.

You had better stay safe you idiot!

.　　　　　.　　　　　.

As the battle raged on other larger undead such as Megalodons and an Elasmosaurus appeared. Jolson did his best to aid Ava on her front. He was no commander, so he relayed what he knew to her during the battle, and she gave the orders.

When the Elasmosaurus appeared, he found himself being the one to face it. He decided that reach and size of the blade was going to matter and changed his Artifact into a massive two-handed scythe. The Elasmosaurus was lightning fast and had incredible reach with its long neck. If this had been a normal weapon this would have been too slow for fighting this thing.

Fortunately, he was able to stay ahead of it and was able to chip away at a little bit at a time. Eventually the decay caught up with it and it was slowed enough that he was able jump and sever the head completely. The body and head both rapidly decayed and turned to dust.

With the tentacles having retreated from below the evacuation had been able to speed up. Unfortunately, the tentacles from above were there to block any escape in that direction.

The undead that had come from above were currently being held in check by the Undines that were on that side but that would not last much longer. Suddenly he heard a horn blow.

FINNALLY! Meterove you better hurry up!

Jolson heard Ava shout, "TIME TO FALL BACK TO THE HUMAN SHIP!"

Jolson called it out as well, "FALL BACK TO THE SHIP!"

.   .   .

Dras was in the lead followed by Terenia and Laticin and a number of Undines and Mermaids as they ran towards where the ship was moored. When they had first arrived, Joleen had negotiated with the Undines after they had calmed down. One of the things she had asked for was a place to dock the ship that would also hide it from below.

She had been worried about more Megalodons or Leviathans, but it turned out that it had been a good plan since it hid the ship from Mia and none of the undead that had been here before the small pier had been built knew about it.

Their group got to the pier at the same time as Joleen's group. The guards that had been assigned to the ship were still there and a quick check was all that was needed to verify they were still living. Everyone headed for the hatch. Dras and Narok staying at the back to guard against the undead that were coming this way.

Laticin was slightly behind them but not directly in the fight. She was to guard Terenia while she used her bow to pick off undead. She wished she could be of more direct help, but she knew that Terenia would be vulnerable.

It did not take too long for Jolson and the rest from his area to arrive. Once they were in sight the guards fell back inside the ship followed by the others. Dras was the last one in and once he had sealed the hatch behind him, he shouted, "We are sealed! GO GO GO!"

Joleen and the rest launched the ship and once they were clear of the dock Jolson called out, "I can see something massive down there. We are currently right over it!"

Joleen smiled, "Drop all remaining depth charges!"

Terenia pressed several buttons and pulled a lever. "All remaining depth charges dropped!"

Joleen said, "Get just below the surface, then get us out of here as fast as you can!"

.   .   .

Mia was enraged. The Sirens that had attacked her had drawn her attention for far longer than she had thought they could. The wounds that they had caused were superficial at best, but they still hurt and were annoying.

She suddenly felt something brush against her from above and she turned her attention that way. Floating down were a dozen large cylinders that were about the size of a person. The second she noticed them they exploded, and pain and rage flooded through her.

HOW!? WHAT!? WHAT IS GOING ON!? MY TENTACLES!!!! WAIT THAT OBJECT!!! THERE WERE MORE OF THOSE ON THAT WORLD THAT DARED TO INJURE ME BEFORE!!!!

Hatred blinded her to her goal and Mia went to chase that thing down and destroy it. Another sharp poke, this time at her left eye, brought her back to her surroundings. There had been one Siren left and it had buried a spear in her eye over and over until it ruptured.

Just moments before she had large chunks taken out of her body and tentacles and now this! Mia grabbed the Siren with a tentacle and rather than simply kill this one to raise it like the others Mia brought the thrashing Siren down to her mouth.

There were rows upon rows of large fangs that surrounded a huge squid like beak. The Siren was too small to warrant eating but this was more about revenge. She threw the Siren in through her beak and swallowed her whole.

Mia looked around now trying to see where that thing had gone. Her search was hampered by her lost eye. There was nothing for it, she was going to have to use the Weaving power she had been taught to try and heal these injuries.

She channeled her power and the flesh that had been blown apart began to writhe and knit itself back together. It could not replace the bits that had been completely pulverized, but at least all of her tentacles were functioning again.

The eye was lost though. She had lived countless millennia without ever being severely injured and now in such a short time she had been mutilated to such an extent!

She was incandescent with rage. Somewhere in the depths of it though she felt something tugging on her. She realized that she was moving but not of her own accord. A fell voice whispered in her mind, *"You must find and destroy the temple!"*

What temple? Who do you think you are to take my body from me!

There was a sense of deep amusement at her indignation as well as her thoughts. She tried several times to wrest control of her body from whatever force was moving her away from her hated target.

Mia found herself at the surface now. She had her tentacles wrapped around the entire structure, tearing it apart as if it were nothing. Once the structures collapsed three stones fell down into the water. Mia felt the being that had control of her body send undead down to find them.

.   .   .

In the distance Dras watched the destruction through the periscope. It had been a desperate battle to get everyone out of there. Fortunately, the number of casualties on their side was extremely low.

Joleen asked, "Dras what does it look like?"

Dras stowed the periscope, "That beast has completely torn that structure that was around the Core down. It is totally gone. The size of that things body is... I have no words."

The Undines that were onboard were all silent. That place had been of great importance to their people for longer than anyone knew. Now it was gone. There was terror in many of their eyes. This was not the sort of thing that anyone was used to, but they were taking it even harder than normal.

Jolson asked Dras, "You saw Meterove before the battle started right? Do you think he is safe?"

Dras nodded, "I saw him going to a door that looked very out of place."

Terenia asked, "What do you mean out of place?"

Dras noted the anxiety in her voice and eyes and said, "It was a wooden door. The kind that you would find on a boathouse in a fishing village. For the life of me I cannot figure out why that would be there."

Jolson said, "There was that bit about the path shaping itself to user. If I had to take a guess, I would say that the trial or whatever is happening is different depending on the individual that goes through it."

Joleen asked, "What would be the point though?"

Jolson shrugged, "Who knows? It does sound like the sort of thing that Flare would set up though."

Joleen asked, "What makes you think that Flare would be the one to set it up?"

Jolson said, "It is her job to hold the barriers of the worlds. If something were to happen here on the Planes, which can access all of the worlds in Creation, she would want a trump card here."

Joleen and the others nodded. That really did sound like Flare. As one they all thought of Meterove. Each one was different, but the sentiment was the same. Good luck.

CHAPTER 32.5
BURGEONING

The plan was working so far. That girl was already growing into something amazing! In no time at all they were on their way to cleansing the Plane of Water. The Kraken was still a serious threat to them though.

The number of minions that it had amassed already was terrifying. What they had managed to do with the limited number of combatants, most of whom had no experience with fighting was impressive to say the least.

There was one more move to make to ensure that this one would go the route that was needed. The question was if she would notice and potentially resist.

What she would be capable of in the future was still up in the air at this point. Would she take the route of leader, or would she take the route of adventure? Her potential with magic was pretty impressive as well. What would she do once she was able to learn how to use it?

The relationship between her and Meterove and the other one was going in the right direction. It did not seem as though there would have to be any more nudges to make sure things ended the way they needed to. The whole of Creation would depend on that.

CHAPTER 33
TRIAL

Meterove stepped through the door and immediately found himself in exactly the place that he thought that he would end up. He closed the door behind him and as it closed the cacophony of the siege vanished, as did the door. Where the door had once been there was now more of the same simple wood planks with gaps between them.

The wood was grey with age and through the gaps you could see sunlight, yet strangely none of the cracks let shafts of light in. The ceiling appeared to be made of the same planks and again, none of the gaps let in shafts of light.

There was a short space from where he currently stood to a corner. Meterove walked down this short hallway until he came to the corner. He took a deep breath and turned the corner.

Infront of him was a large open room, perhaps twenty feet on a side. In the middle of the room and taking up approximately a quarter of the total space was water. It was a bright marine blue, lit up by bright rays of sunshine.

The first thing that he noticed was that there was no sign of how this was supported. The space along the walls was completely bare and the only other thing of note was the object that was floating in the air in the middle of the water. The crimson and silver dagger was slowly revolving in the air.

Meterove walked to the edge of the water and looked closely at the dagger. His vision was pulled down to the water and he noticed that deep in the water there was something that was that same strange shape. It was only a shadow, but it was clearly the same shape.

Suddenly the shape appeared to turn slightly and was now getting larger. It was now growing in size at an ever-increasing pace. A feeling of intense fear took over and Meterove grabbed the key and noticed a staircase along one wall that had blended in with the rest of the wood before.

Meterove wasted no time thinking about it and quickly began running up the stairs. One flight, then it turned at a corner and another flight ran along that wall. After that flight there was another and another and another!

Meterove vaguely wondered how this was possible. There had been no sign of support to begin with. How was there a tower of wood out here and on top of water at that!

Below there was a roar and whatever that thing was burst up out of the water and crashed down on the stairs behind him. Inexplicably the tower seemed to shrink some, as though it was giving that thing another chance.

It was out of sight below, but Meterove could still hear a rushing sound and he did not look back. It suddenly jumped out of the water again and crashed into the stairs clipping his heel on the way down.

This time he got a look at the creature. It looked like a whale with large veins and tentacles fuses along the outside of its body. It also had just the one fin along with the tail. That little bit was all that Meterove wanted to see. He ran as fast as he could.

Time and again he heard it crash behind him, but he finally reached the top and he found a door very similar to the one that he had come through. He went to open it, only to find it locked.

There was a fleeting moment of panic and despair before he remembered. Taking the key that he had just grabbed he opened the door and ran through. Meterove slammed the door behind him and found himself in total darkness.

How does that work? I was running along the wall of the tower. I could see the light shining through the gaps in the boards the whole way up.

No matter how hard his sense of reason tried to deny what had happened the evidence before him was conclusive. All around him it was absolute darkness. Strangely enough he could still see himself and anything that he was carrying, which still included the key.

Meterove attempted to use magic to create light so that he could see where he was going. The light sprang into existence. He could clearly see the light source; however, it was not illuminating any of the blackness whatsoever.

Meterove wished he had not left his main pack on the ship. He dug through the pockets of his coat to try and find something that he could use to make a makeshift torch. After rummaging around he found a flask that he had confiscated from Dras a while back.

He poured some of this over a small cloth bag that he wrapped around his old swords blade. He was going to use some magic to light it but stopped. He did not think it would work but he should at least rule it out.

Meterove used some flint from his pockets to light the cloth on fire. As he was putting the flint back, he accidentally dropped it and when he went to pick it up found that there was no floor in the place.

What the hell am I standing on then? This is really bizarre!

Meterove shouted, "Hello?!"

There was no sound after his initial shout. No floor and from the sounds of it, no walls either. With no other ideas to go on, Meterove started walking. It was odd, since it FELT like his boots were hitting something hard underneath him and obviously, he was not falling.

Meterove kept walking and eventually he saw something ahead. It was a door. Suddenly the door flew open, and the world turned and the next thing that Meterove knew, he was falling towards that door.

He fell down through the door and skidded across the floor of a hallway for several yards before coming to a stop. Meterove groaned as he stood up and went to look back through the door he had just fallen through, but it was closed now.

He walked over and wrenched it open only to find himself out on a platform similar to the ones that had been outside. There was a strange whirling water that was around him. With a start Meterove recognized it for what it was, the giant spiral that was the Core.

Somehow, he was inside the Core, and it was not what he had expected. For one thing there was air in here. It was like being inside an enormous tornado. The door closed behind him and when he opened it, he found that it too led somewhere different than it had previously.

Meterove was curious, so he closed the door, then opened it again. This time there was another long hallway. While looking at it Meterove was struck by a very odd observation. No matter how hard he studied the walls or floors he could not tell you what they were made of or even what color they were.

Leaving the door open Meterove walked back out onto the platform and looked all around. Far below him he could see something. He took his spyglass out and looked through it. While still too far to be sure it looked like some kind of wooden building.

Is that the tower that I climbed earlier? That makes even less sense if you look at it from the outside. If that is down there, then what is up? HOLY SHIT!

Meterove was utterly dumbstruck by the sight in front of him. There was a building that could only be described as a temple. It was built of white marble and as far as Meterove could tell was designed exactly like the structure outside had been, only smaller.

I guess I need to get there. If I had wings, I could just fly, but I have my doubts about using magic in here. I guess I need to keep going.

Meterove took one last look around then turned and walked through the door into this new hallway. There were dozens of doors on either side of it. Like the hallway, he could neither tell the material or color. He tried a few but they refused to open.

He walked down the hall for what seemed like forever. There was a sudden sound of rushing water from the direction that he had come from. He turned to look and saw a wall of water roaring towards him.

Meterove began to run, but it was no use, and he was submerged. As soon as he was in the water, he was now somewhere else. All around him was water but he could see further than the hall would have been.

Wait...was that a fish that just swam by?

Meterove looked all around but the water here was murky, and he could only see a short distance. There was something in here with him though.

There it is again! What are you?

Meterove decided to see if there was a bottom to this, so he began swimming down. The bottom came up so fast that he almost swam right into it. It was muddy with weeds. There was no visible source of light, but he could still see.

Now that he was on the bottom Meterove decided that the best course of action was going to be to pick a direction and go. He stayed close to the bottom since he still did not know what it was that he kept seeing.

He had just gone over a hill when the world flipped on him. He now found himself far from the bottom and once again he was seeing those dark shapes out of the corner of his eye. Whatever was out there was either hunting him or was scared of him.

It would be nice to know which one it was.

He swam on, heading straight for the muddy bottom. Along the way he had more flashes of whatever was out there. Once he reached the bottom Meterove took out his sword.

I am done running from whatever you are. If you are a predator, then you most likely will be attracted to blood. I have an easy way to get you some.

Meterove made a small cut on his hand that let out some blood, then healed the wound. He then moved back several yards and waited. After several minutes Meterove was at least certain that it was not a shark or other ferocious fish.

It still let a chill on his spine though. As he continued to swim, he noticed something. Over to his right there was a rectangular hole. Swimming over to it and looking inside Meterove was shocked to find what looked like stairs.

What are stairs doing down here? There it is again! What are you!?

Meterove was sick of being chased around this place by whatever that was, so he decided to investigate the stairs. He had swum only a little ways down when two things happened simultaneously. The water ended and the gravity shifted, leading him to fall out of the water and down onto the steps, which had switched sides and were now going up.

Meterove grumbled several curses as he got to his feet. He stretched his neck and heard it give several loud cracks. He sighed, "Whoever made this place was an asshole."

The more that he thought about it, the more certain that he was that whoever it was had made it wanted to keep people out. What was the purpose of the keys to get in then? Why had Flare sent them here? It was thinking about Flare that gave him an idea.

I wonder...perhaps that was the reason she did that?

Meterove followed the stairs up until he found himself at another door. This place was really starting the grate on his nerves. He suppressed his anger and opened the door.

"FINALLY!"

The door opened to show an obscene number of stairs, but they led up to the temple that he had seen earlier. Not wanting to think about how much his legs were going to burn by the time he made it to the top Meterove started up.

.　　　　　.　　　　　.

Joleen was sitting with Terenia, Laticin, Claire and a little Snow Woman that had identified herself as Rakira. Rakira had snuck back and hid on the ship. They had only just found her and brought her to Joleen moments ago. The first thing that she had done was have Terenia make the girl some simple shoes.

Joleen was sitting with her left hand on her temple. She asked, "What made you do this? Your people must be very worried about you."

Rakira shook her head the said in a light voice, "My mother will know where I went. As for the reason, well I have met your brother Meterove before today."

Joleen could not stop the surprise from showing on her face. Meterove had mentioned the Snow Women before, but it had not occurred to her that they would meet one of the ones that he had met.

Rakira giggled, "He had called me something like cute or adorable. He was so honest and pure that I took an instant liking to him."

There was an instant worried tension from two of the others. Given who she was they could not just send her away. Still, she was only a little girl. What were they going to do about this?

Fortunately, their concern was unfounded. Rakira said, "I could tell that in some way he was going to be important to my future. I have no idea how at this point but the only thing that I know for sure was that I have heard of the term "big brother" before and that seems to fit."

Terenia and Laticin relaxed while Claire looked a little confused at their reaction. Joleen was also happy to hear that she was not going to have to deal with a little girl with a crush on her brother.

Joleen said, "Getting back on topic, why did you come aboard?"

Rakira said, "I have a strong feeling that this is where I need to be right now."

Joleen decided that she was not likely to get anything more out of the girl so instead she opened up a new discussion, which included the others. She sighed, "OK. Now do any of you have some idea of where we should go to next?"

Laticin looked thoughtful as she said, "Well...there is something in the texts about a temple. I have no idea what this temple is, or where it might be though."

Claire and Rakira glanced at each other, then Claire spoke, "I find that interesting, since I have never heard of any mention of a temple before. However, I have heard of a place that was supposed to be at the Core."

Rakira said, "I have heard of a ritual that is supposed to be performed at a temple, only we have never known where this temple was supposed to be."

Joleen moved her hand to her chin, "That is interesting. Laticin, what else does your texts say about this temple?"

Laticin shrugged, "Only that the temple would only be opened after the trial was completed. I assumed that the keys were the trial but now I am not so sure."

Joleen said, "You think that those keys were meant to be used to open the trail."

Laticin nodded, "Exactly."

Joleen returned her gaze to Claire, "We were all around the Core back there and we never saw a temple. The only thing that we saw was Mia destroying the structure around the Core."

Claire said, "We were around the base of the Core on this side. What about the other side?"

Joleen was deep in thought for a few minutes. That was plausible. She asked, "How long would it take to reach the other side from where we are now?"

Claire shook her head, "Without knowing how fast this ship of yours moves I cannot say. I can say that it would take Laticin months to swim it."

Laticin said, "Unless we take a spiral up."

Claire and Rakira both looked at her astounded. Claire said, "Laticin! How can you suggest such a thing! A person would be torn in half trying that..."

She realized halfway through what Laticin's plan was.

Laticin looked at Joleen and said, "We have lots of Undines with us. They can help calmly direct the ship once we exit the spiral so that it is not torn apart and will even get a speed boost. If we are lucky, we could be at the other side in less time than we have been on this ship."

Joleen stared at Laticin for a full minute before she erupted in laughter. She was laughing so hard that tears were running down her cheeks. At first Laticin was a little offended, but Joleen calmed herself down enough to say, "OH you are absolutely a great match for those two!"

Terenia started to laugh a little as well then put an arm around her shoulders. "Let's get going then! I cannot wait to see what that idiot has gotten himself into this time."

Joleen agreed, "This time though we get to get into it with him. He is not going to hog all the fun!"

CHAPTER 34
RISKS

Demetria stood on an iceberg looking off towards the Core. Somewhere out there was her little Rakira. She was unsurprised when she found her missing. She had glanced at her once she recognized Meterove at that meeting.

The look on her face had been all the indicator that she needed. That girl had somehow known that he was here on the Plane of Water. What that meant she had no idea.

She knew that she should be worried since Rakira was now closer to danger. She knew that she was likely on that ship that the humans had. She had decided to trust that the humans would keep her safe.

It was time to get moving. She needed to head up an evacuation of those that were unable to fight. She needed to make sure that the Snow Women survived this.

Her first order of business was to gather all of the women together at her village. It would be cramped but it would be possible. The easiest way to do that was not necessarily the safest. After worrying about it for a bit Demetria decided that she should take the safer, if slower route.

They would move from village to village gathering everyone together and moving as a group. This held its own risk as well, a big one. If they were attacked while moving and were unable to fight off whatever it was that was attacking, their species would be in jeopardy.

Gwen had come up behind her without her noticing. She was suddenly at her side looking in the same direction. She said, "Rakira is a strong one. She knows her lessons well."

In the end Demetria knew that she was actually worried, despite trying not to show it or think about it. Hearing Gwen acknowledge it that way made it easier to manage the fear that was in her heart.

Demetria said, "I know. I am actually very proud of her, though I will have to scold her something fierce when I do see her again."

Gwen chuckled, "Yes. When you see her again, you make sure that you do that."

．　　　　　　　　．　　　　　　　　．

Joleen was waiting on the bridge. They had just
finished the preparation for heading into the spiral. In just a
few minutes they would ride into the spiral and from there
they would head to where they believed the temple was.

Joleen was nervous about this plan despite pushing
for it. She wished there was a safer route that they could
take. She was getting more and more like Meterove
sometimes but not here. Well, the actual plan was one that
he would love but that was beside the point.

She worried again about how he was doing. Soon
enough they would be reunited. That was what she kept
telling herself. This was going to be very dangerous. There
was also that other Kraken that was on that end.

They had gone over their weapons and found that
they only had six torpedoes left. Joleen was hoping that the
other Kraken was either gone or significantly smaller than
Mia because they did not have much of a backup plan. The
Undines might be able to do something but that was not a
given.

Everyone was ready so there was no more reason to
delay. She called out, "Take us in."

The plan was to go down and approach the spiral from the deeper water so that they would more closely align with the spiral to reduce the chance of damaging the ship. They had several Undines whose only jobs were to patch any leaks that might start.

Ava had taken over the sonar. It had fascinated her, and she had been a quick learner. She said, "We should be entering the spiral in five...four...three...two...one."

As soon as she said one, they felt the ship speed up considerably. Everyone that was not seated was making sure to hold on tightly to something. From the moment they entered the ship began making some really unpleasant creaking sounds.

The Undines were doing their best to keep the pressure of the water from getting too great, but they were getting pushed to the limit. This was one of the faster spirals around and they also had to make sure that they had enough energy left to redirect the ship once they were done.

The creaking changed to popping and in several places the Undines were already starting to put extra energy into making sure a leak did not start. The whole ship was shaking now, and Joleen was sitting in her chair, clinging on for dear life.

Faintly she could hear Ava counting down. She was at thirty-one right now. Joleen really hoped this thing was going to make it to zero. She glanced at Narok and saw that he was staring at her. He looked as worried as she felt.

She heard Ava call out fourteen as if she were miles away. Everything seemed to be in slow motion as well. It was impossible that they had only been in here for seventeen seconds!

Somewhere behind her she heard someone retch and the sound of something splattering. She tried not to think about that too much. She was queasy herself. She had been fighting the sea sickness since the first day with herbs and magic, but this was something else entirely.

Ava called, "Five...Four...Three...Two...One!"

On one the shaking came to a sudden stop. She now saw all the Undines, including the ones that had been on standby begin to channel their power. They were essentially creating a current that existed only around the ship. The goal was to redirect the ship now that they were facing the wrong way.

They had used magic to secure everything that was not already bolted down. The blood was rushing to Joleen's head. The force that was being applied to the whole ship during this turn was tremendous. If she was honest, she really thought that this might break it apart.

Ava called out, "There is a huge object ahead. Based on the outline on the screen, I would be willing to guess that it is the other Kraken."

Joleen wished there was a way to be certain of that or at least to know if their torpedoes were going to be enough. Unfortunately, there was none so she had to decide if it was worth taking the chance.

Dras was down in the weapons room. She knew that if she called out the order that he would have them fired before she would have a chance to rescind the order.

What do I do?

The answer to her was complicated at first. She kept weighing things in her head, even when she heard a slightly panicked Ava call out that it would be on them in in thirty...twenty-nine...twenty-eight."

Then suddenly it became crystal clear. Meterove would just go for it. All in with no regrets. There was something that was ahead of them that was clearly a threat and here she was, hesitating!

There was a communication system that the Leturai referred to as comms on the ship. She turned the one on that connected her to the weapons room and shouted, "Dras fire all remaining torpedoes!"

Not more than three seconds later she heard Dras' voice, "Six torpedoes away!"

The world seemed to go silent, even the sound of the ship creaking melted away. Then there was the sound of six explosions and a shriek the likes of which she had never heard. For ten heart-stopping seconds Joleen waited for Ava to say something. The silence of the wait was the worst.

Ava suddenly laughed, "Whatever it was is now sinking down. Either it is dead or in retreat!"

Cheers echoed around the bridge. They only intensified when the news that they had successfully leveled out was announced seconds later. Joleen almost fell out of her chair. Now that the crises had passed, she was utterly drained.

This was not the end of their journey though, so Joleen straightened herself in her chair and said, "Ava! Do you see anything else in the area?"

Ava turned back to her console and said, "There is nothing that I can see. We are a little ways off from the Core though."

Joleen nodded; she had been mostly concerned with something else attacking but that did make sense. Anything else that might be around to attack them would be waiting near the Core.

Joleen said, "Take us to periscope depth. Narok, find me that temple!"

Narok said, "On it."

Terenia and Laticin came up the ladder. A few minutes later Dras and Claire followed them up. Joleen noticed that Dras had been having a hard time since the meeting keeping his eyes where they belonged. Him following Claire up the ladder was not an accident.

While she wanted to say something she realized that might be a bad idea at that moment. They needed the Undines cooperation right now. Besides, there was no way that all of the women that were on board had missed what he was doing.

That means that they either like it or that they do not care. I guess if that is the case then it is not my place to judge. Come to think of it, he has never once looked at me like that.

Joleen said, "Claire, I hear that you are pregnant. Congratulations! How far along are you?"

Claire placed her hand over her bare stomach and said, "Only six weeks. This is all new to me since this is my first reproduction cycle."

Seeing the confusion on Joleen's face Laticin interjected, "Undines are different than Snow Women and Mermaids. Where we need to find mates to reproduce, the Undines will become pregnant after intervals of time even if they have not been with a man."

There was a shocked silence for a moment from everyone that was not from the Plane of Water. Joleen's first thought was how that was so unfair. What if the woman did not want to have children?

Then something else occurred to her. Her own species had its own unavoidable event as well. Still a woman's monthly cycle was not the same as being forced to have children.

Joleen put that matter aside. This had nothing to do with her. Claire was the one that this affected, and she was clearly happy about it. Instead, she decided to ask another question.

Joleen thought a moment then asked, "How long are pregnancies for your people?"

Claire said, "It lasts for two hundred and seventy cycles."

Joleen looked at Laticin, who said, "The dark and light cycles here."

Joleen said, "Ah, then it is pretty much the same as humans."

Claire asked, "Do you have any children?"

Joleen glanced at Narok as she said, "No. I have been involved in near constant war ever since my father was killed." Joleen paused then continued, "I would like too though."

Jolson stood off to the side watching the conversation. He and Meterove both had known how Joleen and Narok felt about each other for a long time now.

They would have tried to advocate for them even while their father was alive.

Technically as her brothers they did have something of a say in who the man that would take their sister's hand would be. They just chose to stay out of it, at least for the time being. For now, they just enjoyed watching them.

Jolson felt a clicking in his mind. It was very similar to the sound that clocks make. He too yearned for that kind of relationship. He knew that that kind of life was never going to be his though.

In the deepest parts of his mind, he felt a small push. Another voice woke up and began to sleepily speak to him.

But why not? You can do whatever you want! There are no reasons to worry about what will happen to others. You need to worry about what you want. Do what you want to do right now...

Jolson shook his head. It was getting worse.

.   .   .

Olivia and Fayre had gone to great lengths to make sure that they returned to the Shallows as fast as possible. They had stayed on high alert and had killed anything that had moved. Even so, they were far from safe. This was about as far from their home as the core had been.

After discussing it she and Fayre had concluded that the longer route through the Shallows would be safer than the direct route over even more deep water.

Olivia was worried about Claire, but she had to accept that she was an adult. She had made the choice to go with the humans. Olivia was unsure if she trusted them to keep her safe but at this point there was no other option but to trust in them.

A shout from ahead brought her attention back to her surroundings. There were dozens of undead coming at them from all sides. There was only a dozen of them. Thinking quick Olivia shouted, "Get in a circle and make a wall of water to stop them!"

A twenty-foot diameter circle formed then sprang up making a circular wall ten feet high. Moments after the wall was up the undead began hammering on it. Fayre said, "Elaine! Change to offense. Make spears of water and aim for their heads. Be quick about it. They likely mean to keep us from getting back and warning the rest of our people."

Olivia was surprised at how she had not thought of that. If Mia really wanted to kill everyone on the Plane, then it would be far easier if word of the danger never made it back. Olivia had a sudden inspiration and changed the form of her wall so that she could launch a crescent shaped water blade out from it.

She had placed the blade at neck level, and it was extremely effective. Five heads fell from shoulders with just one attack. Fayre noticed and smiled in approval. She then said, "Everyone push blades of water out from the wall into them!"

In a matter of minutes, the undead were destroyed. Fayre looked at the bodies and shook her head, "No time to worry about them. We need to hurry back as fast as we can!"

Olivia did not even respond; she simply fell in step behind Fayre. She had been worried about Claire earlier, but now she knew that it was better that she was not here. Olivia had recognized one of those bodies.

She hid her recognition and pain as best she could. While all Undines were considered sisters there were still those that were closer than others. The woman that she had seen was one that she had been particularly close with. Clara had been close with her and Claire for so long. Now she was gone forever. Tears rolled down Olivia's face.

I hope that you make them pay for this! You came here claiming to be able to do something, so you better not fail!

Moira was swimming away from the fighting as fast as she could. The rest of the Mermaids were behind her except for Laticin. She knew that she had gone with the humans. She had thought that she had seen attraction to the boy that had showed up and had been right. What she had not expected was that Laticin was not just looking to mate with him.

Interestingly, she herself had once had someone that she had loved long ago, but she had been torn from him and it had broken her heart. She never really got over it. Sure, she had gone on to mate with a few other men, but she never forgot the one that she had fallen in love with.

Seeing that look in Laticin's eyes, Moira had simply smiled and nodded to the girl before she turned to leave. There was no way she was going to put her through that kind of pain, no matter what the rest of their people thought.

Elise had been insufferable about it from the moment they had left. She was currently swimming half a length behind her on the left and had not stopped a monologue about how obvious it was that Laticin was not suited to the responsibility of being an elder.

Moira was tuning the woman out. There was no time for dealing with this stupidity right now. They were all in danger. They needed to get back to their lagoon. Moira had decided to try something that was incredibly risky but would get them home before the cycle was over.

The route between the Core and the Lagoon was littered with smaller spirals. She was currently leading them through each of these spirals to utilize the extra speed. The spirals were normally completely vertical, but using the little magic that she knew from her time off the Plane, Moira bent them!

The going was rough, but they were only a little battered by the time they made it back. Elise continued to yammer the entire time. Finally, Moira had enough. She turned to Elise and pointed her spear at her.

Elise was shocked, *"What is the meaning of this?"*

Moira said, *"You have been doing nothing but verbally abusing Laticin and the decisions made by the elders as a whole! Do not think that I have forgotten that you attempted to have mine and Alara's competency questioned! You are a danger to everyone here. Go! If you try to stay, I will see you executed."*

Elise wanted to argue but the look in Moira's eyes said she was serious. Hurt and enraged she turned and swam off. Technically the direction she went was still part of the Mermaid territory but at least she would be out of the way. Moira reflected sadly on what had happened to her former friend.

I do not understand how we missed this side of you before. Is this new or have you always been good at hiding this? Your obsession with the texts and with always being right has poisoned you.

.   .   .

Mia felt the death of her former mate through the weird connection that she had with all the undead that she controlled. She regretted that she would not be able to eat him like she wanted. More than likely, there were sea creatures picking away at his body even now.

The ones that had hurt here appeared to be heading towards something that had appeared on the other side of the core. It was beyond her reach now. No matter how hard she pushed herself she could not get around to that side for several days.

She did have some minions up there though. She wanted to see what was so important that these wretched little things would risk so much to get there so quickly. She was still searching her mind for whatever it was that had taken over her body before as well.

Mia was beginning to think that taking the Ashen Soul up on that offer may not have been the incredible offer that it had appeared to be. She watched through the eyes of her little minions and saw something that was truly out of place.

A huge building was there, floating on the water. There was no land under it. It was a simple thing really but what made it the most intriguing was that it was totally stable. The waves broke upon it as if it were a solid landmass.

She would have liked to send her minions in for a better look, but they were only fish and therefore limited to what could be accomplished. She would have to send her hordes of others up to take a look.

Mia was still quivering with rage at her injuries and her one good eye almost glittered with malice despite its inky black color. She sent out the order and in response, tens of thousands of undead that were floating around her slowly began swimming up to the surface, heading to the nearest spirals.

The sight of her massive form floating in the eerie greenish water with thousands of little black specks all around her was beyond terrifying. The larger undead, the Leviathans, the Megalodons, the Ichthyosaurs would act as transport.

One by one they were loaded on with undead then swam off to fulfill their roles. Mia did not care if she lost them in the process. There were still plenty of their kinds left to turn out there. For now, she needed to decide what her next move was going to be. She needed to rest that was

for sure and eat. The thought of eating always made her
happy. She swam off looking for some larger prey.

CHAPTER 35
TEMPLE

FINALLY!!! THE TOP!!!

Meterove climbed the last of the steps and rolled onto his back gasping for breath. He had tried taking them at a run at first but the sheer number of them meant that he had run out of steam halfway and had to walk the rest of the way.

He knew that time was short, but he was exhausted, his legs burned and he had a pain in his side. He sat up and looked around while he rubbed his side. This temple was quite the site.

It looked like the same stone that the obelisks were made of. The detail that had been put into the workmanship was incredible. There was the same carving in the stone, repeated over and over.

It was three circles, two larger ones that were each connected to the smaller one by a single line. It was only about the size of his thumbnail. It spiraled around the round pillars; it ran along the trim, and it formed a larger picture of the carving in a pattern on the floor. The picture was about five square feet and repeated itself every fifteen feet.

There were arches as well. The top of them had that same design. Whatever that design was, it clearly was important. There were also water gardens scattered around. Water Lilly, Cattails, Lotus, and Canna Lilly made a spectacular display.

Meterove looked around and yet again he saw the spiral all around the temple. There was another obelisk nearby with some writing on it. He walked over to read it.

Bend your knee and glory in the greatness of the guardian of the Plane of Water. He who sleep beneath the waves until the time he is needed comes.

Meterove blinked and read it again, certain that he had to have misread that. Unfortunately, he had read it correctly. Who the hell was this guardian? It was bad enough dealing with one megalomanic with Flare but now they had another one here?

Meterove shook his head and began searching the rest of the temple. It was HUGE. It took him the better part of an hour before he found something. It looked like a huge door. He tried to push them open but considering that they were made of stone they did not give.

Something was telling him that these doors needed to be opened though, so he poured as much magic as he could into enhancing his body and gave them another push.

This time, after a moment of resistance the doors moved. Meterove decided that he might was well put everything into the left door since it seemed to move a little better. One more huge push and it swung open.

There was a gigantic crash as the door crashed down on the other side. Meterove looked through and realized that this led out. Meterove stepped through, but realized too late that the gravity had changed again.

As soon as he was through the doors the world turned ninety degrees and he fell back into the temple. He rolled a few feet before coming to a stop. He was getting really sick of that. Getting back up he walked back to the doors and this time he ran and jumped, pushing off the door frame with his hands.

He vaulted up and onto a new floor, with the water of the plane spiraling REALLY close to him. It was actually a little unnerving. Meterove noticed that what he was on looked similar to where he had just been in terms of architecture, if not detail and scope.

It was a large white stone platform with several dozen pillars ringing it. It looked fairly similar to that temple that the gorgons had been. In the middle of the floor were the two giant doors. Looking at it, he understood why the door crashed now.

Looking around he got another surprise, though this one was very welcome indeed. He could see a familiar long black object approaching. Once they got close enough, he saw some water get manipulated into a type of dock.

While that was being completed, he saw the hatch open, and two women came running out. They ran as fast as they could and threw themselves at Meterove. Laticin was on the left and Terenia was on the right and both had small tears in their eyes as they latched onto him.

After a moment Terenia kissed him, followed by Laticin. They continued to embrace him, even as they calmed down enough to speak.

Terenia sobbed, "I was so worried about you. You are such an idiot! You are supposed to take me with when you do something like that!"

Laticin was a little more composed, "I was worried too! Who knows where that was going to lead! What if you had needed help!"

The reality of it had been that there had been no time for something like that. Even if they had been nearby there was almost no time. Dras had been right there and would not have had time to join him. He knew that the girls knew this and were just letting their feelings out, so he stayed quiet.

While the girls mock lectured him more people arrived. Dras, Joleen, Narok, Jolson were all smiling at him. Meterove saw that there were also a large number of Undines that were disembarking as well.

Meterove asked, "How did you get here?"

Joleen laughed, "I took a leaf out of your book. We rode a spiral here, then managed to kill off the other Kraken."

Joleen decided that it was not worth mentioning that they did not know for sure that was what they had killed. They had not been attacked again so either way it was probably dealt with.

Joleen continued, "Unfortunately we are not out of weapons as well as fuel. We might be able to move for about twenty more minutes under perfect conditions."

Ava asked, "What is this fuel you are talking about?"

Joleen said, "Given that this ship was made by those people that your people sent home for us, I cannot give you the specifics."

Dras said, "What I can tell you is that it was stored in large tanks in their harbors."

Ava said, "So if you could go there could you refuel this ship?"

Joleen shook her head, "Those cities are all under water now. We would need to..."

Joleen stopped and looked at Meterove who had realized the same thing. She had been about to say that they would have to be able to breath under water!

Meterove asked, "Ava, how accurately can you place those portals that allow you to move to worlds and how long can you keep them open?"

Ava thought for a moment, "It depends on the portal. The smaller the portal the easier it is to hold open and the more accurately it can be placed."

Meterove asked, "If I show you a location using magic, do you think you would be able to go there?"

Ava smiled, "Absolutely!"

Meterove turned to Dras, "I want you and Terenia to lead some of the Undines through. If we make the portal at the right spot, we should be able to move that fueling hose through the portal. Once that is done, try and find where they have more of their weapons."

Dras grinned, "On it. Come on Terenia! You can glom onto him more later!"

Terenia reluctantly let go of him, but she made sure to kiss him one more time before she followed Dras and Ava back to the ship.

Once that was done Meterove said, "I looked around a little before I opened the door that led up here. A word of warning the direction of gravity changes."

Everyone looked at him nonplused but he did not bother to explain further. They would see for themselves soon enough. He suddenly noticed Rakira and gasped, "What are you doing here?"

Rakira giggled, "I had a feeling that I would be needed wherever you were so here I am."

Joleen said, "Rakira here thinks she might have the answer to what we are supposed to do now that we are here."

Meterove looked surprised, "Is that so?"

Rakira nodded, "I believe that a ritual that is mentioned in my people's writings is intended for this place. It mentions a temple after all and there is no other temple on the whole Plane of Water as far as any of us know."

Meterove felt relief wash over him. Someone other than him knew what to do so for the first time in a while now, he could be the one following. He smiled at Rakira, "What do we need to do?"

Rakira said, "The ritual needs to be performed on a special altar. We must find the altar first before we worry about anything else."

Laticin asked, "How are we supposed to know where that is?"

Rakira responded, "The only thing that is said about it is that it is called the Great Serpent altar and that we must perform the ritual over the seal."

Meterove said, "Jolson can you go with Rakira and some volunteers to look for this altar?"

Jolson said, "Yes, I think it would be best if Laticin came with as one of them. You may find that you want as many Undines up here as possible."

Meterove has been worried about that as well. There was no way that the Ashen Soul was just going to let them win. Mia had a grudge against them as well. She might just want them dead out of spite.

Meterove said, "We will work on making as much of a barrier as possible. I will stay up here in case we need to mount a defense. Joleen and Narok I could really use your help."

Joleen felt a swell of pride that she was now someone that Meterove wanted around in the thick of the fighting as opposed to being in the background healing. Narok looked slightly worried but remained resolute.

As Jolson went through the door on the floor, Meterove heard a satisfying clunk as his brother likely fell on his butt. The small curse made it even more satisfying. He had warned them after all.

After that Meterove set about directing the Undines in constructing a defensible position. Rather than trying to defend the whole temple, Meterove settled on setting up a barrier on either side of the ladder leading to the hatch. This would connect to the back third of the temple where they would use simple water barriers to make it harder for the enemy to reach them directly.

Meterove only hoped that that Dras and Terenia would be able to retrieve the fuel and weapons. There was no way they were going to have any chance against the beast without some serious firepower.

His own magic was quite potent but nowhere near what would be needed to take down something of that size. It might not be nearly as powerful as the Ashen Soul, but it was just too damn big. Fire had worked well on it before but under the water that was out of the question.

Of course, there was whatever this guardian was. Meterove was worried about what was going to happen once it was awake. All of those trials had struck him as weird. What was the point?

I can understand why it might be kept somewhat hidden. If this guardian is anything like I imagine then it makes sense. The keys would have been enough for that though. Why was the rest part of it?

No matter how hard he tried Meterove could not come to an answer that made any real sense. He had a suspicion about who and what the guardian was but that was only a guess. If he was right that explained that obelisk at least. He found himself thinking of Dras and Terenia again.

I hope you two are safe!

.   .   .

Dras and Terenia stepped through the small portal that the Undines made for them. It was interesting to watch. It took a short ritual like process of five Undines to make a portal the size that they needed.

The first thing that they noticed was that somehow this place was still inexplicably intact despite everything that had happened to it. There was even still air in here. The water levels had gone up since the last time they were here though.

At the time Dras had wished he had been able to blow up the entire facility to hurt the Kraken more. Now he was thankful that only some of the tanks had gone up. He swam over to the tanks that were furthest from the area he blew up before.

He had been worried that either all the tanks blew or that they had destroyed the only refill point. After seeing this place again, he was glad that he had not voiced those concerns. This was their capital, of course they were going to have multiple refill stations!

Dras pointed out the hose to five Undines, who swam over and began making a portal. Dras noticed that he was not the only one that was watching the Undines swim by. Terenia gave him a wink and a thumbs up.

Once the portal was opened it quickly began to drain the water from the area. Fortunately, the Undines were able to make smaller walls that made the process quick. While he was running the hose through, Terenia began searching for the weapons.

Dras stepped through and began refueling the ship. He showed an Undine what to do and went back through the portal. Once through he helped Terenia search.

One of the buildings that he checked held a morbid surprise. He opened the door, but quickly closed it, and backed away retching. The smell clearly indicated that there was something decaying in there. Dras tied a handkerchief over his face that he soaked with his flask.

Dras opened the door again and walked in looking around for the source of the smell. Unfortunately, that did not take long. There were five bodies down in a pit in the middle of the room. There was metal grating over the pit with a hatch that normally would have allowed them to escape. Unfortunately, part of the ceiling had caved in, preventing the hatch from opening.

This building looked like some kind of workshop. Dras guessed that the ramp that led down to the water and the series of pulleys were for bringing some of the smaller ships in here for repairs.

Dras left the building and once he closed the door, he gratefully pulled his makeshift mask off. He wished there was something that he could do for the dead that had been left in there but now was not the time.

A call from his left caught his attention and he saw Terenia flagging him down. She was standing next to a large building near the water. He hustled over and he saw some familiar markings on the door as well as some other security measures, like bars on the windows.

Dras broke the door down and they found themselves in a small room with another door behind a desk. There was a bookshelf with what appeared to be logbooks. Dras opened the door to reveal the inside of a huge warehouse with cranes for loading.

Dras could see more torpedoes and depth charges along the walls. Luckily, they had not been sitting long enough to start rusting. Dras started moving crates while Terenia went to go get the rest of the Undines.

The process of moving the weapons from the warehouse to the temple was tedious to say the least. It took them several hours to move everything. Dras had also found several barrels that were made of metal. Investigating them revealed that they held more fuel.

Dras had an idea or two of what he could do with those, so he had the Undines bring them along as well. Heading back to the temple Dras found that Meterove had the rest of the defenses in place.

Once the weapons had been fully restocked Meterove had the ship hidden near a ways off from the temple. He had toyed with the idea of setting the ship up as a decoy but in the end had decided that it would be best to have it ready as an escape plan.

It was now resting on the bottom with enough Undines onboard to bring it back to the surface once they were done or if things became too dangerous.

They placed the barrels near the edges to act as an early deterrent. The majority of the fighting was intended to take place on the other side of the doors. With no way of knowing what was coming that seemed the smartest move.

They also used rope that they had taken from the ship to weave the gaps of some of the pillars closed. They might not be completely sealed up, but it would either deter the undead from there or at least slow them down.

Something else that Dras had done while on the ship was cook as much meat as he could. He had taken anything that had fat and had it cooked up until he had several quarts of grease. Meterove was not entirely sure what he intended to do with those but there were more important matters to attend to.

Joleen and Narok were going to be on standby inside the temple just past the doors. The plan was to have them ready to engage while the first group retreated past them. Terenia would be near the doors using Grace as a bow and once Meterove gave the signal to fall back she would be the first through the doors.

This was so that she could ensure that the second line was ready and had the added benefit of having her ready to fire off more arrows once the last of the first line were through the doors.

Meterove was currently standing near where they had the ship moored before. He was watching the water, waiting for the first sign of trouble. Dras was on the opposite side, while two Undines were watching the other two.

Meterove had also considered closing the door to the temple but had decided against it. If the enemy found the doors closed, they might open both doors making the bottleneck less effective.

The water around them seemed to grow darker. Where before it had retained a faint blue color, now it was steel grey. There was no doubt it Meterove's mind.

They are coming!

CHAPTER 36
AWAKENING

Laticin walked with Rakira and Claire as they searched the temple. Jolson was leading them, though it was not like any of them knew where they needed to go. So far, they had found many smaller rooms but had yet to find the door that led to the main chamber of the temple.

Jolson assumed that was where this altar of the serpent was that they were searching for. This temple was needlessly big. So far all of the rooms that had been found were empty.

After a while they found another hall that connected to the one that they had been walking for what seemed like forever. Jolson looked down in both directions, but they were both long and full of doors. At the end they both appeared the turn the same direction.

Jolson said, "It looks like we are going to have to split up here. Time is important but try not to separate after this."

Laticin looked to her right, "Claire and I can take this side."

Jolson looked at Rakira, "I guess that means we get to take this one."

Rakira gave him a small smile and giggle, "We had better get going then!"

She began walking and Jolson was forced to hurry to catch up to her. Laticin and Claire started walking the other way. While they searched, they chatted. Claire was puzzled by Laticin wearing clothing.

Like many of the Undines, Claire had used a small amount of her power to weave water into some minimal covering. She was still barefoot and only her chest and hips were obscured. This had been done at the request of Joleen, who had said that it made them uncomfortable.

There were a few who had refused to do so but for the most part the Undines were now covered, even if it made no sense to them. Laticin wearing real clothing was another matter though.

Claire asked, "Why do you have the fabric coverings of the humans on you?"

Laticin shrugged, "Terenia made them for me. She is incredible. So long as she is near something that is connected to her kind, she can manipulate it. She made these because Meterove wanted me to have some protective covering.

Claire asked, "Protective covering? Is that supposed to stop you from getting injured?"

Laticin responded, "According to Terenia, this can stop small cuts from getting through and can even redirect a blade so that it does not hit my vital organs."

Claire looked at the clothing again then asked, "It looks like it would be constricting. I would feel claustrophobic being stuck in that."

Laticin shrugged, "I was kind of at first but now I have gotten used to it."

They continued to chat as they turned the corner. The first thing that they noticed was that it was a dead end after a few more doors. Claire and Laticin both suspected that they were going to have to turn around.

Laticin said, "Let's hurry and check these last few. After that, I think we should hurry to the others."

Claire agreed and they split up to check the last few doors. After that they moved at a jog and backtracked to where they had parted with Jolson and Rakira. In the distance they could hear the sounds of fighting. Meterove had been right, the enemy had not given up.

Laticin stood there for a moment looking wistfully back in the direction that she knew Meterove was in. While she was lost in her thoughts and worries, she heard Claire giggle.

Claire continued to giggle as she said, "I never expected that you would find someone like him. I have little understanding of men, but I think that I am a little envious of you."

Laticin asked, "Why would you be envious of me?"

Claire said, "I do not need a man in order to procreate. This means that the chances of me ever meeting a man that I might fall in love with are pretty much nonexistent. Unlike you, I do not find myself attracted to women as well as men."

Laticin looked sadly at her friend, "You could just choose to leave you know? You could go out and explore, just for the sake of it!"

Claire shrugged, "perhaps, but I have a daughter on the way. I doubt that I could leave her."

Laticin shook her head, "We will think of something. For now, we should get moving. We need to catch up to Jolson and Rakira!"

Claire gave a start and the two of them sped down the hall. They caught up with them at the top of a long flight of stairs. Jolson and Rakira looked up at the sound of them running.

As they came to a stop Jolson asked, "Why are you down here? Did something happen?"

Laticin said, "We came to a dead end. I believe it is on the other side of that wall actually. Also, on the way here we heard the sound of fighting above."

Jolson glanced in the general direction of the fighting then down the stairs. He said, "Quickly! We need to find this altar now!"

The four of them ran down the stairs. They had not given any thought to it until now, but this temple was always at the perfect amount of light. There was no source that could be seen, just like the rest of the Plane. The chamber at the bottom of the stairs was a different matter.

While it was not too dark to see in here it was still far darker than the hall they had just left. The other thing that they all noticed was that this chamber was much larger. Jolson used some magic to help light the room up so that they could see more.

In the middle of the floor, perhaps thirty feet across, was a mosaic of a serpent that was in a circle, biting its own tail. Jolson noticed vaguely that its face looked very much like the Wyrms back on his own world.

There were several statues of similar looking creatures around the room. Given the décor, Jolson guessed that this was the guardian that they were supposed to awaken. There was a small altar on the other side of the room.

Jolson looked at Rakira, "I am going to assume that this is it. From here on out, you are going to have to take the lead."

Rakira took a deep and shaky breath. Jolson noticed that the air was starting to get chilled around her. She was subconsciously picking at herself as she looked at the altar.

She is just a child. She must be so scared right now.

Jolson stepped over and knelt in front of her. He looked into her eyes and ruffled her hair, "You know what you need to do. Take your time and you will do just fine."

Rakira felt two tears slide down her face and freeze. She wiped them away and smiled at Jolson. She said, "You really are his brother. Laticin and Claire, I will need your help as well."

The three women walked over to the alter while Jolson turned to watch the stairs for any signs of the enemy. He could faintly hear Rakira explaining the ritual. He really hoped they would be successful.

.   .   .

Going back a ways Meterove and the others were waiting for the enemy to make their move. It did not take too long for a handful of scouts to make their way up onto the platform. These were killed quickly but the enemy was alerted to their presence.

In no time there were hundreds of undead swarming up from all directions. There were also some larger undead that made Meterove nervous about fighting them near the water. Meterove and Dras fought on the front lines for as long as they could hold out.

When they finally retreated, they each knocked over a barrel spilling the contents all over. A quick blast of magic once undead were nearly on them and there was an insanely hot fire burning. Dras took out his jars of grease and hurled them at a few of the undead.

Meterove still was not exactly sure what Dras was thinking. Soon the grease, which had congealed turned back into liquid then soon it too started on fire. A few of the undead that had caught fire from the grease try and head back into the water, just as the others had.

The first ones to enter the water did not extinguish their flame but rather spread them. The ones covered in the burning grease though caused a small explosion that spread it all over.

WOW! I had no idea that grease could do that!

The two of them fell back while the Undines made various weapons with water. Now was the start of the real battle. It took the undead nearly fifteen minutes to get past the remnants of the burning fuel and the barriers that had been constructed.

Once they did, they were faced with a barrage of attacks from the Undines. Dras and Terenia were on one side while Meterove was on the other. They were getting ready to enact the next part of the plan. The undead were starting to try and cut their way through the roped off areas. Dras and Terenia took to picking off any undead that came near those with bolts and arrows.

The enemy was massing more and more. Meterove knew that they were not going to be able to hold this much longer. He made the decision to fall back. There was no reason to hesitate, so he gave the signal.

Terenia loosed on last arrow before she ran for the doors. The Undines stood their ground though. Meterove did not like it, but they did not have much in the way of weapons for them to use once they were away from the water.

These woman knew what was at stake and were choosing to fight to the bitter end. Meterove's pride made it hard for him to abandon them. He and Dras fought hard alongside the Undines until the last minute. As the women fell around them Dras and Meterove finally fell back through the door.

Once through the door they ran as fast as possible. They made sure they were far enough ahead that the undead would not see the change in direction. Once they were behind the line that Narok and Joleen had set up Dras turned and started firing bolts.

The undead were even more thrown off by the change in direction than they had been. It would have been comical watching them fall and splat onto the floor if they had not just butchered the Undines above. It was every bit as effective at slowing them down that Meterove thought it would be.

Once they recovered, though they hurried to attack. There was only Meterove, Dras, Terenia, Joleen, Narok and ten Undines left. Those that had remained had brought buckets of water down here before to allow them something to fight with.

The undead being bottlenecked and tripped up was the lynchpin of this plan. So long as the undead could only reach them a dozen or so at a time they would be able to hold out for a while.

The battle was brutal. The swarm of the undead was never ending. They fought on no matter how tired they were. Whenever the number of undead became too large in the hallway, he would make a familiar blue fireball and hurl it into the middle of them.

The fire twice spread out of the door and gave them a much-needed breather. They could not keep this up forever though. Meterove would run out of energy soon and Joleen did not have near as much power to her.

Terenia's magic was strong, but it was being used constantly by Grace already. Things were already beginning to look bleak. Still, they fought on. Dras as usual was flashing around the fight.

They were getting pushed back. No matter how many they killed there was always another one to take its place. Meterove decapitated yet another undead as they moved ever further back.

You guys had better hurry. We are running out of time!

.   .   .

Rakira, Laticin and Claire were all kneeling before the large altar. The ritual that they were performing was meant to break through an extremely deep sleep. Apparently, this guardian had been asleep since time immemorable.

The ritual itself involved the three of them channeling their magic into the alter in a specific sequence. Jolson had heard of locks that used a similar method.

Once they had successfully broken their way in Rakira had said they would be able to communicate with the guardian. Jolson could hear the sound of combat getting closer. He was debating on going up to help when Rakira gave a sigh if frustration.

Laticin said, "We can knock on this door all we want but the guardian does not seem to want to wake."

Jolson asked, "How do you even know that it is alive?"

Claire said, "It feels similar to when you attempt to awaken someone that does not wish it. We can feel the presence, but we cannot get it to acknowledge us."

Jolson walked over to the girls and said, "Well it needs to acknowledge us now. The enemy is getting closer by the second and if we fail here who knows what will happen. Flare entrusted this task to us, we cannot fail!"

There was a sudden change in the pressure of the room. It now felt as though it were...full of something. A deep masculine voice echoed throughout the room.

Did you say Flare? Why would mother send tiny specks here? What reason would you have to awaken me?

WHOA! That voice was almost panicked...also I was right. He is one of Flare's actual children.

Jolson responded, "Yes, I did say Flare. We are here because this Plane is in terrible danger of being overrun by the forces of the Ashen Soul."

That does not make sense. How could the Ashen Soul's minions be here? Mother would never send something like you here when I was already here.

Jolson said, "It took a ritual just to break through that little nap of yours. I assure you that the Ashen Soul's minions are here. They are fighting their way towards this room as we speak."

Even if what you say is true, what of it? What do a handful of minions matter against me? There is no reason to disturb me over such trivial matters.

Jolson was getting annoyed with this guardian now. "It is a matter of concern for everyone and everything that lives on the Plane. Your mother would not have sent us here if she did not believe it to be so. Another thing, it is not just a handful of undead. It is likely that there are thousands, all of them controlled by Mia."

Mia? Wait...I know that name. That is the name of the first Kraken. If she has been corrupted, I suppose I have no choice but to fully awaken and take care of the matter. Mother's wrath would be terrible if I failed this task.

Jolson made a mental note about this guardian. He did not want to be one. He was here because Flare had made him, which meant that he was not going to care much about their crisis.

I am awakening now. I will purge that which does not belong here then I will return to my dreaming. The serpent that bites its own tail, Jörmungandr will obliterate them all.

Just like that the presence was gone from the room. The three women looked at each other in glee and hugged one another. Jolson on the other hand was very uneasy.

Jolson said, "The others could use whatever help we can give, they are nearly here."

Their joy cut short, Laticin, Rakira and Claire hurried to their feet and followed Jolson back out of the chamber. Jolson hoped that they would make it in time. He was also very worried about how Jörmungandr had phrased his final words.

They met up with the remaining defenders just up the hall. As they entered the fray, Meterove shouted, "You better have good new!"

Jolson used a large scythe sword to kill and undead then said, "I do not know for sure that it is good, but we did awaken the guardian. It is called Jörmungandr, and it is Flare's son."

The lack of surprise on Meterove's face showed that he too had a suspicion about who this guardian was. He asked, "Why exactly do you think that this might not be good?"

Jolson killed another undead while Meterove killed three more. Suddenly the whole temple shook and the undead that had been relentless in attacking them stopped. This unnerved them all far more than the attack. This temple was stationary even though it rested next to a spiral.

They continued to fight the undead, taking advantage of their sudden pause to dispatch many of them before they could react. Soon the hall started to clear out.

Meterove glanced at Jolson, "There is no way that they gave up here. Do you think that shake was this Jörmungandr moving?"

Jolson said, "There is only one way to find out. We will have to head to the surface and see for ourselves. Something that he said earlier down in that chamber worries me, though."

Meterove said, "You had mentioned something about that. What did he say?"

Rakira was the one that responded, "He just said something about obliterating "that which does not belong here" the something about returning to his dreaming."

Jolson said, "The way that he was talking, it sounds like he did not want to be the guardian of the Plane. He also sounded like he was going to perform his duties to the letter and with the minimal effort needed."

Meterove looked alarmed, "Obliterating all that does not belong here! We need to go now!"

Meterove sheathed his sword and began sprinting out of the temple. The others followed him but only Jolson seemed to understand what he was thinking. Joleen tried to ask what was going on, but she needed her breath for running.

The number of bodies that were littered through the hallways made it exceedingly hard to move quickly but they still made it back up to the doors in just a few minutes. Twice more they felt intense shaking from the temple.

Once they were out on the surface Meterove fired a small red burst of magic down into the water, then began to wheeze, with his hands on his knees.

Once they had caught their breath Joleen asked, "What is going on?"

Meterove said, "What does not belong is subjective at best. For sure though it does not include those of us that are not from the Plane of Water. It might include whatever was not here when he became the guardian."

CHAPTER 37
JÖRMUNGANDR

The shock following what Meterove had said had taken more than a moment to wear off. Joleen and the others that had come here on Flare's orders knew that they certainly did not belong. What made them uneasy was that he implied that perhaps some of the others might now count as well.

While they were waiting for the ship to respond the signal that Meterove had sent Claire asked, "Are you implying that we might be in danger as well?"

The other Undines looked just as skeptical and Meterove shook his head, "No, I think that the Undines are safe. Flare had referred to your people as being the Plane of Water's equivalent of the Spirit Foxes of the Spirit Plane.

The concerns I have involved the others. True they held keys needed to awaken Jörmungandr but there is still a chance that he will not see them as truly belonging on this plane."

While he was explaining this another huge shake rattled them and this time, they were able to see what was happening. Every one of them had their mouths fall open.

Moving out of the water was the largest single thing that any of them had ever seen. It was so big that it made the temple look like a toy. After staring at it for a few minutes Meterove realized that the odd pattern that he was looking at were scales.

Jörmungandr was moving and by the looks of it the guardian of the Plane of Water may well be long enough to stretch around the whole of the Plane. The waves made by its passing were so large that they were forced to make a barrier to keep from being swept away.

It arched part of its long body up out of the water and Joleen was able to see a break in the sapphire scales that made up the top half. The underside was a vivid green and was slightly ribbed. There was also a long series of spines that ran down its back.

How the hell has no one from the Plane ever seen this guy? He is obscenely huge!

The time it took for Jörmungandr to clear the area was nearly as long as he was. Once he was gone the open jawed stares did not stop. Once the ship surfaced and the hatch opened, they scrambled onto the ship.

All of them were eager to be gone from this place. Claire took one last look back. Many of her sisters had fallen there. They would come back to tend to them if they could, but there was a chance they might never know true rest.

Meterove ushered her and the others down the ladder, then sealed the hatch behind him. He entered the bridge and immediately was confronted by a livid Ava.

Ava shouted, "Where are the rest of the girls?"

Meterove shook his head. He knew that she was not looking for an answer to that question. His refusal to speak seemed to anger her though as she continued to shout at him.

Finally, she broke down in sobs, she asked, "Why is it that none of you were killed, only my girls?"

Joleen was the one that answered, "Your sisters chose to stand their ground, rather than retreat. It is possible that they might have lived had they followed the plan. However, I personally think that the only reason that any of us are alive is because of them."

Meterove agreed, "We were getting pushed back pretty far in there. The time that they bought us by standing their ground may be what tips the scales here."

Ava was clearly taking the losses hard. From what Meterove had seen, losses from fighting were extremely rare on the Plane of Water.

This is new to her. They might lose one or two women here and there. To them that IS a large loss of life. They have never had to grapple with losing so many people so quickly.

Looking around Meterove could tell that everyone that was from the Plane of Water was very shaken right now. He knelt down and looked Rakira in the eyes. She just stared back, but there was an unease behind them.

Meterove held her hands and smiled at her. For the first time since he had run into her again, she was acting her age. Letting down the front of the composed future elder she curled against him crying softly.

Of course, you are scared and in shock. You are just a little girl after all. You have already taken on way more than any little girl ever should.

While all of this was going on Joleen took command of the ship and began plotting a course. At first, she had intended to put distance between them and the fight. After she thought back to how big those tentacles were, she knew that Mia was just as big as Jörmungandr.

Fear began to bloom in her mind. What would happen if Jörmungandr was defeated because they did not help. She hesitated a moment longer, then she had them set a course for Mia via a spiral. Once Meterove had calmed Rakira down he released her and walked over to Joleen.

Joleen said, "Do you have something on your mind?"

Meterove could tell from her tone that she was going to be stubborn. Still, he needed to try, so he said, "This is a dangerous plan, Joleen. The fight that we are heading towards is not something that this ship was made for."

Joleen replied, "I am well aware of that. I already know that this is beyond my own means to assist with. We need to though."

Meterove said, "We are risking more than just ourselves." He glanced at Rakira, then continued, "There are some on board that have already done more fighting than they ever wanted to do."

Dras chimed in, "We also have at least one person on board that is pregnant too."

Claire looked mildly surprised that Dras was the one that had mentioned her. She placed a hand over her stomach and smiled at him.

Joleen said, "I understand that. I do not like putting anyone in danger, least of all those that cannot defend themselves. However, if Jörmungandr fails to kill Mia and is then corrupted, the consequences are far worse."

Jolson said, "We cannot let the Plane of Water fall to the Ashen Soul. Every world would be defenseless if that were to happen."

Meterove went quiet. He knew that already of course. He knew, but that did not mean he had to like it. Meterove exhaled softly trying to calm himself. Joleen was right after all. This had to be done.

Joleen watched his reaction with a sad smile. She loved that side of her brother and hated that she was right. She turned her attention back to the matter at hand. She said, "Ava, I need you to get us to the nearest spiral."

Ava took a few breaths to calm herself, then wiped away her tears and sat back down at her station. Soon they were back in the spiral. Joleen knew that this was more dangerous than before. They had less Undines this time around.

The only way this was going to work was if they utilized the safety measures that the Leturai had built in. Soon they were heading through the spiral again. This time, there was significantly more damage to the ship.

During the crossing they were forced to seal off nearly half of the ship. While this was a heavy loss, with the Undines help they were able to make fast repairs. It took only a few hours for the ship to be back up and running.

Once the ship was operational again, Joleen had Ava begin looking for Mia. She assumed that Mia would not have moved too far but would have focused on gathering and sending her minions after them. Soon enough Ava found her. Just as Joleen had feared there were several other large objects alongside Mia.

There were only three others besides her, but Joleen was worried that it might be enough to tip the scales in the fight. Jörmungandr would potentially have a hard time with Mia alone.

Joleen asked, "Do you have any idea what those other readings could be?"

Ava said, "It is hard to say. There are several creatures that Mia would see as useful to turn. However, there very few species on the Plane of Water that are functionally immortal like the Krakens. She would not have any more of her kind this close to her outside of mating. Being as she is undead now; she will most likely attempt to eat them."

Dras mumbled, "Sounds like a lot of the women I know."

Joleen raised an eyebrow at that but made no comment. Instead, she asked, "Can you give me some guesses as to what they are?"

Ava said, "I would hazard a guess at an Ichthyosaur for the smaller one. As for the other two, they could be anything. If I had to guess though, I would assume that they are Leviathans."

Meterove tensed up at that. He had not forgotten their last encounter with a Leviathan. Joleen did not like hearing that. The last Leviathan had taken a toll on them both physically and in terms of their weapons. Now they had to potentially deal with two of them, plus Mia?

Joleen was concerned that they might not have the firepower to take the fight to Mia. There was no way that they were going to be able to win this head on.

Joleen asked, "Is there any indication that Mia is aware of us?"

Ava said, "There has been no movement to indicate that the undead are aware that we are here."

Joleen thought for a moment then asked, "Which direction is Jörmungandr approaching form?"

Ava said, "From what we saw from the temple I would guess that he is approaching from the same direction we did, only he would have to take the longer route due to his size."

Joleen spent a few moments mulling this over. On one hand she was all for doing things the way that she would normally do them. Take it slow and move with precision. On the other hand, the way that Meterove would do things also had its appeal.

Charging in and attacking at the same time as Jörmungandr also had its perks. There was the element of surprise that would help a lot with the odds. The downside to that was that Jörmungandr was both unaware and likely uninterested in, help.

After she had thought about it for a little while Joleen concluded that no matter what she did, there was going to be risk. In the end she had to go with them trying to even the odds without getting too close to Jörmungandr.

Joleen said, "We will wait until Jörmungandr makes his entrance. When that happens there will be a brief window for us to attack them while they are focused on Jörmungandr."

Joleen could tell that Meterove and Dras were fans of this plan. Meterove was still apprehensive about putting the others in danger, but he knew that this was the best course of action. The others were also in agreement.

Suddenly Ava called out, "I see something new on sonar! I think he is here!"

There was no doubt that it was Jörmungandr. He was coming in fast. Joleen shouted, "Full speed ahead!"

.   .   .

Mia had known that there was something special about that temple. She had not forgotten the giant serpent that had been there so long. He had not moved in so long that the thought of him takin action had not occurred to her.

He was coming here now though. She could almost feel the dread that the minions he passed up felt. He was clearly coming for her. She had brought what she could to aid her in fighting him. Alone she might be his equal, but with several of her largest minions here to back her up the scales would be tipped in her favor.

She had not forgotten the little ones that had hurt her before either. She intended to make them pay, but the threat of the giant serpent was too great to let grudges distract her. She moved up some from the depths and prepared to meet him.

There was a low roar and there was a sudden increase in water pressure as Jörmungandr arrived. He was slightly bigger than her but not by much. Mia could see his shock in the way his body tensed up.

There was another roar and he barreled into her, first sending a massive burst of boiling water ahead of him that would likely have severely injured her before. Now, with her body enhanced through undeath, she was only slightly injured by it.

His massive fangs digging into her though, that hurt. She wrapped his body up in her tentacles and began to constrict his body while tearing at it with the spikes inside her suckers. She was keeping her body well away from his mouth. Those fangs would do massive damage to her vitals if they reached her.

As she continued to fight with the great serpent, she became somewhat desperate. Where were her minions that she had brought with her? Why were they not helping her?

In her furry she had not paid close attention to what was going on around her. She searched for her minions and found that there was only one left.

HOW!! WHAT HAPPENED TO THE OTHER TWO!?

That question was almost immediately answered. She saw it. That hateful object that carried the tiny ones! How had she missed it attacking? The answer came to her in a flash of rage and bewilderment.

THE UNDINES MUST HAVE USED THEIR POWER TO HIDE THE FIGHT FROM ME!

There was nothing for it now. Her last minion was a Leviathan, and it should be able to kill them without much trouble. A worry flickered across her mind. They had after all killed off the Ichthyosaur and the other Leviathan already.

The fangs sank into her again followed by another blast of boiling water. This was no time to focus on them. She would send all of her minions that she had left to attack both the little ones and the great serpent!

Joleen was watching the battle unfold through the periscope. Mia looked like nothing that she had ever seen. Her long head, which was vaguely squid like, though with eight fins on the trunk. These fins were also more rigid, with sharp spines along them.

It was really frustrating not being able take part in the fight directly. Joleen had known from the beginning that this would be the case, but it did not make it any less frustrating.

Joleen gave everyone that wanted a chance to look at Mia. Only those of her party, Laticin and Claire did though. They had managed to sneak pretty close then proceeded to attack at the same time that Jörmungandr barreled into Mia.

They had actually lucked out and the one Leviathan had made the error of swallowing some of the depth charges that they had dropped. This had blown the head apart and killed it right as the other two noticed them.

The Undines had helped with the Ichthyosaur. Normally it would have been far too fast for them to be able to be a match for it. Fortunately, the Undines were able to create turbulent waters that threw it off, which allowed them to hit it with several torpedoes.

The Undines had also been doing their best to keep the ripples of their battle from reaching Mia. The later she knew she was losing allies the better. The last Leviathan was going to be more of an issue. It was too large and powerful for the Undines to inhibit its movement. There was no way it was going to make the same error that the first one did either.

Joleen decided that the best thing that they could do was to keep the Leviathan busy while Jörmungandr fought with Mia. Of course, things did not work out quite like she planned. There was the sound of knocking from outside the ship.

Ava whispered, "There is a large cloud of something out there. It was not there a moment ago."

Jolson said, "The interference from the battle may have masked it."

Claire asked, "What is it?"

Meterove said, "You already know the answer to that, just as well as the rest of us. Those are the rest of the undead that Mia managed to gather."

Laticin asked, "Does that really matter? There is no way that they can get in, right?"

Meterove said, "As far as we know, that is true. However, there is still the simple matter that they can throw off our sensors."

Joleen whispered, "I think that they are also the reason the other Leviathan is holding back. I think there is some sort of plan that they concocted."

Jolson thought for a moment, then exclaimed, "SHIT! We need to get out of here now!"

Joleen did not bother asking questions. She shouted, "You heard him! Get us out of here!"

Once the engines kicked in Joleen turned to Jolson and asked, "What is going on?"

Jolson said, "That knocking is all over the ship. It is likely that they were doing it to mask their real intentions. If some of those undead are Leturai, then they know how this ship works."

Joleen's eyes went wide, "Then they would know exactly how to disable this ship!"

Jolson nodded, "Then we would be sitting dead in the water. It would be an easy kill for that Leviathan."

There were many more clunks from outside the ship as they set out. Once they began to move the Leviathan began to swim faster towards them. Once they were clear of the cloud of undead Joleen called, "Drop every depth charge that we have left! Set the sensor for the depth we are at now so they are masked by the undead!"

Joleen was banking on this Leviathan coming up on them quick. The agonized roaring that followed the explosions and the shuddering of ship, proved that she had made the right call.

Joleen asked, "Ava can you confirm that the Leviathan was killed?"

Ava looked over her display for a moment then happily said, "I am picking up the figure, but it is sinking down to the bottom. We do appear to have killed it!"

There was cheering all over the bridge. Joleen did not have time to focus on this now. She asked, "What is the status of the fight between Jörmungandr and Mia?"

Narok looked through the periscope while Ava checked the sonar. Ava was the first to respond, "The fight appears to still be in progress."

Narok said a moment later, "I can vaguely see it. If we are going to do something about it, we might want to do it now."

Meterove said, "If we do I recommend that we fire all torpedoes then turn and get as far away from here as we can. Jörmungandr is not going to be pleased if one of those hits him."

Joleen asked, "Where would we go?"

Ava said, "We could try to make a portal back to your world."

Joleen said, "Start working on it. Once we have a way out, we fire."

Ten minutes later though a confused and worried Claire reported back. Claire said, "We do not understand the reason, but we are unable to make a connection right now."

Meterove said, "I bet you it is because of Jörmungandr. If he is indeed the lord of this Plane, then if he does not want there to be travel from here, he may be using a power similar to his mother's"

Jolson exclaimed, "That's right! Flare creates barriers for the worlds. It would make perfect sense that her children would have similar powers to her own."

Joleen said, "What you are telling me is that there is no way that we can get to safety if things get dangerous?"

Laticin timidly said, "I have a place that might work. We should only need to hide the six of you, correct?"

Meterove nodded, "Your art cave."

Joleen asked, "Is it going to be large enough?"

Meterove said, "Easily. It should also be well enough hidden that we will escape his notice."

Terenia had come up from the weapons room during the conversation. She gave Meterove a confused look.

Terenia asked, "Why are you thinking that we need to find a place to hide?"

Meterove said, "I get the feeling that Jörmungandr is going to wipe the slate clean once he is done with Mia. Anything that does not belong here will be purged. The question is what is he going to interpret as not belonging here?"

There was a pause. Now that they were close to the end, Meterove's words carried more impact than they did earlier.

Ava said, "The battle between Mia and Jörmungandr is still going on. Mia appears to be holding her own."

Joleen looked around everyone and said, "We will head for the Mermaids territory after we fire on Mia. Laticin I will need you to help Ava get us to this cave of yours as fast as possible."

Laticin said, "You can count on me."

Joleen took a deep breath, the gave the order, "Fire all torpedoes! As soon as the last torpedo has left the tube, I want you to get us out of here."

.   .   .

Mia was getting frustrated. Somehow, she had lost her three greatest minions and the little ones were of no use. She was pressing her attack on Jörmungandr, when suddenly there were six blasts of searing pain that lanced through her.

THAT VILE THING!! HOW DARE YOU!!

Jörmungandr did not hesitate to press the advantage now that Mia had been both weakened and distracted. He tensed up his body and delivered another blast of boiling water, then grabbed onto Mia with his jaws. Once he had a secure hold, he began pulling her back to the surface.

Mia began to panic. The tiny ones had injured too many of her fins to be able to resist being pulled to the surface. With an enormous explosion of water, the two of them resurfaced.

Jörmungandr was now able to attack with the full power. Instead of boiling water, a torrent of cobalt flames burst out of his mouth, turning several of Mia's tentacles to ashes. Mia roared in agony but there was little that she could do now.

Twice more Jörmungandr unleashed his flames on Mia. Her tentacles were gone and now the rest of her was being burned away. Even in this state she was filled with nothing but rage and hunger.

WHY!!? Why...why...I should have been the one... I did not get what was promised! I want to devour more!

Once Jörmungandr was satisfied with his destruction of Mia, he went on to focus on the greater part of the Plane. Every line of his scales began to glow with a faint golden light. The horns on his head and spikes on his back began to glow so brightly, they appeared to be made of light.

Jörmungandr growled and released the energy that he had built up. This was a special ability that he and his siblings all had. This purifying aura was the reason that he and his siblings had been made to be guardians. It would spread slowly but steadily across the entire Plane.

Mother had better not complain about me not taking this task seriously.

Despite being covered in a great many wounds from Mia, Jörmungandr did not appear too fatigued. He disappeared below the waves. He had one last thing to take care of before he could return to his rest. That object that had injured Mia would not be damaged by his purification blast. It needed to be dealt with as well.

.   .   .

Joleen had watched the end of the battle as long as she could through the periscope. She had been able to see Mia take a crippling blow from Jörmungandr by having tentacles burnt off.

Now they were racing across the water trying to get to several spirals. Ava had detected something large coming after them on the long-range sonar. Meterove was probably right about Jörmungandr wanting to destroy everything that did not belong on this Plane.

The plan was to take to separate spirals to get to the Mermaid lagoon. They were moving as fast as possible now. Joleen was willing to take a few risks in terms of defense in order to increase speed.

Once they had made it to the second spiral that they intended to cross then pulled up and waited. Once Jörmungandr was detected on sonar they dove into the spiral. The angry roar from behind them was unnerving but also exactly what they wanted.

They were soon coming up to the Mermaid lagoon. Once they were there, they quickly abandoned the ship. The Undines and Rakira were the first to leave. Joleen was not going to risk the lives of anyone else when Jörmungandr wanted them.

Claire and Laticin had refused to leave with the others. Laticin had maintained that they would need her to find her cave. Meterove knew how to get there and was considering saying so but the look in her eyes made him keep that to himself.

Once it was just the eight of them, they prepared to depart but were stopped by the appearance of Elise. She had entered the ship once the last Undine had left.

In her hand she held a dagger. It was clear that she had no idea how to properly use it but that did mean she was not dangerous. There was a manic gleam in her eyes. Her breaths were fast and ragged.

Elise said, "I heard. You have angered the Great Lord! He is coming for you, and you plan to flee. I cannot allow this!"

Laticin said, "Mother, snap out of it! Jörmungandr is not a god! He is just a guardian that the Lady Flare placed here to -"

Elise cut her off, "Shut your mouth you stupid child! You know nothing!"

A beeping from the console that Ava had been running told them that Jörmungandr was coming. Laticin tried to get through to her mother again, "Mother! Please! He is not a god! He does not care about you or anyone else! The only one he cares about is himself and making sure that he does not invoke his mother's wrath!"

Elise became so enraged at Laticin that she was spitting as she shouted, "I am his devout! I will deliver onto him, that which he is pursuing.! I will be rewarded!"

Meterove said, "I am sorry Laticin, but we do not have time for this. He is coming now!"

Meterove stepped forward and Elise lunged at him with the dagger. He easily caught her wrist and disarmed her. She struggled against him, and after he released her she threw herself off him in a rage and tripped and fell down to the next deck.

Meterove took advantage of that and said, "Everyone out! We need to get to the cave NOW!"

Laticin took one last look at where her mother had fallen then followed Meterove out. In her heart she was utterly broken at that moment. Her mother had verbally abused her, attacked her competence, and now threated her physically and intended to sacrifice her for her "god" without a second thought.

They left the ship behind and fled to the lagoon; swimming as fast as they could. Once inside the cave the eight of them waited in tense silence.

.   .   .

Back on the ship Elise was slowly moving up the ladder of the ship. When she fell, she had broken an ankle, so it was very slow and painful work. She was so outraged now that she was yelling, even though there was no one around to hear her.

She raged about the stupid child and the filthy intruders. She condemned all the unbelievers. They were all fools! She would see that they paid for this!

At the same time, she was so euphoric she could hardly contain it. She was going to see her beloved Great Lord! She would get to bask in his glory! Perhaps he might even reward her for her devotion!

It took her awhile, but she had managed to get out of the ship and was now standing next to the hatch, though she was leaning heavily on her good leg. In the distance she could see a great swell of water with two enormous objects sticking out of it.

THAT MUST BE HIM!!!!

All of her pain melted away. She could still feel it but now it was as if it were being felt by another person. She knelt down and began to pray. She was loudly chanting out her prayers.

Jörmungandr broke the surface and Elise was nearly thrown off the ship. He stared down at the ship and when she shouted, "Oh Great Lord! I am your most devout-"

Jörmungandr dove forward and crushed the ship in his jaws. Elise was knocked off and into the water. She had the briefest moment to think before the momentum of Jörmungandr pulverized her body.

I do not understand...the Great Lord...has killed me. I was his most devout! I followed the scriptures! Could I have been wrong? Was...Laticin right? NO! NOOOOOOOO!!! I was so faithful! This cannot be the truth! She must have done something!

.   .   .

The wave of golden energy took some time to spread across the Plane. Wherever it went that which was undead was turned to ash. However, there were far fewer undead left than had still been there when Mia had fallen. After Jörmungandr had believed himself successful in destroying the last of the outsiders he had returned to his slumber.

He did not care that there had been portals that had allowed many of the undead to flee the Plane, as they were aiding in the removal of the undead. What happened outside of here was someone else's problem.

Jörmungandr went back to sleep and the rest of the denizens of the Plane of Water were left to pick up the pieces without the aid of their guardian. Meterove had to admit that Jörmungandr had done his job, even if he had done the least amount of work possible.

791

He was worried about Laticin. That final confrontation with her mother had shaken her. She was far too quiet while they hunkered down in the cave. Terenia had tried to talk to her to keep her mind off of it, but it had been to no avail.

Now that Jörmungandr had likely gone back to sleep Joleen and decided that it was time to head out of the cave and go do some damage control. Their first stop would obviously be checking in on the Mermaids since they were in the lagoon.

CHAPTER 37.5
RELIEF

The situation on the Plane of Water had been successfully taken care of. That had been close. The Darkfire one had taken great pains to assist the Ashen Soul, yet they had still been defeated.

It was unfortunate that so many had escaped but there had been no way to avoid that. That Jörmungandr would be so hostile towards the ones his mother had sent to make sure he did his job was alarming, though expected.

It had been amusing to see him fooled in such a manner. He would be very salty when he learned that they had survived. Flare would not particularly care about his attempt to kill them.

Her only real concern was making sure that the Ashen Soul did not spread. She really could not care less who died in the pursuit of that goal. That might well cost her in the future.

The necessary pieces were slowly assembling. There was still the matter of finding one that was not bound within the influence. There were still other fires though. Perhaps soon they would be able to free the other selves.

There was not much time left to stay in the shadows. These mortals would have to be met with soon. The breaking was already beginning. The end was both far away and too near.

CHAPTER 38
FALLOUT

The Mermaid lagoon was in complete chaos. Everywhere you looked there was panic. The fighting had cost them many lives. They were not a warlike people and the need to fight here had been crucial. Among the dead were Alara, as well as three other elders.

The Mermaids had lost nearly half their number in such a short time. Moira swam around the lagoon doing her best to calm her sisters. The sight of an enormous creature earlier that had destroyed the ship that Laticin had been on had caused a panic.

There were a million things to do and only one of her. As far as she knew the cause of all of this was still out there. She had taken the precaution of pulling all of her sisters back to the inner lagoon. This was where they normally had the children learn how to swim properly.

It was very shallow, almost on the level of the Shallows. The only difference was that this was salt water. The bottom was extremely fine sand. With every surviving member of the Mermaids gathered like this it would be easy to wipe them out with a single attack.

However, Moira saw no other option. The enemy had been whittling away at their numbers for a while now and sitting still was only playing into their enemy's hands.

"Moira! Come quick!"

One of the sentries sent her an urgent message. Her tone had been excited though. She hurried over to the sentries position and was greeted with that best sight that she could have hoped for.

Laticin was there, unharmed and with Claire and Meterove and all his friends as well. Based on the smiles on their faces they had some good news to share. All except Laticin, there was a deep shadow over her.

She pointed to the surface and every one of them followed her up. Once there she wasted no time with formalities. She asked, "Did you succeed!?"

Joleen said, "Yes. We were able to get the guardian of the Plane to awaken and he destroyed Mia."

Moira closed her eyes and started crying. It was over. She gave herself a moment to bask in that news before she continued asking questions. "When you say guardian...does that mean that there is a Great Lord after all?"

Everyone winced at this statement and glanced at Laticin. Joleen said, "Not exactly. It turns out that the guardian of the Plane of Water is actually Jörmungandr, one of the children of Lady Flare."

Moira seemed to wither slightly. She had held onto a little hope that what she had heard before was wrong. She had spent her whole life believing in the Great Lord. She spent a moment reconciling that before she proceeded.

Moira said, "I think that the rest can wait for now. I will tell the others that it is safe to return to our homes. We will also need to contact the other Principal Races."

Claire said, "We dropped off a large number of my people near here. I do not know if they are hiding or if they have started making their way to the Shallows already. I would like to search for them."

Moira said, "I will discuss matters with those who remain here. Once that is done, we will make for the Shallows. With the Core having been destroyed we will need somewhere that everyone can meet, and the Shallows makes the most sense."

Claire said, "Yes, I agree. I will see you soon."

Moira looked at Laticin and said, "I think you should know that I was forced to banish your mother when we first returned to the lagoon."

Laticin looked up shocked, "Why?"

Moira looked sad, "She spent every moment she could trying to convince me that you were either lying about the crisis or that you were trying to use it to your advantage or that you did not know what you were doing. In the end I had to make the decision that was best for our people."

Laticin started crying. The were not just tears of sadness. They were also tears of rage. Despite everything that she had done and shown her, Elise had refused to see the truth. She had even attempted to sabotage her own daughter behind her back.

While Laticin was crying Meterove said, "She confronted us on the ship, just before we were going to abandon it. She was going to make us stay there, to sacrifice us to her "Great Lord" no matter that meant killing her own daughter. As far as I know she died, when Jörmungandr destroyed the ship."

Moira heard the barely concealed rage in his voice. It would not do to enrage this man. He was not at all upset at Elise's death and had she survived, he may well have killed her.

Moira chose to comfort Laticin and comment on how she was glad that she was safe. She had a sneaking suspicion that there was something more going on with Laticin than just her mother's death.

Moira said, "I will be going now. I hope that we will see all of you again soon."

Moira dove under and Joleen asked, "Claire, which do you think is more likely? Did Ava have the other Undines take cover and hunker down or are they heading back to the Shallows?"

Claire said, "Knowing Ava she decided to make their way back. The only complication that they would have is helping Rakira move with them. They would not be able to move nearly as fast and would also do their best to avoid open water."

Laticin said, "Then they are most likely heading for Kyra's Shoals. They are a scattered collection of shallow water. It also has one of the most unique water features on the whole Plane.

Claire said, "You mean Kyra's Falls."

Joleen asked, "What is Kyra's Falls?"

Laticin said, "It is an underwater waterfall. From what I understand it is a rare phenomenon."

Jolson paused and asked, "It is a WHAT now?"

Laticin said, "It is an underwater waterfall. It will be easier to just show you. That is the most likely course that Ava would take."

Meterove shrugged, "We do need to check in with the other leaders and have a more detailed discussion with Moira before we can leave. I personally am ok with doing a little be of sightseeing on the way. I think we earned the right to that."

They let Laticin lead the way. Now that they were back in the water Claire had done away with her "clothes" since she wanted to be able to give them as much of a boost as possible. Oddly enough Dras made sure to place himself behind her.

The Falls were not terribly far away from their current location. Claire used her power to shape the water around their feet into flippers and made their hands webbed. This increased their swim speed considerably.

Meterove, Joleen and Jolson used their magic to augment the others. This allowed them to travel at twice Laticin's normal top speed. The scenery flashed by and in no time, they were at the Falls.

They were everything that Laticin had said and more! The center was dark blue that slowly turned to cobalt at the edges. Around that there was an area of sea green water that could be seen falling into the blue.

Laticin explained, "This is virtually impossible to find anywhere else due to the unique features of the Plane of Water. The closest thing that anyone knows of is an illusion caused by sand moving underwater in a world that Mermaids had visited in the past."

They did not stay too long, since they did have important matters that they needed to see to. Following the shoals for another day they finally caught up with the Undines.

Ava was shockingly happy to see them, and not just because they had Laticin and Claire with them. Rakira smiled the moment she saw Meterove and ran over and hugged him. Joleen could not help but giggle. It reminded her of when Meterove had been young and would get excited seeing her and Jolson return from somewhere.

Now that they were reunited with Ava's group they continued on to the Shallows. When they reached the Undine city it was clear that they had been under siege as well. There was an obelisk that Claire informed them had not been there before near the entrance.

They did not stop to examine it though. They continued into the city. The atmosphere was subdued with no one out in the streets. Eventually someone did notice them, and the cries of joy led to many more Undines coming out.

Eventually the revelry caught the attention of the councilors. Olivia practically sprinted through the streets and tearfully embraced Claire. After she had a few moments to calm herself down she informed them that the Snow Women had also joined them.

Rakira said, "Does that mean my mother is also here?"

Olivia said, "Yes Demetria is here. She will be glad to know that you are safe. Come. We should talk."

Olivia led them through the city to another new building. Along the way they saw many signs that there had been fighting here as well. This new building was clearly meant to be for emergency housing. Once they drew near two women that were watching the door recognized Rakira and one of them went inside for a moment.

Demetria came out a moment later. While she was not running as fast as Olivia had, she looked no less relieved to have her daughter back. They all waited for the mother to finish her embrace.

Once she was done, Demetria said, "I thank you from the bottom of my heart for keeping my daughter safe."

Joleen said, "You should be thanking her for saving the Plane from the Ashen Soul. If she had not known about the ritual needed to awaken the guardian of the Plane of Water we would not be here right now. His name is

Jörmungandr by the way, and he is one of the children of Lady Flare."

A familiar voice said from the crowd, "I have heard that name before."

Fayre had caught up with them. She continued, "It is not something that we often talk about since there is no record about who or what Jörmungandr was."

Dras said, "Well now you know. He is a giant sea serpent dragon, and he is a dick."

The Undines were puzzled, and Joleen quickly said, "He means to say that he is not exactly friendly."

Fayre asked, "What more can you tell us?"

Joleen shook her head, "Moira is going to come here soon. We will address everyone then. We just wanted to ensure that everyone was safe, and that Ava and the others made it back home."

Fayre said, "I appreciate that. I can also appreciate that you wish to inform us all at the same time. We will arrange for some accommodations for you until then."

Joleen said, "Thank you. With any luck the Mermaids will not be too far behind us."

It took a few days for the Mermaids to arrive. Once they did, Joleen gathered everyone together to address them. Laticin and Claire had gone back to their respective people for the time being.

The Undines had restructured the building that had been housing the Snow Women to accommodate the meeting. The plan was to have Joleen address the Principal Races and afterwards to have them ask questions.

Joleen stood on a raised platform the Undines had made for her to speak from. She cleared her throat and said, "Hello. Most of you already know this but my name is Joleen Valaseri. My brothers and I came here to investigate some attacks on our world that originated here. We are working with Lady Flare, and we have handled the threat. The first Kraken, Mia had been corrupted by the Ashen Soul. We have since neutralized Mia."

Once she had finished ,Olivia asked, "How did you neutralize Mia and are you sure that the threat is past?"

Joleen responded, "The threat is most certainly past. We used a ritual to awaken Jörmungandr from his slumber. He destroyed Mia and released a purifying burst of energy that turned every undead it hit to turn to ash. Based on what we have seen the burst has completely covered the Plane of Water."

Courtney asked, "Who exactly is this Jörmungandr?"

Joleen said, "Jörmungandr is the guardian of the Plane. He is the son of Lady Flare."

There was murmuring at that. Many present had already heard that they were working with Flare. They were also aware of the Mermaid texts and of mentions of a guardian. That this guardian was real and that it was the child of Flare was beyond their expectations.

Courtney looked very skeptical, "I have heard of this "Lady Flare" before, but I never put much stock in her being more than a myth. Surely you are not suggesting we believe some fictional beings offspring-"

A loud slap echoed across the room and Courtney fell onto her backside, one hand touching the bright red handprint on her cheek. There was a small trickle of blood coming out of the corner of her mouth.

Fayre was the one that had slapped her. Claire was stunned. She had never seen Fayre hit someone before. She looked at her mother and found Oliva also staring at Fayre openmouthed.

Fayre's voice was mostly calm, though there was a slight tremble and an icy coldness to it. She said, "You will leave now. After everything that we went through, all the lives that were lost, you chose NOW to try and play politics. You have no place on this council."

Courtney's mouth worked soundlessly like some fish. After a moment, the full weight of reality hit her, and she began to cry and ran from the building.

Fayre turned to Joleen, "I apologize Lady Valaseri."

Joleen shook her head, "Think nothing of it. I have experienced the same myself before."

Meterove could not help but be proud of how much Joleen had grown. She may have been his older sister, but she had spent a lot of time hiding behind him since they first set out after their father's death. Now here she was, taking the lead and showing cool leadership.

Joleen cleared her throat, "As I was saying, Jörmungandr is the child of Lady Flare. I would not count on him to protect you though."

Fayre said, "I am confused. You said that this Jörmungandr saved us. Why would we not be able to trust him to protect us?"

Joleen patiently said, "Jörmungandr did not save you. He saved the Plane of Water. His job...his task that was given to him by Lady Flare is to protect the Plane of Water. He will do no more than that. So long as the Plane of Water is safe, anything else is expendable."

The silence that fell once Joleen had said those words was so complete that Meterove was sure he could hear the sound of the waves. Everyone, whether they were an Undine, snow woman or Mermaid was unnerved by that.

Demetria asked, "I actually have something to ask of you Lady Valaseri."

Joleen looked slightly taken aback. "What would you want to ask me?"

Demetria said, "I had the good fortune to have met your father years ago." Joleen was shocked. Demetria continued, "I was able to negotiate safe passage in your empire when looking for men, so long as we did not harm any of the men. Unfortunately, that was only a verbal agreement. I was hoping to get something a little more concrete in the event that something unfortunate happens."

Joleen was surprised to learn that her father had made an agreement like that. It made sense that he would not have told anyone else about it. The more time went on, the more Joleen realized she had barely known him.

Now was not the time to dwell on that though. He had been a good man and a good emperor. She had no problems with his choice to make a deal like this with the Snow Women.

Joleen said, "I would be happy to work something like that out with you."

No sooner had the words left her mouth than Moira was asking, "What about us? Could we also make an agreement of a similar nature with you?"

Joleen smiled at Moira, "You need not worry. I will make agreements with all three races should you wish it. I can also introduce you to several other races of our world that would likely be more than happy to meet you."

Moira asked, "What if I wished to have some of my sisters make a permanent colony on your world?"

Joleen blinked. That was not something she had even remotely expected. Perhaps seeing Joleen's expression, Moira continued, "We lost so many of our sisters. We must take some action to ensure that our kind does not vanish. There may be some of our sisters out there on various worlds, but I would rather know for sure that there is at least one other colony."

Joleen considered it for a moment then said, "I would have to sit down and have a much more detailed discussion with you. Tentatively I can say that it would be something that I would seriously consider."

Moira looked pleased with her response. Olivia was the next to speak, "We Undines rarely leave the Plane, but we would not mind having a friendly agreement with your people as well."

Fayre nodded her approval, "We also owe you a debt that we will not soon be able to repay. If you find yourself in need and we are able to, we will lend you aid."

Hearing all this talk about their world made Laticin's blood go cold. He was not going to stay here. Neither was Terenia. They were both going to leave here soon. What was she going to do once they were gone?

She felt like there was a gaping hole that had suddenly appeared next to her heart. It swallowed it and all of her capacity for happiness. She would lose them and be left with only her pain of losing so many sisters...and her mother.

She did not want this. She had not been particularly unhappy before all of this. Sure, her mother had been a zealot, but Laticin had found some pleasure in life. Her friendship with Claire and her art for starters.

However, from the moment that she had first seen Meterove, she had begun to feel alive in ways that she had never experience before. Here was someone that accepted her for how she was, not how they wanted her to be. He had accepted all parts of her too.

Then there was Terenia. She was wonderful, beautiful, and so incredibly kind. She had to have been hurt by what had happened between Laticin and Meterove, yet instead of dwelling on it, she had chosen to take it as a blessing. She clearly cared for Laticin as much as Meterove did and perhaps in time as, much as the two of them cared for each other.

Laticin looked up at them, standing behind Joleen to her left. They were so kind to her. Meterove was a warrior, true, but the way that he comforted Rakira before was burned into her mind. He had nothing that he was personally going to gain from it, yet he had taken it upon himself to comfort that little girl.

Then her mind moved to the others. Dras was so much like Meterove that Laticin could instantly get along with him. He was fun and also so exceedingly kind. His evident interest in Claire made him of a different interest to her.

Jolson and Narok were both very reserved, but they too had been nothing but kind. Joleen was fiery and sassy. Laticin liked her a lot and while she could not be sure, she thought that Joleen felt the same way about her.

Where she had only one real friend before, she now had many. She also had two lovers. How could she give that up? The answer to that was obvious...she could not. Now that she had thought through this, she knew that she could not, would not, give that up.

Once she said those words in her head, the void in her chest vanished and uncertainty that she had not even known was there disappeared without a trace. She was sitting next to Moira, and she heard the woman whisper something.

Laticin turned to look at her and found Moira smiling at her. It was the kind of smile that she had always wanted to get from her mother. It warmed her heart even more to see.

Moira whispered again, "You will go with them. You have found something that is beyond precious. Do not lose it. Do not squander it. Do not sacrifice it."

Laticin began to tear up. She looked at Moira and choked back a sob as she grasped the woman's hand. She looked into her eyes for a moment longer then switched her gaze back to Meterove and Terenia, only to find them looking at her.

She knew that they could tell what she had decided to do. This was a huge leap for her. She had never even been off the Plane before. Now here she was, making the decision to leave it altogether.

The meeting went on for some time after that. There were a great many questions about what had happened and what they could do to protect themselves in the future. There was also a brief inquiry about the fate of the Sirens.

Once that was done it was already late so it was decided that Joleen and the others should rest for the night and then they would be escorted back to the portal tomorrow.

After the meeting Laticin was standing on a ledge overlooking the Lower Shallows. Claire came up to her and quietly stood there looking out over the scenery. After a few minutes Claire said, "You intend to leave."

Laticin knew it was not a question. She said, "Yes. I have too much pain here."

Claire smiled, "And you have found love that is not going to be here."

Laticin laughed, "Yes, that is probably the larger reason."

Claire said, "As it should be. Happiness must be greater than suffering. I must say that I am jealous. I must admit that I am curious about men now. I wish I could meet someone myself."

Laticin laughed, "What about Dras?"

Claire cocked her head, "What about him?"

Laticin could not help herself, she started laughing. She had hardly any experience at all with men and love, yet it was the most obvious thing to her that Dras found Claire attractive.

Claire still looked confused so once Laticin had calmed herself a little she said, "He finds you attractive Claire. He takes pains to make sure he is in a position to see your body whenever he can."

Claire asked, "Is it not just that men like the female form?"

Laticin said, "If that were all it was, then he would have been staring all over during that meeting. Instead, he had eyes only for you. True I think his eyes wander, but if what I hear about humans is true than that is something that is to be expected."

Claire looked pensive, "What do I do then? I have no idea how things like that work. Do I talk to him? How do I know if I find him attractive?"

Laticin could not help but laugh at her friend's naiveté. True, she was not much better but at least she knew that she had found Meterove attractive right away.

Laticin said, "Come let's go talk to him and I will help you discover if you find him attractive. I imagine you will though. I may not be interested in him, but I can tell you that he is pleasing to look at.

CHAPTER 39
DEBRIEFING

The next day dawned and Meterove and the others made their preparations to leave. They would be joined by two more, both Laticin and Claire would be joining them. Claire was ostensibly going for the purpose of seeing what else was out there. Only Laticin knew her real purpose.

Laticin had taken her to go see the others last night in order to ask them if they might join them. The fact that Claire wanted to leave had come as a surprise. Now that Claire was aware of the reasoning of Dras' gaze she was much more self-conscious.

Fortunately, no one seemed to notice and they happily agreed to take the two of them along with them. The journey back to the portal would go significantly faster if they had an Undine with them.

This time the journey back was uneventful. They saw a handful of sea creatures such as dolphins and various fish but otherwise it was just a lot of swimming. Reaching the portal after several days, Joleen decided that they should rest before going through. It was obvious that she was giving Laticin and Claire one last night on their home before leaving and they were grateful.

While the eight of them sat around their camp Dras asked, "Hey, do you guys remember what happened here on our first day? Did we ever find out what that thing was?"

Laticin asked, "What thing?"

Dras said, "So we came through and set up this tent the first time there was a creature with a long neck that was killed by a giant shark. Then that shark was speared on a massive, spiraled horn that was at least as long as the shark."

Laticin and Claire looked at each other for a moment then Claire said, "The first one might have been some kind of Elasmosaurus . The shark sounds like it was a megalodon. As for the last one I have no idea. The only sea creature that I know of that has a horn is a narwhal."

Joleen asked, "If you know something that sounds like it, then why are you unsure?"

Laticin said, "Narwhals should only grow to about half the length of a megalodon. From the sounds of this beast, if it were a narwhal, it would be larger than a blue whale."

Claire shrugged, "There are so many parts of the Plane that we simply do not explore. Perhaps it was a subspecies of narwhal that was far larger?"

Meterove laughed, "I guess it does not matter all that much. We will not likely be back anytime soon, and there is no guarantee that it is still in the area anyway."

They spent the rest of the night chatting. Laticin and Claire had a lot of questions about Nexus and Yxarion. In the morning they packed everything up and took one last look out over the water then stepped through the portal.

Once on the other side Dras said, "Is it weird that after being wet pretty much constantly, that I want to take a bath?"

Meterove laughed, "No, I get what you mean."

They took a lift back up. From the moment that they had first come through, Laticin and Claire were looking around at everything. First the five portals and the roots of Creation had astounded them. As soon as they were back up at street level, Nexus became their new fixation.

Claire had thought the Undine city grand but compared to this...! All around there were buildings that were far taller than anything, except the Core. The fact that all of this was made of materials other than water was also of great fascination to the two girls.

Joleen led the way and soon they were walking through some familiar doors. Luck appeared to be on their side for once, as Flare was talking to Ricaran when they walked in. The second she saw them she waved them to her office. As anxious as she had to be to hear what they had to report, she waited until everyone was seated.

Flare said, "Well? Based on the amount of time that you were gone and the fact that you look more than a little full of yourselves, that you were successful."

Joleen tensed her jaw and clenched her fists in her lap. She really hated this woman. Unfortunately, Dras did not have a filter.

Dras said, "Careful Flare. You would not want to get slapped again, now would you?"

Flare went red and Laticin and Claire stared at her in shock. Adding to both women's embarrassment Meterove added, "She would deserve another one for not giving us more information about who we were going to be dealing with."

Narok said, "It is fun watching her unload on Flare."

Joleen snapped her head over to Narok. She had not expected him to tease her! She had gotten so used to him following along quietly that she had forgotten he had a similar type of wit as Meterove.

Turning back to Flare, Joleen coughed, "We were successful. Mia was neutralized by Jörmungandr. He also tried to kill us as well. I doubt that you care though I figured I would still report that. All the undead appear to have been purged from the Plane of Water."

Flare did not even blink. She clearly knew that they had found out who exactly the guardian was. All she said was, "That is good to know. Is there anything else that you have to report on? How bad was the collateral damage?"

As much as this woman irked her, she was necessary. Joleen took a deep breath and said, "As best as we can tell there were heavy losses for all species on the Plane. The Three Principal Races suffered a lot of losses. Approximately one third of the Snow Women and Undines and nearly half of the Mermaids were killed. Additionally, the structure known as the Core was totally destroyed."

Flare wove her fingers together and said, "That is both fortunate and unfortunate. With the Core destroyed then the trial is meaningless. That was meant to aid in awakening Jörmungandr. As you have found, he is not the most agreeable. Part of the reason that he was placed there was punishment. He needs to rein in that temper of his. The temple that I had placed there will remain open, thus he is vulnerable to attack."

Flare sighed, her brow furrowing. Joleen was still angry with her for keeping them in the dark, but she could at least sympathize with her on this matter. Worrying about things like this came with the territory.

Flare shook her head and said, "I am sure that you want to get home, however I would like to speak with you on several other related matters."

Joleen felt a wave of anxiety, "What do you mean by related matters?"

Flare said, "We have reason to believe that the Ashen Soul went after each of the Planes. The Plane of Water we know is secure for now. The others though may already be in the early stages of corruption. Then there is the issue of the slavers that have been found poaching all manner of worlds."

Meterove looked surprised, "Slavers? Ones that cross multiple worlds? That would mean that They are using the gates, correct?"

Flare shook her head, "No. Unfortunately, they are not coming through Nexus. These Slavers have discovered the truth of Creation. Usually when a world learns of Creation and how there are other worlds it is when they have become significantly more advanced. Once that happens, they can only explore so far. The Slavers though work for a man named Damien Winters. He is far too powerful for us to attack directly at this time, especially with the Ashen Soul making the moves that it is."

Joleen asked, "Would this man not want to work with us to stop the Ashen Soul?"

Flare laughed, "No, he would not. Damien Winters is incredibly cunning and powerful. This has given him something of a god complex. He would absolutely believe that he could subdue and enslave both us and the Ashen Soul."

Meterove had been quiet while Flare had talked about Damien Winters. He had never known his mother, but the reason for that was because of this man. He felt an odd sense of rage and thirst for vengeance.

He looked up to see that Flare was looking at him somewhat sympathetically. She said, "What you are feeling is natural. While you are only half dragon, you still have some form of our ancestral memory. You are feeling the rage that comes from that."

Joleen asked, "What other threats do you think that the Planes are going to be facing?"

Flare did not argue the change in topic. She said, "There are indications that the Ashen Soul may have made some more agents like Mia."

Joleen did not like the sound of that. She asked, "What do you mean more agents like Mia?"

Flare said, "Exactly like it sounds. Only, the agents that we have managed to confirm are far worse."

Meterove snapped out of his reverie and asked, "What do you mean? What could be worse than something like Mia?" As soon as he said that something awful occurred to him. "Actually, there is something that I wanted to ask you about. We discovered a cavern on our world that held a giant monster that was bound in chains."

Flare looked impatient, "I am sure that it is nothing."

Meterove said, "It was repelling the undeath back in our world."

Flare stopped whatever she was about to say and stayed frozen there, her mouth tensed. After a moment she said, "Perhaps you should tell me more about this monster after all."

Joleen said, "It was insanely large. It looked like a humanoid torso but had mouths with eyes all over it. There were also things that looked like tongues where a head should have been."

Flare exhaled and unless Joleen was mistaken, her pupils were dilated. What was that thing that even she was unnerved by it?

Flare whispered, "The One That Devours Through Sight..." She exhaled, then said, "That is one of the First Ones. Just as their name implies, they were the first creatures that were made in the early days, when Creation had not made many worlds yet."

Meterove asked, "I thought that you were the first? Well, you and the Dragon Lord?"

Flare nearly sneered at the mention of the Dragon Lord, but said, "We were, but the First Ones were the first to exists outside of the Planes and this space. They are nearly as old as us."

Jolson said, "You appear to be afraid of them."

Flare said, "A First One would be capable of a lot of destruction. The Ashen Soul is not likely to corrupt one of them, but they are incredibly dangerous in their own right. If somehow the Ashen Soul managed to find a way to do so, I worry there would be nothing to stop it, save totally destroying a world."

Meterove tensed, "Are you able to do that?"

Flare nodded solemnly, "I do not take that option lightly, but yes, it is well within my power to do that."

Meterove did not want to ask the other question that was on his mind. The look in her eyes told him the answer, he did not need to confirm it.

Dras asked, "If these things are as dangerous as you say, then how was this one captured and chained up?"

Flare said, "The First Ones do not utilize portals to travel between worlds. Rather they journey through the space between them. In that cold emptiness they drift, moving according to their own desires."

Jolson said, "That is useful to know but that does not answer the question."

Flare said, "When they are traveling, they go into a sort of hibernation, where the majority of their power and consciousness is shut down. There is not much of interest on your world to that First One. If I had to take a guess, your world was made after it had started a journey and he was pulled in by it. Once he was there, he was still weak, and the previous magical civilization of your world captured him. If he is still bound, then I would be interested in having both it and its bonds examined."

Dras asked, "What makes you so sure that there is nothing that this First One would want on our world?"

Flare said, "Every First One is different. The one on your world, The One That Devours Through Sight, does exactly what its name says. It devours what it sees through its many eyes. Those things that you described as tongues do function in a similar way, only they "taste" the worlds across creation for what it seeks."

Meterove asked, "What exactly is that?"

Flare said, "Energy. There is nowhere near enough energy on your world to truly interest it. If it could get close enough to your star, it would devour that, but that would still not be enough. The First Ones will move across Creation forever."

Narok asked, "How do we kill it?"

Meterove looked at him and he shrugged, "That thing is a threat to Jol-all of you."

Meterove decided not to comment on the slip and asked, "Well?"

Flare shook her head, "When they were made, Creation was just learning to make things. It would not be for many years that creatures began to experience death."

Terenia gasped, "Are you saying that it is immortal!?"

Flare shook her head, "Not exactly. There is one thing that could kill a First One, but it would be a huge risk to try and transport the First One to it."

Jolson asked, "Why not take it to the First One instead?"

Flare laughed, "For one thing it is beyond anyone's power to move. Also, if we did manage to do so, your world would end instantly."

Meterove asked, "What is this thing?"

Flare said, "I mentioned it to you the first time we met. Creation makes things in balance. This is partially because there is a balance to Creation."

Jolson whispered, "Destruction."

Flare nodded, "If you would like to see it, I could show you."

Joleen said, "I would like to, if only to understand better."

Flare said, "Then follow me."

She waved her hand and an outline of a door appeared in the wall and suddenly it gave way into a staircase. Flare led the way up. Meterove was having déjà vu because of the temple.

Once they reached the top Flare opened a door and they stepped through onto a large cobblestone patio. Once everyone was there, Flare gestured up and everyone gasped.

They were floating high above Creation and above them even further was the most sinister and beautiful thing. It was an ocean of different colors of light swirling around a center that was the deepest black any of them had ever seen.

Looking carefully, you could see that it was sucking all manner of things to it. Even light itself seemed to bend around that blackness.

Flare said, "That is Destruction. It lies there ready to devour everything that Creation makes."

Now that they had seen it in person, they understood what Flare had meant. Everyone went back down to her office and returned to their discussion.

Flare said, "I will dispatch someone to examine this monster to be sure of its nature. Until I personally say otherwise, I do not want anyone near that place."

Considering what she had told them and how they had felt when they had been there, there was no argument to that.

Flare said, "Now that this matter is settled, I need to return to the previous matter. I believe that the Ashen Soul has managed to corrupt some high-level demons, potentially even the Proto Gods themselves."

Jolson exclaimed, "Now we have demons in the mix!?

Flare sighed deeply, "Unfortunately that is what it looks like."

Meterove asked, "What are you trying to get us into Flare? We went to the Plane of Water because there was an attack on our world. I have yet to hear you give any sign that the Ashen Soul has been anywhere else."

Flare looked annoyed, "The signs are there. What about your world? Have there been no incidents with the sky or with fire or underground?"

That last part stirred something in the back of Joleen's memory. After a moment she said, "I remember something a while back. Before our father was killed there was a report from the Dwarves about something that was in their mines I think."

Flare said, "If you want proof that this is still affecting your world, then go there. I am sure you will find something."

The look on her face said that she already knew what they would find. Just as they were about to get up Flare held up her hand.

Joleen asked, "Is there something else?"

Flare said, "You could say that. There is a stranger here on Nexus. He calls himself "The Gamemaster" and he has taken up residence on a new section of Nexus that appears of have manifested itself."

Meterove asked, "Why do you not just get rid of this Gamemaster?"

Flare took a deep breath through her nose, then said, "I would if I could, but the fact that he was able to make a new part of Nexus without my approval means that he has more power than anyone here. I cannot deal with him unless I am willing to risk countless worlds."

Meterove rolled his eyes, "You want us to go look into this guy for you d-"

Flare cut him off, "I do not want you to go anywhere near him! I do not know what he is or what his limits are! I fear that he may be very dangerous! Avoid him! Now you can go."

CHAPTER 39.5
IMPOSSIBLE

This made no sense! How was this even possible! This Gamemaster could only be one individual. This situation was outside of all calculations. There was only one possibility, and it was not one that would ease the anxiety. The Seed would need to be investigated at some point, thought it would have to be someone else that did the investigating.

The fact that he was there now, when Meterove and the others were there made for a dangerous situation. Meterove and his friend were both prime targets for this Gamemaster and his insane games. What kind of prizes was he planning on?

The time for meeting them needed to come now. Without that there was the chance that everything that had been built up until now would fall apart like a house of cards.

CHAPTER 40
GAMEMASTER

Their sudden dismissal from Flare's office had taken them all by surprise. Whoever this Gamemaster was he was like an exposed nerve for her. As they walked past Ricaran's desk he glared at them. Dras made a point of giving him the jauntiest smile and wave as he walked by.

Once they were done with Flare, they decided to show Laticin and Claire around Nexus some. As anxious as they were to get home, they felt that the girls deserved to be shown around Nexus.

Terenia joked that they should head to The Nexus for drinks. Dras tensed up at first but after a moment said, "Why not? That will probably be a lot more fun this time around."

Joleen was curious about what had happened the last time they were there but knew better than to ask. Still the idea of getting some drinks right now did not seem all that bad. There was the question of what Claire would do there though.

She was not the only one thinking about that though. Jolson said, "What about Claire? It would not be a good idea for her to drink alcohol while she is pregnant."

Claire said, "I am confused. Why is that bad?"

Joleen said, "At least for humans, alcohol is dangerous for the unborn child."

Claire said, "Ah, I see. So long as I do not drink anything that has alcohol in it, I will be fine, correct?"

Meterove gave a half shrug and said, "That is true. Alright, I guess we are going to The Nexus."

They made their way over to the bar. The bartender remembered them from last time. He had a smirk on his face as he saw them walk in. Dras had changed some since that time though and now walked up to the bar and asked, "Do you have any more of that "special" bottle from last time?"

The bartender smiled, "Yes, I do. Do you want to start with that?"

Meterove held up his hand, "NO! We will start with some ale for myself."

Each of the others put in their individual orders with Joleen ordering for Laticin and Claire. The bartender was actually quite skilled at making nonalcoholic drinks for Claire. Both she and Laticin were currently wearing clothes that they had gotten from Terenia.

Laticin was wearing a lowcut black dress that went to her mid hip, and a pair of knee-high black boots. Claire was wearing a soft blue dress that went down to her knees and ankle high boots. Both had a slight heel to them.

Meterove had to admit they both look amazing, even if it was weird seeing them in clothing. Dras had been particularly complimentary of Claire. They partied for several hours that night.

Finally with a signal from Meterove that he had the approval to do it, Dras got everyone, except for Claire a round of Ambience. Meterove gave a short explanation of what it would do. Joleen, Jolson and Narok all panicked a little. When Dras asked what they thought it would bring out, and if they did not want that their protests died down. Afterall, how powerful could it be?

.   .   .

The next morning saw Meterove waking up in the room that he had rented at The Nexus, with Terenia on his left and Laticin on his right, though both of them were using his chest as a pillow.

Meterove spent a little while just looking at them as they slept. They had been through some insane ordeals together and apart. It was something of a miracle that they were all here together. That had been part of the reason that he had been willing to come here last night.

After watching the girls sleep for a while they eventually began to stir. Terenia was the first one to wake up, and she had only started to stretch when Laticin awoke as well. Once they were all awake, they went downstairs for breakfast.

When they were heading down the stairs, they ran into Jolson who was acting totally normal. He had apparently had a good night, though he refrained from commenting on anything in particular.

They had barely sat down when Joleen and Narok joined them. Though Joleen looked a little embarrassed with Narok being a lot more physical with her. He held her hand on the way down the stairs and briefly placed his hand on the small of her back before taking their seats.

Dras and Claire were the last to arrive. They were chatting amicably. There was nothing about their demeanor that would suggest that they had slept together. Meterove was starting to wonder if Dras had actually had any of the Ambience at all.

The eight of them waited for their breakfast and chatted about the upcoming day. They would spend today around Nexus and tomorrow they would return to their world. There were many different shops and restaurants that they could spend the day exploring.

It was halfway through the day, when they were walking on the outer most street of Nexus, that they became absorbed in conversation and accidentally went past the street that they had meant to turn on.

Meterove suddenly felt that something was off, and he looked around and saw an area of Nexus that was sitting off to the side of the circular city, like a tiny soap bubble clinging to a larger one.

Only now did he remember what Flare had said about the Gamemaster. Leaning against a small statue of a dragon was a man dressed in a very peculiar fashion, even for Nexus.

He was tall and bald with a thin build. He was wearing a black and crimson half mask that covered the right side of his face. There was no hair, not even stubble on his chin. His head almost looked waxed it was so smooth. It was hard to pin an age on him, but Meterove would guess somewhere in his forties.

He was wearing a formal looking back coat with two large silver buttons on it. Under that there was an expensive looking crimson shirt. He was also wearing black pants and extremely shiny black shoes. On his hands he wore thin crimson gloves and in his left hand he held a black cane with a silver tip and handle. The handle was also shaped like a dragon.

Upon seeing them he exclaimed, "AH! Do I see some new blood for my games!? Hurry, hurry, hurry to the chance of a lifetime. I the Gamemaster can make any desire that you have come true!"

Meterove had to admit that he was curious what about this man had Flare so ruffled. He glanced at the others and saw the same question in their eyes, so he led the way over. The man's face split into a sly grin.

The Gamemaster said, "Well, Hello, hello to all of you! What can the Gamemaster do for you?"

Dras said, "You were the one that called out to us. You tell us what you can do."

The Gamemaster's grin did not slip a bit. He said, "I have games, my dear man! Games the like of which you have never experienced before or ever will again!"

Terenia mumbled, "You have way too much energy for someone talking about games."

Joleen agreed. This man was expressing the same kind of energy as a barker for a carnival. There was something very mysterious about this man. Joleen could not sense any kind of pressure from him. Nothing to indicate why Flare was so upset about him.

Meterove asked, "What kind of games are you talking about?"

The Gamemaster's grin grew slyer, "AHH! That I cannot tell you for that it part of their charm!"

Jolson asked, "Why would I want to agree to play a game if I do not know what game I am going to be playing?"

The Gamemaster gave a flamboyant gesture as he said, "Because you will get some really FABULOUS prizes for winning my games!"

Joleen looked around the small bubble that he had created. There was nothing else there besides the statue that the man had been leaning on before. She was still trying to figure out his angle when she heard Narok speak.

Narok asked, "What is the cost of playing these games?"

The Gamemaster said, "There is no cost to play. There is only one condition that must be followed when playing my games!"

Meterove asked, "What is that exactly?"

The grin on the Gamemaster's face was still sly but now there was a hint of danger to it. He said, "Once you start the games there is no stopping until you finish them!"

Meterove wondered how this man planned to enforce such a thing but rather than test it out he decided to play it safe for right now. Flare was warry of this man, which was enough reason to expect that he had some kind of power or trick up his sleeve that was not worth testing.

Meterove said, "Thanks but I think that we are good for now. We have plans for later and if we cannot stop until we are done playing it would cause us to miss them. Thank you for the kind offer. Have a good day sir!"

Meterove began steering them out of the bubble. As they were walking away, he heard, "I will be here any time that you wish to take part in the most spectacular games ever!"

Once they were out of sight Joleen asked. "What do you think of that guy?"

Meterove said, "He does not come across as dangerous on the surface, but underneath it I think he is incredibly dangerous. There is something about him that seems vaguely familiar but I cannot put my finger on it."

Laticin said, "I do not think that he realized that I have better hearing than a human."

Meterove looked vaguely surprised, "I do not think that anyone, but you and Claire, knew that."

Joleen asked, "Why does that matter? What did he say?"

Laticin said, "As we were walking away after he said that part about the games, he talked to himself a little. He said, "I will see you soon Meterove, Joleen and Jolson." After that it could not hear, but I guess it is safe to assume that it was the rest of our names."

Meterove looked back at the corner and shook his head, then said, "I think we should finish our business here in Nexus without thinking of him anymore. Once we are gone in the morning it will not matter anyway."

They found themselves a restaurant and had a lavish meal. After that they returned to their rooms back at The Nexus for the night. Tonight, they had a simple nightcap before bed.

The next day they had everything packed and ready to go by mid-morning. Joleen led the way up to the Gates. Once they knew they had the proper destination ready to go Narok took the lead with Joleen right behind him. Meterove, Dras Laticin, Terenia and Claire were the last to go through.

Meterove and Terenia each took one of Laticin's hands and led her through. Dras took hold of Claire's hand and walked her through. On the other side there was no signs of a threat, though the fire and lava from the volcanos was a new sight for Laticin and Claire.

Once they had gotten over that, they looked at the Gateway. It was currently night so there was not much for them to see outside of the volcano. After they all stepped through the Gateway the girls were once again astounded.

Joleen looked at them and said, "Welcome to Yxarion!"

.   .   .

They had been back in Yxarion for a little over a week now. In that time Joleen had set up several meetings with the rest of her government, the other races that they were friendly with and the Three Principal Races.

The Leturai had been very interested in meeting the Undines and had worked out a trade agreement. The Undines would help recover the Leturai's cities for them in exchange for goods. The Leturai had eagerly leapt at the chance of getting their homes back.

They had also reached the kind of agreement that Demetria had wanted with the Snow Women. They would be allowed to come as often as they wish amongst the people of Yxarion, provided that the men they coupled with, were willing and unharmed. Additionally, while they were within the empire, they were bound to all the laws. That also meant that they would be protected by those same laws as well.

The Mermaids were given ownership of a large lake in the western empire. It had no human occupants so the lake and the shore around it was seeded to the Mermaids, allowing them to have their own city-state. They had the same agreement as the Snow Women.

It took some time for Laticin and Claire to get used to a world with dry land. There were also far more people around than they were used to. They had not been in Nexus long enough to really get a feel for there but Yxarion was busy enough to give them minor anxiety at first.

It was on a warm evening that Meterove was sitting on one of the many balconies in the palace with Laticin and Terenia admiring the city. They were planning on watching the stars. Ever since she had first seen them, Laticin had fallen in love with the stars.

Tonight, as they sat there waiting for the sky to darken Laticin said, "I know I keep saying this, but I am so glad that I found you. I am so happy being here with you two!"

She was sitting in the middle and both Terenia and Meterove had an arm around her waist. Terenia said, "I know what you mean. When I first met Meterove I was actually trying to drain their life force. To me they were just another threat. Meterove captured me but instead of harming me, he chose to get to know me."

Meterove chuckled lightly, "I had to do something to keep myself awake while being up watching you."

Terenia swatted him playfully on the head, then said, "You ruined the moment!"

Meterove said, "We have been through a lot since then. Battles and traveling to places that neither of us could have ever expected."

They continued to chat as the darkness fell and the stars began to peek out. Meterove could not put a price on this time. He knew that all too soon something new was going to come up. Something that would require him to go somewhere new.

He tightened his arm on Laticin's waist and she looked at him with a small frown. He smiled at her and said, "I was just thinking about when we will get involved in some new dangerous matter of Flare's or when the Ashen Soul will make another move."

This time both women smacked him on the head. In unison they said, "Now is the time that we should be resting and enjoying life!"

Terenia continued, "We need to have fun and relax and not be dwelling on the hard things."

The sat there the whole night watching the stars. At one point their trio became five when Claire and Dras showed up looking for them. Then they became eight once the others showed up. It was a fun gathering; a night where the only thing they needed to do was enjoy being there with each other.

The next morning brought all the joys of Joleen's job as the empress. She did not have nearly as much to do as she used to, but it was still annoying. She would be glad when she could fully transition the empire over to a republic.

It was a little before breakfast that word came that she could hardly believe. She asked the man to repeat it twice to make sure she heard it right. Once she had done that she sent for the others. She made sure to mention that this was a matter of urgency.

It took a little over fifteen minutes for everyone to gather together. While this was fairly quick considering there were eight of them, the wait had felt like an eternity to Joleen.

Meterove was the last one to arrive. He had been assisting with the task of choosing new members of the Royal Guards. He noticed her tension as he walked in. He gave her a half side eye and asked, "What is going on that you wanted us all to rush back here?"

Joleen took a few breaths to calm herself down some. Once she had done that four times she said, "Do you remember that room that was in the Citadel of Time that Valaas and Syr could not enter?"

Jolson yawned, "What about it?"

Joleen looked at him and an excited smile spread over her face, "It has opened."

Milton Keynes UK
Ingram Content Group UK Ltd.
UKHW041905120324
439302UK00005B/314